THE CRUELLEST JOKE

THE CRUELLEST JOKE

WESTON DRAPER

Weston Draper

DEDICATION

You know who you are

Contents

Chapter 1

All it takes is a little push

Bill looked at the time and sighed. He was running late again. Sweat was pouring profusely down his back while the stubborn tooth refused to budge.

"How's it going? Is it out yet?" the patient in the chair whined to Bill.

"Not yet," Bill muttered in frustration. Then came a knock on the door. It was the boss, Dr Samuel Sung. His presence was announced by that narcissistic voice.

"My jaw's gettin' a bit tired," the patient continued whining. The patient was the size of a mountain with solid bone to match. The tooth itself was nothing but a rotten stump with less than air to grip onto.

"Hey Bill," the sound of condescension reached Bill's ears before the man poked his head in, "we've all got patients waiting, it's OK to run a little late but just be careful not to break that root like all the others OK? Just do as I told you earlier, that little fella's gonna be fine if you use my surefire technique. Take it easy, I'm gonna see your next one."

Bill could not understand if his boss had any awareness of just how much arrogance was oozing out of his voice. For someone with such mediocre skill, that maniac thought he was God's gift to dentistry. It was the first patient after lunch break and Bill was already frustrated by breaking a root while attempting to remove a tooth earlier that morning. The more he concentrated on removing the tooth intact, the more anxious he became. That nauseatingly persistent voice in his head kept ringing, "don't break it... don't break it..." The stress which was racing through his head was skyrocketing. If only that megalomaniac boss would just leave him alone. If only that damn persistent voice stopped echoing.

"Hold on, it's almost there" Bill encouragingly said to his patient, hoping that idiot would stop moving his head about.

"Ughhhh", the patient made a loud sigh. Nothing was going well for Bill. He could put up with an annoying boss if they just left him alone. A difficult tooth? Happens all the time, he could deal with it. A difficult patient? Perhaps that could be acceptable under some circumstances but when all of these factors combined, it was synergistically apocalyptic. The icing on the cake was how that narcissistic boss paid him less than the other associates because of some imaginary "sliding scale" based on productivity. How did he end up in this circle of hell?

Miraculously, the tooth suddenly started tilting. OK, Bill thought, this moment was critical because the root tip almost always broke while it was just about to come out. Moving... Moving... millimeter by millimeter... then "click." It was the worst sound that could come out of a human mouth. Fracture. The worst word in the English language. Most normal people probably considered another certain word beginning with "F" as the most impactful word in the English language but for dentists, there was no other word which triggered the most fear. Bill had broken yet another root tip.

It was subtle, but Bill saw his assistant roll her eyes towards the edge of his peripheral vision.

"It happened again huh?" the betrayer muttered right in front of the patient, "I'm going to get Cindy." "Doctor" Cynthia Huang, an arrogant bitch who happened to be the boss's favourite associate and was hence assigned to "mentor" Bill. These subhumans revelled in their mediocrity. The quality of their work was below what most students managed to achieve in dental school. Sure they were fast, but if they actually slowed down and did things goddamn properly it could be so much better. With absolutely zero consideration for Bill, his assistant walked out the door.

"What's going on?" the patient asked with more than just a hint of anxiety.

"Don't worry, a tiny bit of tooth is still inside, it will probably just float to the surface," Bill replied.

"Mr Smith, please wait a while, our senior dentist Dr Cindy will be here in a moment," Bill's assistant returned with a smug expression on her face. Bill had to put up with this all day. Every assistant they provided him with was just a spy. None of the other dentists at the clinic trusted the new hire. They were all God's gifts to dentistry but he was just some poor under-experienced schmuck out of dental school who "needed help tying his shoelaces." Bill knew very few excellent dentists who taught him in dental school. They were a rare breed who admitted their mistakes with humility and taught him what they learned from their own failures. Most of his teachers however were like these narcissists who were as oblivious to reality as dancing ballerinas in a warzone.

Bill stared at the chocolates he gave the assistant that morning. When he first arrived, everybody was hostile so he learned to bribe them with gifts. This made them instantly pliable, so he thought. However, it seemed that all of his efforts were completely wasted. None of them were on his side.

"Am I going to be OK??" the patient further enquired with increasing anxiety.

"It will be fine, this happens all the time, Dr Cindy is a specialist when it comes to this," Bill's assistant continued. That under-educated troglodyte. She did not understand that misrepresenting qualifications was a state level offence which could result in Bill risking his registration. Cindy was NOT a specialist. "A specialist is a protected title" as stated by law which can only be used by practitioners who were registered as such.

"Why didn't I see Dr Cindy in the first place?" the patient continued.

"She's so popular we couldn't fit you in, you sounded like you were in a lot of pain so we did our best to get you in today," Bills assistant replied, completely ignoring his presence.

"What's your name by the way?" the patient asked.

"I'm Wendy, nice to meet you, ha ha," Wendy replied jovially. Yes, her name was Wendy. She was well into her 40s and had less ambition than a primary school musical production. Single mother. Divorced. Took the house from the ex husband and had been working in the clinic ever since the boss took over. She was like his lieutenant, following his every whim and fancy like a cultist. In fact, the clinic was run like a cult. The clinic owner was like a messiah and his associates were the disciples.

"Nice to meet you too, haha, I get it, we gotta give these young'uns a chance don't we?" They were laughing at Bill's expense.

There was a knock on the door. It opened and in came a woman in her mid thirties wearing the grey surgical scrubs with "King's Dental" imprinted on the left breast pocket. That idiot boss thought of himself as a King. Obviously. There was no such Dr King anywhere on the premises or even in the whole of Shellharbour.

"Hi there, I'm Dr Cindy, how are you going?" she spoke with a thick Asian accent. Bill suspected she must have been an import from China who just barely spoke with enough English to pass the dental council exam.

"Better now that you're here," replied the patient.

"How about I have a look?" Cindy asked.

"Bloody tough tooth eh?" replied the patient while opening his mouth.

Cindy looked at the x-ray first then at the patient's mouth. She grasped one instrument, fiddled, then another, fiddled again, a few more times and then said,

"Hmmm... I'm afraid we need to refer you to an oral surgeon. Don't worry, we're not going to charge you. Dr White the surgeon is just down the road, he'll get it out in a jiffy," Cindy said.

"Thanks anyway doc, you're a life saver. What can I do about the pain? Is it going to get better?" the patient asked.

"I'm going to prescribe you some antibiotics, Bill I'm a bit busy so could you write up a course of doxycycline for 5 days and some codeine?" Cindy commanded Bill with disinterest.

"Uhh... sure," Bill replied, barely able to contain the anger.

"Is it normal for roots to break?" the patient asked.

"Oh it happened in my early days but it doesn't happen these days," Cindy replied while glancing at Bill.

He was holding back a severe avalanche of anger. That was the final straw. That arrogant bitch could not have removed the tooth in the first place. The whole clinic treated him like a dumping ground for all their problems. Bill frequently checked what the other associates were doing.

Their tooth extractions - simple cases one after another. Anything remotely difficult and they referred to Dr White down the road who was NOT an oral surgeon. He was yet another narcissist who charged double what everybody else charged because all his practice was based on oral surgery but when Bill found him on the register, it clearly read, "GENERAL DENTIST." The moment the girls heard on the phone, "tooth snapped off", they knew the case was too hard and dumped it on Bill. Then they blamed Bill and ordered him to prescribe drugs dentists do not routinely prescribe.

Doxycycline was normally prescribed for tooth trauma, not general tooth infections. The law stipulated that prescribing outside guidelines required clinical justification. What justification did Cindy have? Ignorance? Then she commanded Bill to prescribe a pain relief medication that was also not recommended as a first option. If the pharmacist gave the clinic a quizzical phone call asking why dentists were prescribing drugs they do not normally prescribe, Bill would be on the firing line. If he prescribed something different, then the patient would be able to notice. Bill was placed between a rock and a hard place yet again.

All of a sudden, Bill was struck with an elevation in heart rate. His hands were shaking and his mind started conjuring gruesome, violent thoughts. How he wanted to just slam Cindy's head against a brick wall until either the wall or her head split open. Whichever came first. He was not fussed. Wendy deserved the Julius Caesar treatment for the betrayal that she pulled on him. He wasted good money attempting to sugar her up. His boss, the staff, the patient, the whole goddamn town deserved to burn. Oh how fun it would be to listen to their symphony of screams as white phosphorous slowly melted away their helpless bodies. A few seconds later, his heart rate slowed down. Without saying another word, Bill picked up a pen and started to write down the prescription, as he was commanded.

Bill had no goddamn choice other than to follow the orders of these fools. He needed this job. It took him 3 months to find his first job but it was even worse than this. Bill could hardly believe it. This job at Shellharbour, was an upgrade. That's right, an upgrade, Bill acknowledged to himself. Bill felt like rock bottom right now yet he had actually experienced worse. Bill gritted his teeth and finished writing the prescription then begrudgingly handed it to the patient,

"Here you go sir, we'll give you a call to check on you later," and get the fuck out of here, Bill wanted to add but obviously could not.

"Hmmm, alright, if there are problems, I'll be sure to let you know," the patient replied as he walked out of the room and right past reception without saying a word.

Bill looked at the time, it was 4pm. This patient was scheduled for 2-2:30pm for a toothache, the next patient was taken by the boss, and was scheduled for a straightforward front tooth root canal that was worth over $1000. Bill had already started the procedure and the patient seemed happy to return but the slimeball boss convinced the patient that Bill was not worth seeing and gladly took over instead. Cindy had wasted another 15 minutes with her fiddling. Bill would have been better off sending the patient directly to Dr White down the road but as the newest member, that was definitely not allowed. Couldn't this recent graduate manage even basic dentistry? However the seniors referred out all the time because obviously they were the arbiters of what was deemed challenging. Now Bill was running half an hour late for the 3:30 patient.

Slowly but surely, the sensation of a severe headache crept into Bill's skull. Just moving hurt his head. He could feel his clinical scrubs plastered onto his back from all the sweat. His hands were shaking uncontrollably. He felt dead tired and his entire body ached as if in sympathy with his fatigued brain. He was in no state to practice but he still needed to put on a fake smile and welcome the next patient who obviously was not happy to be delayed. Bill needed this job. Just three more patients, Bill thought, just do this and go home, Jesus... Jesus...

Jesus. Can I even make it? It was going to be a 90 minute drive home. He was only three weeks into this job so the house he was renting was much closer to his previous job. Rushing was out of the question. Something adverse would happen and then he would be in more trouble. Bill sighed as Wendy said,

"The room's ready, bring in our 3:30," with an emphasis on time discrepancy. He hated that woman.

It was truly agony. Fortunately, the next two patients were healthy and just needed some checking and cleaning. Neither raised an eyebrow at being late. Bill only experienced difficult patients from time to time. It was pretty normal for the majority to tolerate slight inconveniences, after all, medical doctors often ran an hour late or more and they rarely did anything other than talking. However, Bill also realised that the most difficult patients came at the end of the day. This was true yet again this afternoon.

"Karen Waters?" Bill walked out to call out the final patient of the day. An older woman with a deep scowl on her face stood up and marched into Bill's room in a haughty manner.

"Do you always run late? This is what happens when they throw me in the deep end," Karen muttered too loudly to pretend it was a personal musing.

This struck a nerve for Bill. One thing which must never be done was to insult Bill. He was superior to all these subhumans who had never even struggled a day in their lives. He went through hell and back to reach where he was now while these morons walking in the streets each day, even if the intellect of ten of them were combined, they would not ever be able to achieve even half of what Bill had accomplished. To have this old, senile, oxygen thief dare insult him was crossing the line harder than a nuclear explosion. He wanted this lump of useless meat disintegrated. But he needed this job. Fuck. Bill had to contain his anger just that little bit longer.

"I heard you had a crown come off, is that right?" Bill started with the well-rehearsed line.

"I wanted to see Dr Sung today but they said he wasn't available. I just need this tooth glued back on. It's very urgent because I have tea with the parents association tonight. It's 5 o'clock now and I'm in a rush. I feel terrible because Dr Sung only did this crown for me a year ago. If you see him please tell him I'm so sorry for breaking his crown," Karen said with the opposite attitude to what she showed Bill.

"Let me take a look first," Bill replied.

"I don't need you to look, I need the tooth back in!" Karen returned with a personality shift as violent as lightning, reverting back to the haughty attitude she walked in with. This was going to be a disaster.

Bill did not reply, instead he looked at the "crown" Karen had placed on his tray. This was no ordinary crown. It was a cantilever bridge done poorly. In construction, nobody was stupid enough to forget to stack counter-weights. However, in dentistry, lots of dentists did exactly this. It was possible to glue false teeth onto existing teeth. However, only desperate or stupid dentists would try and use a weaker front tooth to support a back tooth originally bearing much stronger chewing forces. Dr Sung was probably both desperate and stupid and designed Karen's bridge for failure. Not only that, the remaining tooth was completely broken off at the gum level. There was nothing left to glue onto. It would be a choking hazard when, not if, it falls out during her sleep and then if she dies, Bill would probably lose his licence.

Bill was almost laughing to himself. The situation was absurd, her demands were beyond the realm of fantasy.

"I can't glue this back in," Bill tried to explain, "look at these photos, see how there's nothing left? There is nothing left to glue onto and it will either fall out while eating or during sleep which can-"

"I came here to have the tooth glued in and now I have spent an hour only for you to tell me it's a waste of time!?" Karen rudely interrupted Bill.

"Unbelievable, I'm going to make sure Dr Sung hears about this."

"I'm only being honest with you, look how big that back false tooth is compared to that front tooth, anything stronger than the minimum biting force could have caused this to happen without warning," Bill tried to explain. It was becoming increasingly obvious that patients like Karen were incapable of understanding basic logic.

"Are you saying Dr Sung did a bad job?" Karen continued, "Dr Sung has been my dentist for the past 10 years, my entire family sees him."

Fuck. Bill now had to defend that moron.

"He did the absolute best that he could," Bill uttered half heartedly, at least this part was true, that moron could not perform better quality dentistry even if his family's lives were at stake, "he must have had no other option." The latter part was a total lie. There were definitely better options just that Dr Sung was not capable or interested in offering them. Uttering such lies felt like rending his soul apart. Sure, lying was commonplace these days but he could not tolerate lying to protect a subhuman. That made him even lower than that subhuman moron.

"I'm already going to be late for my dinner, this has been a waste of time," Karen again insulted Bill. She grasped her "crown" from the tray and melodramatically twisted her head towards the door and walked out, again with a deep scowl on her face. Surprisingly her face lit up as she faced the receptionist and the two struck up a conversation about their families. Useless small talk. Wasn't she going to be late for her dinner? Bill would not be surprised if not a single word out of Karen's mouth was the truth. Bill waited for Wendy to walk out of the room and punched the desk while quietly cursing. That would have to do for now, but he really wanted to punch through a brick wall. He had no time at all to write up the records for each patient this afternoon. There was a mountain of bureaucratic paperwork which served no purpose other than to satisfy an audit from the dental board which would never happen in the first place.

By the time Bill walked out of the clinic, it was already 6:30pm. He still needed to drive for 90 minutes and then cook. There was no time. Bill lethargically opened his car door while attempting to gingerly sit down so as to not aggravate his throbbing migraine. As he started driving, Bill thought back to his previous job in a rural clinic. That was Bill's 5th job and it seemed that every new job had useless morons as bosses and deceitful traitors as staff. He had been all around the country by now and nothing seemed to prove that dentistry was worth doing. The worst job he ever had was the previous job. It was so awful one of the dentists there committed suicide in his Porsche. The clinic supplied Bill with very few patients, so much so that his commission was barely enough to cover rent and food. The only patients he did see were usually related to fixing up the gross negligence of the other dentists at little to no charge.

Morons in the clinics he worked at all did poor quality work and deceived patients into pursuing expensive treatments which failed more often than not. The dentist who committed suicide probably made the most money from convincing patients to undergo expensive work only for Bill to fix up when it ultimately failed. That bastard deserved to die. This new job had plenty of patients and Bill did get paid. The senior subhumans were not doing good quality work but initially at least, it did not seem as if they were as incompetent as the previous clinics. However, after today's display, maybe Bill just did not see the signs. The more Bill reflected, the more Bill yearned for those precious late teenage years studying in the United States. His life was like a dream back then. He had friends he could trust. The teachers were competent, humble and hard working people. If only....

HHHHHHOOOOOOOONNNNNNNNNNK!!!

Suddenly Bill was jolted awake by a loud truck horn. He was staring at the headlights of an oncoming truck. Cold sweat emanated from every pore in his body while Bill reflexively swerved out of the truck's way. That was too close. He had fallen asleep while driving. He had almost died. This was not the first time he had fallen asleep while driving but in the past the tyres driving over the lines on the road created a loud vibrating hum which usually woke him up. Today, he was so tired that nothing softer than a truck horn could wake him up. Well, now he had so much adrenaline coursing through his veins it was impossible not to pay attention. Undoubtedly, receiving such a shock would have consequences.

By the time Bill reached his driveway, the lethargy returned. His heart rhythm returned to normal as the effects of the burst of adrenaline started wearing off leaving him in a weary state even worse than before. Bill could not see much of the property he slept in. It was pitch dark and near freezing outside on an August evening. It did not feel like home. There was nothing but a dilapidated single unit with crumbling, semi-rotten wooden weatherboard walls. For all Bill knew, it could have been termite infested. Yet he had to pay over $400 a week for something that was not fit for human habitation. He had already applied to rent another place in Shellharbour but the cretins working in real estate were slower than a turtle and kept making excuses about how there was some shortage of properties. Bill knew the truth. They just wanted to extort higher rent and therefore higher commissions. He voluntarily offered substantially more than the asking rent yet those bastards were still trying to play mind games with him.

Not only was Bill's headache worse, every heartbeat sent a throb through his head like a jackhammer. After the long drive, his ears were also ringing like he had just been flash banged. Bill placed a foot outside the car and almost fell over. His legs were as weak as jelly and he could barely support his own weight. Bill half walked, half stumbled his way through the darkness only to find the door was unlocked. He was too goddamn stressed to worry about that. As he opened the front door, Bill felt darkness creeping in. The moonlight still offered some illumination but even that was shrinking by the second. The next moment Bill opened his eyes, the sun was blasting through the windows. It was then that Bill realised he had involuntarily lost consciousness and it was already morning. Fuck.

Chapter 2

Hopelessness (I)

Bill looked at the time on his smartphone. There was some nostalgia generated by that bottom tier, free phone one of his dental school friends gave him. It read 6:23am. It then occurred to him, did he even close the door behind him? He lost consciousness so insidiously he could not recall the final ten seconds at all. Bill craned his neck and breathed a sigh of relief after seeing that the door was indeed closed. However, it was not locked. Bill had immense mistrust for the community this house belonged to. Bill had lived in Busan, South Korea; Toronto, Canada; New York City, United States; Poznan; Poland. Never had he ever seen as many drug addicted, tattooed, drunken, dangerous people as the Australian rural countryside. He shuddered to think what would happen if one of those lunatics discovered him in an indefensible state as he was. The gun laws in this country were pathetic.

Bill calculated, his first patient was at 8:30am and the drive alone would ensure that the earliest time of arrival would be 8am. Just like yesterday, Bill had no time for breakfast. Did he have dinner last night? No, Bill recalled, he did not even have a sip of water to drink. Did he have lunch? He least ate a banana, that he knew for sure. This malnutrition was definitely wreaking havoc on his physiological and perhaps even mental health, but he had no goddamn choice. What else was he supposed to do? He had no time to eat let alone prepare something to eat. He barely had time for a shower. There was still a headache, but it was at least 50% milder than yesterday. As long as there were not going to be any more blunders like yesterday, maybe he could still survive today.

Who am I kidding, Bill thought. He was probably going to die from overwork sooner or later. Which day of the week was it? Bill actually had no idea. While standing up shakily, Bill leaned on the shoe drawer for support while taking out his barely functioning smartphone again to check: Thursday August 7th, 2014, 9 degrees celsius. He could probably make it. Just today and tomorrow, Bill thought. Worst case scenario, he could pretend to be working late and ask his boss for permission to stay behind in order to collapse onto the dental chair. It would not be the first time he had done that either. Last weekend, Bill recalled that he slept for possibly 18 hours a day. Perhaps he stood up to have a meal now and again.

The existential dread was indeed painful. This pitiful life he currently led consisted of waking and doing dentistry under extremely stressful circumstances with the only relief being sleep. He had once enjoyed playing video games on the Playstation console. Even in dental school, he had his friends at arm's length who were more than eager to share in the complaints regarding their poor quality education. These days, he was isolated, fatigued beyond measure and forced between a rock and a hard place on a daily basis. Still, what choice did he have? He needed this job. He really did. Nobody could keep moving from job to job forever. There were indeed professional locums but that kind of dentist or doctor agreed from the outset to work temporarily. Each time he left, he either quit in a dramatic fashion or was forced out. Bill was only 26 years old. He would not tolerate another 30 years of this torture. If he could not hold down a job for more than a few months, that was it. He would kill himself then and there.

There was at least enough time for a shower. Bill used to joke to his friends about a "shower in a can," which was basically the famous "Axe" body spray deodorant. He even had a bottle in his house for the sake of nostalgia. Not today though, only the lowest of the low would actually take a "shower in a can" seriously. Bill hobbled to the kitchen on the way to the shower and poured himself a glass of water. He was indeed thirsty, he did not even notice until the water reached his parched insides. There were many jokes about what was truly the nectar of the gods but in Bill's hyper-malnourished state, even rainwater could have been mistaken for that holy nectar.

His hand was shaking, the water was almost spilling out. Goddamn it, Bill thought as he reached inside his jacket pocket to bring out his bottle of "no doze" caffeine pills. He had no time to drink coffee but his withdrawals were so severe that he would not be able to practice without it. He took out two pills and washed it down with the remainder of the water in the cup. Subtly but surely, his hands started to stabilise and even his headache ever so slightly decreased in intensity. Bill walked into the bathroom and looked at himself. His clothes were not visibly soiled. He then sniffed his garments. A hint of the disinfectant the clinic used but not much body odour. A spray of deodorant would be enough. He did not have enough time to look for a new set of matching clothes anyway.

It took a while, but Bill managed to shower, redress and gel his hair. Bill looked at his beaten up smartphone again, it was 7am. He had better speed down the highway then. There were no police checking for speeding until only the 30km region around Shellharbour anyway. Bill paid attention to locking the door this time and sat back in his car to prepare for his long drive again. After entering the highway, Bill checked to ensure the road ahead was straight as far as the eye could see and pushed as hard as he dared on the accelerator pedal. The speedometre inched its way up, 110, 120, 130, 140km/h, then the car started shaking due to the poor quality of the country road. This was probably the limit. What choice did he have?

Bill finally arrived at the clinic without falling asleep this time, fortunately. There was a carpark with four spaces for patients in front of the clinic and a shared carpark with the accountants next to them in the back. The patient carpark was already full. The clock in his car read 8:25 so he still barely had some time left to get ready. Bill hastily parked his old Mitsubishi Magna behind the clinic and checked to make sure he was within the lines - close enough. The car still had the dent on the passenger side front door from hitting the kangaroo a month ago. It drove fine so there really was no good reason to fix it. The car was over ten years old and the repair cost would probably exceed the $3000 purchase price anyway.

As Bill opened the door, Wendy greeted him saying,

"Good morning sleepy-head."

This angered Bill. His hands immediately clenched but he was able to stop his face from flinching, just barely.

"Uhhh, hi Wendy" Bill quietly uttered.

"You've got a busy day today doctor. I'm going to be with Dr Sung today. I'm gonna miss you but you'll be fine with Lucy today. She'll be able to rescue you," Wendy said again with that condescending tone. Bill struggled to contain his anger. The sheer willpower required to stop him from decapitating that torturer rivalled all the gods with all their divine power. She enjoyed provoking him. What else could explain these sarcastic tongue lashings? It was like she took the crown of thorns Jesus wore at the crucifixion and converted it into verbal form, encasing his whole body and scraping every last skin cell off his body only to revel in the pain she was causing. This garbage subhuman only made his day ten times worse by calling in another useless cretin who did nothing but delay *his* treatment. She even had to remind him of arriving so late. These morons were incapable of empathy. Could these people just cut him some slack? If he even forced upon them a fraction of the mental punishment he experienced yesterday, these dungheaps would have driven into a tree and died in car fires.

The only thing these people could "rescue" was their own ignorance. They seemed determined to maintain their tunnel vision approach to life like pigs rolling in the mud. They revelled in it. The best Bill could squeak out in response was a faint "thank you" before walking to his office. Lucy was a young girl who had just finished high school and worked for this clinic since the beginning of the year. She was the least experienced assistant. So not only was she a spy for Dr Sung, she was also the least helpful. At least Wendy was competent enough to ensure that when Bill needed something, she had it prepared. Lucy on the other hand still needed reminding when it came to spotting the difference between left and right upper extraction forceps. It was going to be a long day.

Bill examined his computer monitor and scrutinised the day ahead. Check-up and clean, check-up and clean, check-up... filling, consult, at least the day seemed manageable. Then he opened the files one by one until his heart sank again. Last patient before lunch, Patrick Fitzgerald, 5 years and 2 months. Bill hated treating children. It was especially worse in the rural regions. Because parents took such poor care of their own teeth, their children's teeth were in an abysmal state. Infections and broken root stumps everywhere and pathetic spoilt children who could not tolerate an injection even if it were to save their lives, literally. There were indeed children who died of dental infections. If that child decided to scream his lungs out, Bill might actually go berserk this time.

Lucy then walked in. She would have been a very attractive blonde girl except that she was covered in tattoos. Bill could also see the black fingernails. A typical sign of a drug user. Bill was especially incensed by this class of people. He called them ferals. Just like there were feral animals, there were also feral humans. Zero appreciation of culture, zero intellectual capacity, zero self-awareness of the destructive nature of their lifestyles. Unlike him, these ferals *chose* to take drugs and drink their livers to death. Bill had no choice but to be squeezed between a rock and a hard place. Just looking at her sent waves of revulsion.

"Good morning Bill, our first patient is for check-up and clean right? Don't run late," she said in a whimsical tone with a smile on her face. Was she trying to mock him? How he wanted cut that smile off her face. These people were not just morons, they were malicious morons. Bill was obviously suffering, it was obvious in his facial expression. Yet these sadists kept stabbing him like a chained bear for amusement. Bill felt like saying something equally brainless,

"With you assisting, we're gonna make this day the best goddamn day and ball outta control, Hoo rah!" Bill replied. That gave Lucy a little laugh. If these morons never spoke seriously then Bill would only respond just like that in turn. Fortunately, the check-ups which Bill looked at earlier did not transform into monstrous complications and the morning went by quickly until Patrick, the 5 year old came in.

"Lucy, could you call the kid in, he'll like you better," Bill requested. Bill did not want to even see this spoiled brat.

"Patrick?" Lucy called out as she placed her head outside the office door, "Patrick? Hi muscles! How's your day? Wow, is that a dinosaur?"

This was the kind of garbage, intellect destroying drivel that subhumans engaged in. Bill would never stoop down to that level to entertain some idiot child. As Patrick came in, so did his mother, sister who looked like she was the same age and infant brother in their mother's arms. Not this again, Bill thought.

"Hi, I'm Bill your dentist today, can I look at your mouth?" Bill said while putting on his least intimidating voice.

Without saying a word, Patrick nodded his head. That was a relief, Bill thought. In the past he had dealt with screaming kids. The worst ones were the child actors who would pretend to be scared and rampage for 5 seconds before mummy had to jump back in to cuddle and "negotiate." This could go on for over an hour over something as simple as a filling without requiring anaesthetic. This time Patrick did not hesitate and sat down.

"Hi, my name's Janine, Patrick's mum," Janine introduced herself, "I was looking in Patrick's mouth and there were some brown spots. It's been a while since he's last been. We've been really busy with Jayden here."

"Have there been any other problems? Like for example pain?" Bill replied.

"Um, not pain, have you had any ouchies buddy?" Janine asked while looking at Patrick.

"At kinder, me and Sam were running, I fell down and it hurt," Partick said. Obviously he was not going to provide anything coherent.

"We're talking about your teeth bubs," Janine asked again.

Patrick then shook his head.

"Well a couple of days ago he was saying that something hurt when we gave him some juice, didn't we bubs?" Janine tried to elaborate.

"OK, OK, let's have a look," Bill said.

What Bill discovered inside was a miniaturised version of a disaster movie background set. There was tooth decay everywhere with caked on plaque everywhere. It was one of those typical presentations where the child clearly never brushed his teeth. A thirty second quick, tangential swipe with the toothbrush was not toothbrushing by anyone's standards. Most of the plaque was stained brown and orange and it almost looked like a biological mouthguard of bacteria infesting the child's mouth. Clearly the parents had the intelligence quotient of a peanut and took about as much care of Patrick's oral health as Bill spent on his Mitsubishi. Bill tried to tactfully explain the situation.

"There's a lot of problems happening in Patrick's mouth, I think it would be a good idea to *consider* seeing a kids specialist dentist," Bill tried to explain.

"Hang on, what do you mean by lots of problems? Last checkup the dentist said everything was fine," Janine tried to argue. Bill detested this situation. Children were notorious for all the screaming but the parents were often equally disgraceful if not worse. He was already dreading the waste of breath argument that was about to commence.

"The last checkup was 18 months ago, that's a long time, enough for problems to develop," Bill tried to explain.

"Why do we need to see a specialist? Are they gonna charge through the roof?" Janine further tried to argue.

"I recommend them because they can put Patrick to sleep and do everything at once," Bill tried to elaborate.

"I think Patrick's a bit too young for that. Tell me what his problems are, what can you do today?" Janine demanded.

"He has multiple cavities in his mouth," Bill explained.

"What caused this?" Janine asked

"Usually it's a dietary and lifestyle disease as well as ineffective brushing," Bill elaborated.

This useless argument went on. Janine walked in believing that she was a "good mother" and that feeding little Patrick by effectively offloading a dump truck full of sugar into his mouth every day was for his own good.

"OK, let's just do that filling today," Janine finally settled on one plan of action. Bill hated these kinds of vermin. They neglect their children and want to blame the dentist when something goes wrong taking absolutely zero responsibility for their misdeeds. Even if Bill did this one filling today, there were 10 other cavities ready to go nuclear any second.

"After this filling, I can prepare a referral to see the specialist, you can just have a consultation which will be cheap" Bill tried to explain.

"Why can't you do the treatment here?" Janine was still going to argue.

"Why not see Dr Cindy? She's like a specialist, she's fantastic with kids," Lucy blurted out.

That was another line which must never be crossed. *Nobody*, did not matter if they were Jesus himself, *nobody* was to interfere with the treatment that Bill provided. These morons at the clinic did not have the ability to treat this disaster zone. Bill did not dislike Patrick. Patrick was as close to a victim as it got. Seeing Cindy would be effectively condemning his teeth to an early grave. Beneath his mask, Bill's mouth was baring a horrifying snarl but nobody could see his expression. That bitch Lucy could not keep her mouth shut. Bill had to remind himself. He really needed this job. That was the only thing stopping him from impaling that feral excrement in the face with the pen on his desk. All of these morons seemed to lack the situational awareness to realise that calling everyone specialists contravened the law.

Bill stared daggers at his assistant but he was in the midst of injecting the young patient in the chair. He tuned out the conversation between

Janine and Lucy, but he did hear some parts including, "specialist," "experienced," "she has two kids," "oh St Martins?" It seemed like all women talked about revolved around their kids and their school life. They should have booked them in with Cindy in the first place, why force him to go through this torture? Just add another victim to Cindy's crimes. It would barely make a difference considering how many cases she had already fucked up, Bill thought.

"Stay open, good job, close your eyes and wriggle your toes, just a pinch and the tooth goes to sleep," Bill enunciated the old mantra. Patrick seemed stoic enough, there was a slight flinch when the needle pierced the mucosa but otherwise he was fine. While he was trying to concentrate, Bill heard the sound of screaming. It was not coming from Patrick. It was his infant brother. The ear-piercing howls of a wailing banshee echoed through the room like a thousand needles in Bill's ear. His entire body shook from anger. How was he supposed to focus on a field less than 2mm wide when he was being almost physically assaulted?

Bill gestured to Lucy to usher Janine out of the room. Lucy only returned Bill's gesture with a puzzled expression. That's right, Bill thought, these idiots let the whole family stay in the room all the time. Nevermind the cramped mess it made, nevermind the unruly children smashing into equipment and wreaking havoc. Just let 'em in, Bill imagined the thought process of these morons, just let 'em run wild cause who needs rules? Who needs order? This was the reason these subhumans never produced good quality work. Their laissez faire attitude was reflected in their work. Nobody cared here. Close enough was good enough. Most of the time it was not even close. Goddamn it.

Bill could not say anything. He really needed this job. He really did. As he was preparing to put his foot down on the pedal to activate the drill, Bill noticed his hands were shaking. Was the caffeine wearing off? No, the moment he focused, his hands stopped shaking. He was quivering in anger. All this fury being bottled in could not have been healthy. He really needed this job. Bill activated the drill but as soon as he did that, another howl erupted in the air and this time his hand involuntarily jerked aside. Bill immediately stopped the drill otherwise he would have lacerated young Patrick. Goddamn it. He really needed this job.

"Hush, hush, hush," Janine ineffectually attempted to calm the infant. Finally, Lucy said something. Her ears must have been traumatised by now as well.

"How about I get him something? We have some toys in the waiting room," Lucy said. Although it was not explicitly said, Janine perhaps finally understood the very obvious situation.

"He must be hungry, I'll give him a treat, do you have a rest room? Hey bubs, be good alright, watch over your big brother," Janine said while facing the second youngest.

"Charlotte will show you where to go," Lucy answered, referring to the receptionist.

"Be right back bubs, you'll be alright," Janine said before finally heading out the door.

Finally, Bill thought, some people just did not possess even the slightest sense of human decency. He was about to perform an extremely delicate procedure, the slightest disruption would result in either the drill penetrating into the tooth nerve resulting in infection or a soft tissue laceration which would result in a torrent of bleeding. That inconsiderate subhuman could not even consider the wellbeing of her own son, Patrick, who had a drill in his mouth. Bill placed the high speed handpiece back into its receptacle and picked up the slow speed drill. As he did so, the sister shifted her attention to Bill because mummy had left.

"What's that?" the sibling asked. Goddamn it.

Bill hated children. One problem was exchanged with another.

“Uhhh, this is our cleaning device,” Bill tried to explain. It was hopeless.

“What’s that?” the sibling said again this time pointing to another tool.

“Come have a seat, let Dr Bill do his work,” Lucy said, surprisingly not being completely useless. Fortunately, the child walked away. However, that did not last long. Within seconds, her attention span was reset and she was thumping her feet up and down with heavy footsteps by her brother’s feet next to the chair. Goddamn it, Bill thought. Just as he thought that, Bill noticed his hands were quivering yet again, this time even harder. It was not just his hands, Patrick was also quivering. His jaw was opening and closing. Patrick was reaching the limit of his patience as well.

It took almost an hour. Bill had finally made it. Patrick was already shaking his head left and right. Clearly neither of them could go on any further. Bill threw the instruments on his tray and stood up. Janine had not come back, as expected. He did not expect her to be able to settle down the infant that easily. Without saying a word, Bill walked out of the room and subsequently out of the clinic. He could not trust himself to remain calm. Every single crevice of the building was filled with tempting objects inviting him to inflict violence. It was incredibly alluring, but he needed this job. He just had to leave.

Bill blinked. Bill stared at where he was walking. He must have been walking for at least five minutes. The clinic was a distant dot, he could barely make out the sign at all. Bill looked at his barely functioning phone. It was 1:40pm. He knew his next patient was due at 2pm. He did not pack any lunch but hopefully he would be able to have another banana or whatever was available in the fruit bowl. If he were lucky, maybe one or more of the girls would have some leftovers. Each day there was at least one staff member who bought take-away and left some behind. Once he was even lucky enough to have a whole abandoned burger. Bill could have bought his own, but take-away was not cheap. Neither did Bill have enough time to prepare his own food. Bill sighed, turned his head and started walking back.

As he walked through the door, Bill noticed Dr Sung walking out of the staff room. Seeing Bill, Dr Sung started talking,

"Bill, come this way, I just wanted to check on how you're going." This was obviously not going to be good. Bill assented with a weak voice and started following Dr Sung down the hall to the largest surgery in the clinic. It was also the front window surgery.

"I had a very unhappy Karen Waters on the phone this morning," Dr Sung began, "She is usually such a lovely lady but she seemed extremely upset this morning. She also left us with a 2 star review. Let's bring it out."

Bill had a sinking feeling in his throat.

"Here we go, she wrote, 'Don't ever see the new guy, Dr Bill Parker. I had an emergency but he was extremely rude and refused to see me. Just told me to shut up and go home. I trust only Dr Sung who has been my dentist for the past 10 years. Doesn't matter how bad your emergency, just wait for Dr Sung to be available. He's worth the wait!" Dr Sung read out the review.

"I wasn't there myself, but I heard from Wendy that you did indeed refuse to treat Karen. We are a Christian practice. We are here to help people. Christ would never have turned away a person in need. What would your father and the almighty father, Jesus, think about what you did to Karen yesterday?" Dr Sung continued.

Wow, Bill thought. He tried to honestly and sincerely help that bitch of a woman last night. He probably even saved her life. But it seemed that people don't give a FUCK about their own wellbeing and would gladly risk a choking hazard just because their dog shit brain could not think in any other way. Not only that, she made a false allegation for all the public to see. In addition, that fucking traitor Wendy corroborated the false allegation solely to inflict pain. That vindictive, malicious, evil, vile, horrendous abomination of a breathing sack of excrement. Bill's heart rate was again skyrocketing. His entire body was shaking. The universe was arbitrarily punishing him. Why was he born into this torture chamber? What did he do wrong? Bill tried to say something to defend himself but all he muttered was an incomprehensible croak.

"Look Bill, I looked at the photos and I agree that the crown couldn't be recemented, but you gotta be able to communicate effectively," Dr Sung continued. With that, Bill's anxiety attack seemed to abate gradually.

"I would have said, 'I'm sorry Mrs Waters, I would glue it on again if I could but it would fall off within seconds. Now we don't want it falling off during your parents' night would we?' and then she would have been fine. We can't have these kinds of mistakes being repeated. I don't want to lose you Bill, I think you have great potential but please, you have to work on it. We're all here to help you. I know in the city getting a bad review is nothing much but this is a much more tight-knit community, you can't afford to have a poor reputation," Dr Sung continued. Bullshit, Bill thought. He said exactly that and even showed the photos repeatedly. However, Bill did not entirely disagree with his boss, it could have been his tone or body language or whatever. He just did not connect with Karen. Plus, the team here was *not* here to help. They had succeeded in doing nothing but isolate and entrap Bill into disasters time and time again.

"It won't happen again sir," Bill said obsequiously.

"I'm sure it won't. By the way, I would love to see you at our Sunday service. I know you live really far away but when you manage to get a rental here, come join us. I hope I'm not being too affront about it, I assumed you were Christian given your Korean background like me," Dr Sung continued. Bill was only pretending to be a Christian. During his childhood, hell, even during dental school, Bill was a Christian but by dental school, most of the brainwashing had worn off.

"Yes I do follow the teachings of Christ. I'd love to join your congregation. Right now, that damn real estate agent is playing mind games, she should be messaging me any time now," Bill lied.

"I hope to see you there," Dr Sung said, "ahh, look at the time, your first patient's here, better get to it."

Bill needed this job. He would pretend to be anything Dr Sung wanted. Bill was near certain that he would be fired if Dr Sung found out he was not a true believer. That Karen incident was a warning. Anything, *any* tiny excuse and he would be out of here. Bill really needed this job. As he walked out of the surgery, Bill actually felt moisture in his eyes. He was on the verge of tears. He struggled to fight back against the wave of impending depression. This was more than just being caught between a rock and a hard place. Not only was he trapped between the rocks, there was another rock crushing him from above his head, like a three directional sandwich. It was not legal to discriminate based on religion or ethnicity. But tell that to these morons. They would not be able to understand the law even if a lawyer battered them over the head with a legal textbook.

Bill had zero time to eat yet again. He had no goddamn choice because of how desperately he needed this job. Bill dejectedly staggered over to his surgery and collapsed onto his chair. He sat, slumped over and took a few deep breaths while his assistant was still away at lunch. He did not want others to see him in this state. Some day, all these people who wronged him will get their just deserts, Bill thought. As he started hearing footsteps outside, Bill sat up straight and checked his afternoon - goddamn it. Yet again, he was seeing patients his boss or the other dentists were "palming off." There was almost always a good reason why other dentists sent patients his way. They pretended it was to provide him with more income but that was a gross lie. So far, he could only recall receiving patients who were problematic. They were rude, frequently failed to arrive or their treatment needs were probably too "unproductive" and complex for the morons to handle anyway. Even better, a combination of everything.

The first patient, Natalie Burns, usually sees Dr Sung, x-rays and photos were all taken, Bill mused. Good, Bill thought, at least he managed to check the patient properly. However, one red flag caught Bill's eye. "Patient arrived 15min late" was plastered on her file. Goddamn it. He knew it. Bill dug deeper, he needed to at least check what was needed. X-ray - all good, no decay, photo - a few stains here and there, some gum recession, nothing really needed addressing. Who knows what she was in for, Bill thought, must be something cosmetic. She was a healthy looking 30 year old and they all wanted tooth whitening. Bill clicked on Dr Sung's previous notes, pitifully insufficient according to dental board regulations but all older dentists wrote one or two sentences as their notes. Bill knew Dr Sung typed with two index fingers. Can't teach old dogs new tricks, Bill mused. So much for God's gift to dentistry.

Dr Sung's notes read as such:

Pt presented for fillings, lignocaine block, 46, 47 cleaned fissures, filled. NV

36, 37.

Anyone from the general public could look up dental board regulations. It was essential to record consent which included an explanation of the advantages and disadvantages of any treatment performed. His notes had none of that. No indication of filling material type, no indication of how much anaesthetic, no indication of which parts of those teeth were filled. That guy was taking so many shortcuts even the Chinese Government would want to consult with him. Not only that, none of those teeth actually required fillings. They were obviously stains. It was unbelievable. In fact, Dr Sung condemned himself by taking pre-operative and post-operative photos. Bill recalled the conversation he had with Dr Sung on induction day.

"If you see any stained molars, 9 times out of ten once you drill in you can still see the brown mark underneath. Then you take a photo and show it to the patient, tell them, 'see, there was decay underneath!' and they'll be grateful," Dr Sung said. Bill thought he was saying that in jest. The decision to drill into the teeth locked the patient into a lifetime of replacement fillings which would gradually increase in size as time went by. Diagnosing decay which needed filling was more complex than "seeing brown." Bill did not take him seriously at the time but it seemed like that moron was more than just stupid, he was unconscionably stupid. Goddamn these animals, Bill thought. The nurses once bragged about Dr Sung's debt. What was wrong with this world, Bill thought, in the past people bragged about their wealth but these days they bragged about their debt. Debt made you rich these days. The more indebted you were, the richer.

He had seen it time and time again, whether it were car loans, mortgages or even just flat out gambling. These animals wasted all their money on conspicuous consumption. They placed themselves and potentially everyone else at risk of financial ruin just to show off to their friends. If Joe Bloggs had a two storey mansion, then *I* must have a three storey mansion. If Joe had a Mercedes then *I* must have a Lamborghini. Without exception. Dr Sung was for sure late for a loan payment again. Why else would anyone seriously drill into stained teeth recklessly? What car did that guy drive? Bill searched his memories. So far the boss always left before him. Bill always sat back to deal with the mountain of notes properly. There was both a Range Rover and a Maserati out the back. Could have belonged to the accountants. Bill was not sure.

What infuriated Bill more was Dr Sung's invocation about Jesus Christ only minutes ago. So much for being "Christian." Koreans were all like this, Bill thought. Every one of the so-called "Christians" he met, especially his own parents, were incredibly insincere about their beliefs.

So they preached about "helping" people and "loving thy neighbour." Where was the love here? In what way was over-treating in order to pay off the car loan "Christian?" The hypocrisy was so blatant it was visible from the moon with the naked eye. This criminal scum *dared* lecture Bill about Christian values? It must have been in Korean DNA to be so fanatic about proselytising but simultaneously be so dishonest. This extreme level of self-deception required a galaxy sized brain. Some black magic was employed to partition the brain cells pretending to believe in religion from the brain cells generating unconscionability.

In fact, Bill changed his Korean name from Jin-Woo Park into William Hastings Parker because he detested his own Korean ancestry. Statistically, white names on curriculum vitae were rejected less than Asian names. This was scientific fact. It only backfired once when he attended an interview at a clinic with two British dentists. Those morons just stared blankly at Bill for 5 seconds before asking, "what's your nationality?" Dentists were not lawyers but these cockroaches imported from the broken NHS system were more ignorant than a newborn. If he wanted to, he could have reported them to Fair Work, the government ombudsman, for discriminating based on ethnicity. It was against the law to discriminate based on ethnicity. While in some ways Bill wanted to use the law against them, the law was also pathetic. What was wrong with advertising, "We want white dentists only?"

Lucy stepped in and wordlessly started setting up the equipment required for fillings. Bill was dreading this. Hopefully the patient would not even turn up. Otherwise, he would be forced to drill into healthy teeth. Bill did not care much about the patient's wellbeing. She could have died on her drive here for all he cared. But Bill could not tolerate being forced to do something he did not want to. He felt like there was a gun pointed at his head. If he went against his compulsions, that metaphorical bullet would be fired and cause him unceasing internal agony. In the past he struggled to eat, stay awake and even wake up.

Just keeping his eyes open triggered intense headaches and dizziness. He had to lie down and sleep. It was the only relief he could get.

As Bill waited, the door opened and he heard the words he was dreading,

"Hi I'm Natalie here for my 2 o'clock appointment," a female voice sounded out. She actually arrived on time.

"Hey Lucy, I'm hell tired, could you call our next patient in," Bill requested.

"Sure," Lucy replied as she started walking out, "Natalie? The doctor is ready for you."

"Hi, nice to meet you all," Natalie greeted the team.

"Hi, nice to meet you. I have been informed by Dr Sung that there are a couple more fillings to do. He's very busy and I heard that you needed this done ASAP so he couldn't fit you in today," Bill continued.

"No worries, how long is this going to be? I just gotta let my partner know," Natalie asked.

"It's going to be 2 fillings on the left, maybe an hour?" Bill replied.

"Alright, gimme one sec," Natalie said while dialling her mobile phone. How rude, Bill thought, at least show some common courtesy stepping into my office.

After her phone conversation, Bill examined the patient to confirm his suspicions. Just as I thought, Bill thought, her teeth just had some grooves which looked brown, no sign of real tooth decay at all. He was truly pushed into a corner now. Bill examined the fillings done by Dr Sung last time. Of course they were flat and featureless, as expected when in a rush but at least that had no impact on the longevity of the fillings. What did bother Bill was the gap in the margin on the filling next to the gum line. Dr Sung always did those types of fillings, known notoriously in the dental world as buccal cervical fillings, in a matter of less than 5 minutes. He never tried to control the bleeding from the gums so almost without exception there would be contamination and a gap. The filling was never required in the first place but now it was even more difficult to brush effectively.

Bill really needed this job. He could not dare upset the boss again. If he dared even slightly imply that the fillings done were unnecessary, the patient would complain. That could happen if he decided to dismiss her without any treatment right now, even though that was exactly what she needed. If he actually did those fillings, both his mind and body would punish him unceasingly for who knows how long. Fuck it, Bill thought. He had to bite the bullet. His headache would worsen, he might not even be able to eat. Maybe he would be compelled to shower 5 times this afternoon instead of the usual 3 in order to wash away the agony. He might even punch a brick wall. Whatever. He just had to bite the bullet. Bill did exactly as he was told.

It was agonising, excruciating even. However, Bill still followed the script.

"Let's bring up Dr Sung's photos. See those brown marks there? That's what we gotta fill today," Bill said exactly as Dr Sung had instructed. Towards the middle of the procedure, Bill took some photos as well,

"Wow, it was dark underneath as well, we're lucky to have caught them early," Bill regurgitated more of the filth. At least his fillings would have some proper anatomy, unlike Dr Sung. Bill sighed after he put down the last instrument. This was his life now. He had no goddamn choice. He was forced yet again to look for another job. It was impossible to continue like this week after week. Bill could only imagine what would happen. Someone was going to die. Could be himself, he did experiment with suicide in the past even before coming to Australia. He could lose control of his body and stab someone, literally. How long would it take to find another job? How long was a piece of string? Until he had a solid offer, he still really needed this goddamn job.

Although Bill managed to see the rest of the patients that afternoon without any major incidents, his mind and body were both depleted. Just like yesterday, he was experiencing an agonizing migraine on top of his head spinning. His legs felt like jelly and his back ached. The caffeine was wearing off because he did not take a lunch time dose, hence his hands were shaking like he had Parkinsons. Fuck it. He was not going to write any notes today. There was a limit to how much his mind and body could handle. His stomach was grumbling and he could feel the malnourishment ravaging his internal organs. Bill just thought about it, he had not gone to the toilet since morning, nor did he drink any water. It had been several days since he last defecated too. These days, he was almost always constipated. Perhaps it was due to malnutrition. He was certain that if he did not have anything to eat right now, he was going to die by tomorrow morning.

He was a dentist. He was supposed to be earning a high income. Instead, he could barely afford to pay rent and food let alone actually enjoy any of his money. After moving around the country 5 times, almost all the money he earned was wasted. Not only that, the money he earned felt like blood money. Each dollar was draining out the blood of his body, poisoning him and reducing his lifespan. How could he afford to spend his own blood? Society was a metaphorical vampire sucking him dry. The nurses who were paid $30 an hour including super, were enjoying luxurious lifestyles. Bill's nominal remuneration was supposedly higher, except for one moron former boss who paid Bill as much as a nurse. Despite that, Wendy drove a brand new Toyota Rav4. Lucy had a near brand new Mazda 3. Charlotte and the other three assistants also drove vehicles less than 3 years old. Only Bill drove a $3000 clunker from 2003. If those girls hit a tree, they could probably walk away but if Bill did that, the car would become his sarcophagus. These same girls bought take-away every couple of days and drank themselves into oblivion at night. Tattoos did not come cheap either.

Was he even living in reality? Bill stopped believing in God back in dental school but this world was even more sick than a godless hell-hole. This was a special hell designed specifically to punish Bill. Bill was paid a commission in every job except his first job where the boss considered him an "employee" and was perhaps the only boss that paid any superannuation. Although that job only lasted a few weeks, at least income was guaranteed. Afterwards, Bill learned the lesson that 40% of $0 was indeed $0. In this current job he sometimes even earned $1000 in a single day but if he died because of the job, what use was that money? Jesus.. Jesus.. Jesus, Bill thought. If only Jesus were real, he would never have let this society degenerate into this mess.

Bill had no choice but to drive into the local McDonald's drive through. He wordlessly walked out of the clinic and drove over. Of course it was jam packed. The utility vehicles from the busy tradespeople in town queued up for almost 20m outside the drive through window. Bill sighed. He was going to have to wait. Bill again started reminiscing about his childhood. In New York, the staff were so efficient that he once had his McChicken meal delivered to the counter *before* he even finished saying "large McChicken meal." People were rude and never greeted each other but Bill preferred that to all the insincerity here. If only people were to shut up and mind their own business, Bill thought.

"Welcome to McDonald's, may I have your order please," the drive-through worker announced through a large window.

Bill was jolted out of his reminiscing.

"Uhh hi, I'd like to get eight cheeseburgers and two soft serves," Bill ordered.

"So that was eight cheeseburgers and what sorry?" the server seemed confused.

"Soft serve," Bill said it slower and louder

"Sorry?" the server still did not understand.

"SOOOFT... SERVE" Bill was almost shouting now.

"Umm..." it was useless.

Someone behind them started shouting too, "He wants some ice-cream honey, a cone!"

"Ohh, a soft serve cone," the serving girl finally understood, "so that's 8 cheeseburgers and 2 soft serve cones? That will be $9."

Bill faced this type of racism before. In order to become a permanent resident, he needed to pass an English proficiency exam. There was a racist elderly woman who pretended she could not understand his American accent. Regardless of being in the United States or Australia, not a single white person struggled to understand him other than racists. Those exceptions occurred when they saw his face. So much for all that social justice bullshit, Bill thought. Society had such racist attitudes towards him so it was perfectly justified for him to treat others with the same views. He hated pretenders. People who lied to themselves were the worst liars of all time. If they lied to themselves, they would lie to others even more. All those cockroaches who could not "understand" his perfectly adequate English only did so due to their racism which they never dared admit. He was not coming back to this McDonald's if this piece of shit racist bitch was going to serve him again, Bill thought. Even the car behind him with the infernal engine noise still understood him clearly. It was because they did not see his Asian face.

Bill had nothing more to say to that cockroach. He swiped his card and took the bag. He may as well start eating now. Bill was used to dangerous driving. He did not have enough time to eat at home so he often drove with his legs on the steering wheel. There were no cars on the road this late anyway, only the odd car now and again. Hell, it was safer than that time he fell asleep, Bill thought. If he were eating, at least it occupied his attention span so that he would not be falling asleep. In fact, this type of dangerous driving was keeping him alive, so Bill thought. Bill was ravenous. He gulped down the ice cream and ravaged the cheeseburgers like there would be no tomorrow. He was fortunate McDonald's had a $1 cheeseburger promotion today. If he were able to sit down and eat, he might have ordered 20.

After Bill arrived at his dilapidated house, Bill this time was conscious long enough to lock the door properly behind him. He even made it to his sheets before collapsing. Bill did not have a bed. They were too expensive and he was used to sleeping on the ground. This house had hard wooden flooring so Bill needed to place a few sheets of linen as a cushion. Within seconds, he lost consciousness. Only one more day until the weekend. Then he could properly restore his failing mind and body.

Chapter 3

From the depths of despair

Bill looked at his half-broken phone, it read 6:00 am, Friday 15th August 2014. He managed to make it one more week through purgatory. Bill spent at least 30 minutes every weekend half-heartedly applying for jobs in Melbourne. This time around, he planned on searching every single advertisement on Seek, Dental Job Search, Facebook, contacts, any avenue he could think of. Bill needed to be covert about it because he still needed the money from this job. Today, he had enough time to properly shower and have something to eat. There was some mild lingering headache from the previous night but nowhere near its peak. Bill never wanted to experience that again.

That weekend prior, Bill did nothing but drink. He woke up, drank, fell asleep again, drank some more. Alcohol was really cheap in Australia. There was a special on at Liquorland so Bill bought a pack of 48 cans of Victoria Bitter for $60. Bill did not have any pretensions when it came to alcohol. It all tasted the same and all produced the same effect as long as he drank enough of it. Bill knew he had work to do. However, the speech that Dr Sung gave Bill destroyed him emotionally. It was like someone took a sledgehammer and pulverised his very will to live. Bill thought about tying a knot with his tie onto the hanging rod for clothing fixed into the wardrobe. Heh, Bill thought, this house was probably so dilapidated that even if he *tried* to hang himself, the rod or walls would break. He could not kill himself even if he tried. Bill only managed to act after being forced to wake up for work on Monday.

Bill went through his routine. Pour some water, take a dose of caffeine, shower, dress and unusually take the additional step of retrieving the jar of peanut butter from the shelf. Bill looked at his bread, he bought it on the previous weekend over a week ago but the climate was fairly cold so it was hopefully still safe to consume. Bill inspected the packet only to find a faint trace of mould on the very end of the bread. Fuck it, Bill thought, it was the very last piece of bread, the rest was probably OK. Bill retrieved three slices of bread and spread the peanut butter on it. One piece was definitely not enough, the peanut butter was so firm it would rip through it like a heavy duty excavator. Two slices would be barely acceptable, three would be safe.

Bill gulped down the peanut butter and bread concoction. Nobody would call that a sandwich, not even close but it still tasted just fine. In fact, that was nowhere near enough peanut butter to be satiated so he took out the largest spoon in the drawer and scooped up as much peanut butter he could with one scoop and ate it straight out from the jar. For something that was so cheap, it tasted hell good, Bill thought. Bill did not know if he would be able to eat anything for the rest of the day so he needed something to energise him. Bill looked at his phone again, 6:50am. Not bad, Bill thought, should be plenty of time today, no need for speeding.

After arriving, Bill continued with his routine. Say hello, endure the mockery, check the books, prepare for the worst... He could never get "used to it." Bill did not find any obvious red flags on his books but the first patient was booked in for a half hour consultation for reviewing an extraction he did. Bill recalled the patient, it was a straightforward extraction, but the patient was on a government voucher so it was no surprise their mouth was a disaster. Bill would not be surprised if another tooth somewhere else flared up all of a sudden. Bill hated treating government vouchers. The government had a disastrous public dental system which was so useless they were better off just dismantling everything. Bill was an American at heart. He knew, no, it was just plain fact that everything the government touched turned to dust. As far as Bill knew, the public system probably was not even going to pay him. They were so pathetic, money probably came in only once every half year or so.

"Heya Bill, I'm back with you today," Wendy, Bill's most hated assistant announced while walking in. Bill grimaced and gave a barely audible grunt in assent. Within a few minutes, the first patient arrived. This time Bill wanted to check for himself what the patient was in for so he personally called out the patient's name,

"Mandy?" Bill greeted.

"Yes," the middle aged woman replied. She stood up and even before she entered the room she started complaining. "I went to the doctor a few days ago and he told me that there was an infection where you pulled me tooth out last week. I was in pain all last week and finally the pain's going away. It's only started calmin' down after I took the antibiotics," she continued explaining in a thick, broad Australian accent belying her lack of education.

Bill's blood pressure instantly skyrocketed. This useless, unemployed subhuman who was obviously a drug addict, received *free* fucking treatment and came here just to complain? Who was this motherfucker who told her she had an infection? Bill wanted to waterboard this cretin in front of him so she could reveal the name of that medical practitioner who planted these fantasies inside her head. Then he could burn down that fucker's house with his whole family inside. Cockroaches breed cockroaches after all. He could not let the little ones grow up to cause more harm to society. Mandy, the addict ruined all her teeth and now wanted the dentist to take all the responsibility. Bill never once stopped slaving and was receiving constant punishment for his hard work. The harder he worked the poorer he got. Only recently did he have a positive cash flow. Only a week ago his bank balance was $0. All this hard work and nothing to show for it. But this thing, was it even human? This thing received free handouts at the cost of Bill's life blood. This thing was consuming Bill's life.

"Ok, let me have a look," Bill said. Mandy made a "Hmph" sound and opened her mouth. Bill saw what he expected. There was some ulceration and a patch of white, typical of bone exposure caused by excessive smoking and alcohol consumption. Bill routinely advised patients to not drink or smoke for at least 24 hours but this degenerate in front of him was one of those who immediately started smoking the moment she walked outside. Dry socket. It was not an infection. Medical practitioners knew *nothing* about the mouth. Bill never once attempted to treat diabetes or heart disease because he was not a doctor. Why did that moron try to practice dentistry then? Bill hoped the antibiotics gave that thing in the chair some serious side effects. Maybe a clostridium difficile infection that would render her bedridden for months on end. She deserved it and that piece of shit doctor ought to be sued for fucking up another patient with blind treatment, Bill thought.

Bill's head started throbbing again, that headache was returning and his hands were quivering, again. Bill wanted to physically kick this patient to the kerb but he still had to keep it together. Just a little while longer.

"You're feeling better now so if you have any problems, let us know," Bill said while motioning with his head towards the door.

"That's it?" the patient replied, "Jesus I expect better service from my hairdresser."

This time, even Wendy was sympathetic to Bill.

"We get people like that, I was there when you did the extraction. She's harmless, everybody knows she's one of the town drunks. She's just upset she couldn't drink properly for a couple of weeks," Wendy said to cheer Bill up.

Bill waved his hand to dismiss the matter while he was fuming inside.

There were lots of unanswered questions. If such a patient were in such pain, why was she not booked in to him so he could talk some sense into that idiot? He told all the patients to call up if there were any problems but so far he thought there were no problems because nobody came back to see him. Bill was about to spiral further into anger until his phone suddenly started vibrating. He looked at the half cracked screen, it was one of the numbers for which he sent out a job application.

"Hold on Wendy, we still have 10 minutes until the next patient, I gotta get this," Bill said.

"Oooh, a call from the girlfriend eh?" Wend teased.

"Ha ha," Bill pretended to laugh. That was actually a sore spot for him. He did once have a girlfriend only for her to betray him. Women were all liars.

"Hello this is Bill," Bill answered the phone.

"Hi! This is Amanda calling from Mega Dental on Collins, how are you?" greeted the voice from the phone. Bill's anger immediately dissipated. Collins Street, Melbourne. This was as close to his dream as it could get. He placed almost zero effort and copy/pasted a generic cover letter to apply for this job because he never thought in a million years they would say yes. It was the longest shot he ever attempted but here was a genuine opportunity.

"Oh how are you?" Bill responded.

"Very well thanks. Our Boss Dr Andy Chen loved your application and just so happens we're looking for someone. I understand that you're all the way in Sydney right now and we do need a face to face interview, but before we do that, how about we offer a phone interview as part of the screening process?" Amanda continued.

"No problems, I'm good right now if you are," Bill said half in jest. Bill did not care what happened to his patients here. Even if this were a small chance, he would leave this hellhole in an instant.

"Not right now unfortunately, Dr Chen is quite busy but he is free at 1:30 during lunchtime, how about then?" Amanda asked.

"That's perfect," Bill replied. He was going to finish on time even if he had to walk out of the room. What were they going to do? Fire him? Bill did not care any more. For the first time in a month, Bill had a smile on his face.

"We'll chat at 1:30pm then, bye," Amanda said.

"Bye," Bill replied before hanging up.

With newfound determination igniting a flame in Bill's heart, he glided through the series of check-ups and fillings until he dropped down the instruments triumphantly after the last patient.

"Alright Jason, let's bring you back for another check-up in 6 months, Wendy, I'm heading out," Bill announced then walked out of the room. Was it so abrupt that it sounded rude? Perhaps. What did it matter? He was going to leave this dump anyway. Bill walked past the various surgeries and opened the rear exit door. He headed straight for his car and closed the door. This was perhaps the safest location where he could have the phone interview without the viper's den finding out. Well, there really was nothing to do now but to twiddle his thumbs, Bill thought. Bill took out his smartphone, it was 1:11pm, zero missed calls. They said 1:30pm and Bill knew he was going to run slightly late past 1pm but fortunately he had much time to spare.

Bill had to do something to occupy his time. Bill looked at his contact list. He had only a few friends in dental school. Since February, he had not spoken a word to any of his friends. Not even a single text. Bill harboured no insignificant amount of guilt for being incommunicado. He was sure they tried to contact him but he could not even check due to changing his phone number so frequently. He had no goddamn choice, it was out of necessity to save every dollar. That was just an excuse, Bill realised. He bought dozens of prepaid SIMs at Woolworths when they had a clearance but the real reason he did not contact them was because he just felt an overwhelming sense of shame. With each passing month, the barrier he voluntarily erected became increasingly rigid to a point where suddenly replying out of the blue while trapped in the deepest pit of despair was absolutely horrifying. He had to wait until he made something of himself. He either returned to Melbourne triumphantly, or in a coffin. There was no other acceptable option.

The only classmate he spoke to was a fellow Korean who for a short period of time worked as a competitor only a few kilometres down the road from Dr Sung's clinic. They enjoyed complaining about their clown bosses. He went by the English name of Henry and he did not last long before moving on to greener pastures. Why would anyone want to stay in this purgatory? Bill missed his gang. Aside from Henry, there was the angry Cheng who Bill missed most of all. Then there was the recent addition Tom who he met while working. Bill was feeling semi-conscious. Reminiscing about the past felt good. The grim reality was that every new day felt worse than the one before, rendering each day the worst day of his life. The best parts of his life *only* happened in the past. The gang accomplished so many interesting experiences that Bill would treasure for the rest of his life. Bill started deliriously drifting into his memories of the meals they shared, the debates and arguments they had (especially involving religion), the classroom shenanigans...

RRRRIIIIIIIING!

Again Bill was jolted awake by the sound of his phone. Bill felt infinitesimally light headed from his semi-conscious drifting but he felt alert enough to have this interview. Bill pressed the button to answer the phone.

"Hello this is Bill speaking," he answered.

"Hi Bill, this is Andy from Mega Dental on Collins, how are you going?" the voice sounded through the speaker.

"I'm very well thanks and you," Bill continued.

"All good. I heard that you're working all the way over in New South Wales, how're you going there? Thinking of returning to Melbourne?" Andy asked.

"It's OK here but nothing beats Mel-*borne*. I've been halfway around the world and all the way across Australia, Melbourne is the best city I have lived in," Bill elegantly blasted with his adopted theatrical tone. Despite living in Melbourne for 5 years, Bill always pronounced the city's name the way a tourist from America would say it, with a heavy emphasis on the "bourne" part, like Mel- BORN. However, he was serious. Bill loved living in the United States, he even liked Manhattan citizens better than Melbournians but that city was old and dirty. Overall, on balance, Melbourne was indeed the best city he had lived in.

"Ha Ha Ha," Andy laughed, "I agree, Melbourne is indeed the best. You graduated from Melbourne right? Your CV said so, that means you must know Terry Huang? He has been with us for many years now," Andy continued.

Terry, that was a name Bill had not thought about. He liked that kid. The lecturers used to say that he lacked a single bad bone in his body. Bill pitied that kid because he was bullied so much. His gang occasionally communicated with Terry but only very infrequently. Bill last spoke with him on good terms so he was fairly sure he could count the kid as an ally.

"Oh yeah, I remember Terry, medium height, glasses, likes crackin' jokes," Bill said, "tell him I said hi."

"Ah great, you'll fit right in. Most of our dentists here are Melbourne graduates. Could you give me a brief run-down of what kind of dentistry you have been doing? You did write that you have been working in private practice," Andy continued asking. Bill knew he could not write down the fact that the longest he could hold down a job was a few months.

"I've been halfway around the country, there is nothing I haven't seen," Bill loved his sophistry, there was some truth to it after all.

"Ah great, that's what you get from working in the country, so many patients aren't there? In Melbourne though, we see quite a lot of implants and orthodontic work, have you done any of that?" Andy asked.

"Ahh as you know, I don't have 40 years of experience like dem child labourers heh. Believe me though, if I could have been practising dentistry in the womb, there would be nothing stopping me. I've seen those procedures live and the first thing I'll do is to book in and do some implant and ortho courses," Bill replied like a politician.

"That's great, we're a team here and if you want to learn, I'll send cases your way. I would really like to see you in person and I want to make it worth your time. At the moment, I can only offer two days a week, but we're going to be opening another clinic some time next year and then we can give you more days," Andy finally made the offer.

"You tell me when, I'll be there immediately, sir," Bill replied with a strong emphasis on "sir" and absolutely zero hesitation.

"I don't want you rushing with a plane ticket or anything, so any time I'm working would be fine. I'll be on both days on the weekend, you can come any time," Andy continued.

"I'll be there first thing Saturday, sir," Bill jumped to reply.

"Haha, I love your enthusiasm. I'm probably going to have some time during our lunch break, so pop in and have a look at the place some time around 1 ish, cya then," Andy signed off.

"See you soon," Bill replied.

It was locked in. Bill did not care how much money he was to spend on an air fare. He was getting the hell out of this dump. He would even drive all the way there if there was nothing available. The smile on Bill's face spread into an unmistakable ear-to-ear grin. I'm coming back bitches! Bill thought to himself. Mel-*bourne*, Bill thought in his American accent as well, the greatest city in the world, bar none. The girls were so hot they were responsible for global warming, Bill thought. He was going to return as a hero. The world had punished him enough. He deserved this win. Finally, Bill thought he had grasped the threads of fate and wove them in his own favour.

Bill slid out of his car and started walking back to the clinic. He opened the door and quickly entered the sterilisation room and put a mask on his face to hide his grin. Good, Bill thought, nobody had seen him. He needed to keep this a secret. Two days a week was nowhere near enough money to support him. 40% of $0 was still $0 and there was no doubt that his income from those two days would indeed be close to $0. It was frustrating, but Bill still needed this Shellharbour job. Hopefully not for much longer. As Bill started walking towards his surgery, he heard the chatter emanating from the staff room. It was still lunch break so it was unsurprising that the nurses were still eating. Bill looked at the time on his smartphone, 1:43pm, the interview did not take long. He was going to book the plane ticket right now.

Bill was a maestro at finding the cheapest fares by now. Webjet, Wotif, airlines' own web pages, Bill did a thorough search of all of them. He did not care how much he needed to pay, he was going to board that damn plane no matter what. Nonetheless, Bill still enjoyed the thrill of finding a good bargain. There. He found it. 10pm red eye flight from Sydney to Melbourne. It was only $89, a far cry from the $213 it would have cost for a flight the next morning. Bill had to finish on time today. His suitcase full of suits was still unopened since moving the last time. He just needed to prepare some toiletries and drive straight to Sydney. He could make it. 4 hours was enough time to just barely make it. Bill took out his debit card and booked the flight and accommodation.

To be safe, Bill also signed into his email account to verify the invoice. Bill never memorised his password. It was a string of 16 random letters, symbols and numbers which he needed to write on a piece of paper just in case he needed to access any of his accounts while away from home. "R*LmpPAY2x$RMN(z" was going to be hard to type. Bill failed twice before finally typing in the correct combination. Bill scanned the page, air fares - check, hotel - check, wait a minute, Bill thought, that snake oil pedalling real estate agent finally responded. The landlord finally accepted the lease arrangement. It was a bit late now but Bill might as well accept. It would take potentially months for his client base in Melbourne to build up to an acceptable level. Bill typed in his response. He did not want to risk waiting too long for someone else to steal that lease.

Bill checked his appointment books. A whole afternoon of fillings and extractions. Bill hoped for the best. If something fractures, just palm it off to Dr White, Bill thought. He did not care any more. Bill walked into the staff room.

"Hey Casanova, chatting with the hot date again eh?" Wendy teased, "did you have your lunch?"

"Heh, come on now, you girls are the only ones I think about," Bill replied in jest.

"Oooh, Wendy's single you know," Lucy said in jest. Bill subconsciously dry wretched. There was no way he would let that used up whore come anywhere near him.

"I'm broke, I can't afford a wife," Bill said half sarcastically, although the bitter truth of that statement sent minor tremors of anger through his head, "I can't even afford lunch. You gonna eat that?" Bill pointed towards the half eaten burger. It was 5 minutes from the end of lunch break so Bill knew this was a good time to "snipe" the leftovers before they went in the bin.

"No, you can have it," Lucy replied. These females were always worried about weight loss. Perhaps they should have lived more like him, heh, Bil laughed to himself.

Bill grabbed a knife and shaved off a centimetre of the burger that had been in contact with Lucy. Even Bill had standards. He would not want to have contact with that feral saliva. Who knows, Bill thought, he did not want to catch Australian bat Lyssavirus, the rabies equivalent endemic to Australian animals. That's right, Bill thought, Lucy was indeed an animal.

"Look at Bill caring for the environment. There's not gonna be any food waste here in our clinic," Wendy chimed in jest. Bill poured himself a cup of water from the tap and washed down the remnants of the McDonald's burger. It was mostly cold but still tasted better than the unadorned peanut butter sandwich he made himself. Not bad, Bill thought as he disposed of the plastic cup and headed back towards his surgery.

Bill zoomed through that afternoon's patients like he was on cruise control. In his mind, he was rehearsing what he was going to say. Bill had only used his pre-written script less than a month back to interview for this job. After going through so many interviews, Bill recognised the questioning patterns prospective employers asked. Interviews were incredibly useless at discerning how well a new hire would perform. Everybody lied during interviews, it was just a game. Hence, there must be a winning strategy like any other game out there whether it be chess or Call of Duty. Bill rehearsed in front of the mirror just like his favourite orator of all time - Adolf Hitler. Say what you want about that guy, Bill thought. Bill felt that Hitler's dedication to theatrics and emotionally stirring speeches helped inspire Bill immensely. Bill actually met a lot of success obtaining jobs by combining the skills of Adolf Hitler and Don Draper, the fictional advertising executive from the television series Mad Men. He needed to channel Hitler's energy and Don Draper's cool, effortless arrogance.

What do you do when X goes wrong? How do you retain loyal patients? What are your hobbies? These questions were always asked. Bill contemptuously laughed at the morons who actually believed in such a system of screening applicants. Bill could have hired an actor and fed him lines through an earpiece. Just being good looking and confident would have a 99% chance of securing any job as long as someone cleared the cover letter and CV hurdle. God, society was invented and run by subhuman animals. Bill admired the Japanese for their engineering, however they screened their job applicants based on how well their Kanji handwriting appeared. It was amazing how such an intelligent society could have the collective mental retardation of believing that a person's handwriting was a window to their intelligence. Bill hoped Japanese people never saw white doctors whose handwriting appeared worse than an infant's scribbles. Not only that, they strictly wanted rehearsed answers only. In fact applicants purchased standardised job application question and answer textbooks. The entire world was fucked, Bill thought. But hey, since it was all a game, Bill would find every damn cheat, exploit and strategy available to take advantage of the game.

The second last patient of the day. Curved root, older, burly male patient, heavy decay. It was a recipe for disaster. Bill did not care any more,

"So Sean, this tooth has a big hook and it's gonna break when I pull on it," Bill informed the patient, "but don't worry, I'm going to prescribe some antibiotics to see how the pain goes. If it still hurts, then you can see Dr White who is an expert at removing teeth." Bill played it smart, he would not be caught calling another general dentist a "specialist." Bill also stopped caring about referrals. With any luck, this patient might become a headache for Dr Sung who definitely had nowhere near the skill to remove that tooth intact.

"Fair dinkum mate, I kinda wanted to drink with me mates tonight at the pub anyway, wouldn't want me mouth bleedin' like a bastard anyway," Sean replied. The man appeared to be almost 50 but that did not stop these people from drinking their lives away. Wendy on the other hand seemed to give Bill the death glare. Bill knew his time here at King's dental was limited. If he did not get fired, he would voluntarily leave anyway. He could not wait to leave this festering cesspit of malignant filth.

As the clock approached 5pm, Bill put down the instruments for the last patient. Enough was enough. The clean was done so he dismissed the patient then walked out the clinic after issuing a faint "goodbye" to whoever he saw on the way out. Dental record notes? Fuck it. Attending the interview in Mel-*borne* was more important than satisfying the monkeys down at the dental board who were too busy to audit someone in Whoop Whoop anyway. Bill was basically on auto-pilot. He cruised back to his rotted shack and triple showered, put his toiletries in a bag and shoved it inside his already packed suitcase. To be safe, Bill scooped out half the peanut butter remaining in the jar and gulped it down. He had to at least have some nutrition. Barely skipping a beat, Bill headed back to his car and started driving towards Sydney.

Bill was used to this by now. Park at a train station, ride the train to the airport, get past customs, then board the plane. It was even better that it was so late because the domestic lounges were mostly empty. International travellers were still milling around like an ant colony but it was fortunate Bill was not one of them. Of course, Bill was searched again while crossing customs because non-whites always looked suspicious. He had been through this numerous times already. He was basically still on auto-pilot. Just go through the motions, Bill thought. By the time the plane landed, it was already 11:15pm, a minor delay but almost on time. Bill did not need any check-in luggage so he headed straight out and hailed a taxi to his hotel.

The cheapest suite he could find was $150 a night. It was nothing fancy but for the price Bill was expecting something better than this. Every single hinge creaked like a growling beast. The white paint was faded and yellowing and there appeared to be mysterious stains on the bed sheets. It was disgusting so Bill took the towels from the shower and covered his clothing before pulling the sheets over his body. He would probably need to wash his clothes another three times with bleach before it was safe to wear. Bill sighed, hotels never cleaned their sheets anyway. They probably only changed them if someone defecated on the sheets. Then it would be too obvious so they would be forced to change them. Nonetheless, within a few minutes, Bill was already sound asleep.

Chapter 4

A new hope

Bill marched along Collins Street with a spring in his step. It was good to finally be back in Mel-*borne*. Everyone was ignoring him on the street just the way he liked it. One of Bill's nightmares was to run into a patient he had treated. There was always this sense of foreboding just in case the patient was unsatisfied with some aspect of his care. Besides, they were there to have him treat their teeth, not their mental health. He did not care and did not want to know what they did in their spare time. He was almost certain he would have treated psychopaths, child molesters and white supremacists by now. He approached that thought like the US military, "don't ask, don't tell." Bill did not recognise a single face on the street. This level of anonymity was what normal should be.

Ahh, Bill sighed in relief for the first time in months, the familiar tram intersection of Collins street and Swanston street. It was marked by the impressively gothic building on the corner. Collins street was full of pretty girls pursuing the lowest common denominator, Bill thought. If Bill could use sex appeal to sell dentistry, he would exploit it to the maximum. No matter what clinic Bill worked at, female dentists always billed more than him by a very, very wide margin. It was like comparing a rabbit and a turtle in a real life race. So much for the "gender wage gap," Bill thought. The clinic he was walking towards was a bit further down to the west so Bill crossed the road from the tram stop and briskly proceeded towards his destination.

That morning, Bill showered 5 times just to be safe. If the health inspector brought a UV lamp to inspect that hotel room, they would probably order it to be incinerated with nuclear fire. Bill was going all-out this time. His suit was bespoke, there were cheap tailors online who accepted custom orders. The belt - LV of course. He also packed his special Chanel for Men perfume. While Bill often neglected to buy food, he would never neglect his wardrobe. Bill loved his suits. After meticulously grooming his hair, placing facial foundation (it's not just for women, Bill thought) and putting on his specially packed shining leather boots, Bill donned his Burberry trenchcoat as the final layer before heading out.

The hotel was not directly inside the CBD but it was close enough. With just a few minutes' walk from the tram stop, Bill arrived at his destination. It was a multi-level building. The entrance was nondescript just like most of the businesses in the area. There was a Mega Dental logo on the directory plaque fixed against the wall in the foyer. Second floor eh, Bill thought, there were elevators but it was pretty crowded. Bill preferred the solitude of stairs anyway. Bill climbed the stairs only to be greeted by a large illuminated sign with the words, "Mega Dental on Collins." He was finally here.

Bill looked at the time, it was 12pm, he was early. It was only good manners to be early, plus he could have a tour of the clinic. He walked towards the automatic doors which let him through. There were two women at the reception desk. It was quite large, at least 5 metres in length. The outward side was covered in polished chrome while the top was polished marble. Everything was shining. The floor was polished marble, just the way Bill liked. There were two wide cylindrical pillars made of polished marble again adorned by Roman-esque ornate pilasters. Opposite the reception desk was a large, square window as tall as an adult. Although it was only the second floor, it was still a pretty decent view of the city beneath.

Bill greeted the reception team,

"Hi, my name is Dr William Parker, I'm here to speak to doctor Chen," Bill said to the nearest available receptionist.

"Oh yeah, I heard you were coming, doctor Chen is busy now, he's got a few more patients to go. You can have a look at the clinic while you're waiting, my name's Lakshmi by the way," the girl introduced herself. She had a mild Indian accent. The other receptionist was on the phone speaking in some Asian dialect, probably Chinese Mandarin from what it sounded like.

"Sounds good. Busy day today?" Bill decided to have some form of small talk to gather some more intelligence.

"It's OK, we're not swamped but everyone is working hard at the moment," Lakshmi replied, "Are you from Melbourne?" She probably caught on to his accent which was intentionally, very American.

"I've studied in the US before but I did dentistry in Melbourne," Bill replied, "what about you?" Since he was pretending to have some small talk, he might as well tag that on.

"I'm from India, I studied there actually, I'm currently doing my ADC exams," Lakshmi answered, "you might know some of our other dentists here, they're mostly from Melbourne Uni." Great, Bill thought sarcastically, dentistry was already massively oversupplied with unnecessary graduates but here was yet another foreigner deluded enough to believe she could strike it rich as a dentist in Australia. She did have at least *some* form of a dental degree no matter how questionable it was. Just that alone made her magnitudes more competent than the feral animals in the countryside.

As Bill was thinking that, he heard a familiar voice,

"I'll see you in 6 months, bye." Bill looked over, it was Terry Huang from dental school. Bill unenthusiastically said to Lakshmi, "Good luck with your exams," and headed towards Terry.

"Yo nigga T, what up fam?" Bill greeted Terry enthusiastically. Despite being fairly racist, Bill did admire the dialect used by black communities in the United States. After watching so many Hollywood movies, he was quite enamoured with their mannerisms.

"Oh hey Jin, wait, *you're* William Parker?" Terry replied quizzically.

"The one and only. I'm like Jesus, back from the dead, here to save you all," Bill proclaimed.

"Ha ha," Terry gave his usual "innocent young boy" laugh, "cool, you made it. Andy asked me if I knew this Bill Parker guy and I said no then he got all suspicious lol! How's Sarah by the way?"

That triggered a very painful memory for Bill. Bill once loved women. He felt like his sole purpose in life was to settle down with a good woman. He idolised their beauty and femininity. He spiralled down the typical delusional fantasy about women being delicate flowers. Truly the fairer sex descended from goddesses. For a long period of time, Bill read sociological studies about female behaviour, desires and sexual preferences. He researched online and imitated conversation tips and courtship strategies. It was a game after all so surely there was a strategy to attract the woman of his dreams. However, his previous girlfriend, Sarah, crushed his heart. One day, she just stopped contacting him. He knew exactly why. It was two months after graduation and Bill had no employment prospects. He had lived past his usefulness. All along, that bitch was only interested in his potential. She made a snap judgment that his potential was reduced to zero and so did her sexual interest in him.

"Ni-Guh, promise me one thing. Don't you fucking start about women. Those bitches ain't worth shit. I ditched the bitch and now I'm here to work, work, WORK!" Bill gave Terry a fairly stern warning.

"That's true lol," Terry replied. Bill knew that kid would understand because of how severely he was bullied by female students.

"How've you been nigguh? I missed yo ass after all this time," Bill said.

"Pretty good, haha, that was my last patient before lunch, I'll show you around," Terry invited Bill.

"Sounds good fam, lead the way," Bill replied while following Terry down a corridor lined with surgery offices.

"That's Andy, he's always busy, but he'll be finished soon," Terry said while pointing out the boss's surgery. "We've got the digital CEREC scanner here too, it's pretty good, you can do crowns really fast. I just did one for that patient you saw on the way out. Here's our OPG machine, here's the steri, here's the staff room.."

The tour went on for a short while. Terry explained that it was tough after graduation. He could not find a job for three months and actually went on government subsidies in mid-March. His case manager actually asked him to study and become a chef instead. Terry said he felt extremely depressed. Bill felt infuriated. Terry was a hard working domestic student. Born and raised in Australia. He was innocent yet was bullied unreasonably and undeservedly. Then as a final twist of the dagger, the same country that treated him so cruelly *dared* say to his face that his entire 25 years of life until now was completely wasted. It was not easy studying to become a dentist. Terry studied until midnight as if it were normal throughout high school to obtain the marks required. Dental school tortured both of them. Then society dared turn its head and say,

"Tee hee, jokes on you, should have just quit high school and learned to cook instead guys!"

The universe exacted a great punishment from Terry but ultimately rewarded him with this job. Terry said that he was on the way to earning over $100k by the end of next financial year. He was happy and doing well. Bill could tell from the tone of his voice. Terry used to be timid and quiet. Now he seemed fearless yet maintained that facade of innocence. It was almost like he found a way of weaponising innocence. Now that Bill was here, it felt like the universe was apologising to both of them and rewarding them as a form of recompense. The two men sat in the conference room discussing their recent experiences until the door was opened by Dr Chen.

"So I see you two are acquainted with each other," Andy announced his entrance.

"Yeah, haha, I had no idea he changed his name. He was called Jin-woo back in dental school. Bill Parker, I never would have thought he would choose that, sounded pretty weird, but now it suits him," Terry said.

"It does suit you, nice to finally meet you in person, I'm Andy by the way," Dr Chen started the interview.

"Nice to meet you too sir," Bill replied with a military salute. Some people found it weird that Bill gave military salutes. To Bill, it was only natural in order to show respect. In fact, if he greeted dignitaries while standing, he would also click his heels.

"Thanks for making the trip down here, how was it?" Andy asked.

"I'm used to it. I've been all around the country," Bill responded. Meanwhile, Terry headed out of the room.

"That sounds great, you seem so enthusiastic, I like that, we're in the process of expanding right now and one of the dentists unfortunately had a cancer diagnosis so we will need you to start working pretty soon at 40% commission, next week if possible. I wasn't sure if you could make it this weekend so we didn't have any patients booked in for you," Andy continued, "I'm planning to open a new clinic possibly towards the end of this year. In fact, they're working on construction right now. It's going to be in Carlton, pretty close to the dental school. You're used to that area by now right?"

"Yes sir," Bill replied.

"Once it opens, I can probably give you all of Monday to Friday as the lead practitioner," Andy continued. It almost sounded like a dream come true. To be able to pretty much become a lead dentist in a clinic so soon after graduation.

"Tell me a bit more about your experiences. What's your country practice like? Do you see lots of patients? Do you prefer big cases?" Andy asked.

"You know what it's like in the country, there's hell caries everywhere and people come in with an attitude like they should all be treated for free. I see like 10 patients a day, sometimes 15," Bill answered diplomatically.

"Here our books are mostly well filled but you won't be seeing 15 patients a day to begin with! You did lots of extractions right?" Andy continued interrogating.

"Yeah, broken teeth, wisdom teeth, baby teeth, you name it," Bill replied somewhat in boast.

"Great, we see lots of wisdom tooth cases here. We also have a CEREC scanner, have you used it before?" Andy asked.

"I've given it a try in dental school," Bill replied only semi-truthfully, he did manage to watch a demonstration in dental school.

"It's fantastic, instead of sending to the lab, we can do crowns in less than an hour, you'll love it," Andy recommended. "We're also very different from the countryside in terms of demographics. There's a lot of overseas students and young people. They're very tech savvy these days and shop around a lot. What strategies do you use to retain your patients?"

"My patients love me. I develop a relationship of trust between us. If I tell them whatever I touch turns to gold, they'll trust me. All those cheap insurance practices out there, Bupa, NIB, HCF, it's the easiest thing in the world to steal patients from them. Unlike those clinics, I actually care about the quality of my work. You see, I am a bit compulsive but I have worked hard to turn my compulsions to my advantage. Patients know that there's no way in hell I'd let them walk outta my surgery with trash in their mouth. If there's anything I can't do, I refer to my colleagues," Bill replied.

Bill loved his theatrics. What he said was not entirely a fabrication. He might have exaggerated slightly but the gist of it was true. Andy continued asking a few typical questions like Bill's hobbies and family background. All irrelevant garbage, Bill thought. It seemed like Dr Chen was not trying to do a psychological evaluation or anything significant. The job was as good as in the bag. Finally, Andy Chen wrapped up the interview.

"I think you'll really enjoy working with us. I hope it's not going to be too much of a burden flying in and out of Sydney. Are you planning to come work with us full time?" Andy asked.

"Absolutely sir, now that I'm back in Mel-*borne*, I'm gonna work till you carry me out on a stretcher. My life is gonna all be about work," Bill replied, "I've gotta say, it's good to be back. You know, those rural dentists in the countryside don't even know how to do dentistry. They're so backwards they're still using hand files for their endos and they tell *me* I'm the crazy person for learning about rotary files."

"I like your enthusiasm, enjoy your stay in Melbourne and keep doing those courses. If you want I can contact Sirona to organise some CEREC training. It's so easy, you'll never need to argue with a lab again. I've gotta rush to my other practice in Kew, nice meeting you, I'll let the girls know to make space for you next Saturday, all good?" Andy finally sealed the deal.

"Yes sir," Bill replied, while holding out his hand to shake on it.

Mission accomplished. Bill was elated. Not even the *marines* could get him outta here now, Bill thought. You would need goddamn Seal Team Six to carry him out in a body bag, Bill thought. In his rush to organise his Melbourne trip, Bill had neglected to book a return flight. Bill had to admit, if he did not get the job, maybe he would have just jumped off a building or something. After all, he knew how to get access to the dental hospital roof. A small corner of his mind was prepared for the worst but now he had won. Booking a flight back to Sydney was easy. There was always going to be at least one flight available. Bill did not care, he was just going to walk up to the airport and buy a ticket then and there. He had done it before. But before that, he was going to spoil himself with a proper meal.

After arriving at the airport, Bill managed to secure a ticket for a flight at 8pm, 4 hours from now. There was a McDonald's at the airport. Bill walked up to the counter and ordered his favourite,

"Hi, could I get a family McValue box?" Bill ordered.

"So that's the 4 burgers, family sized chips, 4 drinks value deal? What burgers would you like?" the serving girl asked with a mild level of incredulity.

"Give me 2 Big Macs and 2 Chicken and Cheese and I'd like 2 cokes and 2 waters for the drink," Bill continued.

"Alright, so that's 2 Big Macs, 2 Chicken and cheese, 2 cokes and 2 bottles of water? That would be $20 thanks, cash or card?" the employee continued.

"Card please," Bill replied. Bill tapped his card and waited for his order.

Bill was indeed ravenously hungry. Bill did not know when he would be able to eat again. Not just a snack, but any food at all. He lacked both the time and money. Today was special. He deserved to reward himself so he was going to eat enough for a week. It took him the greater part of an hour but he did indeed finish everything, including the beverages. It was going to take one hell of a long time to digest, Bill thought. With so much food to digest, Bill felt no short supply of lethargy and discomfort. To be safe Bill set an alarm to wake him an hour before boarding. Bill had one more problem to settle. That barrier he erected between him and his friends, it was finally time to demolish it. He was back and ready to face his friends with pride. The phone numbers were still stored on his phone even after repeatedly changing SIMs.

Bill trusted Cheng probably the most out of his friends. Bill empathised with Cheng's struggles. That nigga was unfairly treated by the world just like me, Bill thought. He might as well give it a try. Bill scrolled down to Cheng's number on the contact list. He hesitated for a second or two, but now was not the time for regrets, it was do or die time. Fighting back the hesitancy, Bill pressed down on the screen.
"Hello?" the line reached through, although there was loud background noise.

"Guess who bitch," Bill said.

"Wow, you're not dead? We've been trying to call you for ages bitch," Cheng replied, "I'm driving right now though so the signal might break up. There are quite a few signal dead zones here."

Bill knew Cheng was probably driving back to his dental clinic in the western Victorian countryside. Bill remembered that Cheng was actually one of the first people to find a job despite developing such a poor reputation at dental school. It was all because of the useless retards persecuting him, Bill thought, that guy deserved to be employed first as an act of defiance.

"Why the hell have you been radio silent for half a year bitch?" Cheng asked.

"It's a long fucking story, oh my god, you'll never guess what the fuck I've been through. But I'll tell you one thing fam, we gotta meet up in person to explain all this bullshit that's happened," Bill said.

"What happened to your girlfriend?" Cheng asked. Bill thought it was odd that two of his classmates asked him the same question in one day. Bill was probably the least likely person to have been able to find a girlfriend considering just how poorly he fared in dental school. Perhaps Sarah was the most interesting thing to have happened to him from the perspective of his friends.

"Oh my god, don't bring that bitch up. You gotta promise me one thing, PROMISE ME!" Bill shouted. His outburst did attract a few stares from the passing strangers.

"How would I make a promise I know nothing about," Cheng asked.

"Women are all trash, they make you think you had something real but in the end it's aaaaaaaall fucking fake. All a bunch of fucking lies. 'Dem Ko-reans are pieces of shit, NEVER fucking get involved with 'dem Ko-reans," Bill continued.

"So you two broke up then," Cheng tried to ascertain.

"Oh my god, promise me Cheng," Bill tried to sound serious by saying Cheng's actual name, "don't you fucking dare waste your time trying to pursue women. If I ever see you trying to simp or go white knighting in some fucking bullshit relationship, we are fucking through you got it? WE ARE FUCKING THROUGH!" Bill could not help but lose control of his emotions. Sarah left him crying alone at home overdosing on alcohol. That pain was so intense, he wanted to deep fry her entire rotten Korean family alive. Nothing he could physically inflict was as painful as the pain she caused him.

"Calm down idiot," Cheng's voice rang through the speaker while onlookers were increasingly wary of the mental patient screaming into his phone, "look at me, women go running the moment they see my face. I *wish* I had the ability to piss you off that much."

"I'll tell you about it later, face to face. That bitch is dead and buried," Bill said.

"Wh- khhhhh g," Cheng's voice started to fade. It seemed like his car was travelling through a dead zone. Then the line disconnected entirely. It was only 5:30pm, a long time to go. Bill dialled the number again - it failed to connect. Bill sighed, this was exactly what was expected from country driving. Bill waited a couple of minutes then tried again, this time it rang through.

"I told you so, that bit there is always a dead zone, WTF have you been doing all this time? The last time you messaged us, you said that you were homeless and tried to sleep in the clinic you worked at and relied on the old 'shower in a can,' " Cheng asked.

"I've been all over the country, but this time, I'm back bitches," Bill said, "after all this time, I've finally gotten back to the best city in the world, Mel-*borne*."

"It's *Mel-ben* you idiot, we keep telling you we're not in the United States any more," Cheng reminded Bill.

"Fine, Melbourne then, I'm gonna be working with Nigga Terry, remember that kid? You have no idea, that kid is now Wolf of Wall street, he's ballin' through the roof," Bill explained.

"Yeah I remember him, haven't talked to him in a long time," Cheng continued.

"Cheng, listen to me, I have been to hell and back. For a long time, I couldn't contact you because I was in a position of instability. You seemed so happy that you found a job. If I started talkin' about all this shit that's been happening in my life, you and Henry, I would have fuckin' ruined your lives making my problems your problems. Remember what I said about my life in Poland? It was even worse, I wanted to kill myself, but that's all in the past now. I almost gave up but I have discovered. You have control over your life. I know it's fuckin' hard and takes a long ass goddamn time, but we have more control over our lives than what it can feel like. Look at me, I'm finally back in Melbourne! It's *exactly* like I remembered. The best goddamn city in the world. The women here are so hot they're responsible for global warming!"

"Yeah I remember Poland. You were at Syracuse undergrad, forced to study bullshit arts subjects despite being a science major so you thought you could get a dental degree faster in Poland but that shitty university couldn't teach for shit and you decided to transfer to Australia," Cheng replied.

"I was drinking myself to death in Poland but at least I could wake up without a headache. But this time it was worse because for some reason, my head cannot stop hurting. I don't know if it's cause I'm an old piece of shit or caffeine withdrawal or malnutrition or some other bullshit," Bill elaborated, "it's hard to admit that I'm becoming an elderly cadaver. Listen Cheng, I believe in you. You can change your life too, come back to Melbourne."

"I would if I could but there's no fucking jobs bitch," Cheng retorted with more than just a little sense of hostility.

"OK, OK, I won't bring it up but please, just think about it. Back in Poland I thought that my entire life was a mistake but look at me now. Listen fam, *you* can control your fate. It might surprise you how much control, even if it's just a little bit, that you have," Bill said.

"I'm OK with this job, it doesn't pay much but 40% of $0 is still $0," Cheng mentioned that lesson again.

"I know, which is why I'm still gonna go back and forth between here and Shellharbour but as soon as Andy Chen opens up that new clinic, I'm gonna ditch that shit," Bill explained.

"By the way, I thought you hated Melbourne, what's with this sudden love obsession?" Cheng asked, seemingly mollified.

"You have to understand, that year I spent at Syracuse, that was what I thought Melbourne Dental School was going to be like. Back in the US, every single lecture was given by a PhD qualified professor. There were no garbage postgraduate fags teaching us because of understaffing or budget cuts. The school ran smoother than a fuckin' Formula 1 engine, a masterpiece. We had a private on campus hotel, shuttles, free gym, free lunches, all for *less* than the goddamn rip off bullshit school fees that Melbourne Dental School charged. Back then $1 AUD was worth *more* than $1 USD. This country should be fucking embarrassed that we had to pay *more* than an Ivy League education for some bullshit that was just barely competitive with Poland. The only goddamn thing that shithole MDS did better than Poland was that you spoke comprehensible English, not as well as the real English spoken in the US of A but close enough. How would you feel if you went to a proper goddamn university then paid *even more* to attend some shithole which couldn't even hire lecturers to teach and half the time have no supervisors while trying to treat patients?" Bill stated.

"Whatever, I agree with what you're saying but why the change of mind?" Cheng asked.

"You know, aside from Melbourne Dental School, the place does remind me of New York except it's cleaner. If you took the people from Manhattan to replace the assholes in the streets here, it would be perfect," Bill replied. The two continued reminiscing about their dental school days before Bill explained what actually happened during his radio silence.

"Alright, hey I might be reaching another dead zone, after that the signal gets really patchy beyond Ballarat," Cheng warned.

"I need to go soon anyway, let's meet up next Saturday, I missed yo ass, no homo," Bill asked.

"Alright, see ya bitch," Cheng said.

"Bye bitch, don't forget to add me into the Textsecure group chat," Bill returned. The phone line then disconnected. It was 7pm now. Bill felt better prepared to board the plane now. Most of the gastrointestinal discomfort was gone now. He was checked again for explosives and drugs (of course) and waited to board. It was a short flight of less than an hour without delay this time. By the time Bill returned to his hovel, it was already 12:15am. He would be sleep deprived the next day but so what, Bill thought, the Shellharbour job barely mattered any more.

Chapter 5

Not even the marines can get me outta here!

The same struggles persisted with his King's dental job. More tooth fractures, more complaining female patients and more betrayals from the staff. Bill wanted nothing more than to see all the animals here suffer in pain but he still needed their money. He was angry but this time he had something that he did not feel before - hope. All of a sudden, that torture was nowhere near as effective as only a few days before. Afterwards, Bill did manage to finally visit the real estate office to finalise the lease arrangements for a property here. Unfortunately the only property they had was a double story house costing $550 a week. It could not be helped. Bill drove up to the Wembley's real estate office and walked in. The receptionist greeted him,

"How can I help today?" she asked. Her name was printed on her badge, "Shelley."

"Hi, my name is William Parker, I received an email about a lease agreement?" Bill replied.

"Oh yes, just wait a moment, Margaret our property manager will be with you shortly," She explained.

What came to greet him was a middle aged woman on the higher end of the body-mass index.

"Hi, nice to meet you in person, come and let's finalise the lease," she explained. Bill walked into a small office with a document in triplicate present.

"Please have a read and sign all the spots which we have highlighted," she continued. So Bill read the document and signed where he needed. Nothing seemed out of the ordinary. Next was to move his belongings over. Bill actually did not own any furniture. No refrigerator, no washing machine, nothing which had the potential to impede his nomadic lifestyle. He had no goddamn choice. His life was so unstable he wished he could afford to buy some furniture and enjoy some luxuries in life. The agent handed him the keys so Bill took them and drove down to his new home. He did not have the time last week but he needed to cancel the lease for his dilapidated hovel.

Bill inserted the key and unlocked the front door. This property was an actual suburban house, not just a run-down unit. 1970s brick veneer, double storey, lawn and grass and garage, just like a typical California Bungalow. What immediately assaulted Bill was the cacophony and sheer terror of a black mist of insects flying through the house. Bill took out his camera and started recording. He was paying $550 a week for this infested piece of shit.

"What the hell? This is your typical house in Australia, people. This piece of shit costs $550 a week. Look at this. Wait, is that mould? Fuck! OK let's go up the stairs. I swear, this has got to be some murder house or some shit, someone must have died in here for all these insects to appear. See this? What the fuck, more goddamn flies." If he ever created a social media account, this was going in. He was going to need some Raid insecticide.

* * *

By Friday, Bill had served his time in purgatory and had booked the return flights and hotel accomodation for his first days working in Melbourne. He was more eager than ever. This time the hotel was much better quality but still cost $150 a night. The only problem was that it was in the suburbs. There was one suburb that Bill wanted to live in more than any other, that was South Yarra. This hotel was not in South Yarra, it was in Glenferrie. He had to catch the Airport Shuttle then the train to reach it. Fortunately the hotel concierge still worked at 11pm to usher Bill in. The sheets also did not have mysterious stains on them. He was going to be sleep deprived the next day but he had no goddamn choice. Money did not grow on trees.

Bill had always lived within walking distance of the dental school so he rarely ever caught public transport. Unfortunately, now he was forced to experience just how poor it was. On the weekends, there were substantially fewer trains than the peak hours of a working day. The train ran late as if the driver were ordered to have a sleepover at every stop. Bill did manage to make it before the opening time of 10am, if just barely. Bill trudged through the doors triumphantly and said hello to Lakshmi who he recognised.

"Good morning doctor, welcome," Lakshmi said, then she turned towards the Chinese receptionist and introduced her, "this is Mandy, she was too busy to speak to you last time."

"Good morning, nice to meet you," Mandy introduced herself.

"What's my day looking like today?" Bill asked.

"We've booked in 4 patients for you, the first patient is at 11," Lakshmi replied.

"Alright, I'll go and introduce myself. By the way, how many people are on today?" Bill inquired further.

"We have 6 dentists on today besides you," Lakshmi explained.

"Alright, I'll go introduce myself," Bill said before heading towards the surgeries.

"Hey, welcome, the boss is always a bit late, he rushes about all the time between clinics," Terry came out to greet Bill.

"Nigga T what up? Do I get an induction or something?" Bill asked.

"Last week was your induction lol. It was the same for me, he basically told me to start working the day after I interviewed. You'll get used to it," Terry replied just as another tall male walked past, "Hey Luke, this is Bill, we went to dental school together."

"Oh hey," Luke introduced himself, "welcome to the team," before walking off towards his surgery.

"Luke graduated way ahead of us. He's pretty good. Brian is my mentor and my hero, he rescues me a lot lol. There he is, this is Bill, do you remember him?" Terry continued the tour while introducing his hero.

"Oh hey, I don't remember your name but I have seen you around the dental school," Brian said as an introduction, "welcome to the team."

"I've seen you around too, do I get a mentor too?" Bill asked.

"Haha lol, it's just a joke, I'll be your mentor haha," Terry said, making Brian express something resembling either a grin or a grimace, it was probably a bit of both. "The two girls Lauren and Linda are always late. Lauren is the Asian one, you'll like her. Linda is the tall blonde, she's pretty but... kinda dodgy lol."

Bill walked into the surgery marked with his name. He asked Terry,

"Do I get some sort of login or something?"

"Just use mine, I was using the boss's sign-in for a couple of weeks before he gave me one, did you set up your provider number?" Terry asked.

"Not yet, those assholes at Medicare take forever," Bill replied.

"Then use the boss's number for now," Terry said while keying in his credentials on the computer. The fact that the IT network was a little disorganised did make Bill hesitate somewhat but he was not worried. The clinic used "Precise" dental management software. Bill knew that dealing with them was difficult and slow. It was normal to not bother preparing new dentists with login credentials until the clinic was sure they would stay on.

Bill looked at the bookings. There were nowhere near as many patients as King's dental but they were booked in much longer and appeared to require more complex treatment. Check-up, wants braces, second patient had a toothache from wisdom teeth, the next one was for root canal and last one was also a toothache. It was the city after all, people cared more for their teeth so it was natural they would want to save their teeth with root canal treatment rather than remove everything. Bill realised it was already 10:10 and the two female dentists had not arrived yet despite their patients already waiting. It seemed that no matter where he went, female dentists seemed to get away with whatever they wanted. Bill sat back down and started reading the files of the patients in the other dentist's books.

The three missing dentists finally arrived within the next five minutes. Andy walked past Bill's room and greeted him,

"Hey welcome, you have a few patients today, it's not bad. Just remember, every year it just keeps getting better and better." With those words of encouragement, Andy walked away to treat his patiently waiting patient. With nothing better to do, Bill walked out of his surgery and greeted the incoming female dentists. Terry was right, Lauren was not unattractive. He could tell she was probably late from putting so much effort into her appearance. Bill said "hello" to both of them. Lauren replied, "Hey, you must be the new guy, welcome, I'll be seeing you around."

Linda replied with a, "Good morning" and walked away.

Bill went through the next day's books as well, only 2 patients booked in. Both check-up and clean. Terry had 6 patients, so his books were more than half filled. The other dentists were about three quarters filled. It was definitely a different experience working here. While he was waiting, Bill decided to watch some videos on wisdom tooth extraction. He was a professional at dental video education because Melbourne Dental School was too incompetent to actually teach anything. Most graduates should have been more appropriately considered graduates of the YouTube dental school. What kind of desperation drove the school to have an ex-dentist who had next to no clinical experience to teach them how to drill and fill teeth? Having to learn the basics after graduation was far too late and just grossly irresponsible.

Towards 11am, another Indian woman walked in and introduced herself,

"Good morning, I'll be assisting you today, my name is Rania."

"Good morning, are you also doing the ADC exams?" Bill asked with a sneaking suspicion Rania was also a graduate from India trying to work in Australia. If she were, that would potentially make his life easier.

"No, not any more, I did study dentistry in India but I tried twice already. Instead I'm studying dental hygiene part time so I can become a hygienist," Rania said. Bill once tried applying for a job as a hygienist as well. Bill could never forget the older hygienist woman who interviewed him. She was obviously underqualified, after all all hygienists took a 1-2 year course which did not even teach basic anatomy sufficiently to administer local anaesthetic. However, that woman had the most arrogant attitude and displayed a collection of hygiene tools with a haughty "hmph" to suggest that she thought Bill could not even use them.

"Good luck with that. It's good that you're also a dentist, I always expect the best out of myself and anyone around me," Bill said, reverting to his usual rhetorics.

"Haha, I'm sure we'll be fine today," Rania said with some jest.

The day passed quite quickly without the drama of Bill's Shellharbour purgatory. With so much free time in between patients, Bill was able to spend as much time as he liked per patient. This was essential. Bill detested being forced to compromise. His compulsions drove him into that state close to an anxiety attack if he were forced to compromise. Whatever needed to be done, Bill must do it his way. Bill looked at his daily billings. $1400 for just 4 patients, not bad. In the country each patient was allotted such a short amount of time that Bill could not help but perform less work on each person. At this rate, Bill would actually be able to make a net profit from coming back to Melbourne even with so few patients. He even finished early with plenty of time to write his cursed notes. The future was looking brighter by the second.

Bill walked around to Terry's surgery. He was finishing off his last patient of the day. Bill listened to his conversation,

"... the crack seems kinda deep, if we leave it alone, the tooth might split apart and then we can't save it. We can do a metal crown which lasts the longest but costs a lot of money since we need to send it to a lab. Then you need to wait two weeks for them to make it. Or, we could make a CEREC crown which is not as durable as a metal crown but it's cheaper and obviously looks like an actual tooth,." Terry finished the conversation with that innocent child-like laugh.

"Makes sense, I'll book in once the tooth settles down," the patient said before walking out.

"Yo that was some Jordan Belfort shit right there," Bill remarked, comparing Terry to the Wolf of Wall Street.

"Who's that lol?" Terry replied innocently.

"The Wolf of Wall Street," Bill replied.

"Oh, I haven't seen that yet," Terry replied.

"It's like your ancestors were used car salesmen or something. I'm gonna meet up with Cheng, remember that kid? You should come with us," Bill invited Terry.

"That angry guy? I haven't seen him in a while, it will be fun," Terry responded, "just let me finish these notes then I'll be ready."

In fact it was Cheng who showed up at the clinic first. Bill looked away from his phone when he heard that familiar voice. There he was, asking the receptionists for Bill.

"Nigga what up, I missed yo ass, no homo," Bill said walking up to Cheng, "by the way, I asked nigga Terry to come along with us, you cool with that fam?"

"Whatever," Cheng said, "I just came back from a roadtrip to NSW and I'm driving back to work on Sunday so I have plenty of time." The two kept chatting until Terry came out.

"You took your time, let's go to that nearby ramen place," Bill said. Nobody disagreed so they headed down.

"... Then that crazy idiot said, 'if we did a root canal, there would be no more problems,' that piece of shit didn't listen to a word I said and then he complained that I didn't just wave a wand and Harrious Potterous

Alakazam! BAM and the tooth is fixed, I hope he drives into a tree," Cheng said in the midst of the trio complaining about their worst cases with bowls of ramen in front of them.

"Yo Terry, can you tell me what Linda does that makes her so dodgy? She was rude and arrogant just like all the other goddamn female dentists I've seen but the clinics I've been in, the females were 10x worse. The clinic owners were also hell arrogant," Bill said.

"She's a bitch, I was running just a little late and she goes and steals my next patient. It was a root canal patient as well," Terry said.

"That piece of shit Sung asshole did the same thing to me but he's the boss so I had no goddamn choice," Bill interjected.

"Yeah, Linda does that all the time. She did that to me multiple times now I don't even talk to her. She also charges for a temporary splint for $400 and lies to the patient, she pretends to 'check if they're grinding or not' but then charges for a proper lab made splint for another $450 regardless of what the temporary one looks like. Then she just chucks in fake item codes all the time, especially charging extra for temporary crowns and once she even charged a "desensitising per visit" item code 27 times in one visit lol," Terry elaborated.

Bill could not help but feel envy. Without a doubt, Linda got away with these unconscionable practices because she was female. She just exploited people who were stupid, vulnerable, or both. Bill had not even heard of dentists charging for a temporary splint. The proper one was far superior yet she charged almost the same price for an unnecessary and vastly inferior product. Bill never stooped to that level. He was a true professional. He did not care if his patients died in their sleep but the work he performed, even the fee charging, must be up to his standard.

"Does she actually do good work?" Bill asked.

"Lol, no," Terry said with that innocent smile on his face, "Andy caught her several times charging for subgingival debridement after spending at most 15 minutes leaving behind all the calculus. I've also had to replace lots of her fillings that fall out." That pretty much condemned Linda in the eyes of Bill. Treating a patient with severe gum disease took well over an hour, perhaps even several. But for Linda, it sounded like she just threw in fake charges and pretended to treat the patients. The morons back in Shellharbour complained about everything Bill did. But, he was proud of the fact that out of possibly dozens of fillings he placed, not one needed replacement, not even one. The opposite was true of the other dentists.

"She's lucky she's female. She only gets away with it *because* she's female. What about Lauren?" Bill asked.

"I don't know, she doesn't steal my patients lol so I don't know much about her. She's hell busy all the time, way busier than me," Terry replied.

"See? This is what I mean. People like us, we have to work like we're in Auschwitz but these goddamn females, aaaaaall those morons out there come in to look at a pretty face and they're like, 'hurt me harder! She can do no wrong! All is forgiven!' These females don't need to do good quality work. In fact, where I've been, *none* of the female dentists I've seen do *any* good quality work. They get to slice and dice and get away with it while us men who do things *properly*, we get fucking sued," Bill lamented.

"Yeah fuck that. Back in dental school, one teacher kept telling me that employers kept screaming, 'I want caucasian female dentists only! Caucasian female!' Like what the fuck is this bullshit? We're meant to be dentists not some fucking brothel," Cheng furiously chimed in.

"Caucasian female? Fuck 'em, where I've been, and trust me, I've been all around Australia, all those rich old white men, they want to see Asian females only. These old, fat, bald pieces of shit, they've all got some Asian fetish. You know how Asian women have washboard chests and look all underage and shit. All those old fuckwits want to be touched all over their face by those tiny, child-like fingers," Bill elaborated.

"Asian female? Where I've been, nobody wants to see Asian dentists. In fact, my boss said there were patients complaining to him, 'can't you get some proper white dentists?' We actually have an Asian female dentist, I wouldn't say she's 'balling'," Cheng argued back.

"That's cause she must be hell ugly. Maybe she's trans or some shit. Don't trust those Mel-borne Dental School morons, you can't trust anything but the truth you see with your own eyes. And unlike you, I have seen so much shit you won't even believe, especially when it comes to race. Tell your boss he *should* hire some white dentists. There's nothing wrong with that," Bill put his foot down.

"Haha lol, I think Bill is right about Asian female dentists. Lauren is busier than Linda. Linda has to resort to dodginess and screwing me over in order to ball," Terry stated in support of Bill.

"Whatever. You say this shit but you do realise that the majority of the population here in the CBD are Asian students. That's probably why Lauren is so busy," Cheng issued his analysis.

"Maybe, I see a lot of students and it's true that Linda doesn't see as many. Maybe it's because Linda can't speak Chinese lol," Terry surmised.

"Yo, your client base is fucked up. You know students are hell unreliable. I don't speak Chah-nese either. Why can't we just be honest. White doctors should see white patients, Chah-nese doctors see dem Chinese and Korean doctors see Korean patients. Females should see female doctors. What's wrong with that? I don't want to see some moron who gives me dirty looks. They're going to be suspicious of my every move, all ready to make some fucking allegation the moment they see something they don't like. All this equality bullshit has fucked up society. I know for a fact that when Euro fags bring their Euro faggotry into *this* country, they ain't gonna accept the way we do things here. They have that NHS and socialised healthcare garbage and expect *me* to slice and dice just like they're used to in their fucked up Euro shitholes. *Just* patch it up, *just* slap it on, they have no fucking clue what they're doing and they expect *me* to lower myself to their subhuman level? Fuck. Off. This is why those Euro fags should only see Euro fag doctors and Chinese assholes should only see Chinese. I've seen lots of patients from the US of A, and you know how many problems I've had with them? Zero," Bill opined as he hand gestured a "zero" symbol while placing extreme emphasis on the last word. "These NHS fags come to *this* country and expect us to bow and kowtow to their level of faggotry? I once went to an interview in WA where these two NHS assholes kept asking me questions about my ethnicity for five minutes straight. Those two morons just kept looking at me with dirty looks on their faces. They must have thought I was some white guy. You see, changing my name worked but these morons were hell fucking passive aggressive racist. I'm OK with being racist but this country forces people to pretend not to be. I got fucked over just because these two Euro fags didn't write, 'White doctors only'. I wasted a whole fucking day at my own expense getting there. What's wrong with writing on the ad, 'we only want white doctors. If your eyes are this narrow fuck off'? I see nothing wrong with that. In fact, that's the *only* fucking way society should be. Instead we have to be passive aggressive and everyone pretends they're not racist but I proudly admit that I AM RACIST! So are you two by the way, everyone should admit it. So I hope for everyone's sake we don't just see goddamn Chinese students all the time."

"Nah, it's alright. We see a lot of office workers too haha. I'm not racist, I like to see everyone haha," Terry lightheartedly quipped.

"No, no no, you don't get it. We *need* to be openly racist instead of all this passive aggressive bullshit. I can state for a fact, 100 percent, you two speak hell good English. Despite that, haven't you had white morons pretend they couldn't understand you after they see your face?" Bill asked.

"Uh... I'm not sure, maybe. Some guy once stared blankly because he expected me to sound like a FOB," Cheng referenced the "fresh off the boat" racist stereotype, "but was so shocked he looked around the room to see if there was another white guy."

"I haven't really, I don't know, maybe, definitely at least once but I can't remember lol," Terry also contributed.

"You see what I mean? Everyone is fucking racist but society says 'racism is bad!' and now everyone's gotta pretend they're not racists and they're *forced* to do this passive aggressive bullshit. We *need* to have open racism. If someone hurls shots directly at me, at least I can fuckin' defend myself. Instead, some passive aggressive racist bitch failed me for my IELTS bullshit. Almost cost me my citizenship. Then only a few weeks ago, and this happens lots of times by the way, some McDonald's bitch pretended she couldn't understand me when I asked for a soft serve. I know for a fuckin' fact that she was being passive aggressive with me cause the car behind me, it was a large as hell pickup trick with an engine sounding like a jet engine. But that asshole behind me could understand me *perfectly*. You know why? It was 'cause he couldn't see my face. This is a fuckin' disgrace. All these bitches just look at my face and assume I can't speak English worth a damn so they *intentionally* refuse to understand me. If we had open racism, then that bitch would refuse to serve me and get some Korean ho to serve me instead. There's nothing wrong with that. It's the way things *should* be," Bill pontificated with conviction.

"Maybe you're right, I sometimes feel like that lol. Poor Bill, maybe you were just dealing with bad people. Everyone's much nicer in Melbourne. What do you think of the other dentists in the clinic?" Terry asked. Bill spent some of his spare time looking through the books of the other dentists to check their work. Occasionally some dentists took x-rays to check their work, sometimes they took photos. Although it was not definitive, it did at least suggest if anyone was unscrupulous.

"They seemed aiight, I like that Luke guy. Man of few words, I like that. Brian does some pretty good endo. I don't know about the boss though, he sounds like he corrupted you bro, you used to be so innocent, now you're like Jordan Belfort," Bill replied. Terry laughed at that suggestion.

"Maybe he did corrupt me. Dental school was the worst. When Centrelink told me to become a chef, that was soul crushing. But he gave me a job in the end and I learned a lot from that guy. I don't have to worry about dental school or Centrelink any more thanks to him," Terry explained.

"I get the vibe you guys' boss is a bit of a sales rep," Cheng offered his opinion as well.

"What about Lauren Chan? You think she's pretty?" Terry asked.

"I will never look at women the same again after Sarah. Do me a favour, don't you guys dare get into a relationship. Women are incapable of being genuine. All they do is lie," Bill argued.

"Can you tell us what actually happened?" Cheng asked.

"Alright, but keep this to yourselves. Remember back when I first met her? That girl came up to *me*. I knew it was strange because you two saw me trying to pick up girls for years and all of them just ignored me. Well it turns out that ho was the same. All Koreans are Christians. They're not like white Christians either, they're all hell into it like a disease or something. 'Dem Ko-reans are just fake Christians too. All that bullshit about "love thy neighbour" and "give to the poor," it's all fake. 100% chance that bitch was fucking some Chad with a big dick the moment she left me or even before she left. Problems started happening around graduation. She wanted to go party and get high with her friends. I told her repeatedly, do not take drugs, do not drink alcohol. So much for her Christian beliefs, she only pretends to believe them when necessary. One night, she left a party obviously drunk and smelling like weed. We got into a huge argument. From that point onwards, it was pretty much over. We still met up and she even introduced her family. Her brother was some piece of shit pharmacy graduate and he was looking down on me for not having a job. I hate it when subhuman animals DARE fucking look down on ME!" Bill was audibly shouting now. He was obviously incensed. "That piece of shit, I just wanna give him some of Putin's favourite polonium, Novichok, up his asshole. That whole family was looking down on me. Even if you combined all of their intellect, they wouldn't even be able to accomplish half of what I have done to get where I am NOW! Goddamn it. In the end, all of a sudden Sarah just started ghosting me. I turned up at her door after a week but her mother just said to go away." It was clearly a painful memory for Bill.

"I heard that Sarah is working in Melbourne. You might even meet her lol," Terry suggested jokingly.

"Oh my god, I don't wanna see that bitch again for the rest of my life. That man who loved her, that piece of shit simp is DEAD. I killed him. Jin-woo is dead and buried. If you ever see her, just tell her Jin-woo is dead," Bill said.

"Or you can start balling like Mr Belfort here and walk up with a wad of cash and a pimp coat on and make them regret what they did to you," Cheng suggested.

"You know, you are a genius, that's why we're good friends. I might just do that one day," Bill said with a radical uplift in tone.

"I'm here in Mel-*born*, and I'm here to stay! Not even the MARINES can get me outta here! You gotta call Seal Team Six and I'm not goin' down easy. They gotta carry me out in a fuckin' casket!" Bill exclaimed with great enthusiasm. "I'm here to work, work WORK! I'm here to do nothing but WORK! You guys need to do the same. We're gonna ball through the fuckin' ROOF! Hoo-Ra!"

"Are you seriously gonna work 7 days a week?" Cheng asked.

"I don't give a fuck. You see all these lazy assholes walkin' on the street, they're all screwed. Totally screwed. You think this country has a future? All these welfare fags getting all the handouts. Fuck those guys OK. I'm gonna be the one with money when this country falls. All this real estate and CDO securitisation garbage you saw in the US, we're just copying them word for word. This country is gonna fall but I can promise you one thing, the United States will be the last, *last* to fall. But me, I'm gonna be there to watch these animals fucking kill each other in front of my lawn," Bill proselytised. "Especially you Cheng, your boss is ripping you off. Who the fuck pays dentists $30 an hour?"

"Shut up bitch, you think jobs grow on trees?" Cheng rebuked.

"Alright, alright, you gotta come back to Melbourne man," Bill responded.

"And how many patients are you seeing?" Cheng asked.

"Look, I just started OK, just look at Terry instead, soon I'll become just like that nigga, Jordan Belfort ain't got shit on me!" Bill continued. "Terry, I love you man, but you can do much, much worse. Listen, out in the country, I've seen some dodgy shit you would not even believe. Those snake oil barons out there just take photos of stained teeth and tell patients, 'look it's brown! That's bad!' then they drill in and say, 'look, it's brown underneath too! Lucky we caught it early.' You should bury Linda to the ground with next level dodginess. That bitch ain't got SHIT on those snake oil barons out there." That generated a chuckle from Terry.

"Enough fantasising, so what's happened to the rest of the class?" Cheng asked.

"Don't ask me ni-gguh, I haven't spoken to anyone but you, no homo," Bill stated.

"Haha, I only heard from people I've met at courses. The white kids from our class, they're balling like crazy. I heard that some people have set up their own clinics. I also heard that Cho-Seung and Tae-Hyun got arrested in Singapore lol," Terry explained.

"See what I mean? Koreans have corruption written into their DNA. They couldn't slice and dice in Australia so they decided to go running to the nearest Asian dump that recognises their degree and what do you know? They just can't help it," Bill pontificated.

"You're Korean yourself... Or are you special? Are you a North Korean prince in hiding or something?" Cheng mocked.

"Shut up. There are no Korean men like me. I'm way ahead of the curve. I've overcome my fucked up Korean DNA and ascended into a stable genius. We're all stable geniuses by the way, don't you two fucking forget that," Bill handed down his judgment.

"I wish I could be balling as hard as Blake Llewellyn, I caught up with him at this recent course and he said that he was seeing 20 patients a day doing 15 minute checkups and cleans. He was definitely earning over $300k a year, at least. I remember that he always worked really fast back in dental school," Terry sourly explained.

"Fuck that kid. He should just come out of the closet already. Stop worshipping that faggot. You know he gets all his patients from Grindr," Bill shut Terry down.

"He's married lol," Terry riposted.

"So what? I can have my parents arrange a fake marriage within a week. You wanna bet?" Bill denounced.

"Why DON'T you then?" Cheng goaded.

"Oh my god, isn't it fucking obvious? I told you, all dem Ko-reans are subhumans. I will *never* stoop down to that level. And neither should you. That Llewellyn guy however, that piece of shit needs to put on VR gay porn in order to fuck his wife. And don't you talk about speed. All the dentists that do shit quickly, 100% of them are all shit. Zero exceptions. Believe me, I've seen it all, I can say this with 100% certainty. I remember back in Dental school, this Llewellyn guy was leaving caries and fucking teeth up left right and centre but he was too delusional to care. I NEVER want to hear any more bullshit about fast equals good. You hear me? If you keep saying that low IQ shit, then you're gonna go on my list," Bill threatened.

"Lol, what list is this?" Terry probably should not have asked.

"Well Terry, if you get on this list, you'll get *exactly* what you got comin' for you. Guess what happens to people with low IQ? Cause the people on the list, they're all low IQ subhumans," Bill menacingly stated.

"Uhh... OK, I won't say that again," Terry timidly retreated.

"Good, fuck that guy, if you keep pulling that Jordan Belfort shit, you can drop that Llewellyn guy like a featherweight. You gotta aim for that heavyweight UFC shit my ni-gguh," Bill stated.

For all his self-confidence, Bill was still worried. Despite how much he hated working in Shellharbour, his income was *incomparably* higher there. The trio talked a bit more then paid the restaurant and allowed Terry to head home. Bill however did not want to catch public transport if he could avoid it.

"Yo bitch, you owe me, remember how much I helped you back in dental school? Can you gimme a ride? Come on man," Bill pleaded.

"That depends on how far you need me to drive you, I'm not driving all the way to Epping for your homeless ass," Cheng replied.

"You live in the Eastern suburbs right? My hotel is just a few kilometres outside the city, next to uh, what was it, Glen... Fer something station? It's on that ghetto ass Lilydale line," Bill said.

"You mean Glenferrie station?" Cheng confirmed.

"Yeah, just drop me off there," Bill said.

"Whatever, it's kind of on the way home," Cheng replied. Hence, with a short walk, the two reached Cheng's new car.

"Did you keep in contact with anyone during all that time?" Cheng asked.

"Hell no fam, you're the first in the gang I've contacted. I saw Henry only because he worked for some guy competing with us down the road. But he ditched. I also met this white guy, Tom, he was just like us. He's got these Aryan looks, Hitler would have been proud but he's all ashamed of that shit and pretends to be some SJW apologist. But that kid helped me a lot, I learned a lot of shit from that guy while we were working for Howard Chan in Shepparton. In fact, after we both ditched Chan's clinic, he gave me some intel on Shellharbour. I keep talkin' smack about Shellharbour, I bet that's why that guy ditched the place, but it's hell better than working for any of the other places I've been so far. Isn't that a tragedy? Dentistry has gone to hell. Mel-borne is the last city standing. I don't know what kinda boss you have but that Howard Chan guy, he's such a dodgy ass piece of shit. He had the magical ability to transform each tooth into cubes whenever he did a crown. You wouldn't believe that shit, he would just go zip, zip, like with an angle grinder. You remember how back in dental school it took us hours to do a single tooth whereas that guy finished in like 20 minutes. His crowns came back with 4mm gaps and he says to the patient, 'we'll just keep an eye on it.' You don't even see that shit in India. But Tom, that kid just said 'yes sir, yes sir' 'cause of his cucked D N A." Bill spaced out each letter of "DNA" with great emphasis. "I told that kid back in Shepparton, 'you gotta ditch this place' but he just got angry at me. What the fuck was wrong with that kid? I was trying to help him. You were saying the same shit just before. Come on man, I'm just trying to help you get a better job. After that, I ditched and found another job in WA, but that boss was a piece of shit too. Later Tom said he ain't working for that dodgy snake oil baron any more, he's gone to Cobram, which is just a misspelling of Whoop Whoop and they haven't figured it out yet. Jesus, that kid also needs to come back to Mel-*born*," Bill remarked at the end of his exposition.

"It's Mel-*ben* idiot, you just can't flush that US tourist out of your system," Cheng reminded.

"Mel*bourne* alright? I missed all yo asses, no homo. I'm back in Melbourne bitches! Did you see any good lookin' country hos? Country towns are a total wash. They're all hell feral. Drugs, cigarettes, alcohol, and all hell arrogant attitude despite, *despite*, none of them feral pieces of shit going to university. They can't even do an arts degree. In Melbourne university, those arts chicks were like models. They were so hot, they were contributing to global warming!" Bill exclaimed.

"They wouldn't date your creepy ass idiot, remember how much you failed?" Cheng brought Bill back to harsh reality.

"Well that's cause they're arts students. You get 3 of them together and they can't even do *half* of what I've managed. What do you think would happen if I just walked up to them and said, 'what's your price?'" Bill mused.

"You would get accused of sexual harassment and get thrown in jail idiot," Cheng issued more doses of reality.

"You never know. Those hos be broke *as fuck*, just give them a little push, like the Joker said in Dark Knight, all they need is a little push, and those hos gonna be begging for money. Just you wait, this country is gonna fall and those thirsty hos gonna be begging for my dick," Bill declared.

"Nobody wants that pencil dick idiot," Cheng joked.

"Shut up, you tall as hell but you don't know how to use your height to your advantage," Bill argued, "if I were as tall as you, I would have women lining up in the streets."

"Keep dreaming bitch," Cheng served more brutal reality.

The duo continued their banter until reaching Bill's destination near Glenferrie station.

"I'll see you next time, you coming back to Melbourne next weekend?" Bill asked.

"I don't know, only if I feel like it. I'm hell tired from all this driving. I'll let you know," Cheng answered.

"God speed," Bill said before walking away. Bill thought he might as well start contacting the gang on group chat. He took out his smartphone and typed through the cracked screen:

What up bitches? Miss me? I'm back in the greatest city in the world. I stayed radio silent because I was in a position of instability. Now nothing can get me out of here, not even the marines!

That was enough for now. The future was looking bright for Bill. Tomorrow he would likely see a couple more emergency bookings. Such patients did come, but to a lesser degree than the countryside. How long would he be able to keep up this fly in fly out lifestyle? Bill did have his doubts but as long as his body could keep up with it, he would keep going. Then as soon as he started seeing as many patients as Terry, he could finally leave that Shellharbour hellhole forever.

Chapter 6

A criminal lack of self-awareness

Bill worked by flying in and out of Sydney for three months. He was still seeing around 4-6 patients per day in Melbourne so that definitely was not enough to sustain his income. The hotel fees and air fares were also starting to take a toll on his efforts to accrue money. Bill checked his half broken phone again, it was now 1:13pm Saturday November 22nd. He only saw two patients that morning but he was still lethargic from the extensive travelling. Bill was planning on continuing with the discussion on Textsecure group chat with his gang last night on the merits of the free market economy but his drooping eyes were signalling otherwise. Bill loved the unleashed free market but Tom always countered everything he said. It was pretty annoying and Bill lacked the energy to argue back at times like these.

Bill stared at the OPG x-ray on the computer for the past wisdom tooth extraction patient. He was planning on writing notes when his eyelids became increasingly heavy. Without warning, Andy Chen walked in to greet Bill.

"Hey Bill, one of our weekday dentists, Allan is planning on dropping a couple of days. He said that he's planning on working in the suburbs so I'm wondering if you want to pick up a few days. I asked the other dentists first because I know you're busy working up in New South. How is that job going by the way?" Andy asked.

"It's alright. I'm busier over there but I have to say, gosh, rural dentists don't know what the hell they're doing. This clinic, is by far, the best clinic I've ever worked in," Bill reverted to his rhetorics again, triggering a slight chuckle from his boss, "I was always thinking of moving to Melbourne, in fact I've been looking for apartments to rent already. I just wanted to save up some money first but as soon as I do, I can start dropping days from Shellharbour."

"Let me know when you make a decision. Don't worry, come back to Melbourne, Christmas season is our busiest time! Allan told me he's dropping the days in 2 weeks," Andy elaborated, "You've got my number, I gotta head off, enjoy the rest of your afternoon, have a go with the CEREC!"

Bill was torn. If he worked for 4 days here in Melbourne, his income would probably drop by 50%. Considering the flying in and out costs, he would barely be earning minimum wage. In fact, he was phoning Cheng almost every second night for 2 hours or more at a time constantly deliberating back and forth regarding when to quit King's dental. So much so, the preoccupation over money overshadowed the cruel antics of the boss and staff at King's dental. If that purgatory stopped being so annoying, then it was possible to perhaps work there long term while flying in and out. Bill really was torn. This was a watershed moment. It was like fate, the universe and his own heart were all beating with one rhythm, guiding him towards the inevitable decision to leave Shellharbour. The only matter was when. If only the universe made just one more sign, he would make a firm decision.

That night, Bill phoned up Cheng again.

"Guess who bitch?" Bill spoke into the phone.

"Why do you keep calling me? I'm in the middle of gaming," Cheng replied.

"Come on man, why you gotta talk like that? I miss yo ass, no homo, and I need your advice on what the fuck I should do," Bill said.

"We talk about the same thing over and over again every night, can you keep it short this time? Has something happened? Did you kill someone in the chair?" Cheng said with no insignificant amount of irritation.

"Alright I'll keep this quick but there's gonna be some big changes. Some guy's gonna be dropping days at Mega and the boss asked me if I would pick them up. In the past we've only talked about dropping Shellharbour while looking for another Melbourne job but this time, I don't have to, I could be working 4 days and live in South Yarra, the baller suburb," Bill explained.

"Aren't you hell crawling? You said you only see about 4 patients a day, sometimes not even billing $1000 for the whole day," Cheng asked, throwing some water onto the fire.

"There are cheap places in South Yarra too, there's this single bedroom apartment which only costs like $250 a week, that's what you pay for that big ass country house," Bill continued.

"I pay $210 a week idiot, and it's a 3 bedroom house," Cheng said.

"That's what you get in some feral country town, but with rent as low as $250, I can still come out on top even with just 4 patients," Bill said.

"Then what are you waiting for? Tell that asshole boss you're gonna quit. Put on your pimp coat, gold rings *and* gold chains then tell him 'I quit bitch,'" Cheng recommended.

"Don't you think I want to do that? But I've got no goddamn choice, I need that money. It's actually not so bad any more, they're mostly leaving me alone these days. One more year, no problems, I'll just walk out, but my bank account is almost *zero* right now. If I quit, I'll be right back to square one. In fact, even worse than square one, I'll be back at square one after working like a fucking slave for another year," Bill complained.

Cheng listened to Bill's whining for another hour. He had had enough. Enough was enough at a certain point.

"Shut up idiot, you've said this 100 times already. Why have you kept phoning me without listening? I'm not your therapist, they get paid to listen to your bullshit just so you can ignore their advice," Cheng finally said.

"Come on man, why you gotta talk like that?" Bill pleaded.

"You've already made your decision. You never listen to me anyway so you're merely seeking my validation. You have my approval, go and ditch that piece of shit Shellharbour gig and crawl in Melbourne, at least you won't be so angry all the time," Cheng said.

"Alright, alright... Jesus, Jesus, Jesus... Alright, I'm gonna go for it when I'm back next week," Bill said.

"Bye bitch," Cheng ended the conversation.

"Go back to your wanking," Bill returned.

* * *

As if fate were complicit, the following Monday after work, Dr Sung summoned Bill to his surgery for a "chat."

"Bill, I have been hoping not to have this conversation with you but I did say on the day we met that after three months we would re-evaluate how things would proceed," Dr Sung chastised in the same condescending tone he used as if speaking to a 2 year old. "It's actually been over three months and I've been trying to push this back but it's about time we handled it. Remember Natalie Burns? She was such a lovely patient but only a week ago, she came back with a chipped filling. It was one of the fillings you did. The chip was small so I just polished it and reassured her but this shouldn't have happened. My fillings don't chip like that. She was extremely upset at how long you took and how much you charged. Normally fillings only take about 20 minutes to do but you took an hour for two of them and charged her full price. If the patient requires more than $500 of work which can be done in one visit, I normally give them a discount. This is the Christian way. Money isn't everything Bill. In Matthew 19:24, he said '...it is easier for a camel to go through the eye of a needle than for someone who is rich to enter the kingdom of God.' I did say we were a Christian, family practice do you recall?"

Bill's temper instantly flared. That motherfucking, goddamn subhuman cockroach! How *DARE* he criticise *MY* work?! Bill thought. Those fillings should NOT have been done in the first place yet he *forced* them on Bill and now he criticised Bill for charging a *fair* goddamn price for a fair job performed? That piece of shit subhuman rushed through all his work like a psychopath which resulted in chipped, broken, lost fillings left right and centre and they were all dumped on Bill to fix often at ZERO fucking cost. Bill had to do free fucking work for that megalomaniac and he *dared* accuse Bill of all this garbage? Now that shit-for-brains wanted to bring religion into the argument. It was a sign of a complete nutbag to start vomiting out Bible quotes. Oh this was going to be good.

"Yes you did," Bill replied with his orbicularis oris half twitching between a smile and frown. His anger was already dissipating. Instead of being angry, this show was transitioning into a comedy. Only a top tier retard with IQ as low as room temperature would have such little self-awareness.

"To be honest, I was hoping you would accept my invitation to join the church I attend. You said you were busy with another job which I did not object to - it's your life, your choice, but I really did expect more from you. The girls have been telling me that you still keep making the same mistakes. Our patients are our life blood yet you keep sending them away whether it's for referrals or being rude to them. I was willing to give you a chance to learn in the past 4 months. However, it seems like very little has changed. I'm afraid you're just not a good fit for our practice," Dr Sung continued with his verbal diarrhoea. "I'm really sorry to say this but I'm afraid we have to let you go."

By now, Bill was laughing on the inside. This was indeed fate. What did he expect? Subhuman animals will always be subhuman animals. Did anyone expect chimpanzees to stop throwing shit? Did anyone expect dogs to stop eating shit? These animals at King's Dental would struggle to even compete with dogs on an IQ test. They possessed the bare minimum IQ which enabled them to consciously breathe but anything beyond that would overheat their brains resulting in combustion. Trying to make these animals work in dentistry was like trying to run Windows 8 on a Pentium 1 processor. Just couldn't do it, Bill thought, just couldn't be done, can't make the impossible, possible after all.

"Yes sir," Bill said half smiling.

"I'm sorry so see you go but this is goodbye. I will be reallocating your patients for this week to the other dentists. I wish you luck in your future endeavours," Dr Sung concluded.

"You too," Bill gave a military salute and walked out of the room.

By now, Bill's anger had entirely dissipated. This was the sign he was looking for. It was almost perfect. It would only have gone better if

Bill were the one handing in a letter of resignation with an orchestra behind him. That would be quitting in style. Cheng played the violin so perhaps Bill could have hired that guy to add some more glitz and glam. Too late for that, Bill thought. The first thing Bill did after driving home was to phone Cheng.

"Bitch guess who," Bill initiated the conversation.

"Not again, what do you have to share this time?" Cheng asked.

"I've got big fucking news, you know how I said that this was fate? Well guess what," Bill counter-questioned.

"What? You killed someone? Don't waste my fucking time on anything less urgent," Cheng responded in jest.

"I'm ditching Shellharbour," Bill explained, then he tried to recall in as much detail as possible the conversation he had with Dr Sung.

"That guy sounds like a moron," Cheng replied, "doesn't he know that discriminating against people's religion contravenes the Fair Work Act? You know you can go to Fair Work and create a nightmare for him just for fun?"

"Forget it, that guy did me a favour. In fact, after seeing that shit, I can state with 100% certainty, that for *all* Koreans, there's something wrong built into their DNA. All that shit you see Koreans do, it's all genetic, they're born defective," Bill asserted.

"You're Korean, you do realise," Cheng advised.

"I've been fighting this garbage DNA my whole life. After all this time, I can confidently say that I have overcome my disability. I have risen above my Korean DNA and so you have you by the way. You don't do anything like 'dem Chahn-nese," Bill said with great emphasis on splitting the word "Chinese" into two syllables, the same way a Southern United States native would speak.

"So what you gonna do now?" Cheng asked.

"I need to ask for a favour alright? It's just gonna be temporary. You gotta help this homie out, you owe me bitch. At the moment, I'm actually homeless. Nuh uh uh uh pleh - before you say anything, it's not like I have any goddamn choice. I'm already preparing to have an inspection at that South Yarra apartment. When I'm working in the city, I'm gonna be renting some hotel rooms but *only* on the days I work. I can't afford to be renting *and* paying for hotels with only 4 days at Mega. I'm cancelling my country house lease today but I know those assholes are going to fuck me over. I definitely can't afford to fly in and out. Out of the fucking question. Until I can sign the South Yarra lease, I'm gonna be broke as fuck and I need to crash at your place on my days off," Bill pleaded.

"I'm gonna be really racking up my civic duty points housing a homeless guy. Well it's not as if anyone else lives there, and it's a big house. But it's pretty fucking messy because I don't clean the place. Also don't walk around the neighbourhood since it's a small town, they're gonna think we're gay or something. In Melbourne nobody's gonna care but gays get thrown out like they do in the Southern US states here in Beaufort," Cheng said.

That's right, Bill thought, Cheng worked in some far away country town beyond Ballarat. It was impossible to stay with Cheng all the time because driving for 2 hours to and from the city for work was too much. With the savings he had right now, it was very expensive to stay in hotel rooms for $150-200 a night for potentially a month continuously. Even worse, it was peak holiday season. There would probably be nothing available other than backpackers' accommodation centres. Bill would rather die than sink down to that level. Also, it was impossible to find a decent hotel room during the week of Christmas and New Year's. Not for a reasonable price.

"You're a good friend fam. You know I would die for you, you know that right?" Bill said to Cheng.

"Whatever, you say that to lots of people," Cheng returned.

"Only to us four, fuck everyone else. One day, when the world burns in nuclear fire, I want to be the one pressing the button, and I want all of you in the room with me," Bill said.

"Just tell me when you're going to come over," Cheng said.

"I don't know, I need to pack my shit, hire some sort of storage for my car and belongings, and get rid of this bullshit rip-off lease," Bill advised.

"Whatever, bye bitch," Cheng said.

"God speed son," Bill returned.

With that, Bill turned on the ignition and drove home. He had an antiquated laptop which was considered high end 8 years ago but was completely outdated junk today. It did the job so Bill did not complain. Bill worked through the task list. Search for car transport, because he was too goddamn tired to drive for 8 hours to Melbourne, search for short term car storage, book air fares, book the hotel, contact Wembley's real estate to cancel the lease which was not going to be cheap either. It could have been a month's worth of rent or until they found another tenant. So much to do, Bill thought, but he did have plenty of time. He still had until Friday before the deadline to return to Melbourne but Bill wanted his separation with Shellharbour to be complete like a divorce. He never wanted to return to this purgatory again. He did not want to hear about it, say its name or even think about it again. That's right, Bill thought, the next flight would be the last time he would make this trip. He might as well savour the moment.

"Uh hello," Bill spoke into his phone, "Is this Margaret?"

"Yes, this is Margaret from Wembley's real estate, how can I help," Margaret replied.

"Hi, I'm calling to notify you that I plan on moving out as soon as possible, what's your protocol?" Bill continued his line of questioning.

"I'm sorry to hear that you're moving out so soon. You signed up for a whole year's lease. There will be a termination fee in addition to the bridging fee until we can find another tenant. At this time of year, everyone is travelling so much it's going to be hard to find any permanent tenants," Margaret explained.

"Alright, no problem. Just email me the sum amount and I'll come pay it. Use my bond to pay for the cleaning services and keep the change," Bill said, because those fuckers would find some way of stealing his bond anyway, there was no point even trying.

"Aaaalllright, just leave it to me, I'll get everything sorted as soon as I step into the office tomorrow," Margaret responded, "anything else I can help you with?"

"No that will be all, good night," Bill concluded.

"Bye bye," Margaret said in turn. It was all coming together, Bill thought.

* * *

"Knock knock, guess who," Bill said as he knocked on Cheng's door.

"I'm coming bitch," Cheng said to welcome Bill. Bill heard the door click and it revealed Cheng standing in a narrow carpeted foyer with a room directly to the left and the lounge to the right.

"I brought some gifts my ne ge," Bill tried to use the Chinese expression, "��" which was pronounced very similar to his favourite expression. In his hand, he held a KFC two piece feed. It included chicken, chips, Pepsi, bread roll and potato & gravy.

"Thanks bitch, this doesn't make us even though," Cheng replied, inviting Bill in.

It was Thursday evening. Bill sorted out most of the paperwork on Tuesday and dropped off his car in Sydney on Wednesday so it could be delivered down to Melbourne's temporary garage. He only managed to pick it up today before driving it down to Beaufort. It took 90 minutes, but Bill was used to that distance from working in Shellharbour. Bill explained what was happening at Mega dental. The new clinic, the other dentists and the poor behaviour of some other dentists there. There were two unused bedrooms so Bill had no problem staying out of Chen's way. It was pretty easy.

"How long are you gonna stay here for?" Cheng asked.

"Don't kick me out fam, you owe me remember," Bill joked.

"I don't owe you shit bitch," Cheng replied.

"Next week, those South Yarra fags, they call themselves Barrington real estate, they said they'll give me a tour of some cheap ass apartment on Hope Street, I'll submit my application as soon as possible," Bill explained.

"You can stay here when you need to but if you become a permanent fixture you better pay some of my rent bitch. Plus, this is hell far, you seriously gonna drive 2 hours each way for work?" Cheng asked.

"I've had to deal with much worse, it's only temporary," Bill replied. The two chatted some more then went to sleep.

The next two weeks at Mega dental were much busier than Bill expected. Dr Chen explained to Bill that Christmas was the busiest season by far. Instead of 4 patients a day, Bill was seeing close to 10 patients a day, almost as busy as some country practices. Bill did indeed feel like he was "balling through the roof."Considering he was now working 4 days a week with almost full books, Bill had not even the most infinitesimal quark of regret remaining. Goodbye and good riddance to Shellharbour, Bill thought.

The clinic was forced to close on Christmas day due to inane government rules about restricted trading. Cheng had once explained the story of Frank Penhalluriack who was arrested for Sunday trading as recently as 1982. What a fucked up legal system, Bill thought. The two men tried to drive to the nearest McDonald's in Ballarat, it was a wasted hour long return trip because even they were too lazy to open. They had to eat Cheng's rice cooker deluxe, a misnomer considering it consisted of throwing in random vegetables and meat without any seasoning. Perhaps a bit of salt. Cheng was ultra-practical and preferred to cook "hands free," Bill admired such thinking, something which took women hours to do, Cheng could do it with a flick of a button while taking a shower. Good taste was overrated.

This time, obtaining a rental property was much easier than the useless morons he was used to dealing with in country towns. The inspection went well enough. The landlord accepted the offer easily as well. The place was a dump but Bill did not care. What was most important to Bill was the 3141 postcode. Unfortunately because it was holiday time, everyone was forced to take leave so moving in would be delayed until after the first week of January. Nobody followed religion properly any more but everybody was quick to use religion as an excuse to take a holiday. Bill would have loved to work on Christmas day if only he could but the ridiculous labour laws of this nation were unbelievable. Boxing day and the following weekend were very busy days for Bill.

Ever since Allan dropped Thursday and Friday, Bill was now working a continuous 4 day work week. Things could not have been better.

* * *

Bill looked at his new smartphone. Why not get a new phone? Bill had some level of stability now and he could afford to use something that was not on the verge of collapse. It was a new iPhone 4 which despite being outdated, it was still Apple and on a $25 a month plan with unlimited calls, it seemed to be a pretty decent deal. It was 6:10pm Monday January 5th 2015, he had spent the day moving some of his old dental school belongings from the storage into his new apartment. Bill dialed the number for Cheng,

"Guess who," Bill spoke into the phone.

"You know, I always pick up your phone calls but you never pick up mine. Once I saw a meme about a situation where a terrorist kidnaps someone and asks them, 'I'll give you a chance to live, phone up any contact you like, but if they pick up, we'll shoot you.' I know I'm gonna be 100% safe because you never pick up my fucking calls," Cheng replied.

"Come on man, don't put it that way, can you hear a difference by the way?" Bill asked.

"Not sure, you sound like you're shitting on the toilet," Cheng replied.

"I'm not, why you gotta say that? I got a new phone bitch, iPhone 4 cause I'm a baller now. You hear the difference?" Bill continued.

"That phone's hell old, we're already up to the iPhone 6, it just sounds echoey," Cheng replied.

"Must be the acoustics, I'm in my new apartment using my new phone bitch, this is what success looks like, one day, you'll be ballin' too, just ditch your piece of shit country town already," Bill insisted.

"Why don't you shut the fuck up? If there were a job available right now in Melbourne with full books and 40% commission, I would ditch right away but you don't see that shit growing on trees do you?" Cheng rebuked, sounding somewhat upset.

"OK, OK, but next time you're here in Melbourne, we're gonna celebrate alright. I'm inviting everyone. I know for a fact that Tom is doing some Lonely Planet holiday bullshit drinking himself to death down in Melbourne this Christmas. Henry's back too, his family always has this Christmas thing cause they're fake 'Christians.' We should all go out for a party, on me," Bill offered.

"Fine, whatever, as long as you're paying," Cheng replied.

"Let's lock that shit in," Bill decided.

* * *

Bill looked at his shiny phone, it was Wednesday 6:57pm, right in the middle of summer and the sun was still a couple hours away from going down. Bill found the gang already present outside Dainty Sichuan Chinese restaurant on Toorak road. Henry looked gaunt, almost like skin and bones. Tom looked like he always did with that smug air of superiority about him. Bill immediately adopted a haughty swagger as seen in Hollywood Mafia movies and extended his arms out as if he were about to hug them.

"Look who it is, ha ha haaaa," Bill expressed a melodramatic fake laugh, "Tom, Henry, I'm back bitches. Cheng, sir."

"Are you back or are you just going to disappear again?" Cheng joked.

"I had my reasons," Bill replied, "I wasn't ready to establish contact until now, everybody else was doing well around me but I had a million problems. I couldn't bring my problems back here. But those days are

DEAD, I'm back Melbourne! It's gonna take Seal Team Six to get me outta here!" Bill continued.

"Hello Jin," Henry greeted, "it's been a while, I hope you are well."

"Come here man, I missed yo asses, no homo," Bill said while hugging Henry, although Tom seemed a bit uncomfortable so Bill backed away. Did that guy secretly hate Asians? It did not matter, everyone was a racist, especially Bill.

"What are we waiting for? Let's go in!" Bill announced.

It was a long time coming, Bill thought. He had suffered so many trials and tribulations. He *deserved* this. Bill and Cheng loved spicy food but Tom and Henry could not handle it. Cheng did the ordering because he spoke Chinese but that idiot did not speak it well enough and accidentally ordered a fish that cost $170 because he heard $70, which was actually per half kilo. The gang discussed their trials and tribulations, with Bill taking up most of the rhetoric. It was a touching reunion, Bill thought. 2015 was going to be *his* year. All the pieces lined up perfectly, as if guided by the invisible hand of fate. From here, his life was going to improve, or so he thought...

Chapter 7

All that glitters is not gold

It was Thursday and Bill was half-way through his patient list in the morning. He was fully booked, the Christmas/new year's rush was not yet over. Bill examined the patient file for his next patient, it was Anusha Gupta, in for her whitening treatment. Bill had never performed in-office tooth whitening before. It was antithetical to Bill's quest to perform evidence based therapeutic treatment. Bill did her checkup and clean last week. The patient had perfectly healthy teeth, any desire for cosmetic enhancements were a complete waste of time and money, but she wanted it so who was he to say no. Unfortunately, Bill needed to rely on his assistant this time so he asked,

"Rania, have you done in chair bleaching before?"

"That's what the next patient is in for right? No worries, I'll set everything up," Rania replied while walking out the room to retrieve the whitening kit.

Meanwhile, Bill walked down the corridor to usher in his patient. Bill remembered that last week, he specifically told her,

"I'm not sure what codes we're using so I *can't*,' with *immense* emphasis on the "can't", "give you an accurate quote. What I can do is give you a sample quote, because there are a couple of codes which I know for certain will apply, how many times or whatever other codes, I'll know on the day of treatment."

Bill was also certain that he explained the general complications, including the typical cold sensitivity which would be temporary. He never performed the procedure before so he did not know how well patients tolerated it but his colleagues who had performed it dozens of times told him that almost everybody felt a bit too sensitive to tolerate the entire hour of treatment. Most patients lasted about 45 minutes of bleaching. There was no way in hell he would forget to warn her about his colleagues' most common complication.

"Anusha?" Bill announced while looking for an Indian woman.

"Good morning, how are you?" Anusha replied, almost sounding Australian. She told him that she came to Australia when she was late in her studies, so Bill guessed it was probably around high school. She seemed to have eliminated most traces of her Indian accent but not completely. She obviously practiced with great effort to sound as Australian as possible. Bill responded with a solemn, "Good how are you" and guided her towards his surgery. She looked like she was in her early 30s and was placing an extreme emphasis on cultivating that "young urban professional" appearance. The older Australians had a term for this kind of people, "yuppies." Bill was technically a yuppie himself by definition but this woman behaved like she was Glen Close from "The Devil Wears Prada." She dressed with the typical female pant suit and persisted with that air of superiority as if she had achieved something spectacular. Bill was not sure which movies she watched but whichever movies she did, she paid way too much attention. That kind of behaviour was *not* normal. The elderly were right in the way they disliked yuppies, this woman behaved like a dwarf among midgets. Probably some human resources figurehead given some semblance of power over helpless employees and translating that delusion into real life, as if she *deserved* to be treated like a queen.

Bill had met lots of actually successful people. They did not behave like that. They had won life, they did not care about the opinions of the masses. This woman was severely overcompensating and just watching her walk and tilt her head in that overtly arrogant manner aggravated him immensely. Bill went through the rough overview of the procedure and started setting up. Bill looked at the time, it was already 10 minutes into the appointment and he had not started bleaching yet. Rania had told him it took an hour but Bill felt increasingly insecure about his time management. He had no choice but to look at the instructions given in the whitening kit. Ok, the blue thing goes here, the cotton wool goes here, this liquid thing goes here, but how thick should I put it? Bill thought to himself.

The procedure was not hard, but it took a hell of a long time and there was no possible way to speed it up because the blue lamp was programmed by proprietary software to shine for 15 minutes for each cycle. Did it actually do anything? Bill had placed 37% hydrogen peroxide solution on the patient's teeth. In dental school, nobody taught him about any light activated peroxide, that shit was pretty dangerous just by itself, Bill thought. Fortunately for his time management, Anusha only managed to tolerate 3 cycles but Bill was already running 10 minutes late.

"I think that's enough, my left teeth are feeling a bit sensitive," Anusha informed Bill.

"That's OK, most people last as long as you have so that's normal," Bill replied.

"Will I be OK?" Anusha asked. Bill had no idea, his colleagues told him that the sensitivity was temporary, but how long? One day? One week? One month?

"Avoid hot and cold foods and drinks and it will be fine, it's temporary," Bill reassured Anusha while sounding somewhat insecure.

"Uhh, OK," Anusha seemed to lack confidence.

"If you have any problems, just let me know," Bill replied before Anusha departed.

Bill tried to piece together the codes Terry had suggested to reach $350, the promotional price. He was already 15 minutes late so he decided to help Rania set up hoping to reduce the waiting time for the following patient. Within a minute of sending the code through to reception, Ellen the Thursday receptionist walked in holding the receipt for the sample quote Bill provided last week.

"Bill, Anusha was complaining that she was only quoted $180 last time," Ellen said. Bill's biological furnace immediately flared. That fucking bitch. He very definitively told her that it was *NOT* a goddamn quote because he did not have the right codes. But, that was not all.

"She was getting a bit aggressive, she said she works for Theranus insurance and that she knew how all this worked," Ellen continued. Bill was cornered. He could argue but the next patient was waiting. The next patient deserved their allocated time and so did the 3 other patients after that. It would be a domino effect of running late one after another. Even if he won the argument, that bitch would probably cause problems for him because she worked for Theranus. Bill hated those fucking useless, rent seeking, ponzi scams masquerading as insurance companies. They had the power to arbitrarily audit him at any time and even finding the tiniest, most miniscule error could cause an endless headache. It was not humanly possible to make zero mistakes. Why the fuck did dentists invite these subhumans to get violate them without Vaseline?

That fucking bitch schemed this from the last visit. Bill thought he escaped most of the subhuman behaviour from Shellharbour but it seemed that there were vile, subhuman animals everywhere. He tried not to expose his anger to Ellen but it was hard.

"Jesus just charge her whatever. I don't have time for this garbage, can you handle it?" Bill spoke with immense irritation causing Ellen to furrow her brows ever so slightly more. He was a dentist, it was his job to make sure patients receive quality treatment, not to handle financial matters. Dentists usually called receptionists the "door bitch," their role was to be like cerberus, Hades' 3 headed guard dog. If they did their goddamn job that fucking immigrant bitch would *not* be able to make threats like this. But noooo... the staff outside were less like cerberus and more like poodles with cowardice to match.

Ellen did not seem happy but she had herself and that subhuman patient to blame. Bill walked past Ellen by the door and called out the next patient while averting his gaze from the subhuman Anusha. Ashleigh, the next patient, apparently needed some tooth glued back on. The man who responded appeared to be in his late 40s, probably some boardroom type figure who did not seem happy. His greeting immediately placed him on the wrong footing with Bill,

"Listen mate, I've got some business to attend to pretty soon, I just need you to glue this back on," he said while holding up a Maryland bridge. Bill instantly knew it was going to be a problem. Dentists called it a "Maryland" because the University of Maryland popularised the concept of attaching a ceramic tooth onto a metal plate which glued itself onto the tooth next door. They were horrendously unreliable and Bill never wanted to touch any of that desperate garbage. Regardless of the fact that a prestigious United States university contributed to its practice.

Bill already had a speech in mind for situations like this. Whenever crowns or other glued in prosthetics fell off there was a reason. Not only that, attempting to glue them back on almost universally proved to be less reliable than the first attempt. Why? Something known as the ravages of time. Bill explained all of what he just thought and added,

"I cannot guarantee any longevity, it could last a few days or a few years."

"It's already been glued back on twice, I know the whole spiel," Ashleigh responded. Bill thought this asshole patient interrupting him resembled that arrogant immigrant before. They both overvalued their own societal contribution and this man was somewhat effeminate, probably homosexual. Bill was once taught hatred for any person who was not cis-straight by his "Christian" parents, but after being reverse-indoctrinated by his gang of dental school friends, Bill relieved himself of his hatred of gays. They never bothered him so Bill did not care. However, if this gay man decided to make an enemy of Bill now, he was in a great position to resurrect some of that indoctrinated enmity.

Bill examined the prosthesis - it had layers upon layers of caked on glue. It fit onto its corresponding tooth seemingly well. Whatever Bill did, he would do it properly otherwise his compulsions would drive him insane again. He wasted the next half hour gently removing the caked on garbage and glued the tooth back on.

"Be careful, you can't bite anything hard with that," Bill reminded the patient.

"Yeah, the previous dentist also said that, I've been really careful, it lasted three years," Ashleigh replied.

"You never know," Bill replied while looking at the clock on the wall. He was now running 30 minutes late. Bill guided out Ashleigh while preparing to explain the situation to the next patient.

"Jessica?" Bill called out as a young blonde girl started to stand up, "I'm running a late but I'll be with you as soon as I can."

"Are you sure? I've been already waiting for half an hour. How much longer?" a seemingly disgruntled Jessica responded. Bill hated these situations. He tried his best to run on time but situations like this were out of his control. If he could wave a wand and run on time all the time he would do that but how could he know how complex the cases would be before he had even seen them? He had no fucking reason to apologise, Bill thought, it was *not* his goddamn fault he ran late despite his best efforts. It physically hurt him to say it but he still forced it out,

"I'm sorry for running late, I will be as quick as possible," Bill replied through gritted teeth and white knuckles. Jessica did not respond while she sat down.

Bill hurried back to his surgery. He made a mess trying to clean up all that old cement and the glue he used was not easy to tidy up either. Again, he tried to help Rania clean up and set up for the next patient. It took them both about 5 more minutes. Unfortunately, it seemed Jessica was not willing to wait that long as she was gone. Bill walked up to Ellen and asked her only to have her respond with,

"She just left, I tried to call her name as she walked out but she just ignored me."

Fuck. Bill thought he had escaped the worst of it in Shellharbour but misfortune always came in bundles. When it rained, it poured. The silver lining was that it was lunch time now but that did very little to mollify Bill.

That very afternoon after work, Brian came into Bill's office.

"Hey man, I saw your patient this afternoon. You were fully booked so the receptionists booked her in with me. I did have some free time. I think her name was Anusha... Yes that's right. She was actually crying, she said the whitening felt like torture, it seemed weird, did she kick up such a fuss during the whitening session?" Brian asked. Again, the furnace was lit. Bill could almost feel his head spinning, his fists were clenching. All he could think about was taking a sledgehammer to Anusha's skull and splitting it apart like a watermelon. Brian's facial expression was not one of anger, at least he seemed to understand that it was the patient exaggerating the whole story. Why else would he ask about the circumstances of the matter?

"No, she just said it was sensitive," Bill responded.

"She was a bit of a princess so I gave her some LA and she seemed OK after that. In the past when I've seen patients with extreme sensitivity, they're usually jumping in the chair, it's pretty rare though," Brian added.

"She was just a fucking bitch, you helped me out bro, I know you got my back. I got your back too, don't forget that, I'd die for you bro," Bill added half in jest.

"No worries, I just wanted to let you know," Brian said before heading back to his surgery.

Unfortunately, that week contained more trauma for Bill. The day after, as he was finishing his third last patient, Ellen sent Bill a message to read. It was a complaint from Ashleigh.

> *Bill, your patient Ashleigh came back saying that his bridge fell out again. You were busy so we booked him in with Terry who glued it on again. Ashleigh seemed quite upset, he said that the previous cementation lasted three years so it should have lasted another three years.*

Bill instantly flared up. He wanted to smash the computer with a baseball bat then make mincemeat of both Ashleigh and Ellen. What the fuck was that woman thinking? How does interrupting him now of all times help? It was not urgent, she could have waited for the day to end. Now all Bill could think was murder. Not only did she write this garbage to him, she also recorded it in the patient file. Bill read the patient file, the communication was also recorded by Terry. The patient was complaining, blah blah blah, Bill thought. Terry had already recorded and saved it, why did she have to tell Bill and then write it down again? It was like a medical office covering the entire surface of a patient's paper file with "warning" stickers, because some idiot felt 1 or 2 was not enough.

Even that was not the end. After finishing the last patient, Terry hobbled into Bill's surgery and informed him about the aftermath of Ashleigh.

"I saw your Maryland bridge patient, he said you glued it on yesterday but it fell off again so I glued it back on." Bill had to resist the urge to smack Terry. How many times did he have to relive that garbage? In a quiet, menacing voice, Bill said,

"I've already heard, I don't want to hear or speak about this garbage again." Terry did seem somewhat perturbed and left Bill to sort out his notes. That kid, what the fuck was he thinking? That smirk on his face, he always had that fucking smirk. If he used it on patients, fine, but Bill did not want to see that asshole laughing at *his* expense. Jesus, Jesus, Jesus, Bill thought.

It did not take long for the long dagger of fate to cruelly twist itself for a third time in Bill's heart. Next Thursday arrived and Bill was eating some of the staff's leftover Mcdonald's. That was still the unfortunate reality, Bill thought, despite living in a better suburb and enjoying an improved lifestyle, he still lacked the time or money to prepare his own lunch. As Bill walked towards his surgery, Bill saw Terry was hobbling back to his own surgery and with the same aggravating smirk issued more bad news.

"Did you check our Google page? Someone left a bad review. I couldn't find their name but it sounds like the whitening patient you and Brian saw last time," Terry said.

"Terry, can you be fucking serious for once? I don't know if you're laughing at me or not, can you just act like a fucking professional?" Bill snapped at Terry. Terry appeared more than somewhat wounded this time and immediately wiped the smirk off his face. Bill did not know what infuriated him more, the fact that the immigrant bitch complained or this idiot could not stop gloating for a single fucking second. Bill shook his head and looked up the clinic on Google.

There it was, a one star review under a "Claire Sinclair." That bitch did not even fucking try to think of a believable name.

> *Do NOT see Dr Parker. He quoted me $180 for whitening then charged double, clearly ripping me off. The experience was horrendous, I was suffering excruciating pain throughout the treatment. I've had whitening done before and it should not be like this. Dr Parker clearly does not know what he is doing.*

Oh. My. God. Bill thought. He could not believe it. That fucking arrogant subhuman cockroach. How he wanted to punish that bitch. Nothing he could do would be adequate. Pour acid over her family maybe? Or perhaps a good old death by 1000 cuts? There must be some pharmaceutical method to *enhance* pain because the human nervous system would not be able to register enough pain to adequately punish that animal. If only he had the magical power to resurrect her because killing her once was not enough. Going "medieval" on her was nooooowhere near enough, he was just getting started baby.

Everything in that review was a fucking lie and that bitch knew it, Bill thought. She planned and schemed to scam money from him. For $180, the clinic was making a loss. It would probably not even pay enough for the staff, whitening materials and lease. Bill may have performed the procedure for the first time but he did not do it wrong. It was way over the line to say he "does not know what he is doing." Having false allegations thrown at him was even worse than directly committing a crime against him. Brian confirmed that if it were so painful, the patient would be fucking showing it. This bitch barely made a peep during the procedure. She was putting on an act for attention.

Bill was an immigrant himself, but he paid a hefty price and he continued to make substantial contributions to society both as an essential worker and in tax dollars. Bill did not automatically hate immigrants, but subhumans cheating their way through the system really made his blood boil. Bill's parents had paid over $500,000 AUD by the time the tuition, cost of living and bureaucratic immigration costs were all considered. Bill went through the proper fucking channels and did everything by the book. Bill was slaving away treating and preventing infections which result in hospitalising over 60,000 Australians a year and indeed sometimes even killed people. Bill was literally saving lives. What did that bitch do?

She probably spent her time harassing low level employees as some human resources charlatan after graduating from some useless fucking arts degree in university. These fucking subhmans *harmed* Bill directly and indirectly. It gave proper immigrants like Bill a bad name and not only that, *stole* money from him directly. That useless oxygen thief paid some fuckwit to push papers onto another fuckwit and cheated her way into citizenship after paying close to a tenth the price Bill had to. It was cockroaches like her and the cockroaches who aided and abetted that kind of behaviour which were destroying the nation. Bill felt like his vision was starting to blur. His heart was thumping in his chest. That persistent headache which hounded Bill for weeks on end during his Shellharbour days was back. His balance felt altered and there was a creeping sense of vertigo. Bill wanted to murder her in the most horrendous way possible right now. Protected behind a computer screen, she must have felt invincible. She would not dare say that to his face.

* * *

By Saturday lunch time, Bill was still feeling light headed, the headache was still partially remaining. Then he received a knock on the door. It was the boss. Bill did not know how to respond. That terrifying anxiety was creeping back into his heart. He needed this job even more than Shellharbour. Until now, he was actually enjoying this job. Life was going *well* for once.

"Hey Bill, I saw what happened with that bleaching patient. I actually replied to the review explaining that we have no record of them ever coming. People like that are a pain in the bum, I've had to deal with that a couple of times in the past as well. How are you feeling?" Andy asked.

"I'm still taking it in, you know, I hate false allegations, especially coming from females, whenever I get complaints, it's almost always, female," Bill responded.

"Yeah, she does seem the type. She was even too cowardly to put her real name on there. Go figure. I'm going to contact Google to see if they can remove it. On very rare occasions, they have helped out. I hope you're feeling OK, some patients are just crazy. Kinda gets me upset just thinking about it. 20 years ago there was none of this happening, it has become much harder these days but you're still so young and despite this, the future is still looking really bright," Andy continued.

"Yes sir," Bill replied, somewhat calmer seeing that this boss made much more sense than his other bosses.

"Don't worry, all of us here know you were in the right, enjoy your afternoon and don't forget the CEREC, I'm gonna head to my other place now," Andy finished off.

Bill felt much better that afternoon. Unlike his other bosses, Andy seemed to not only support him, but acknowledged his struggle. Andy seemed to possess far more self-awareness and did not pretend he was some god practitioner, unlike Dr Sung and his whores. Who knows, dirty Korean assholes all pretended to be morally uptight but the illegal sex industry was booming harder than a nuclear explosion in South Korea. Dr Sung probably did have sex with illegal underage prostitutes. The past week was a dose of reality for Bill. Dentistry was always going to bring trouble. If he could recognise crazy patients by waving a wand, he would be rejecting them all but it was impossible. He would definitely order the receptionists to stop booking in re-cementation cases to begin with.

On Sunday, Bill made his decision. He needed to learn how to convince patients to take on expensive treatment just like Terry and Linda *without* them creating a fuss afterwards. In fact, Henry had recommended going to a course by some charlatan called Dr Theodore Bent. The name reminded Bill of Thomas Bent, Australia's most corrupt politician, Cheng seemed to mention that guy's name whenever their Textsecure channel started degenerating into politics. Bill would not have been surprised if they did come from the same genetic line. Being unscrupulous was hard coded in the DNA. There was a course coming up in a couple of weeks in Melbourne. Bill phoned Cheng.

"What you want this time bitch?" Bill heard Cheng's voice.

"Come on man, don't talk to me like that, I'm your friend," Bill replied with their usual antics, "remember how Henry was talking about that dodgy guy, Theodore Bent? He's running some snake oil program, it's only in a couple of weeks. I know you hell interested cause you wanna do some crowns and shit too."

"What do you mean?" Cheng asked.

"Remember Terry? Don't you wanna ball like him?" Bill asked back.

"Bro, I only get paid $40 an hour, the boss finally decided to up my wages but I'm still making dog shit out here, doing fancy work just makes my life more difficult," Cheng replied.

"What if you got a job that paid you properly? Come on man, this is preparation for the future. I don't wanna go alone, the kinda dentists that are gonna be there are all hell dodgy. I need you as my body-guard. They probably hell dangerous and shit but you hell tall ma ne ge, nobody's gonna do shit if you're there," Bill explained.

"I'll think about it," Cheng replied.

Bill was determined. It was not fair that all the others made more money than him. It was not just due to the number of patients, it was the billing per patient as well. Terry, Linda, Andy, they all charged patients more by doing more fancy work. Bill was going to "ball through the roof" just like them. After all, he had another secret plan which benefited substantially from coming to Melbourne. Upon finishing his last dose of the human papillomavirus vaccine, he was going to pay for sex. Prostitution was legal and regulated in Victoria, unlike those underground Korean exploitation brothels. Bill was not going to die a virgin. Women had treated him harshly so he had no choice but to pay for it. Bill liked to joke about Cheng's height but Bill knew Cheng would go to this course anyway. After waking up on Monday morning, Bill booked and paid for Dr Bent's "Ethical dental salesmanship" and booked in his final vaccine.

Chapter 8

Born again sinner

"Yo what's up my ne ge," Bill hailed Cheng as they arrived in the RACV club hotel foyer. Cheng eventually agreed to meet with Bill to do the "Ethical dental salesmanship" course. He would be due to drive out west Sunday evening tomorrow so there was plenty of time today.

"This better be worth it, the education points are entirely non-scientific so most of it won't even count towards the dental board requirements," Cheng replied.

"Fuck the dental board, we're here to learn how to ball through the roof remember, Henry said it paid for itself," Bill reminded.

"Yeah... Yeah... whatever," Cheng replied as the two headed towards the elevator for the second floor.

"Let's pretend that I'm seeing Rob as a patient," Dr Bent explained while performing air dentistry, "I'm just going to have a look now Rob... Hmmmmm," Dr Bent made an exaggerated "Hmmmm."

"Now this is the stage where I plant the seeds in the patient's head, I might also call my assistant over, hey Becky come have a look at this, and she'll say, 'wow, that's serious,' once I agitate the patient, he'll know, that crack is damn serious. This is when you use my tried and true formula," Dr Bent continued explaining. The methods actually resembled much of what the other dental sales techniques some other companies tried to teach, although Dr Bent did package it better for most dentists to be able to replicate. Dr Bent went on to explain more of his technique in detail before summarising it.

"Now Rob, we could do a simple filling. The advantage is that it's quick and cheap and who knows it might be OK for a short while, but the disadvantage is that it will break easily and catastrophically. When it does, it'll probably happen at the worst time like Christmas dinner or on that long anticipated cruise you've been talking about. The alternative is to do a crown. The *disadvantage*, is that it's expensive and you need to wear a temporary for a while. The *advantage* is that it will last and protect the underlying tooth. What would you like to do?" Dr Bent explained. "Remember, it's very important to explain the cheaper option first and really emphasise the disadvantage. Whereas when you talk about the desired option, you need to mention the disadvantage first. The patient will think you're being honest and then you quickly shift to the advantage. Remember how you set up the disadvantages from the cheap filling before right? The advantages of the crown must directly address the fear you have created. Ending on that notion is much more effective than shocking the patient with how expensive it will be. By the time you finish, they would have gotten over that," Dr Bent continued explaining.

Bill thought back to that time Terry convinced a patient with a cracked tooth to do a crown. That kid was doing exactly as Dr Bent was saying. It seemed that being unscrupulous was built into people's DNA. Terry seemed to independently come up with this salesmanship technique. Either that or he was corrupted by the dentists around him. Linda probably did the same too. Who knows, Andy might have been the same, Bill thought. The course then required the dentists partner up in groups of three and practice those lines on each other. It was more humour than education by that point but the course did succeed in organising Bill's thoughts. He was going to use these techniques just like the other dentists and "ball through the roof."

It was 6pm after the course, Bill and Cheng walked towards McDonald's to buy Bill's favourite family value box.

"That guy was hell dodgy, I read somewhere there was some dental board investigation over him because he was doing some sort of 'mercury removal' program that resulted in massive tooth breakdowns and shit," Cheng said.

"Those retard hipster 'holistic' guys deserve that shit anyway. 'Oh my teeth have holes, instead of looking at *myself* and cut out dumping sugar in *my* mouth, I'm just gonna blame chemicals and have some wanker slice and dice my teeth because he said words I like.' Those kind of subhumans deserve to live with the consequences of their actions, YOU told me that ma ne ge," Bill replied. "That shit works though, trust me, it's like a nuclear weapon. You have to be careful when to use it, I know you like to play it safe and shit."

Their conversation continued into McDonald's while Bill started ordering.

"What burger you want fam?" Bill asked.

"Surprise me bitch, I don't even buy McDonald's these days, hell far to drive," Cheng replied.

Bill finished ordering then the two sat down on the nearest table.

"Just between us, I plan to go with plan B, you know what that means?" Bill asked.

"What?" Cheng responded.

"Remember how I used to try and pick up women in Uni? Well that shit doesn't fucking work. Women only go for feral pieces of shit. You see around us? Look at those hos, look at the slobs they have for boyfriends. Those pieces of shit are wearing garbage, look at that," Bill explained. There were indeed a few couples eating in McDonald's, of course none of them were wearing suits like Bill. Ripped jeans, faded shirts, tattoos and tattered sneakers were fairly normal attire.

"If you wanted a woman so bad, why don't you dress and behave like them?" Cheng asked.

"Oh my god, don't you start with me. I am NOT a fucking subhuman slob. I will NEVER stoop down to THEIR LEVEL!" Bill was half shouting again. "Look, look, look Cheng, it's not just that I don't want to, I *can't*, don't you get it? I *caaaan't*," Bill explained, drawing out the word "can't" for added emphasis.

"What the fuck do you think women would think if they see my short Korean ass dressing like those subhumans? They would probably have me arrested like you always say would happen to me. Their pussies start dripping when they see some white, slob maxxed asshole dress and behave like a fucking criminal. Like a criminal," Bill said, while making an exaggerated scowl and moving his arms with melodramatic flair on the last sentence. "Charles Manson has like a hundred females hungering for that mass murdering psycho dick. Whereas me, they treat me like I'm a fucking disease. The Universe, society, God, Allah, Bhudda, Jesus, whatever the fuck, it's just been decided, I am an unwanted piece of shit. I have no goddamn choice. Believe me, I have tried every fucking thing. I have done my research, I tried every single strategy. I've adopted every single persona possible. It. Doesn't. Work. Trust me. I have done *everything* possible. You know me, I'm not someone jumps to conclusions without having tried every fucking possible option."

"So what is plan B then?" Cheng asked.

"Remember Jamie Ong back in dental school? That arrogant as fuck Singaporean dude? We used to try and enter this dodgy place called Red Lantern in South Melbourne," Bill explained.

"You desperate piece of shit, you've finally decided to go there haven't you?" Cheng asked.

"In the past, the brothel madame used to charge money just to meet the girls but now their website is advertising free entry. I've been preparing myself with the Gardasil vaccine. I'm gonna go tonight and I'll tell you all about it. If it's good, I want to see you there as well," Bill replied.

"I don't want to get stabbed bitch, those places are run by criminals, who knows, you could get shot in a drive-by," Cheng warned.

"Haha, wouldn't that be something, not the worst way to die on top of a woman," Bill reasoned.

* * *

Bill was extremely nervous and excited at the prospect of possibly having sex. He had no idea what to expect. Back in dental school, he never actually went into the proper brothel lounge, he did not see any of the women there. There was plenty of parking this late in the region close by to the Red Lantern so he parked his car there and walked a short distance to the brothel. It was not very discreet, Bill thought. The building was situated in view of a main street and had a large double door entrance. Bill paused at the door. He actually did not have the courage to open the doors. Bill took a couple of deep breaths and thought about it for a second. He reminded himself that he had tried literally everything. There was no possible way in *hell* a woman would consent to having sex with him besides him paying for it. That anger tipped the balance and Bill worked up the courage to finally open the doors and walk in.

There was a middle aged woman at the counter who greeted Bill,

“Hello, were you looking for anyone in particular? Have you been here before?” Bill was not sure what he would be asked so he was somewhat surprised at how direct the brothel madame was but he replied “no” to both questions.

“We have 5 ladies available tonight, one is in a booking right now. If you would like to meet the ladies, step through there,” the madame explained.

Bill obeyed her instructions and walked through into the lounge. Sure enough, there were women around. However, none of them were as attractive as what Bill imagined. Bill was hoping for tall, thin leggy blondes or red haired girls with large breasts. He was hoping there would be women fit to be fashion models, or at least close.

Bill coined the term, “would-be model,” a woman who was so beautiful she would have been a model if not for one noticeable flaw. It could have been a scar or perhaps being a bit too short. However, none of the women that night were what Bill would call “beautiful.” Bill thought, if any of these women were to offer their services for free, Bill would not hesitate. He was not repulsed, despite some of their feral tattoos and cigarette smell. However, it was *really* expensive paying for their services. The last thing he wanted was to pay $300 for just one hour only to feel like it was wasted. Bill felt somewhat uncomfortable so he sat down on the nearest black faux-leather sofa.

As soon as he did, the women started coming forward to introduce themselves. It was a business after all, they needed to make an income. However, this was the *first* time women voluntarily approached Bill. For all of his life, women treated him like a leper. Even if these women were attracted to his money and not him as a person, it still felt good.

“Hi, my name is Piper, how are you? Would you like me to go through my services?” there was a black haired woman wearing a skimpy leather outfit covered in tattoos.

"Uhh sure," Bill replied, without paying attention. She would have been rather attractive if it were not for the tattoos. Bill hated tattoos on women. It was just desecration. It made no sense for someone to think, "I want to express my individuality! So now I'm going to self-mutilate and appear just like all the other billion tattooed women who also express their same "individuality!" If the Kardashians suddenly went for laser removal therapy, then all these empty headed morons would also rush to remove their tattoos. So much for "individuality."

The four available women each introduced themselves but only one caught Bill's attention. It was a blonde haired girl of medium height. She was not fat, but definitely not thin either. After the women had completed their introductions, they all went away back to where they were either sitting or chatting to each other. Bill decided to make the second move himself so he stood up and walked towards Holly.

"Uh hey, could you tell me a bit more about yourself," Bill asked.

"What would you like to know?" Holly replied.

"I think I kinda wanna go with you, you mentioned your special services included the girlfriend experience, what does that involve?" Bill asked.

"The girlfriend experience is kinda the opposite of the 'porn star experience.' What you see in porn is not the way people normally have sex. The girlfriend experience is more sensual, intimate as if I'm your long term girlfriend. We'll go at your pace and do what you're comfortable with. We can do lots of kissing, cuddling and of course, sex," Holly explained.

"This is actually my first time in a brothel, actually, my first time having sex," Bill explained.

"That's alright, don't be nervous, I have dealt with clients like you before, I'm sure we'll have a wonderful time tonight," Holly responded.

For the first time in his life, Bill actually felt valued. This woman was trying to convince *him* to have sex with *her* and not the other way round. This woman was soft spoken, warm and affectionate. She seemed so kind and gentle. In fact, Bill did actually start to feel more comfortable around her than just a minute ago.

"Alright, I choose you tonight," Bill accepted her offer. Holly smiled and led him towards the counter where Bill paid the required amount in cash. The two headed toward the room they would be using and Holly said she would conduct a "health check" first. Bill questioned the effectiveness of that considering these women were probably not doctors. Holly then instructed Bill to take a shower before she left for a few minutes to collect the package full of condoms and lubricant.

Holly started removing her clothes. She did have a nice, curvy figure, Bill thought. Bill hated fat women and tattoos, Holly was neither. Bill did spot one tattoo on her thigh but it was not very distracting. All women in Melbourne had tattoos these days. Holly smelled nice and her body felt warm and soft. Holly cuddled Bill like she was his girlfriend, just like she promised. They kissed, her mouth also had a minty taste, probably to hide the musk of cigarettes and alcohol, Bill thought. Holly proceeded to perform oral and place the condom on. She opened a packet of lubricant and placed some on her labia. Of course she would, Bill thought, in reality she would not actually find him attractive, he did not hold that against her for the time being though. Then Holly proceeded to seal the deal, so to say.

However, something was wrong. Bill had watched plenty of romantic Hollywood movies, not all by his own choice, but he did nonetheless. This scene did not match any of the expectations he had. There was supposed to be something special when it came to skin on skin contact. His heart was back to its normal rhythm. The excitement had worn off and while Holly did feel warm and soft, he honestly thought his own self-pleasure in front of internet pornography felt better. Bill wrapped his arms around Holly as she moved up and down. It actually felt a little boring, Bill thought. What he touched seemed less and less special and reminded of him touching an inanimate object, except this one moved.

Bill recalled back in high school, he went to an inter-school, United Nations re-enactment exercise at the real United Nations building in New York. There was a girl from another school he partnered with who literally made his heart skip a beat. He felt warm and fuzzy inside for the two days they worked together. Even at night, he felt his heart tremor at just the thought of her, and no, it was not sexual. Seeing or thinking about her smile, momentarily made her the light of Bill's world. Bill even remembered feeling that special fuzziness when petting a young puppy his parents once gifted him and his long lost sister.

There was none of that today. If Bill could describe it, when he touched Holly, he felt as special as touching carpet, or even just the wall. A sexy, soft and warm wall but nothing more than that. As if to shake Bill out of his reverie, Holly asked,

"Would you like me to keep going? Are you enjoying this?"

"It feels good, but you seem a bit tired, how about we have a cuddle again?" Bill suggested.

Holly moved herself from being on top of Bill and laid beside him. She moved her arms around Bill and the couple cuddled as Bill suggested.

"So that's what sex feels like huh?" Bill half jokingly said.

"How was it? Are you close to cumming?" Holly asked.

"Let's pause for a sec. I want to know more about you," Bill asked.

Bill enjoyed the sex but no more than what he would have in front of the computer. What he was preoccupied with was the attention that Holly was showing him. Was it real? Of course it was not, he was paying her, but... what if? What if she meant the words he said?

“Do you think I’m good looking?” Bill asked. Yes it was a cliche, but that question was burgeoning around his throat waiting to erupt any second.

“Of course, look how wet my pussy is,” Holly responded with a pretty generic response. Of course she would say that, Bill thought, he needed to provoke a genuine response.

“Tell me what you like about me,” Bill asked.

“You have a handsome face and a nice body,” Holly responded.

“Really? I don’t work out at all, I’m not like Arnold Schwarzenegger,” Bill questioned further.

“I’m not a big fan of massive muscles like you see on body builders,” Holly explained. This was getting nowhere, Bill thought, she wanted to earn his income again so of course she would not insult him. He needed to dial it up.

“I don’t know about you but all I see online is big dick, I can’t help but think women all want big dicks but I only have a tiny Korean dick,” Bill goaded.

“It’s not about the size, it’s about what you do with it. In fact, if it’s big, it makes me sore and then I can’t even continue working,” Holly responded. All generic responses, Bill thought. This conversation really was going nowhere, perhaps he could find out more about her. Bill was expecting some abused, drug dependent mental asylum escapee working in a venue like this, but by all accounts, Holly seemed fairly normal. Neurotypical, one would say.

“Do you normally find your clients attractive?” Bill asked.

“Sometimes, after a while, it is just a job,” Holly replied.

"How many clients have you seen? Have you fucked any grandpas?" Bill asked with obscure but genuine curiosity.

"I don't keep track, I've been in the industry for a couple of years now. My clients come in all sorts of ages and sizes," Holly explained.

"Tell me about yourself, what brought you into this line of work?" Bill asked.

"I'm doing this on the side for some extra income, it's not cheap living in the city you know," Holly replied before Bill interjected with another question,

"So you have a main job elsewhere? What do you do?"

"I work as a nurse actually, it's pretty stressful and the pay is kind shit. I travel over from New Zealand to do this job, lots of girls fly in and out," Holly replied with a humourous tone.

"That's right, I hear a lot of nurses say that, I see a lot of tooth grinding and cracked teeth, you have a little bit of that too," Bill added, perhaps accidentally revealing too much of himself. Holly was a little taken aback but she figured it out fairly quickly, "that's true I guess, your day job must be related to teeth then, either that or you're super observant and look at nurses' mouths all day," Holly remarked again with some amusement.

"I'm a dentist, I work in the city, in fact, you can look me up and book an appointment with me. But I don't do free consultations, if you want my opinion, I charge $300 an hour," Bill replied.

"Haha, I do probably need to see the dentist soon," Holly responded.

The two kept discussing their private lives, perhaps somewhat inappropriately as discretion would normally be part of a brothel's modus operandi. Bill did have a notion of this realisation but he was too engrossed in Holly to pay attention. They talked about their interests, hobbies, travels and education. It almost felt like a real date, just naked. In fact, these generic questions were the norm when Bill once tried speed dating. During those speed dating sessions, Bill recalled the women did not even pay one iota of interest. He might as well have been invisible, just a space filler until they could see the next white man. Unsurprisingly, after trying it a few times, he always ended up with zero matches. This experience on the other hand was mind-blowing. Holly actually paid attention and responded to his every word. All of a sudden, a buzzer sounded. Bill had completely lost track of time.

"Thank-you," Holly replied through the intercom, "that was our 5 minute buzzer and you haven't even cum yet, I completely lost track of time."

"Hold on, hold on, do you need to see anyone afterwards?" Bill asked.

"No, I don't have any pre-bookings tonight," Holly replied.

"How about we go for another hour?" Bill insisted. Bill actually prepared $600 just in case because he thought his first time should have been done in style with a threesome. That fantasy did not eventuate but he was glad he withdrew enough money.

"That's fine, if you're up for it then I'm up for it. You can stay all night with me if you want," Holly added with a smile on her face.

"I would love to, but I'm not that rich," Bill said.

"You probably have loads of money, I won't tell," Holly replied while striking a seductive pose, in reference to Bill's profession.

"Haha," Bill chuckled, "that's only true for *female* dentists, I bet you would make double what you earn here if you were a dentist."

Bill was under Holly's spell, he knew that it was a lot of money, but he did not care at this moment. He took out his wallet and further paid Holly who wrapped a towel around her chest and briefly exited the room to settle the account before returning.

"Now where were we?" she announced while entering and removing the towel. Gods, Bill thought, the more he looked at her, the more he was entranced. Bill realised that time was too easy to waste so he was going to dial it up.

"I know this is gonna sound weird but can you slap me in the face?" Bill asked. Holly did seem somewhat taken aback but Bill was sure he was not the only one to make such a request. Considering that "50 Shades of Grey" made sexual violence mainstream, Bill thought, this was nothing.

"I don't want to hurt you," Holly replied somewhat uncomfortably.

"My dad used to do much worse, just a gentle pat," Bill requested, so Holly gently swung her hand against Bill's face.

"Hit me harder, that was nothing," Bill instructed. Holly swung again. It had slightly more impact.

"Harder!" Bill commanded. Holly was looking increasingly uncomfortable but she still abided by his instructions.

"Ow that's starting to hurt," Bill complained, this time Holly seemed visibly upset.

"Was that too hard? Sorry," Holly hurriedly muttered.

"I love that, don't stop, do it again... uh uh uhh!" Bill stuttered to halt her, "just a little softer, but also tell me I have a small dick, say, 'tiny Asian pencil dick!"

"You have a tiny Asian pencil dick!" Holly exclaimed while slapping Bill.

Bill was seeing stars now,

"OK, OK, that's enough," Bill instructed.

"Are you alright? Please tell me you're OK," Holly asked, looking at Bill's red handprint marked face with severe concern.

"I'm good, you did a good job. Now I want you to insult me, tell me I'm a useless Korean piece of shit, tell me to go back to where I came from," Bill requested. This time, Holly had enough. That was crossing her line.

"Umm, I don't feel comfortable with that racism," Holly explained.

"I'm sorry, I didn't mean to make you feel uncomfortable," Bill apologised. This time, he was not so upset with apologising, he did mean it, at least a tiny bit.

Towards the end of the session, Bill did indeed finish while inside Holly with the condom on. However, Bill felt no different, no, it was actually less pleasurable than stimulating himself in front of internet pornography.

"That's it?" Bill accidentally said out loud, "that kinda felt anti-climactic," Bill remarked. Holly immediately seemed to be taken aback. It was like dark clouds shadowed over her facial expressions.

Holly slowly and weakly muttered, "I'm sorry it was a letdown." Seeing Holly suddenly lose composure seemed like an expression of genuine emotion. Maybe she did care about Bill. Maybe sex workers did care about their clients. Bill clutched onto that desperate spark. He would have to keep testing them in the future. It was a long shot, but maybe he had a chance.

"No I don't mean you, I kinda expected this explosion of emotions, but it feels just like me wanking at home," Bill said further.

"Everyone's a bit different," Holly said before taking out a plastic bag, tissues and removing the condom. After cleaning up, Holly cuddled around Bill and said, "I had a wonderful time, how about you?"

"Me too, cumming wasn't that great but you were amazing, like a goddess," Bill praised. That drew a chuckle from Holly.

After a few minutes of cuddling and kissing, the buzzer rang for the second time. The two showered and dressed before saying their goodbyes.

"I hope to see you here again soon, remember to ask for Holly," Holly said before kissing Bill goodbye.

"I won't forget, you were the best thing that's happened to me in my whole life," Bill proclaimed. He felt genuine when he said that. This night was indeed the best night of his life. He felt like a new man, as if the final puzzle piece finally clicked into place revealing an experience which completed him, moulded him into this final perfect form. Bill walked out of the brothel reborn and ready to start a new life.

* * *

The next day, Bill phoned Cheng during lunch break and gave a cryptic message.

"Guess who bitch," Bill talked into the phone.

"I'm guessing you did it last night?" Cheng replied.

"Hold on, hold on, this is an *insecure* line, I had *therapy* with a tall blonde doctor last night, you know how much I like tall blonde doctors," Bill continued.

"I see what you mean, you phoning me up to brag now?" Cheng asked.

"I need to see you ma ne ge, we can only talk about this in person," Bill advised.

"Alright, I can meet you on the way out of Melbourne tonight," Cheng replied.

After Bill finished work that day, the two met at the Grattan Street KFC. It was the closest one to the dental school parking lot.

"... All my life, I've never been able to experience that until now," Bill exclaimed.

"Not even with your real girlfriend?" Cheng asked.

"Don't remind me of that bitch, Holly was more real than that fake "Christian" bullshit ever was even though I paid that ho," Bill replied. "I feel like I've been reborn, you know how those fake ass Christian priests dunk people in the water? Well that's what's happened to me. The old Bill is DEAD. Holly has made me into a new man. You have no idea how good it was, there's a reason all men want to get laid, you have to try it yourself man."

"Not if I want to survive," Cheng replied.

"Oh my god, fuck those criminal owners, you like pizza right? You know how they're all owned by the criminal fucks, doesn't stop you from having pizza," Bill argued. Bill explained everything that happened the previous night in excruciating detail.

Bill was a poor storyteller and could not keep telling the story without constantly and repeatedly diverting down unrelated tangents. Cheng was becoming increasingly impatient as he needed to drive for another 90 minutes after having their meal.

"Hurry up and get to the point, Jesus, you're like dial up internet here in Australia man," Cheng insisted.

"OK, OK, damn it, hold your horses," Bill said before finally finishing the story after a whole hour of unnecessary tangents and semi-rabid ramblings.

"I feel like life is worth living now. I've discovered a new purpose. Those women I met last night, they treated me kindly unlike my mom," with a heavy American accent on the word "mum", "my own sister and Sarah and all the bitches who have ruined my life so far."

"That's cause you paid them or they were expecting payment idiot," Cheng said.

"So what? They still showed interest. I have money, therefore I am attractive whereas those lying whores on the street, who are we kidding, all women are whores it's just that some are *honest* enough to work in a brothel. Those lying whores on the street see me like a fucking cockroach when it's *THEM* who are low IQ cockroaches! Goddammit!" Bill almost shouted again.

"Who knows, maybe Holly does find me attractive," Bill chuckled while clutching onto that miracle.

"Whatever, as long as you're happy and functional," Cheng replied, "you've been crying on the phone to me for months so keep doing that shit so you don't need me as a therapist which I'm horribly under-qualified for."

"Shut up nigga, I don't need any of that psychotherapy bullshit, I've found what I've been missing my whole life, I'm a new man bitches, everyone watch out, there will be no stopping Bill Parker now dammit!" Bill proclaimed with intense excitement and conviction.

"By the way, why the hell did you tell her all about yourself? Why did you pull a Petraeus? You know that idiot who leaked all that secret intel to some journalist he was trying to bang?" Cheng asked.

Bill was immediately struck with regret. General David Petraeus, the once commander of the US armed forces who leaked highly classified military intelligence to some reporter he met one night. A man who disgraced himself and the entire nation over a serving of alcohol.

"Come on man, I just told her the same sorta stuff she told me, it was a fair trade," Bill attempted to defend his desperate position.

"From what you told me, it sounded like those hookers were just saying what you wanted to hear so how would you even know if anything she said was true? You told her about your actual job and that you're some big shot dentist earning $300 an hour. You know how the legal system fucks over men like you and now you're just giving her ammunition to go after you?" Cheng rebuked. It was true, Bill was far too loose with his tongue and now realised the hole he had dug for himself. "Haven't we agreed, the less people know about you, the less ammunition they have to fuck you up because we all know, when the chips are down, humans are just animals who turn on each other. You said that yourself, your words not mine," Cheng relentlessly chastised.

"Alright, alright... Jesus, Jesus, Jesus... Fuck, goddamn it. You weren't there, it was like she had me under her spell. I couldn't help it. I know you want it too nigguh, you just too afraid to admit it. You need to get yo virgin ass over and stop this bullshit about becoming a wizard," Bill desperately defended.

"Don't say I didn't warn you idiot," Cheng replied.

"Alright, I get it already, I won't pull another Petraeus," Bill hastily replied, perhaps too hastily without consideration for what was to follow.

Chapter 9

Hope or hype

As a surprise to nobody, Bill's happiness was short lived. Bill repeatedly phoned up the Red Lantern but Holly was never available. It did not stop him. Bill engaged in their special services every week for the next month, once even going twice in the same week. He tried different brothels, there were lots of them around both South Melbourne and the central business district of Melbourne. He tried different types of women, some tall, some short, some curvy, some very thin, some with black hair, some with red hair. Bill tried the same things he did with Holly, all of them drew the line at the racist insults. Some drew the line earlier at moderately hard slapping, some women slapped Bill harder, just the way he liked it. It was heavily draining on Bill's earnings but he did not care. He never experienced such bliss in his entire life. Unfortunately, everything came to a grinding halt due to one unfortunate choice.

One red haired girl appeared to be stunningly shapely in her figure hugging dress. She said her name was Victoria and only after she took her clothes off did Bill feel regret. She had the outlines of a six pack and she proudly flexed her biceps in front of Bill. Bill felt a sense of revulsion just looking at her. He was not here to fuck a man. He paid good money, he still had to finish though. It turned out that Victoria was a proud hobbyist body builder. That left Bill traumatised but he had learned his lesson. Women knew how to dress in ways which accentuated their beauty and hid their flaws. He had to make the assumption that the more modestly they dressed, the more they had to hide. After that night, Bill looked at his finances, this habit had to stop. Otherwise, he would need to increase his income yet again.

* * *

Coincidentally, Andy Chen stopped by Mega dental on Saturday and had another proposal for Bill.

"Hi Bill, how are you going?" Andy asked.

"I'm good, how are you?" Bill responded, this time actually genuinely, despite Victoria.

"Bill, I love your enthusiasm. I've got something that might interest you. I don't want to push you too hard though.... At the moment, our Carlton development has been delayed, long story, some contract disputes, rain, unions, it's frustrating. It probably will be another 6 months before we can start you in Carlton. However, just so happens, one of our dentists at Kew will be returning overseas so we need someone to take over 3 days a week. If you like it there, we could have you there permanently. It's in the suburbs so it might be closer to what you were used to in the countryside," Andy offered.

Bill thought about it, he would be working 7 days again. But the reward was, he could have more funds to pay for sex. Bill was putting his favourite activity on pause for now but if he earned more money, there would be no doubt he would do it more. For some reason, Bill felt like he was compelled to visit brothels. Sex was becoming increasingly boring but the stimulation of female attention was something more addictive than a drug. This was the universe's way of rewarding him from being so deprived ever since high school.

"You know what Andy, I think I'll go for it. I said I was here to work, work, WORK! I mean it, the more work the better," Bill replied.

So on Monday, Bill found himself driving down to the wealthy, heavily Asian populated suburb of Kew. Kewey family dental, what a ridiculous name, Bill thought. Perhaps it was not as suburban as Andy described, the clinic was situated next to the shopping strip on High Street. Parking was difficult, but nowhere near the extortion racket of central Melbourne. Bill observed his surroundings as he opened the door. Unlike the Collins street practice, this place was much older, less like a shining shopfront and more like a suburban house, that was probably what Andy meant, Bill mused. Inside were a row of chairs next to the wall directly in front and a rectangular reception desk to his right as he entered.

"Hi there, you must be William, am I right?" the receptionist asked.

"Yeah that's right, call me Bill," Bill replied. Bill instantly disliked her, the feeling was probably mutual. Bill could have sworn he heard a "hmph" sound the moment she finished her sentence. Last year, Bill would probably have surged with anger but due to his recent night time proclivities, Bill felt less hostile.

"Nice to meet you today, I'm Jane, you know, you'll be the only male dentist on your days," Jane explained with a smug look on her face.

Bill was becoming increasingly irritated. Was that some sort of warning or a threat? Everywhere he had been, Bill saw the female dentists billing much more than he did. Was there some sort of expectation that he needed to match? Did they expect him to bow and kowtow to their every demand otherwise he would rock the boat?

"Uhh, good to know, as you can tell, I'm worth more than 2 men combined," Bill joked with a sarcastic chuckle.

"Haha, funny man, let me give you a tour," Jane replied. Bill could tell she was faking it all. Already, he felt like a fish out of water. If he were to be surrounded by females, he did not belong, Bill thought to himself. His presence seemed to offend females unless he paid them to tolerate him, Bill repeated his well established empirical knowledge.

Bill had the impression the clinic was old and did indeed remind him of the torture chamber from Shellharbour. The first patient was a regular patient seen by whoever was returning to their home country. Bill looked at their file, recent fillings, no x-rays, needed a checkup and clean, seemed typical enough, Bill thought. As he was reading the records, a young Indian girl came in and introduced herself.

"Hi, I'm Anita, nice to meet you," Anita introduced herself.

"Hi, I'm Bill, you're my assistant today?" Bill asked.

"Yes, I'll be assisting, how are you? Is everything here easy to get used to?" Anita continued.

"Yeah, should be OK, we use the same computer software, boss is the same," Bill replied.

"He only works on the weekends so I don't see him much," Anita explained.

"Heh, he's a busy man, by the way, who else is on today?" Bill asked.

"There are two other dentists on, there's Anna and Diane, they're only working in the afternoon though," Anita explained. Typical, Bill thought, female dentists only needed to work half the day to earn more than him. "You can meet them this afternoon, they're very nice."

Everyone said that about each other. In fact, in dental school, one of his better clinical supervisors used to say, "fob off the patients you don't like with the specialist you also dislike. Tell them the 'specialist is so nice.'"

"Sure," Bill had no other way to reply, "tell me a bit about yourself, are you also a dental graduate?"

"Yes," Anita replied to which Bill thought this was becoming quite a trend, "I'm not doing ADC though, too much money wasted already, I'm starting my studies to become a therapist."

"Those ADC faggots are just useless, we don't need 'em, they should hire *me* to do the testing," Bill joked.

"Haha, yeah, I do feel that the test is unfair," Anita replied. Bill did not dislike Anita as she did not show him any attitude, yet.

After the first patient arrived, Bill called her in and started to look in the mouth. This time, even his recent frolicking was not enough to quell his anger. What he saw astounded him. There were obvious gaps in the fillings where he saw chunks of food and debris getting caught. The same fillings which were apparently placed less than a year ago.

"Uh Lauren, is it OK if we take some x-rays?" Bill asked.

"Is it safe? What is it for?" Lauren asked. Bill sighed internally, he had to have this useless conversation again. If he could "get away" with never taking x-rays he would but the US dental association consensus spelled out in explicit wording just how important x-rays were.

"They're not compulsory," Bill explained, in fact no dentistry was compulsory, some people deserved to lose all their teeth. "However, I can't see in between teeth or underneath fillings. The consensus is to check with x-rays regularly at least every 2 years, maybe every 1 year if we see lots of problems."

"Why wasn't I informed about this before?" Lauren asked.

This instantly raised Bill's blood pressure. It felt like Shellharbour all over again. He was unceremoniously dumped into a hostile environment where he was singled out the moment he walked in through the door. The person who saw the patient previously could not fill teeth if their life depended on it, she was probably female, Bill thought. Not only that, she never bothered to do just the basics with diagnostics for whatever reason and as a direct result, Bill was now *forced* into a position of being the uncomfortable, "pushy" dentist. He was *forced* to defend the incompetence because that was considered "normal" here. There was no diplomatic answer.

"I don't know why the previous dentist did not ask to take x-rays for 6 years but where I come from, the United States which has some of the best universities in the world bar none, x-rays are absolutely compulsory, most clinics require patients take x-rays before the dentist even looks in their mouth," Bill explained. "If you don't want to take x-rays, that's fine. Here in Melbourne, which is the best city in the world, I know everyone does things differently."

Lauren did not seem entirely satisfied with the answer but at least she seemed much less upset. She was no longer frowning at least, Bill thought.

"Alright, how many x-rays do we need?" she asked.

"I only need a couple as a minimum, one left and one right," Bill replied, "the cost is $50 each, a total of $100, your insurance should cover most if not all of it."

"OK then," Lauren replied, this time a bit more confidently. However, the moment Bill started seeing the results of the x-rays, he knew he was better off just pretending x-rays did not exist.

"What's that?" Lauren asked, pointing to an obvious black gap between the white filling and the grey tooth. It was this moment that Bill realised, "I'm fucked."

Bill listed his options inside his head. Option 1 - just be honest and explain that the previous dentist did a trash filling. The disadvantage was that Jane and all the other dentists would probably pull a Julius Caesar level betrayal on him just like Wendy and torture him within an inch of his life. If that were the case, Bill might be forced to commit homicide. Option 2 - lie and pretend that everything was fine as Lauren did not have the special skills to read x-rays. That option was not going to work, the defect was so obvious even a 5 year old in kindergarten would be able to realise the previous filling was garbage. Option 3 - invent some *bullshit* to defend and pretend the previous dentist's work was acceptable.

Bill's headache suddenly returned. His heart was pounding, his vision was wavering. Worst of all, Bill's mind was keenly focused on the sharp objects on his tray. What kind of bodily damage would that do? Bill had many times used such sharp instruments to carve away tooth and gum. What happened if he applied the same techniques on someone's eyes? Would it be deep enough to penetrate the rib cage? Oh the massacre would make Hitler look like a Sunday school picnic, Bill thought. His mind was flashing murder four times a second. In fact, the more gore and violence he imagined, the more his headache abated. Killing one person was not enough, he wanted to take a chainsaw and line up all his enemies in a row and pop half of his body out of an open top convertible to saw every one of his enemies in half. Bill wanted nothing more than a bloody carnival right now.

Bill was *forced* to choose option 3. He was *forced* to invent some ridiculous defence for the previous inept subhuman in order to keep his job. Unlike Shellharbour, Bill *enjoyed* working at Mega. He did not want to lose that job in order to desperately keep himself from starving. He voluntarily submitted to continue working at Mega out of pure joy.

However, this personal sacrifice was taxing him mentally to the point of near collapse. He was *forced* to tolerate this for now, but any more of this and Bill would have to say "no" to Andy. Bill swallowed hard and replied,

"You see, sometimes there could be a small gap which is made to look worse than it is on the x-ray because it's a 2D examination of a 3D object. If we take it at a different angle, it would barely look like anything, probably just some thick lining of glue. Just keep an eye on it for now, but if you're more comfortable with replacing it, no problems, we can do it any time," Bill spoke through gritted teeth. There were more problems though. This woman had tooth decay almost everywhere. Bill knew he would only create problems if he recommended doing some more fillings even though that would be the textbook appropriate advice. "There's more I wanted to discuss, you see those black spots between teeth? We also need to keep an eye on them, take another x-ray in 12 months -"

Bill was cut off before he could finish,

"Are you telling me I need fillings everywhere? I spend so much time looking after my teeth, I occasionally need a filling but only the odd one. I've never had x-rays taken before in my life for dentistry. All of a sudden you tell me I need like 10 fillings?" Lauren spoke with immense intensity.

"Look, I'm not saying you need 10 fillings," Bill tried to explain before Lauren interrupted again.

"Then why did you show me this? Can't you just tell me if I need fillings or not?" she demanded. Bill wanted to choke this entitled subhuman but he knew that would put him in prison. He was not here to teach dentistry 101 yet this under-educated cockroach was trying to interfere with him merely attempting to act in *her* goddamn best interest.

"I'm only saying that you're at risk of developing holes," Bill attempted to talk some sense into her.

"Is there anything that can be done? You said I don't need fillings but now you're saying we can't do anything?" Lauren continued spraying her verbal diarrhoea.

"We have to address the underlying cause of this level of tooth decay. This is not normal, tooth decay is usually a lifestyle disease with high risk factors including sugar between meals," Bill continued.

"So basically you're saying it's all my fault and I should stop eating? I can't believe this, I've never experienced a dental visit like this before" Lauren rudely interrupted again, this time with anger in her voice. "I'll be honest, I don't feel comfortable continuing with this discussion. I'm going to be late for work if I stay here too long," Lauren added before picking up her bag from the courtesy chair next to the wall and storming out of the room.

Anita and Bill blankly stared at each other. Anita seemed sympathetic and did not say anything. Bill's hand was quivering in anger. If it were not for his immense mental strength rivalling Atlas himself, he would have slammed that insect patient's head against the wall so many times there would be nothing more than a broken wall and red mist. Bill sat listening to Jane saying,

"He's new here, don't worry, we have plenty of other dentists who've been here for a long time. You've seen Dr Anna and Diane before, would you like to see them again?"

That was the final straw. If Bill did not leave the hostile environment right now, he was going to murder someone. It could have been him, suicide was not off the table. Maybe. Bill could not rest knowing that he failed to take at least one life other than his own before he died.

Without a word or a care in the world, Bill left the clinic and had a walk. The sun was shining and were it not because of the torture he just received, he might have enjoyed this walk. At this moment in time, this outside exposure was the thin barrier holding Bill back from becoming a rampaging mass murderer. Jesus, Jesus, Jesus... Bill thought. Bill knew from the moment he walked in that he made a mistake. That last patient indisputably confirmed it, 100%, "beyond a reasonable doubt." Bill was enticed by his recent night time escapades which now seemed pointless if he had to sacrifice this much of his mental wellbeing to be able to afford it. It was too late now. He could not simply turn around and say no to Andy who seemed to offer this job in good faith and honest dealing.

Bill returned to the clinic with Jane giving him a scornful, "you're late." Bill wordlessly continued after returning to his surgery. There were no more patients at that level but the clientele was one Bill did not respond well to. Bill was not a family dentist. He only liked a certain type of patient who would instantly click well with him socially. That excluded all children, most women and most elderly, which happened to be the near entirety of the Kew clinic's client base. Melbourne was home to mainly overseas students studying in the tertiary institutions around the region, Bill much preferred that. Kew felt like Shellharbour 2.0, an unceasing nightmare. That day, all Bill saw included children, elderly, women and just one male patient who was 20 years old but the mother came along to the appointment to do all the talking anyway. What the hell was wrong with this world, Bill thought. Am I even living in the real world? Is this some sort of unwaking nightmare?

* * *

Bill looked at his iPhone, it was now April, a few months since he made the regrettable decision to start working at Kewey. True to his predictions, paying for sex was now barely enjoyable at all. Bill initially thought that sex workers were the kindest people in the world. They treated him with kindness when nobody else did. Now Bill was so used to them saying the same garbage again and again, it felt so disingenuous it was almost insulting. His torture at Kewey only made it worse. He could not enjoy what felt like the best thing in the world any more. Bill was treated as a dumping ground for all their problems. Defective filling? Of course Bill can fix that up. Problem patient? Handball it to Bill. Lost a temporary? Bill would do it all for fucking free. Bill could not stand it. The patients did not like him so he had few bookings, that was bad enough but he was *forced*, goddamn *forced* to clean up everyone else's shit for fucking free, Bill thought.

Then came the favours. Bill used the same tactics to appease the staff at Kewey as he employed in Shellharbour. He bought them chocolates, alcohol, even occasionally shared snacks for lunch. All he got in return? Goddamn fucking favours they expected *him* to perform.

"Bill could you please carry this to Mega?"

"Bill could you drop this letter off in the mail box?"

"Bill could you please watch the desk for a sec?"

Bill could think of nothing but murder on a daily basis. Aside from sleeping, it was the only thing which offered any relief for his unceasing headache. For all he did for those subhumans, all they did was ask for more favours. How could he dare say no? One foot stepping in the wrong direction and he was back to the Shellharbour situation where he was a cornered rat.

That's right, Bill thought, he was just a fucking sewer rat to these people. If they were subhuman, what would that make him? A sub-sub human? Something worse than fucking dirt? At home, Bill struggled to fight back tears. Life was actually improving, things were on the right track, Bill thought. Why did life have to be so cruel? Like a roller coaster, Bill was forced from one turning point to another. Life fed him some sweet nectar only to viciously tear it away to truly teach him how painful torture could be. Bill was amazed at just how oblivious those subhumans were to his suffering. Bill showered them with gifts but they took that as an invitation to take advantage of him. That was *not* fucking normal.

Had he not done enough for them already? It did not take a genius to realise the concept of a fucking *fair trade*. He was not their friend, he was not even a colleague, they were just assistants and administrative staff. They were not even in the same league as him, they could never be friends.

Bill thought, you wouldn't even ask a friend to do goddamn favours for no benefit every fucking day. That violated the concept of free trade so heavily, it was akin to raping fair trade until it exploded into a bloody mess. Yet, he was powerless to do anything. What a fucking joke, Bill thought, he was the dentist keeping this goddamn circus running yet he was basically exploited like a cornered rat. Today was no exception, Anita brought her friend in to resolve a toothache and to a surprise for nobody, it was considered normal to offer a substantial discount. Bill knew there would be trouble just from thinking about it. Bill knew the value of his work. It was worth much more than what those female dentists did. Yet, he was being *forced* to discount his work. That was beyond the pale.

"Good morning Bill, how are you?" Anita asked while stepping into Bill's room. "You'll be seeing my friend today, thanks so much for seeing her, I told her about how thorough you are."

"Uhh... no worries," Bill begrudgingly replied. He could not express how he truly felt, that would have him arrested and sent to a padded cell, he was sure. Bill looked in the appointment book, it was half empty, as expected. The first patient was scheduled at 10am, Ankita, that must have been Anita's friend.

"Is your friend Ankita?" Bill asked.

"That's right, she's a bit nervous so just be gentle," Anita said with what Bill interpreted as a smirk. Bill was already feeling apprehension from the impending explosion.

By 10:10am, Ankita had finished registering her details and completed the medical questionnaire. Bill was already upset at just how hard he attempted to finish on time but patients arrived whenever they wanted and took forever to complete some basic details which would normally take no more than a couple of minutes.

"Ankita?" Bill called out.

A young woman who looked like she was in her mid 30s stepped up and greeted Bill. Anita and Ankita greeted each other warmly with elevated spirits the moment they met, erupting into mindless small talk. Just get on with it, Bill thought, the sooner he could send the patient out the door, the less he would need to put up with this garbage.

"So Ankita, I heard that you were having a toothache on the upper left?" Bill asked.

"Yes, it started paining a week ago and now it feels like I can't open wide," Ankita spoke, using the typical expression "paining" that Indian people always used. Bill examined Ankita and confirmed what he thought, severe decay on the wisdom tooth. It was definitely an extraction case.

"So uhh... it looks exactly like what I thought, the upper left wisdom tooth has a very large hole, I'm gonna need a special x-ray that goes around the head to have a proper look at the roots but it's gotta come out," Bill explained. Bill then heard Anita say something in her native tongue and both of them had a slight chuckle, then Ankita moved her head left and right, the way Indian people nodded. At least she was accepting of his treatment plan, Bill thought.

After taking the x-ray and explaining the process, Bill started the procedure. The tooth was immediately loosened with minor pressure, it felt like it was able to pop out any second so Bill applied the forceps and gave it a pull. Then he heard the sound he dreaded time and time again. Click. It was a very minor sound, perhaps not even a sound, just a slight tremor felt through his fingers. Bill looked at the tooth, it seemed to look intact but there was a suspicious flattening of the root which lacked the typical round tip natural to most roots. There could be a fragment of root remaining. Bill honestly was not sure, he tried to check.

"Suction," Bill stated coldly to Anita. Anita did not seem concerned at first as there was no change in her facial expression. Bill was feeling his blood pressure skyrocket. There was bleeding everywhere which was a typical situation involving long standing infection. No matter how hard he vacuumed or attempted to irrigate the area, he could not see anything.

After struggling for several minutes, Anita's tone changed.

"Is it all out?" She asked.

"Hold on, I'm trying to check," Bill replied with no insignificant level of irritation. Bill continued to struggle, this time using surgical tools to feel for any abnormalities. After several more minutes, Anita asked again,

"Did the root tip break?"

Goddamn it, Bill thought, couldn't she see that he was trying to figure that out? Bill kept struggling but Anita kept repeating, "Is there any root remaining?"

With each passing minute, each verbal prod from Anita felt like daggers impaling his skull. His headache was already overwhelming and Bill felt every single heart beat like a bass drum battering his skull with blunt force. Couldn't that bitch just give him a goddamn break? He was trying to concentrate on a fucking impossible situation, could she not tell that she was not fucking helping? Goddamn it! Bill just wanted to murder everyone in his vicinity. His hands were shaking and his head felt like it was being split asunder. His anger was surging faster than he could handle. He never asked for this. He did not want to see friends or family of these morons, he did not do fucking favours and worst of all he was not some goddamn slave doing free work all the fucking time.

"Bill, what's happening?" Anita asked again. This time, Bill had enough, he dropped the instruments on the tray, ripped off his mask and stormed out of the clinic without a single word. He had to do this. Even if he stayed behind to utter a single word in response, that one second could have been enough to elevate his anger to a point where he would lose control and start committing homicide right then and there. He had no goddamn choice but to leave the warzone as soon as possible for not just his own protection, but to save the lives of all those he left behind. He still had some more patients that afternoon, he did not know how he would be able to get through them all. He was in no condition to practice any dentistry. Bill took a deep breath and continued walking. Just like the other day, it might have been a good day to walk outside if it were not for the explosion he had just experienced.

Bill had been complaining to his Textsecure group forum about his predicament. He expected some empathy but after taking out his iPhone to check his messages, Bill was left equally as infuriated.

"Storm in a teacup", "Don't let such small things bother you", "you can say no"

Even his trusted friends were unable to understand him. Was he even living in reality? Was someone clandestinely feeding him crazy pills? Bill texted back -

"Don't you fucking dare. Have you not read a fucking word? I have no GODDAMN CHOICE! FUCK! Just appease, appease, appease... Bow and kowtow, yes master, kick me harder, my face misses your boot! FUCK NO! FUCK YOU! You're either WITH me, or AGAINST ME! THERE ARE NO NEUTRAL PARTIES!"

Bill thought he could at least rely on some sort of bedrock, some foundation he could lean against should he be threatened by the whole world. Yet, his tone deaf friends were trivialising his struggles. "Oh it's just nothing for me so it should be nothing for you too," that was all their subhuman brains could think. So much for empathy. Tom kept insisting "psychopathy bad, empathy good" so where was the fucking empathy for Bill? None of them could understand just how much damage Kewey was doing to him mentally *and* physiologically. Just like Shellharbour, he was returning home every day and collapsing in bed without any food. He was unable to pass stools without a proper diet, his hands were shaking every day. Any time he was not seeing patients, he closed his surgery door and instantly fell asleep. He could not keep his eyes open even if he tried. What a fucking joke, Bill thought. In fact, Bill tried to be empathetic. He went along with the Kewey charades because he wanted to pretend to be a "good" person by Tom's definition. Where did that get him? He was *that* close to committing murder. If he behaved like a psychopath who possessed the dark triad of so called "bad" personality traits including psychopathy, narcissism and Machiavellianism, he could probably have avoided everything.

If only Bill behaved like a manipulative psychopath from the outset and never gave the staff any gifts. He would have lied and manipulated them into believing he was as dangerous as a cornered rat. If he could have made them fear him, *none* of them would dare ask him to do any favours. If only he were Hitler incarnate, nobody would dare betray him and talk behind his back like in Shellharbour. Not unless they wanted to be gassed by Zyklon B. Instead, he only damaged himself by openly inviting this treacherous exploitation. "Dork triad" Tom would always write mockingly, well Bill would no longer pay attention to that idiot's ramblings. There was only the dark triad. Fuck empathy. What was that guy's problem? Was he wracked by white guilt 24/7?

Before long, Bill realised just how far he had walked from the clinic. His next patient was due at 11:30am, it was already 11:05. Bill sighed.

He had no goddamn choice but to start walking back. For the rest of the day, Bill did not say any word other than "suction" to Anita. It was another typical day at Kewey, fixing other practitioner's broken fillings, seeing unruly children and elderly more fit to be cadavers than living beings. Bill left after the final patient without typing any of his notes. Who cares anyway? The dental board could take away his licence and he would not even care right now. He would enjoy killing whichever vermin dared target him with an audit. Bring it on, Bill thought. People lived in this world with no goddamn respect because they were so desperately keeping their heads above water with their poor financial decisions. They had no concept of what it was like to live as a person who had nothing left to lose. Bill was such a person. These cockroaches need to learn what it's like to mess with someone who's got nothing left to lose, Bill thought, *he* was going to show them just what it was like.

By the time Bill arrived home, his head was throbbing like it was being used as a bass drum mallet just like this morning. This time, just like Shellharbour, he barely made it to his "bed" which was more aptly described as a few sheets laid down on carpet and instantly lost consciousness. Again, Bill did not even check if his front door was locked. He was too goddamn tired to check. When Bill opened his eyes again, there was sunlight pouring in. Bill looked at the time, it was 6:53am, just barely enough time to shower. This was so painfully similar to Shellharbour Bill felt like weeping. Despite being in Melbourne, he was isolated, abandoned even. There was no backup. He almost died yesterday and today he needed to go back to the warzone and pretend nothing happened. Fuck.

Chapter 10

Fate (I)

Bill had almost given up but he realised he was mistaken. He felt like he was in love. The girl in front of him introduced herself as Erika. She was a mixed Russian and Korean girl. The moment they met, Bill was taken aback by her beauty. Even if you tried a million combinations, you would not be able to get this unique work of art, Bill thought. Bill laid down next to her after they talked about their origins. She was born in Canada and actually studied within walking distance of the high school Bill once attended. She was only 19 years old and Bill was 27 so them meeting long ago would have been impossible. Bill could only imagine the awkward meeting between a 17 year old version of himself and a 9 year old girl. Bill would have been old enough to be a babysitter, he thought.

However, this was fate at work. All the pieces lined up just right. Bill stared at her perfect bronze skin and petite figure. She was a work of art from head to toe. Erika noticed him staring and gave Bill a shining grin. Gods, her teeth were perfect too.

"You like what you see?" she asked in a provocative voice.

"Heh, by the way, your teeth look almost too good to be real. I'm a dentist, I can tell that they're a work of art," Bill praised.

"You think so? My mum is an orthodontist in Canada, she did my teeth," Erika replied. This was a sign. Not only did they come so close to crossing paths in Canada, she came from a dental family. This was beyond a reasonable doubt, fate at work.

"She did one hell of a job, but I can't comment much since I don't know what you looked like before you had your treatment," Bill explained.

"They weren't *really* bad but I didn't like how some of them were a bit rotated," Erika replied.

"I don't do any orthodontics but I'm planning to start doing some Invisalign, if you ever want to see me, you can find me at Mega dental," Bill enunciated almost unconsciously. He realised he was indeed pulling another Petraeus but it just kept spilling out. He was defenceless in front of this goddess.

"Haha," Erika chuckled, "I'll think of you if I ever need any treatment."

"You know, long ago we were within walking distance of each other. I studied back in Toronto for a while," Bill continued.

"Wow, we really must be fated to meet, haha," Erika chuckled. Those words were seared into Bill's mind. She even said it herself, Bill thought as the two returned to physical intimacy once more.

For the next two months, Bill booked with Erika at least every two weeks, sometimes every week. He felt like he was just on the verge of feeling that special something he once experienced during his high school mock UN re-enactment. When he touched Erika, he still did not feel his heart aflutter like he once did, but he was so entranced by her beauty he could have sworn that emotional response was just around the corner. The way she talked, their background circumstances, everything lined up perfectly like the way a key aligned the pins in a lock. He felt like perhaps this girl was showing some genuine emotional connection with him. No matter what, he had to act.

* * *

"Guess who bitch?" Bill spoke into his phone after Cheng picked up.

"What is it this time? You're interrupting me again," Cheng chastised.

"Come on man, I'm your friend and I need yo genius writing skills," Bill requested.

"What are you planning this time? You finally planning on releasing that manifesto? Your own 'Mein Kampf?'" Cheng asked.

"It's not like that, but it's coming, don't you worry. Anyway, I met this doctor at therapy who was the best doctor I've ever seen. I think I might have a shot, this is like fate but I need your help mah ne ge," Bill explained.

"Something we can't talk about without a secure line again?" Cheng goaded.

"Let's meet up next time you're back. You're coming back to Mel-*born* this weekend right?" Bill asked.

"It's Mel-*ben* idiot, how many times do I have to keep telling you? I might drive back this week, but you owe me bitch," Cheng replied.

"Fine bitch," Bill assented. Bill knew that Cheng was cheap and enjoyed Kentucky Fried Chicken. A small price to pay for his help in securing Bill's fated goddess.

That Saturday night, Cheng picked up Bill from the free parking spaces near Melbourne University to discuss his strategy. As Cheng drove, Bill discussed with Cheng his script.

"What the hell dude, why have you written a script for this ho?" Cheng asked.

"Didn't you read what I wrote on Textsecure? Erika is a like a fucking work of art, she is one in a billion. You can mix all the Russians and Koreans and you wouldn't be able to get a combination as unique as her. When I was in high school, we were separated only by walking distance. This is fate, she said it herself. It's beyond a reasonable doubt," Bill explained.

"Do you even know what beyond a reasonable doubt means? You do realise this legalese bullshit is just code for what the judge thinks? If some asshole judge says, 'beyond a reasonable doubt' he is basically the judge, jury and executioner for what is deemed 'reasonable,'" Cheng interjected.

"Shut up with your legal bullshit, I know what I'm talking about. This is a long shot but it's my last fucking chance. I've tried fucking everything and it's all been a wash. All the fucking hos want to go out with slobs. I've had no fucking chance but this is different. This is my last chance, I won't get another shot like this *ever* again, do you understand?" Bill continued.

"Fine, whatever, how many last chances has it been now?" Cheng goaded again.

"Shut up, you don't fucking understand, now help me with this shit," Bill said.

The two arrived in South Yarra and Bill invited Cheng into his apartment.

"What the hell is this dump? This looks like a repurposed hotel room because the business failed," Cheng could not help but speak the truth.

"But it's South Yarra damn it, the best suburb in Melbourne," Bill defended.

"What's the point of living within this shitty post code? We barely found parking and it's only because it's night time that the time is unlimited. For the same price you could be living much better off in almost any other suburb," Cheng debated further.

"It's only $250 a week here, you won't be able to find anything at this price this close to the CBD," Bill moved on the defensive.

"Yeah but it looks like a meth lab, you literally have pills lying everywhere, the bathroom light doesn't even work, do you actually shower in the dark?" Cheng continued lashing Bill with the truth.

"I'm too goddamn tired to clean this place up, I have no goddamn choice," Bill replied with exasperation, almost giving up.

Cheng read Bill's script, it was like a Korean soap opera.

"When we first met, I knew you were something special, like fate ordained it. Ever since our first meeting, I have not stopped thinking about you. The thought of being with someone like you has given me the courage to bear the suffering of this cruel world..."

"Dude, are you seriously going to say this garbage in front of a woman you're trying to attract?" Cheng asked.

"Help me then goddamn it," Bill snapped back.

"Why do you have all this melodramatic, edgy cruel world shit? What kinda girl wants to hear that garbage? Neckminnit you're gonna spin some emo 'ice-cold fire bullshit,'" Cheng mocked.

"Fuck you bitch, help me damn it! I want to tell her about how similar our backgrounds are. She needs to understand that because all dem other hos and I have *nothing* alike. I'll never meet someone like Erika again and there's no chance she'll meet anyone like *me* again," Bill explained.

"OK then bitch, if you want to say that then why don't you actually say that?" Cheng asked.

"I need to make it flow idiot, that's why I need your genius," Bill requested again.

"You're the one who's actually experienced having a real girlfriend, you should have more expertise than me," Cheng said.

"I still need your help, my mind is like a fucking blank, I can't think of the words," Bill said.

"OK, why not say something like, 'unlike all the other girls, you're special, I've never encountered a girl who's so understanding, I guess that must come from how similar we truly are,'" Cheng suggested.

"You are a genius, that's why I need you ma ne ge," Bill said. The two fleshed out more of Bill's desperate speech for 2 further hours.

For the next week, Bill rehearsed in front of the mirror every night. Just like his favourite orator, Adolf Hitler, Bill needed his speech to be both theatrical and emotive. The next Saturday night after work, Bill caught public transport back to his apartment. He did his usual triple shower. Aftershave, hair gel, foundation, deodorant, perfume, suit... Bill was meticulous about his appearance. Tonight was the night. He needed to present himself at his best. Bill drove directly to South Melbourne and entered the Red Lantern requesting he see Erika. He had pre-booked so she was ready the moment he arrived. Bill only wanted to be the first. The thought of having another man enter this woman before him was disgusting beyond belief. The girl would be "ruined" and that would be unacceptable.

"Hi, did you have a booking or would you like to see who's available?" the receptionist asked Bill.

"Um, I made a booking to see Erika," Bill replied.

"You must be Bill?" she asked again.

"Yes, I booked for 8pm," Bill replied.

"Why not have a seat in the lounge, Erika's not here yet, I'll let you in once she's ready," she informed Bill.

"Alright," Bill responded as he walked towards the lounge. These working girls never arrived on time, they probably spent eternity tinkering with their make-up. Bill sat down and started mentally rehearsing his lines as he waited. Before long, Erika walked into the lounge and greeted Bill.

"Oh hi! I'm so glad you came to see me again! I missed you!" Erika greeted Bill warmly with a hug and kiss on the cheek.

"I've missed you too, I can't stop thinking about you," Bill replied.

"So... how've you been? Would you like some water?" Erika asked.

"No thanks, I've had enough. I've been good, how about you?" Bill replied.

"Yeah, it's been pretty good," Erika replied. Bill knew this conversation was pointless but he still liked to maintain the air of civility. "Come follow me," Erika continued while she led him to her chosen room.

Erika went through the usual. She performed the "health check" which was essentially a cursory glance at Bill's privates under the light then took his money. She instructed Bill to shower while she departed to collect the "care package." At this point, Bill's heart was thumping in his chest. The past week had been full of the same outrageous suffering endured at the hands of Kewey staff but this time, his pervasive thoughts about Erika dulled his senses to the point where he did indeed perceive Kewey as a storm in a teacup. Who knows, perhaps Tom, Henry and Cheng paid for sex as well in order to keep their placid attitude towards staff. Everybody has some sort of coping mechanism, Bill thought. Bill had already showered three times so his current shower was more just going through the motion of washing. After all, he did not want to scrub himself too thoroughly or the perfume would wear off.

Erika returned with the care package within a couple of minutes of Bill drying himself. Erika smiled mischievously and voluptuously teased, "feeling ready big man?"

"I was ready the moment I saw you downstairs," Bill replied. Erika unceremoniously gripped her tight, figure-hugging one piece skirt and drew it over her head then casually tossed it onto the ground. She undressed herself with practiced efficiency it seemed, Bill thought. Wow, Erika was looking especially radiant today, Bill thought. The way her breasts jiggled as the elastic material slipped over them was to die for. His eyes focused with laser precision and etched that memory in for all eternity. Bill looked down, of course, she was not wearing any underwear. Bill sat down on the bed while Erika walked over to lean on top of him, then started kissing. Bill reciprocated and embraced her warm, soft body and gently guided her down to lay down beside him. They cuddled and kissed for what felt like several minutes until Bill decided to strike.

"Hold on, I want today to be special," Bill spoke.

"Oh, so what did you wanna do?" Erika enquired with a facade of sultry curiosity. Bill took a deep breath and repeated it to still his racing heart. His chest was pounding so energetically it was like a percussionist's solo.

"Okay, okay, before I begin, please just listen, I'm not here today just to have sex, we can do that later, in fact, I find the act of sex kinda anti-climactic. What I'm about to say I've never said to anyone before. Promise me you'll listen to everything," Bill began.

"Is that how you feel about me? I thought you loved sex," Erika said while pouting.
"Come on, I didn't mean that, I'm here for you not just sex," Bill replied before continuing.

"The moment I met you, I knew instantly you were my first choice. You know, I'm quite picky about who I choose, I sometimes have girls come back to introduce themselves again or even three times. Sometimes I would just sit there and ask the madame at the desk to give me some time to think. However, the moment I saw you, I didn't even wait for the other girls to introduce themselves, I wanted you," Bill continued, while noticing Erika had an alluring flick of the corners of her mouth forming an incredibly seductive smile.

"Oooh, thank-you, aren't I great?" Erika teased, then gently laughed at her own humorous humble bragging.

"I thought, Oh My God, this has to be fate. We *had* to meet on that day, that time. Just think statistically how unlikely it was for the two of us to meet at *that* moment. Everything had to go right. I had to finish work exactly on time, you had to be free at just that moment. Every moment in each of our lives, every action taken, every decision we made led to that moment in time happening *just* right. There are 7 billion people on Earth and the universe placed the two of us to be together at that moment. If I were late by just a minute, the guy behind me would probably have chosen you. There would have been a 0% chance the guy behind me would have chosen someone else. Thinking about this makes me think, "Gosh, all that suffering in my life happened for a reason." If even the tiniest detail happened differently, we would not have met.

That suffering was 100% necessary for that moment," Bill began enunciating his passion driven speech. He was nowhere near completion.

"When I look at you, it's like I'm looking at a work of art gifted by God to mankind. Even if you got a million Russians and a million Koreans together, they would not be able to produce a child even close to what you look like. In fact your unique genetics are so impossibly rare that not in a million years of mixing would there ever be someone who looks even close. Just think about it, me being able to cross paths with a special person like you who will never walk the face of the Earth again. This is waaaay too much to be a coincidence, this must be fate. You know, I studied in Canada once. When I was in high school, I studied in Toronto. To think that back then, we could have been living within walking distance of each other. I guess we just were not fated to meet back then. Who knows, if your bus were late, if my friend's car broke down, if anything happened differently, we might have met a long time ago. For all we know, maybe we did cross paths at some point and did not realise it. Although, if I saw someone like you on the street, I probably would not be able to forget. It was like fate was teasing us, bringing us so close yet so far, then finally meeting properly this year," Bill continued. Erika however, was silent. Her face became essentially un-moving. Bill was not sure what to make of it but he knew he needed to press on.

"Then I saw your teeth and I sensed that there was yet another connection between us. You told me that your mom," Bill had a heavy accent so pronounced "mum" in a very American way, "was an orthodontist in Canada. I gotta say, she did one hell of a job. I can tell that your mom is someone who values perfection in her work. That's something we both have in common. It's not often you see dentists who actually value the quality of their work. As you know, I admitted that I'm a dentist so I know good work when I see it. Most dentists are a bunch of morons. They think, "Look at me, I have a piece of paper therefore I can do no wrong, I'm helping people!" Trust me, I've worked all over the country,

I don't know what Canadian dentists are like but over here in this country, it's full of morons. This is what makes you and I so special. It's in your DNA to do your best, and I can tell, the service you provide is top notch. Since you inherited your mom's DNA, it's also in your DNA to accept nothing less than the best," Bill continued his ranting.

"That first day we met, I knew we had a special bond. Sure, your mom and I are both dentists, but so are millions of people. What makes you so special is the fact that you and I come from the same type of ancestry. No, I'm not talking about being Korean, I'm talking about that special pursuit of perfection that's locked into our DNA. I bet your mom and I both chose dentistry because we're driven to use our hands to craft beauty and fix the impossible. It's not every day you come across people like us. I recognised the mark of a perfectionist the moment I saw you. Someone like you will never exist again and you can say the same about me. Just think about how close we were to never meeting. That would be a *tragedy*. I've always booked with you because I cannot even think about having sex with any other woman. I said before that sex was anti-climactic because it's true. When I cum, I get a much more intense finish watching porn but being with you is so different. When I'm with you, I don't care about the sex, it just doesn't matter. I enjoy your company. When I'm with you, I feel like all my suffering was worth it. It gives meaning to my struggles. Without you, I feel like I just want to end it all. My God, having to deal with so much shit every day in this joke of a society and to have nothing to show for it? I have to admit, the day I met you, I felt as if dentistry was going to destroy me. I told you how I've been all around the country only to see morons everywhere. Melbourne was different, until I started working in another clinic that was just like the rest of them. But then I met you. Being with you made me feel like all those problems were just washed away. I knew then and there that fate was guiding me. I felt like if you were by my side, I would not even care about any of that, I would tolerate any garbage," Bill was almost finished. Erika's face became more indecipherable. Bill took a couple of deep breaths and finally made his proposal.

"I hope you can understand how special you are. With other girls, it's like I'm touching carpet. I feel absolutely nothing. But with you, I feel alive. I don't care what this brothel says about clients and all that bullshit. They call you girls independent contractors so hey, I see no problem with what I'm asking. I've been hearing about this site called Seeking Arrangement and all this recent stuff about contractual relationships. I'm not asking you to stop working in a brothel just for me. Maybe one day we can become something more than just a contractual relationship but I'm asking for you to please consider, just consider, the option of seeing me as a private client for longer sessions outside this brothel. It's a *tragedy* that we can only meet inside a brothel. It just feels wrong. Fate brought us together and it's sending us a message. We can take things slow, what do you say?" Bill finally asked.

Erika appeared to be noticeably uncomfortable. Bill almost regretted his words before he finished. Surely, sex workers as good looking as Erika would have had men propose to her all the time. Bill had heard of plenty of real life cases online where men eventually developed real life relationships with sex workers. Some even married. What he just did was not outlandish, Bill was absolutely certain of that. For almost half a minute, Erika seemed to be silent, until she finally spoke,

"Ummm... I only see clients inside the Lantern, if you like you could book longer sessions," Erika gingerly muttered with an awkward smile on her face.

Bill was denied. Bill's heart felt like it stopped. Bill was essentially frozen. The shock of rejection sent him into a state of near catatonia. Was that it? She took such a long time to respond and all she said was that trivial response? What was happening here? Bill's vision started to blur and without noticing, his mouth hung open seemingly unable to close. His head started to rapidly spin as if he were about to faint but Bill's consciousness was not releasing its punishingly painful grip. He was being forced to stay awake to process the rejection. The agony was unbearable. Why? Why? Why? Why? Why? What did he do wrong? He did not ask that bitch prostitute to become his girlfriend. There were thousands of women advertising themselves online for private paid sex. He just asked for that. After he poured his heart out, it was ripped to shreds like papier mache.

Erika started moving and performing her services in awkward silence. Bill knew what she was doing, he could see and feel it after all, but it just did not register in his mind. He paid no attention even when he orgasmed. The world was a blur as if Bill were on auto-pilot. It was not until Bill drove back to his drug-den apartment that he finally became lucid.

"FUUUUUUUUUUCK!" Bill screamed, "FUCK! FUCK! FUCK!!!" Bill howled in agony while bashing his right fist against the car door.

"Why does it have to be me? Jesus, mother fuck, goddamn! FUCK!" Bill continued howling. Bill felt like he was being immolated. The pain was unbearable. His eyes also burned. It was too late, there was already overflowing moisture leaking down his face.

There was nothing left. Erika was his last chance. His life was full of suffering until now and Erika represented the one and only escape to salvation. Through her, he gained motivation and strength. She provided meaning to his suffering but in the end that was all fucking fake. None of it meant anything. She was just another fucking lying whore. Fate was intentionally torturing him like rescuing a North Korean political prisoner and showering him with luxury in the United States, only to send him immediately back to North Korea. Bill felt like that North Korean torture victim. He was given a taste of happiness only to have it violently ripped from him just to teach him how shit his life was. Erika was his last chance. Logically speaking, if he had no more chances of forging a better life, then this was it. His life had peaked, this was "as good as it gets." Yet, his life was just fucking awful. If this was "as good as it gets," then suicide was the only option. This was not a conclusion influenced by mental illness. It was cold hard logic.

Bill did not want to commit suicide yet. If he died now, the orchestrators of his suffering would not have experienced the same pain that he felt. It was unthinkable to take the only life he valued, his own, before that of others. He deserved at least some sort of revenge before he departed this world. However, if life was this painful, he did not think he could make it until the next morning. Bill took a few deep breaths and texted his friends on the Textsecure group chat.

"I fucked up. I confessed to a lying whore. It was a waste of fucking time. I am done. If you don't hear from me or if I end up in the news, now you'll know why."

Bill pressed send. Bill looked at the time, it was 10pm. He spent the past 30 minutes just in his car suffering in agony. Bill was not sure if he could make the walk up to his apartment. He did not live on the ground floor after all. He felt so lethargic he might collapse on the stairwell like he did in New South Wales when he had barely made it into his apartment.

Bill then heard his phone ringing. Surprisingly enough, it was Tom, the last person Bill expected to call. He had not spoken aloud to Tom for close to a year now.

"Yeah, hello?" Bill answered.

"I read your message on Textsecure, what happened?" Tom asked.

Bill took a deep breath. Bill was somewhat displeased at Tom's attitude last time he tried to help that kid escape from Howard Chan's vile clutches. Bill did feel some gratitude for that kid giving him employment intel. Begrudgingly, Bill informed Tom about what happened.

"What did the sex worker do? Was she angry?" Tom asked.

"I couldn't really tell. The bitch did look kinda uncomfortable though.

"Don't use that kind of language to describe women," Tom immediately retorted.

"Excuse me? What the fuck?" Bill replied in surprise. Bill could barely believe his ears. Bill did recall Tom being a bit of a left leaning liberal (with a small "L") but today's attitude made him appear like some feminist sympathiser extremist.

"You need to think about it from her perspective. Show some empathy. She was there to do her job which should not involve men propositioning to her," Tom spoke in a somewhat confrontational tone.

"Don't you use that tone with me. I said what I did because it was the truth. I'm not trying to say what I did was right cause it didn't fucking work in the end but someone as good looking as her would have men confessing to her all the time," Bill defended himself.

"What other men say to her doesn't matter, you shouldn't be like them," Tom continued chastising.

"Oh My God, why the fuck did you call me just to throw this garbage at me? I don't have to listen to this. You know Tom, I always thought you were a smart kid but ever since we couldn't speak face to face, man to man, you have become increasingly confrontational. Every fucking thing I say or do you feel compelled to argue with, what the fuck is your problem? I've always felt these closeted Nazi vibes coming from you. I know for a fact that you hate Asians, just be fucking honest for once in your fucking life," Bill replied, becoming increasingly agitated.

"Ok, calm down, just don't do anything that might cause harm to yourself or others," Tom replied.

"It's not like I want to," Bill responded, "let's get one thing straight. What I did today was not harming anyone. You don't get to lecture me with all your white guilt, social justice bullshit. I know you're racist just like I am. Don't try to deny it. For once in your life, can you just fucking speak honestly? What the fuck is your goddamn problem?"

"You said that she was very uncomfortable. In a sexual setting, even though she is a professional, she was still in a vulnerable position. Making someone uncomfortable in such a setting is almost an assault. If anything worse happened it may even resemble rape -" Tom was then cut off by Bill's explosive reaction.

"WHAT THE FUCK! WHAT THE FUCK!!! JESUS FUCK WHAT THE FUCKING HELL DID YOU SAY?" Bill screamed into his phone while violently assaulting his car door with his right fist. "I CONFESSED MY LOVE AND YOU FUCKING TELLING ME THAT I RAPED HER? WHO THE FUCK DO YOU THINK YOU ARE?"

"No, I didn't say you raped her -" Tom tried to claw back his statement.

"FUUUUUUUUUUCK YOOOOUUUU! YOU DARE CALL YOURSELF MY FRIEND? FUCK YOU!" Bill screamed before slamming his thumb on the disconnect button and hurling the phone down onto the thankfully carpeted floor of his car. Bill felt homicidal rage churning inside him like a tsunami. Tom talked about empathy all the time but apparently empathy for Bill was illegal. Every other fucking human on Earth deserved empathy but not Bill.

All of a sudden, Bill heard his phone start ringing again. If it was Tom, he would not be picking up. Bill bent down and picked up his phone only to see it was Cheng this time. At least he still had a true friend left, Bill thought. The others did not support him while Cheng never stopped supporting him.

"What you want?" Bill asked.

"So it sounds like your confession didn't work," Cheng assumed.

"No it didn't fucking work. I am fucking done," Bill said.

"What did she say?" Cheng asked. Bill then explained briefly what happened.

"Turns out she was just putting on a service," Cheng replied.

"She's a fucking lying whore," Bill corrected.

"Well you can't expect someone you're paying to say nice things to turn around and start insulting your small dick and ugly as fuck face," Cheng reasoned.

"You're right, but I thought this time she was different. Who the fuck am I kidding. That Tom kid, he said I fucking RAPED her just by confessing my love. Do me a favour, don't fucking talk to that piece of shit if you want to live," Bill threatened.

"What the fuck, what did he actually say? Nobody is retarded enough to say, 'you raped her' after hearing your story," Cheng asked.

"I can't remember exactly but he said something about how I can't use certain words because they're fuckin' BAD. Then that kid accused me of fucking ASSAULTING the bitch just by making her feel uncomfortable??!! WHAT THE FUCK WAS HE FUCKING THINKING? THAT FUCKING LIBERAL CUCK TALKS SMACK ABOUT ME USING BAD WORDS THEN HE IGNORES WHAT HE JUST SAID! FUCKING MOUTHS OFF TEN TIMES WORSE THAN WHAT I SAID??!" Bill screamed into his phone while slamming his fist against his car door.

"That kid needs a reality check. He's been isolated in Whoop Whoop for so many years it's like he's learning to become a cult leader. What you said was perfectly fair. These women face confessions as a normal part of their job, you can't pretend that it's wrong. Some of these women get actually sexually assaulted at work, you can't compare a love confession to physical assault," Cheng elaborated.

"You're a good friend Cheng. You've always been good to me. Erika was my last chance. I knew it was a long shot but now that she's fucked it up, it's all over. Tell me why I shouldn't just go out and start murdering tonight," Bill threatened.

"What the fuck, why does one rejection make you feel like you need to start murdering people? She's just a whore. You tell me you fall in love with every second whore you bang, you can't take this one girl so seriously," Cheng reasoned.

However, Bill was hitting the absolute rock bottom in his pit of despair. He felt tears in his eyes for the second time that evening.

"You don't understand, it's all over. I've tried everything. I thought Sarah, my "real" girlfriend had genuine feelings towards me, it was all fucking fake. Women pretend to be like fucking saints and princesses but in the end it's all just lies. I just wanted something real. I tried testing the hookers with all my crazy shit and maybe I tricked myself into believing it was real. I tried dating, I tried that pick-up bullshit in dental school, I even tried fucking speed dating. You won't believe the trash quality females that rejected me there. In the end, it was all fucking fake. I am done. It's time to wash my mouth out with a revolver. You know, maybe gun control does work 'cause if it were easy to get guns in Australia, I would have washed my mouth out with a revolver years ago, heh," Bill disturbingly confessed.

"You're jumping the gun there, maybe too literally. So what if it's all fake? Look at all those rich people divorces. For most, marriage is just prostitution with extra steps. Remember that guy on YouTube who said, if you're gonna fail, fail early so that you can move onto something better? The kind of "death do us part" true love bullshit only exists in fairy tales. You've been watching too much Disney propaganda dude. You do realise Hallmark, that company that sells toilet paper as celebration cards, funds all that true love bullshit otherwise how else can they sell their toilet paper? Those cards are hard as hell, my arse would sting like a motherfucker after wiping it with Hallmark. I bet in reality, less than 10% of relationships and marriages out there are the type that you want. Most long term marriages only exist because of mutual benefit and they're probably fucking other people behind each others' backs anyways. Ever heard of grey divorces? Older couples are divorcing like they're on fire and divorce lawyers are raking it in. For all we know, those long term marriages have consenting affairs because after a few years of marriage, couples don't fuck each other at all any more," Cheng tried to calm Bill down.

"That doesn't fucking matter. I don't accept anything less than perfection. Ideals exist because they are unattainable and I will *never* stop trying unless I've tried fucking everything and there's nothing left. Once I know I've tried every possible way there is, then I will know it's over. Right now, that's where I am," Bill replied.

"Are you seriously going to start killing over a woman? You said yourself that you're so much more important. That you're superior. If you want female attention that badly, why not just make female friends and fuck the occasional hooker once in a while? You said you did not enjoy sex so why do you even go to brothels?" Cheng probed further.

"You know, you're right, you make a lot of sense. Fuck these goddamn subhumans, they ought to know their place," Bill replied.

"You also said that you took on the Kew job so you could go to brothels more often. It sounds like there's no point keeping that job if you find sex so disappointing," Cheng recommended.

"You're always right, I should have listened to you all along. This was a total fucking waste of time," Bill realised.

"Hookers are there to provide a service, that physical therapy is real, all that true love garbage, that's bullshit. Imagine if she accepted and then you get yourself emotionally invested only to find out yet again that true love was all bullshit," Cheng theorised. "True love isn't real. Hell, love isn't real, it's a mental construct. If some gold digger pretended to love you then she died without you ever finding out it was all a web of lies, does that make your "love" any less real? What makes it real in the first place? Until they finally betray you, it's somehow all real up until that point? Were you just pursuing honesty in the end? Are you turned on by honesty? Or perhaps you were just interested in the pursuit and the more beautiful the woman, the higher your score?"

"You're always right," Bill replied in defeat, "fuck this shit, I'm going to quit Kew tomorrow."

It was almost 12am. Bill still had not left his car. The two of them finished their conversation. The pain was still strong but at least Bill had a plan of action now. Dejected and heartbroken, Bill dragged his depleted body up the stairs and into his apartment. He barely had enough energy to lie down on his improvised bed and within seconds, he lost consciousness.

Chapter 11

Hopelessness (II)

Bill arrived at work more depleted than Ethiopia's economy. Bill depressingly looked at his books, he was at least three quarters booked. It was going to be a long day. Bill barely had any sleep last night. No matter how hard he tried, he could not stop his brain from replaying Erika's painful rejection. Even worse was Tom twisting a metaphorical dagger into his heart. Bill bared his soul and placed *himself* in a vulnerable position by confessing yet that bastard Tom tried to twist the situation into some feminazi fetishist fantasy and tried framing Bill as a rapist. How could he sleep under those conditions? Did he even fall asleep at all? Maybe he achieved some state of semi-consciousness which only made things worse.

Bill did not greet anyone, not the receptionist, his assistant or any of the other dentists today. They might as well have not existed. His head was throbbing and he felt like he was about to faint. Bill started moving through the patients with extreme lethargy and reluctance. He saw five patients that morning and could not help but inform two patients that he could not do the complex procedure today and requested they book again another day. Bill knew that they probably would not come back. Andy Chen might be upset about it but Bill did not care. He did not have the mental or physical strength to do anything fancy like wisdom tooth removal today. Bill was not even sure if he had the capacity to talk to another five patients let alone operate on them. After sending out the final patient before lunch, Bill closed the door and sank into his chair harder than the Titanic.

Bill looked at his right hand, it was shaking as usual. Bill had forgotten to take his caffeine this morning. Come to think of it, Bill did not even remember to pack his caffeine pills into his mini-briefcase for work. He gave his assistant today strict instructions not to bother him so she had better spread the message to the rest of the clinic not to knock on the goddamn door. There was something he was determined to do today. Bill reached into his pocket and took out his phone. He deftly unlocked the screen and found the number for Andy Chen. The boss was too busy to pick up, as expected. Bill found it unpleasant to discuss important matters through text. He found that people misconstrued his words all the fucking time, especially like that Tom fucker. He needed to talk face to face to minimise that. He could accept the compromise of speaking through the phone for semi-important matters but text alone was absolute garbage. However, today he had no choice.

"Please call me, I would like to discuss leaving Kew" Bill typed with his thumbs. After reading it a few times just to make sure, Bill hit the send button. As soon as he did that, Bill felt like any vestige of energy he had evapourated like a drying puddle. His eyelids felt like they were struggling in a weightlifting competition. Slowly but surely, his eyes closed and Bill started drifting back into that uncomfortable zone of semi-consciousness while being harassed by his memories of last night. If only he could actually sleep. Sleep was the only thing that could keep the pain away but he could not even achieve that. Bill could imagine deluded morons like Tom telling him, "*just* stop thinking about it, *just* stop being depressed, *just* be normal." There was no end to subhumans like Tom. The assault on Bill's head was not fucking voluntary. He could not *just* stop thinking about it. Tom just had to make things worse. It was unbelievable that Bill once called that kid a friend.

Bill was jolted back into full consciousness by the ringing of his phone. Bill looked, it was Andy Chen. Bill answered, "Hello?"

"Bill, I'm surprised you texted me about Kew, all the girls there say they love you and so do the patients, do you really want to leave?" Bill's boss asked.

"Yes sir, I don't know what the staff have been telling you but I've been taken advantage of since day one. I've been working 7 days a week for all of this year and I can't keep going on like this," Bill tried to explain.

"I'm worried about you man, how are you going to look after yourself? You're not working in the country any more so will you be OK just working four days? I see you're building your books up which is good... but we're not quite ready for Carlton to be open yet," Andy explained.

"Don't worry, it's not about the money. It's been almost 6 months like you said, I can wait longer for Carlton to open, no problems," Bill replied.

"I'm just looking out for you buddy, but I support whatever decision you make. By the way, how come you want to leave Kew? Jane was telling me just how well you two get along," Andy asked.

"Don't trust anything Jane says, she's one of the reasons I'm leaving," Bill replied.

"You must have your reasons, I gotta go now but I want to talk more about this when I see you again next Saturday. When were you planning to leave Kew?" Andy asked.

"I'll be real with you bro, I wanna leave as soon as possible but I know you need to find someone to replace me. I hope two weeks can be enough," Bill requested.

"Alright, you gotta do what's right for you, I gotta go now, cya," Andy signed off.

Bill sighed. He wished for Andy to hurry up. In this state, Bill doubted he could last a single whole day at Kew, let alone two more weeks. Somehow, Bill miraculously managed to work through the patients that afternoon. Unfortunately, as he was about to leave, Terry walked in with some unsavoury news.

"Hey did you see our Google page? Someone left a one star review about you today," Terry came in saying.

"Oh My God, Jesus, Jesus, Jesus, can't this fucking wait? I feel like I'm about to faint," Bill complained.

"Oh, sorry, I think it's shit as well but I thought you should know. When it happened to me and nobody told me about it, I found out after the patient complained to the clinic and I felt really shit," Terry explained.

"I just wanna go home, fuck this shit, what did they say?" Bill frustratingly relented.

Bill typed in "Mega Dental" and clicked on the clinic on Google Maps. There it was:

I saw Dr Parker today and he looked like he was so tired it was like he should have been in hospital. I felt very uncomfortable thinking about having someone that tired operating on me. I had to reschedule and couldn't remove my wisdom teeth today. This should not be acceptable. - Angela

"Goddamn mother fuck," Bill cursed.

After leaving work, Bill stood on the tram and saw that Cheng texted him. He was going to pass by this afternoon on his way to the western countryside. Good timing for a debriefing, Bill thought. Not long after Bill arrived back at his drug-den apartment, Cheng drove by. Bill sluggishly walked out and greeted Cheng.

"You look like a zombie bitch, what the fuck happened?" Cheng greeted.

"Goddamn, mother fuck, it was a total wash. I know I still owe you KFC and shit, don't worry, you helped me a lot, even though it was a waste of time. We did a fair trade," Bill returned his greeting.

"So what are you gonna do now?" Cheng asked.

"I told Andy that I'm quitting Kew today. I'm not going back to see that bitch again. Fuck brothels, I don't enjoy sex but I feel *compelled* to do it. Don't you get any urges? You don't know what it's like to have real sex until you actually do it for real. You wouldn't understand," Bill explained.

"It doesn't sound that good from what you say, plus it's hell fucking expensive. You know how little money I'm making? I'm a fucking employee and the ATO takes away half my income before I even get my hands on it. Plus I'm in the country with nobody to help me, I have to pay for all this education to teach me dentistry from scratch since Melbourne Dental School is a piece of shit that should be replaced by the University of YouTube. At least then we can have consistently high quality content instead of good teachers abandoning their lectures and getting replaced by morons who shouldn't be qualified to count sheep," Cheng ranted.

"You wouldn't understand. I'm hell broke too but I have no goddamn choice. After a while, I just feel this urge, I can't fucking help it. It's just biology. You said yourself, 'you can't beat biology,'" Bill replied.

"Well, you haven't answered my original question, what are you gonna do? You still gonna bang hookers?" Cheng asked.

"I don't fucking know. All I know is that fucking kid, Tom, he is dead to me. Do yourself a favour, stop listening to that kid. He acts all smart and everyone is beneath him but believe me, he's full of shit just like all the other morons I've met. I guess I owe that kid for the intel he gave but I don't give a shit about anything else about him," Bill replied.

"He probably just has trouble expressing himself. He always does that online then behaves completely differently face to face. It's probably from being in Whoop Whoop for too long," Cheng reasoned.

"Fuck that kid," Bill cursed again, "you know, I've finally realised, society treats me like a monster but it's not my fucking fault I've turned out this way. Tom is an active member of that part of society which has made me the monster I am today. He is part of the problem. You're either with me, or against me, there are NO NEUTRAL PARTIES!"

"You know that's the kinda logic the Nazis used, pretty much any authoritarian regime uses," Cheng replied.

"Then that's what the Nazis did right. Hitler did nothing wrong other than to lose the war. Don't kid yourself, we'd be all living much better if Hitler won the war," Bill declared.

"Better for white people and yo ass would be in Auschwitz II, Electric Boogaloo right now bitch," Cheng mocked.

"Don't pretend that you disagree, the Nazis weren't monsters, they did what was necessary. Genocide improved the economy, in fact we need genocide right now. People like me need to subjugate all these fucking morons ruining this nation," Bill continued.

"If anyone would be in charge it would be some rich guy who can afford to deceive people into voting for them just like Hitler, and they would put yo ass in a death camp and give you Zyklon B that you love so much," Cheng replied.

"Fuck those rich Boomer assholes, I'm talking about a world *better* than this world. I should be in charge, I'm the only one who can do it properly. This world is falling because useless fucking cockroaches are subjugating ME. It's fucking doomed, this country, society, all those goddamn useless pieces of shit, they're all fucked. I see all these morons on the street walking around pretending that everything is going to be OK, FUCK THEM! I just want to stand in outer space and look at the Earth, on fire. Everything should just fucking burn in nuclear fire," Bill maniacally declared while cradling his head in his hands and rocking back and forth inside Cheng's car.

"Genocide might be a little extreme, I think you'll get little satisfaction killing random people. If anything, you should focus on getting revenge on those who wronged you directly, instead of Tom, who's probably some closet aryan supremacist," Cheng tried to reason with Bill.

"I just want this pain to stop," Bill uttered weakly, he felt like he was on the verge of tears again.

After unloading the heavy emotional baggage off his chest, Bill recounted in detail what happened on the night of the confession. In some ways, Cheng was almost like a psychotherapist to Bill. Psychologists never cared about their patients beyond superficial grandstanding. They all pretended to be Jesus incarnate but talking never cured anyone. In fact, their business depended on patients returning. At the end of the day, without a profit, no business could continue operating, even not-for-profits existed to make a profit one way or another. The health benefits of patients were merely a byproduct of protecting their bottom line.

For the next 3 days, Bill barely managed any quality sleep. The mental assaults were not slowing down. Night after night, he would lie down and Erika's rejection would break his heart repeatedly, followed by Tom shouting "RAPIST" in his face. Every day, he would drift in and out of semi-consciousness. His head never stopped throbbing and his hands never stopped shaking. Bill barely recalled walking to the toilet to relieve himself. Bill also barely remembered showing up to work at Kew either. He was actually thankful his books were near empty. He used to hate Jane for allocating patients to the female dentists but for these three days, he was not in the mood to see even one patient. This went on until Saturday when Andy finally managed a face to face discussion with Bill.

"Hey Bill, are you sure about dropping your days at Kew?" Andy asked.

"Yes sir, 100%. I don't care how long it takes for Carlton to open," Bill replied.

"You mentioned that you didn't like Jane but what actually happened?" Andy tried to probe further.

"Don't trust what any of the staff say. They never liked me and I never liked them. That clinic was meant for females only. I was targeted on day one and I never felt comfortable there. I heard that another male dentist at Mega tried working there once but quit after just a month" Bill explained.

"Yeah, I remember, but Eddy quit Mega as well not long after. I didn't think that was Kew's fault. I was hoping to bring some more male dentists in to the change the vibe of the place," Andy elaborated.

"I understand sir, but the way things are over there, you're gonna need Seal Team Six to make any meaningful change. Every time I listen to Jane, she's always telling the patients to see the female dentists. My books are always the emptiest, no surprise there. If that were the only thing, that would have been fine except they all keep treating me like a dumping ground for their problems. Half the time I end up doing free work, then they bring all their family in and expect *me* to do it all for free. I do them so many favours but they still keep asking for more. How is this even possible? I'm not a goddamn courier. Every goddamn week I'm bringing stuff over," Bill finally let it off his chest.

"Wow, I never knew this, I gotta have a word with Jane about this. That sounds rough man, I promise to fix this, are you sure you don't wanna stay on?" Andy attempted to rectify the situation.

"I'm 100%, I am not going back there," Bill resolutely stated.

"I understand where you're coming from. I have some good news though. I'm confident we'll be able to open Carlton before the new financial year. It's time we talked about your books. You said that you were open to being the head dentist at Carlton, would you like to work Monday to Friday there? We're planning to make the place run for 7 days a week just like here at Mega," Andy asked.

"Sure, I'm glad to have the opportunity to become a leader," Bill emphasised his gratitude regarding the reception of responsibility.

"Good, but I do warn you, as a new clinic, there probably aren't going to be many patients. I'm paying everyone 40% but without a retainer. If you would like a retainer, then we'll need to change to an employee contract and the most I can pay would be 30% commission, but of course all the additional benefits of leave entitlements and Super would add up to 40%," Andy offered.

"I don't need a retainer, I'll get paid what I deserve. Super is a scam anyway, plus I don't take holidays, as you know sir," Bill replied with extreme confidence.

"Ha ha, that's what I think too. I'm glad to see we're on the same page," Andy continued.

"By the way, have you found anyone to work on the weekends? I don't wanna leave Mega altogether so I still want to keep my weekends here," Bill asked.

"We don't have anyone yet. It's no surprise, the economy is booming and everyone expects to walk into a job with full books. It's hard to find dentists or staff these days. If you know anyone, I'd be glad to take them on," Andy offered. Bill realised that fate was dealing its hand yet again. Bill did indeed know someone who could fill the vacancy.

That night, Bill invited Cheng out for the much anticipated KFC payment. For the sake of nostalgia, the two met at the Carlton KFC closest to the circus which pretended to be a dental school.

"Yo bitch, you have no idea what happened today," Bill started off the conversation.

"What?" Cheng asked.

"Andy is pretty much handing you a job, he said today that he was looking for someone to start working weekends in his new clinic which is gonna be right round the corner from here. I gotta say, it's pretty ballsy to put up a clinic right next to the dental school, it's like giving those MDS faggots the middle finger," Bill explained, with "MDS" referring to Melbourne Dental School.

"Right, but it's new so there's probably going to be zero patients," Cheng replied.

"Come on man, you gotta come back to Melbourne, just look at Beaufort, your idiot boss is ripping you off, once you start working here, you should just quit working for that moron and come here, Andy pays 40%, how much do you earn?" Bill questioned. Cheng appeared to start becoming agitated.

"Fuck you, I had no goddamn choice. I get paid $50 an hour, it's shit but 100% of $0 is $0 which is what I'll be earning if I quit that job," Cheng replied.

"Look, I love you man, you've always helped me so let me help you. I see you slaving away seeing like 15 patients a day, you bill like $2k each day at least and the guy just pays you $400? How can you live with that? Come on ma ne ga, just quit that job and -" Bill continued before being rudely interrupted.

"Shut the fuck up already! Do you think jobs just grow on trees? I can't afford to sit around earning $0 for months on end!" Cheng all of a sudden started shouting.

Bill thought that Cheng was increasingly becoming like Tom. He was just trying to help this kid and he started reacting the same way Tom did when Bill tried pushing Tom to look for a better job, which Tom did anyway after being pushed too far...

"Calm down, I'm just trying to help you. OK, you don't have to quit, but maybe once you start seeing more patients, then quit. You'll be working 7 days like me for a while, but it's not so bad as long as the fucking work environment isn't filled with traitors and morons. You'll be working with me so it would just be like old times. Come on man, I know from Terry that there are at least 10 other Chinese dentists from our class alone who are working two or even three jobs travelling to the country," Bill pleaded, "in fact, there are a couple of morons working even further than you. There's at least one guy in Ararat and another in Horsham. Come on, this is how people normally work their way back into Mel-borne."

"This is bullshit. Whatever, I'll ask your boss for the weekend position but I can't afford to quit working in the country for a long time yet," Cheng replied. Bill felt relieved. If he could bring some more of his friends here, even Tom, maybe he could start a new chapter in life. At the end of the day, Bill did not stay mad at Tom. Cheng was probably right, that kid probably was as misunderstood as Bill was most of the time.

* * *

Another week had passed and Bill finally stopped working at Kew. However, the pain still would not stop. It was becoming milder, only slightly, or perhaps it was just Bill becoming more accustomed to the pain. Sleep was still difficult. Some nights Bill actually felt like he woke up from proper sleep, before returning to a state of uncomfortable semconsciousness that could not be called "sleep." For the first time in a long time, the first Monday he did not have to work, Bill just laid down in bed drifting in and out of that semi-conscious state. He was too tired to get up but also too angry to fall asleep. By Tuesday, Bill had enough of the drifting and decided to finally get up and do *something*.

Cheng donated his old scrapheap Athlon X2 5600 computer from 2009. At least it could still run a basic Linux operating system, Bill thought. There was no hope in hell it could run Windows 8 and still be useable. The cheap system's scrapheap fans howled like a banshee but at least it worked. Bill started searching Reddit forums for other men with similar experiences to him. Bill followed link after link until he arrived at this strange page called, "Incels." The more Bill started reading, the more it made sense to him. These were a bunch of angry, rejected men who society deemed unacceptable. They were so called, "involuntary celibates."

Bill read one post after another. These men were rejected based on their height or disabilities. There were divorce raped men, in other words men who lost everything in divorce. There were men who committed suicide and left their thoughts before finally washing their mouths out with a revolver. Bill had finally found his kindred spirits. There were lots of fake posts and trolls but several stories struck him hard. There was one man who said that he was at a Halloween party and had a werewolf mask on. Apparently there were lots of women around him who enjoyed his company. However, the moment he took the mask off, they disappeared. Should have kept the fucking mask on, Bill thought.

Another post indicated that when surveying online dating website users, men rated 50% of women as being average in appearance or better. No surprise there, it was stating the obvious. However, women rated 20% of men as being average in appearance or better. That really struck Bill hard. Bill had given women the benefit of the doubt. He believed that women were not shallow and were interested in men's character rather than appearance. The media and Hollywood always portrayed men as shallow and sex mad, but reality was different. This was revolting. The women surveyed on dating sites must have been young women in Bill's age bracket. These were the women Bill would need to try and attract to engage in a relationship. Reality only showed they were *far* more shallow than men. It really was hopeless. Asian men especially were rated as least desirable, even by Asian women.

There was another man talking about this widespread meme about Tinder, the smartphone dating app which matched people depending on whether or not they found each other attractive. Some man paired with a woman who said, "Ewww," when he admitted he was less than 6 foot. Then he asked her how much she weighed and the woman exploded in rage and unlisted him. Apparently when this meme was shown to females online, they completely sided with the woman in the meme with absolutely zero self-awareness of how shallow they were. Men could not change their height whereas women could just shed a few pounds. Bill studied bone distraction osteogenesis back in dental school. Relapse was a bitch. Men couldn't grow taller even with surgery, not for long at least. Here's a standard, now make it double, Bill thought. Typical.

There were also countless cautionary tales of divorce raping. Bill even started to learn about Australian divorce law, or "Family Law" as the politically correct morons would called it. Judges used the phrase "best interests of the child" as an excuse to arbitrary punish men because men were just declared inferior caretakers compared to women based on gender ideology. Women used their children as bargaining chips to take more from men, no surprise there. Apparently, men were innately violent, brutish rapists who had no right to be with children. If women had full custody then they would also receive the maximum child support. Can't pay? Prison. It was worse than Bill thought. There was more, a study in 1997 found that 96% of children under age 4 were given sole custody to the mother. Even at age 17 when kids could actually think for themselves, the legal system still forced 82% to live solely with their mother.

Bill thought, not even dental specialists could boast a root canal success rate of 96%. That was an insane figure. Most men probably do not want to see their kids, that was understandable, but not 96%. Bill was starting to see a pattern. For the next two days, Bill did nothing but stroll through forum after forum. From Incels, he was also introduced to MGTOW, or Men Go Their Own Way and Red Pill, which was a Matrix analogy from the scene where the main character was ordered to choose to swallow a "blue pill" and forget everything or take the "red pill" to awaken in the real world. It was not as if these posts introduced Bill to new ideas. Bill knew that these problems existed but to this severity? He was well and truly living in a diseased society. Misandry was the norm. By being a man, Bill had a target painted on his back. In this society, in any Western society, he was an enemy by default. It suddenly all made sense.

Bill had been lied to his whole life. Cheng was right. He watched too many Disney movies. Opium for the masses. Psychological drugs pacifying society and maintaining the gynocentric status quo. He was fed propaganda since birth about how women were the "fairer sex" and could do no wrong. They were all princesses to be protected. Except that was all bullshit. Women were the orchestrators of all the ills in his life. Women had rejected him because of factors *beyond* his control. If only they would just get to know him and *just give him a chance*. Except they would not. Any woman would prefer to have sex with some Chad or Tyrone, new terms he learned from Incels referring to white and black men respectively who were apex sexual specimens. In the eyes of women, Bill did not even exist. In woman-vision, they only saw a fucking rat. Bill was just a talking rat to these cockroaches.

Bill tried to actively reject the red pill. Throughout his life, he had tried every possible strategy to disprove the truth. He was as empirical as a scientist experimenting every way possible. He held onto the hope he could prove that the incels' hypotheses were wrong. Rejecting all the false hypotheses would leave him with the null hypothesis; that women were indeed angels to be revered. All the painful experiments ended in failure. The null hypothesis must be unilaterally rejected with extreme conviction. There was no other conclusion.

If only Bill were told the truth earlier, he could have avoided so many problems in his life. These revelations started to slowly numb the pain Bill was feeling. By Wednesday night, Bill was finally able to sleep properly for the first time in weeks. For the first time in a long time, Bill felt emancipated. That headache he was feeling was perhaps the cognitive dissonance he felt. He was taught that women were all angels, but why did they treat him so badly? His mother lied and cheated, so did his sister. His "girlfriend" probably cheated anyway, how else was she treating him so flippantly? Whores took his money and used comforting words to trick him. He was abused and mistreated endlessly by women and somehow they were all angels? His brain was feeling the pain from the lies clashing with reality. Finally, Bill felt like an alcoholic opening his eyes after achieving sobriety for the first time in years. It would take much longer for the pain to go away, but at least he could sleep properly now. Every waking moment was painful, but finally, he was able to achieve some relief by sleeping.

This became Bill's life for the next few weeks until Carlton finally opened. Work became easier to handle for two reasons. Firstly, Bill actually enjoyed working at Mega, it was the best dental clinic he had worked in. Secondly, Bill finally had time off. The moment Bill arrived home, he would have his "triple shower" then jump on the manosphere forums. That was another term that Bill learned about, the manosphere was the collective term for men's rights groups voicing their opinions. It included Incels, MGTOW, Red Pill and now Bill was discovering yet another group called the "Black Pill." These men were far more extreme than any of the others. They believed that society was fucked beyond all recognition and death and rebirth was the *only* option. Even then, humanity itself was doomed so nuclear fire was perhaps in the best interests of everyone, Bill thought.

One fateful Saturday July 4th, Andy finally approached Bill and informed him,

"Hey Bill, I hope you're ready 'cause Carlton will be having its grand opening next week."

"Yes sir, I'm feeling excited," Bill exclaimed.

"You do look a lot better. I heard from the other dentists that there was something about a girl. I understand, better luck next time, you're a good catch so don't give up," Andy tried to cheer Bill up.

"I don't think I'll be doing that again, women and I don't mix, just like oil and water," Bill declared.

"Don't sell yourself short, you just gotta be patient. Your friend Cheng came for an interview as well, he was working in the country like you! I'm so glad we were able to fill our openings so quickly, it's all coming together. I gotta go now, don't forget to try our CEREC! I'm no longer charging any lab fees for it!" Andy said before leaving. Yep, Bill thought, this was the beginning of a new chapter in his life.

Chapter 12

Hopelessness (III)

It was not long before Bill walked into the newly minted halls of Mega on Cardigan, right behind the Royal Dental Hospital of Melbourne. As Andy promised, it was the first week of July 2015, just past the end of financial year. Bill scanned the interior with his eyes. Not too shabby, Bill thought. It appeared that Andy liked consistency and modelled the place almost exactly like the layout of the original Mega Dental. The main difference being that there was no oversized window the size of a full grown adult. Just a plain old small window as expected from a suburban house. Bill eyed the burger shop over on the other side of the road. He sometimes walked past it during his dental school years but he would never waste money on overpriced hamburgers like that.

Bill entered his shining new surgery and signed into his Precise management software. No patients. No surprise there, it was a new clinic after all. There was a clinic around every street corner here next to the city, not to mention the dental school starting their own scam clinic next to the Dental Hospital. So much for free market competition, Bill thought. Typical socialist scum taking *his* taxpayer dollars from the Government to set up a clinic then charge patients private fees. Too bad the students and teachers from the dental school could not do dentistry to save their own lives. Bill shut the door and opened up YouTube. Well, what else was there to do? The pain from existential hopelessness was still there but not as severe. There was substantial "manosphere"content on YouTube and Bill had endless time to watch. Things were going to improve. After all, he was placed in charge with his self approved team. His situation was on the way up...

... Only it did not happen. It was almost two months after opening and Bill was still seeing zero patients. Apparently there was one patient booked in tomorrow for just a checkup and clean. He actually dropped 2 days at Collins Street for this. He was working 7 days, but earning 60% of what he used to make just working 4 days at Collins Street. It was 3:30pm, Bill thought it was time to call it. There were not going to be any bookings for the rest of the day. He had spent the whole day watching anti-feminist videos. It was becoming clear to him that he was being hunted. Bill worked hard his whole life to get where he was but it was beyond a reasonable doubt that women were promoted proportionally to their incompetence.

He was the one who cleaned up all the messes made by the female dentists. He was the one who was repeatedly rejected by anyone he found attractive. He was the victim this whole time, abused by his sister, mother, "girlfriend." He was lied to, fed horse shit propaganda, manipulated and subjugated. His bank account was threatened with freezing by the Australian Tax Office because he had not paid tax for over a year. Bill had completely ignored paying his taxes because he was so tired he could not even get a chance to use his computer until he quit working at Kew. By then, tax was far too distant on his backburner for him to even register it as a concern. The tax office was demanding almost everything he had in his bank account. All that travelling, moving from clinic to clinic, that was hell expensive. The meagre remnant of his money was going to become the welfare supplement of useless admin staff who ought to be given the Zyklon B treatment. If only Bill were Hitler, he would immediately implement an all encompassing genocide.

The harder he worked, the poorer he became. This was not even a joke any more. The "manosphere" was right. Bill finally managed to realise the grand death spiral of society. It started with giving women the vote. The moment they did, women started voting for supremacy, *not* equality. All that bullshit about equality was political doublespeak for subjugation. Modern society was dominated by misandry. As a straight male, he was an enemy of the state. Men built this great city of Melbourne. Men built every fucking city. Men did all the hard labours keeping everything working. One video in particular pointed out that the maximum weight allowed for occupation health and safety limits was less than the weight of a toddler. Women were fine with picking up toddlers like a dumbbell kit but would not get off their arrogant derrieres to start working in construction to fix the "gender inequality" in the dirty, critical jobs society needed.

All the women working beside Bill earned much more than him yet still kept complaining about "equality." Bill had had enough. He was surrounded by a diseased society. He was the only sane, rational person around yet everyone labelled *him* the crazy one? Who the fuck turned him into a monster in the first place? Why did society never take responsibility? The answer was undoubtedly because women dominated and thus doomed society. He should have realised it sooner. Morons like Tom obsequiously smashed their heads on the ground inviting radical female psychopaths to stomp on their faces. People like Tom were the enemy. Tom had become Bill's Goldstein, like the enemy of Big Brother from Nineteen Eighty Four.

Bill did not have a single female friend. Whenever Bill thought about feminism, Tom's face was aggressively plastered into Bill's imagination. Tom's face naturally resembled a target. People like Tom ignored the vile machinations of the radical feminist political movement and their malicious tendrils metastasising throughout the western world's culture and political systems. Bill found the perfect term for such people today. The "manosphere" called them "NPCs," or "non-player characters" which were basically robotically programmed digital characters inside a video game who were only capable of responding in one way no matter the stimulus.

Bill heard a noise, it was his receptionist knocking on the door.

"Hello Bill, did you want to close up now?"

"Uhh... Yeah, I'll be going soon," Bill replied after being snapped back into reality from his reverie. Bill looked at his screen, it was 4pm. He was lost in his thoughts for half an hour. Looking at the YouTube home page, every single video recommendation was some form of "manosphere" or anti-feminist content. The algorithm picked up on that pretty quickly, Bill thought. Bill packed up his belongings, there were not many, after all with zero patients, he barely unpacked. As Bill walked out of the automatic doors, he said a quick "bye" to the receptionist. The assistant had already left half an hour ago.

Forty minutes later, Bill walked from the station into his local Woolworths to buy his food for the rest of the week. Unfortunately for him, or fortunately depending on his mood, the Woolworths was located close to a 24/7 gym and there was no end to stunningly gorgeous women in tight gym clothes walking in and out. Today, Bill did not want to be aroused. He was so lost in his own thoughts that he completely forgot about the presence of beautiful women here. Still, Bill questioned why there were so many attractive women living in South Yarra. The young patients he saw were so destitute, they were almost a waste of time to treat. Young people naturally had less money yet South Yarra was among the most expensive suburbs in Melbourne. There must be a lot of sugar daddies, Bill thought, a collection of cadavers being propped up by these goddess tier gold diggers.

Suddenly, that craving was back. He felt compelled to return to the brothel. Goddamn it, Bill thought. His money was going to be lit on fire by the tax office and now he could not even concentrate without women assaulting his thoughts. Bill recognised this pattern. He would try to avoid thinking about women for a while then his monkey brain would start aggressively assaulting him with thoughts about women. He could not treat patients under these compulsions. He had no goddamn choice yet again. He was compelled to do it. Bill hurriedly completed his shopping. It was an easy task after all, he knew what he needed to buy, especially since it was dependent on whatever was discounted. Bill power walked back to his apartment with a bag full of groceries and dumped it all in the fridge. Even though they were prostitutes, Bill still needed to present his best self. That involved undertaking the triple shower, shaving, perfume and foundation. That shit was hell good, Bill thought, foundation worked as well for men as it did for women.

That night Bill did not really care how attractive the woman was, she just needed to be not unattractive. There was a brunette named Sadie who had a "down to Earth" face, was not fat and did not have any visible tattoos so she was good enough. Again, the session was not very stimulating. Sadie was a nice girl and she was trying hard to please him. He was happy he chose Sadie but he still felt nothing beyond arousal which honestly was not even on par with online content. Not only that, Bill suddenly felt extremely lethargic after leaving the brothel. Bill almost fell over as he stepped inside his car. It was not easy supporting his body weight on one bent leg. Bill had to catch his breath after sitting down. Then it hit him.

A wave of painful memories flooded Bill's head. It was like getting hit by a truck loaded with past trauma. The pain was intense, his head felt like it was on fire. Dental school - time and time again, the beautiful oral hygiene girls ignored his advances. Sarah - betrayed and dumped him like a used plastic bag. Speed dating, Erika, classmates he tried to impress, the painful reminders just would not stop. One after another, the waves cascaded and pounded against Bill's fragile, brutalised heart. Yet, it would not stop.

"Why?" Bill thought. "Why did it have to be like this?" Bill started to feel moisture gathering at the edges of his eyes. "Why couldn't we have met outside a brothel? Would she have even seen me as a human being outside the brothel?" These thoughts rampaged like a tympanist on methamphetamine in Bill's head.

Sadie's kindness reminded him of Erika and Holly. They were all so nice to him. They treated him like a human being. Bill knew now that if he had met any of these beautiful women outside of a brothel, they would not even acknowledge he existed. He was less than dog faeces for these women in real life. They would intentionally step around him to avoid getting their shoes dirty. Was it really $300 an hour all that was separating him from being treated like an animal? Bill felt the tears drip down the sides of his face. He could not help it, the pain was that intense. The "Chads" referred to by the "manosphere" all dressed like slobs. They would not be able to understand true style if it hit them like an oncoming train in a tunnel. Bill placed so much effort on his appearance but it was useless because he was short and lacked a fucking gorilla jaw. Give it another 100 years and evolutionarily speaking, men with jaws less than a cruise liner hanging off the head would be put in cages for being sub-human.

Bill was abused, tortured, emotionally raped by society every fucking moment and all because of the way he was born. And yet that fucking monkey brain forced him to seek female attention spending the precious resources he fought to earn just to twist the dagger further and further into his heart. Bill hated himself almost as much as he hated females right now. This was God's cruel joke, Bill thought. Bill decided to call Cheng for some comfort.

"Answer the phone dammit!" Bill half shouted.

"You know, you're the idiot who never picks up yet you want me to be at your beck and call 24/7. It's almost 10pm and I need to prepare for the drive back to Melbourne tomorrow so get to the point," Cheng chastised.

"Come on man, come on, don't be like that, please..." Bill pleaded, this time sobbing while complaining into the phone.

"Ughhh... what is it this time? Fell in love with another hooker?" Cheng sarcastically replied.

"IT'S NOT LIKE I FUCKING WANT TO! GODDAMMIT!" Bill actually shouted this time. "I can't help it, I'm fucking compelled to do it."

Bill continued by explaining what happened in unwarranted, explicit detail.

"Dude, can't you just accept that you're paying for a service? That service is physical in nature and nothing to do with emotions. Sure, normally people feel satisfaction afterwards, but that's an emotion only arising due to their physical needs being met, you're expecting way too much out of this," Cheng criticised.

"I know goddamn it but I can't fucking help it! I wish I were like you Cheng. How the hell do you not want to murder every fucking person despite going through similar experiences? I remember you were the angry one at dental school, and I thought, 'Gosh, if I were that kid getting fucked over by the dental school like that, I'd become a mass murderer then and there,'" Bill enquired.

"What can I say, fuck life, I've given up on life now, all I'm trying to do is make enough money to retire. I've been fucked over so many times, I'm no longer spending any effort to do anything these days. I don't care how women see or treat me, I don't care what society thinks as long as it does not interfere with my retirement," Cheng explained. "It's almost 11pm now, how long are you gonna keep me here?"

"Alright, alright, fuck you too. You know you need these talks as much as I do bitch," Bill replied, "go fucking wank then, I gotta get back too."

Bill dejectedly hung up and drove himself back to South Yarra. The pain was unrelenting and no less intense than an hour ago. Bill turned his donated computer on and went back to the manosphere. Oh this was a good one, Bill thought. Another Tinder experiment where the original poster found pictures of male models then pretended to be a paedophile, Nazi, ex-prisoner, murderer, racist, you name it, Bill thought. The females matching these male models just did not care how outlandishly evil these fake men were. They would still have sex with them based purely on that chiselled gorilla jaw and a six pack. He had to laugh at himself. Cheng was right to criticise Bill's obsession with these subhuman animals. His monkey brain forced him to go to brothels but at least Bill realised it was just an animalistic urge. These Tinder women would risk getting murdered and raped simultaneously just because the person pretending to message them had gorilla jaws and a six pack. Then they would gush about the Chad's "personality."

To Bill, these Tinder women represented females as a whole. The algorithm showed him nothing to contradict that. To him, they were all prisoners to their biological urges. Completely and utterly incapable of acting outside of their NPC sub-routines. These animals had less control over their monkey brains than even he did. Yet they would crow endlessly about "loyalty," "where did all the good men go?" and quote bullshit like "eat, pray, love." They were not self-aware in the slightest. The first step to treating mental illness was awareness and acceptance. Yet these animals revelled in their mental illness like pigs with their snouts caught in the trough. They had the gall to turn around and start blaming men like *him*. The same kind of men these women treated worse than excrement and subjugated for malicious amusement on a daily basis. The more online algorithmic content Bill consumed, the more he agreed. The pain started to slowly dull itself by 3am in the morning. Maybe he could try to fall asleep now.

Bill woke up late the next day because what did it really matter? He was not going to have any bookings until the 2pm checkup and clean anyway. Who knows, maybe that patient would cancel and it would be a waste of time for him to even show up, Bill thought. Bill sighed, it was already 11am and his phone did not have any messages. If anyone booked in his receptionist would have messaged him. He might as well take his time. By the time Bill arrived at the clinic it was already 1:50pm. Bill took out his optical assistance device, loupes with a head light, then signed into the computer. Within a few minutes the patient arrived.

The patient was apparently some 35 year old female immigrant from Norway who wanted a chip on their tooth fixed. Bill looked inside her mouth, there were fillings everywhere. In fact, there were fillings piled onto other fillings on the same teeth for almost every back tooth. It was a miracle she even had teeth. Bill sighed. Typical socialised healthcare on display. When people were removed from the consequences of their own actions, this moral hazard arose causing idiots everywhere to start abusing their bodies as much as they liked. Hard working enslaved tax-payers footed the repair bill. Bill gritted his teeth thinking about his $70k tax bill which included late submission penalties. If people treated their mouths like a dumping ground for sugar, what did they expect? Not only that, when dentistry was socialised, it was apparent beyond a reasonable doubt that dentists only produced trash quality work like what was in this woman's mouth. He had seen it time and time again with the National Health Service from the UK.

Bill cursed under his breath while taking a full set of photos using the pen sized camera attached to the dental chair. The woman was beginning to look agitated. The problem was one of the poorly performed "repairs" done by some idiot Norwegian dentist in 5 minutes fell off, as expected. Bill could just repair it like the previous idiot but then it would fall out in less than a year. Then this moron in the chair would come back and make a complaint about how much she paid and how much Bill was ripping her off. People like this should just stay the fuck in Norway and continue having their shitty socialised dentistry negligently performed while slicing and dicing the mutilated remnants of what were formerly "teeth." These Scandinavians were indoctrinated into believing that it "could be just patched up, no worries" and felt entitled to free treatment.

"What is taking so long? Can't you just patch it up? It's not even a big filling, I'm going on a business trip next week," the patient asked, causing even more irritation for Bill than she was personally feeling. Bill sighed internally. He was fucked. Her statement instantly confirmed that she was an indoctrinated, entitled NPC moron incapable of thought.

"I'm sorry, but I can't just patch it up, see all that brown and yellow?" Bill said while pointing to his photo, "those fillings there are already leaking, if I filled this tooth today, my filling would just drop out in a few months and the remaining fillings could come out with it."

"I'm sorry, I don't understand, why can't you just patch it up? It's what's always happened in the past," the patient continued, this time seriously irritating Bill.

"I know that's what the dentists in your home country did but in this country, we do dentistry properly," Bill firmly replied.

"You still haven't answered my question. You've been looking in my mouth for 15 minutes," the patient said while looking at her watch, "just to tell me you can't fix my tooth?"

"I'm not saying I can't fix the tooth, I'm trying to explain that we can't just 'patch it up.' This tooth needs all of the fillings on it replaced or even a crown later down the track," Bill tried to explain with substantial exasperation.

"That costs a lot more doesn't it? You don't even need to answer, I know it is," the patient continued arguing.

"I'm not saying you have to do a crown, but you at least need to replace all that old filling on the tooth. In fact, I took so many photos because so many teeth are in a similar -" Bill attempted to explain but was cut off.

"I'm not here for some sort of smile makeover, I just wanted that one tooth fixed!" this time the patient was clearly being rude. She sighed and muttered, "God, this is useless."

"Get out," Bill clearly had enough. Bill did not care if she paid or not. He stood to *lose* money if he gave in to her fantasies. Wordlessly, the patient walked out and Bill closed his door refusing to listen to that annoying whining any longer.

Bill really hated Europeans. Bill thought of himself as an American through and through. Europeans pretended to live in perfect societies with their hard line left wing socialism and arrogant attitude. The reality was what he saw today. If Bill were to become the dictator of Australia, he would definitely remove all public dentistry. Today was the typical result of those idealistic morons in Europe giving handouts to everyone like candy. If Europe were such a perfect idyllic society, why the fuck did that bitch have to come here then? Bill rarely *ever* encountered Americans living in Australia. They had no reason to immigrate to an inferior nation. Europeans on the other hand, they were everywhere, just like plastic pollution in the oceans.

Bill's headache returned. His anger was raging violently. His heart was pounding and his hands were shaking and his vision was blurring. His emotions were so intense that even his vision was being affected. Endless images of gorey violence started flashing through his mind. How easy would it be to kill that bitch? Unfortunately, he would get caught and that would be the end of his revenge path. If that bitch continued arguing with him, who knows, could he have resisted choking her to death? She was one lucky bitch because she was fortunate enough that Bill was not performing tooth extraction. There were any number of sharp instruments that he could have used to give her an instant lobotomy.

Bill woke up Saturday morning with the same headache he fell asleep with last night. Mega on Collins was different. His books were three quarters filled again. At least that was good news however Bill's headache threatened to consume him. Would he be able to get through the day without fainting? Before he could bring the first patient in, Bill saw a message from reception.

"Dr Bill, could you please check your messages, there's a patient email addressed to you, please let me know how to respond" it read. The first patient had not yet arrived, they were supposed to be due in 5 minutes so Bill might as well check his emails.

To whom it may concern,

On May 7th, I saw Dr William Parker to glue my veneer back on. However, it only lasted a month. I went back to my normal dentist who told me that Dr Parker did not glue it on properly and it cannot be glued again. My dentist said that if it were him, he would take responsibility and make a new veneer at no cost. I am a law student so I know my rights. I feel that if indeed Dr Parker did not glue my veneer on properly, he should take responsibility for his failed treatment.

Regards,

Brian Carlisle, JD student.

Bill was instantly triggered.

"GOD FUCKING DAMN IT!" Bill shouted as he smashed his fist against the plastic laminated bench. Bill wanted to find this subhuman cockroach who planted this false narrative in that moron patient's head. Oh how he would enjoy taking revenge. He would deep fry the dentist's family alive and feed them to pigs then slaughter the pigs and blend their corpses with their recent excrement into a shit slurry, then have it dumped in a nuclear waste dump. Death by a thousand cuts was too lenient. If only there were a way to feed them long term opioids so that they become sensitised to pain and *then* cut them into pieces to truly relish the pain. All Bill could think about now was killing. Kill, kill, kill. So many people needed killing.

"Don't EVER book fucking re-cementations with me again. That piece of shit patient is fucking lying. His fucking moron dentist fucked up the veneer in the first place and now he wants to blame me? I will sort this shit out" Bill wrote back to the receptionist.

"... OK doctor, I will leave it with you" was the reply.

Bill knew that patient would come back to haunt him. He took pre-operative photos just in case showing how poorly the ceramic veneer was fitting. Veneers were the easiest type of ceramic work to fit. Sure, getting the look right was hard but it was not fucking hard to fit a flat fucking surface on a front tooth but the sub-human dentist was not even able to fit it properly. Bill also took post-op photos to verify that it was glued on *correctly*. He stressed repeatedly and showed the patient why the veneer fell off in the first place but of course it was in one ear out the other. That moron was not an actual lawyer but still wanted to pretend he was someone important. Bill had treated actual lawyers who showed more self-awareness than that moron. Bill just wanted to kill them all.

Unfortunately for Bill, the reception team also appeared to treat his orders like farts in the wind. 4pm new patient booking: "Crown came off." God, fucking, dammit! How were these morons even capable of breathing? How low could their IQ get? He had just ordered them NOT to book fucking re-cementation patients in and yet *the very same day* they did the complete opposite. Bill escorted his 3pm patient out and marched up to the two receptionists on today. The one who messaged him this morning was Hanna, a young Chinese receptionist and the other was Katrina, a white boomer Australian. It was hard to keep track since they were replaced so often.

"Ladies, did you not see my message this morning?" Bill asked using his quietest voice possible despite his seething anger.

Hanna replied, "I'm sorry doctor, the patient said he was desperate and needs it glued back on today. All the other dentists are fully booked. What would you like me to do doctor?"

"It's too late to cancel, just leave it," Bill uttered in defeat. Days like today, he was reminded yet again: he was the enemy of the state. He was a short, unwanted, straight male in a society which deemed him a hazard just for being born. He was truly doomed. There was no hope.

The next day was no better. At lunch time, Bill was alerted by Hanna again that there was a complaint made against him. Bill's headache was raging like a tsunami yet again. He wished he did not have to deal with this garbage. He had yet to resolve yesterday's complaint and another piled on. He had no goddamn choice. If he did not look at it now, he would have no time later on. If he forgot about it, chances were the patient might escalate their challenge further and write a negative review humiliating him in front of everyone including the general public.

Hello,

My name is Luwalhati Leong, I see Dr Parker yesterday and he did a root canal procedure on my front tooth. That night, my face become more swollen so I went to my GP. My GP say that Dr Parker need to prescribe antibiotics. Why didn't Dr Parker prescribe antibiotics?His treatment make me worse. I believe I deserve refund.

Bill felt the surge of anger rising within him again. God, fucking, damn, it. There was no end to the cockroaches Bill needed to kill. Killing the entire world was not enough. If only he could resurrect everyone and kill them repeatedly again and again. Bill had told that bitch antibiotics did not crawl up inside the tooth where the infection was coming from and it was not recommended. It was hopeless instructing people who barely spoke English. He stressed repeatedly for that bitch to come back if there were problems and he would fix it. He was treating the patient "by the book" and was punished for it. This was a fucking joke. That fucking general medical practitioner had no idea what the fuck they were talking about. On one hand if the bitch got a reaction from antibiotics, the Dental Board would crucify him for harm arising from inappropriate antibiotic prescription. Despite following the rules, some ignorant moron GP fucked him up.

Bill wished he could crucify that GP, literally. Bill was not legally permitted to march in and start interfering with their treatment. Yet those morons were allowed to fuck up his life. Bill knew as much about treating pancreatic cancer as those subhuman cockroaches knew about treating teeth. Yet those fucking morons never showed any fucking humility in front of Bill. They wallowed in their arrogant ignorance and looked down on Bill like a fucking rat just like women did. Bill was reminded yet again of the moron GPs in Shellharbour who told patients they had "infections" because they were too fucking retarded to have the humility of admitting, "I don't know what I'm looking at" when seeing normal healing tooth extraction sockets. These people were all going on his list. Some day, just some day whenever it may be, these animals were going to get their just deserts.

Bill arrived home that day with the worst headache he had experienced since the Sadie incident. Life was just hopeless. Things were on the way up, Bill thought. Everything lined up perfectly like it was fate. He found a good clinic to work in, and to this day, despite the problems, it was still by far the best clinic he had worked in. He was given more autonomy and even a leadership role in the new clinic. His friends from dental school, some of them at least, were around him. This was even better than he could have hoped for when he started dental school. Yet, dentistry had innate problems that just could not be resolved. They were problems caused by this diseased society stuck in a death spiral. Bill leapt back into the Incel forums and was now an anonymous posting member of the community. He was not just going to sit around any more.

He altered the events so that it had nothing to do with dentistry or Mega, obviously. Just another man having his life ruined by women and society in general. Bill had no goddamn choice. He was just one man surrounded by an endless sea of enemies whose malice oozed out like pus from a violent infection. They enjoyed torturing him, like sharp prongs on a wounded bear tied to a pole. This must have been how MacBeth felt when the entirety of Scotland turned on him. Then it struck him. He could use women's feeble minded animalistic desires against them. He read stories online of struggling doctors becoming overnight millionaires by performing liposuction and nips and tucks.

Bill searched online, Botox and dermal filler courses for dentists. He was surprised he did not think of this earlier. All these desperate women young and old were willing to hand out endless amounts of money to inject poison into their faces while they would feel outraged at having to pay just $200 to prevent their tooth from disintegrating into a mush filled infection volcano. If this was the modern dental patient, then as it was well known, when in Rome... do what the Romans do. The course cost $2000 for two days and the soonest availability was next month located... in Sydney. Bill was well acquainted with travelling to and from Sydney so that made barely any difference. Within a few minutes of typing in his details, Bill was now an attendee of the next Australian Dental Association approved cosmetic injectables course.

The Monday following, Bill contacted his indemnity insurer on how to manage the patient complaints. They were fucking useless of course. He was transferred to some idiot who was an elderly specialist but no legal training, of course. He had some poncey English name, was it Reynold? Archie? Something along those lines. The insurance company was supposed to issue clinical *and* legal advice but this guy failed to do both. They instructed Bill to write a letter of apology himself and give the refund out of his own pocket otherwise their underwriter would threaten to increase his premiums.

"Yeah mate, you gotta refund them to shut down the complaint as fast as possible because if they ever decide to escalate the situation, the dental board or lawyers can make your life a nightmare. Not only does the problem then take years to resolve, it could potentially cost hundreds of thousands of dollars," the idiot on the phone tried to explain.

Fuck. Bill paid thousands of fucking dollars every year and yet these morons told him to solve everything himself. At least have their fucking dedicated lawyers draft their own damn letter. In the United States, indemnity insurers handled everything from start to finish so that dentists could spend their time doing actual fucking dentistry. This joke of a nation run by morons needed some genocidal cleansing immediately. Then there were the thousands of starving "no win no fee" lawyers out there to make a quick buck then pocket all the payout so that in the end their clients were just bargaining chips to steal money. Not that Bill cared about their victims/clients. At least he could perhaps demand to know the identities of the bastard dentist who fucked up a simple veneer and threw him under the bus and the negligent moron GP in exchange for the refund money.

It took a week of back and forth before his indemnity insurer finally agreed to the contents of the apology letters and offers of refund. In the meantime, Bill found another one star review under his name.

Don't see Dr Bill. I came in with loose crown and just wanted it glued. I know that gluing again not as good as first time but last time it lasted one year. Dr Bill only lasted 1 week. He was arguing with me telling me I need new crown but I had to keep saying no. I don't like this push, push selling on me. Dr Bill did bad job on purpose to make me do new crown. - Elvis Pres Lee

Not only could they barely write English, they also left a fake name. Bill knew exactly who it was. He knew that afternoon crown re-cementation patient booked in by Hanna was going to be a problem. Some fuckwit Thai dentist made a crown that not only did not fit, there was massive decay underneath which Bill tried to tell the moron who would not listen. He was not surprised. Bill was only surprised that he did not start murdering people already.

* * *

Bill arrived in Sydney at 8am October 17th 2015, on a surprisingly chilly spring morning. Unsurprisingly, the course began with discussing the controversy that was surrounding the developing adoption of cosmetic injectables by dentists. It was Dr Theodore Bent in the headlines yet again pushing cosmetic injectables too far and triggering a backlash from the dental board. The course trainers made it clear that cosmetic injectables were only allowed to be administered by dentists in the oral and jaw joint regions. Of course Dr Bent did not care and would inject it anywhere the patient asked for. Some of the dentists attending brought their own patients in to learn injecting on. Bill learned very little useful information from the course other than how to inject. If he were in charge of the dental board, he would outlaw cosmetic treatment. But society treated him like a diseased rat so how could he argue against adapting to the circumstances?

Bill returned to his hotel room and sighed. This was what he was reduced to, scraping the bottom of the barrel. He was taught to supposedly "prevent and treat infections and pathologies" in dental school. Yet he was here trying to learn how to make a 25 year old girl's non-existent wrinkles vanish and give her Kim Kardashian's fake swollen lips. The world loved Dr House from the television series. If Dr House were a dentist, he would scream at a demanding young girl who chipped her front tooth to get out. A chipped front tooth did not "need" filling but because society deemed appearances to be more important than health itself, reality was different. Time to grab out that angle grinder and drill that small chip into a large chip so a longer lasting filling can be done. Or even better, drill its guts out so a ceramic crown or veneer can be glued on only to fall out again. If that was what society demanded from him, then who was he to say no? Patients never listened to him anyway.

It was way too early to sleep so Bill thought he might as well try out the Sydney red light district in King's Cross. He never went there despite being in Sydney so many times before. It was just a short train ride away so within ten minutes, Bill was already standing at King's Cross station. Bill Googled the nearby brothels. From experience, Bill found that the reviews did not matter, what was more important was how many girls they had working. The more girls, the more popular the venue and hence, more likely younger, attractive women would be drawn to the venue. Before long, Bill decided to visit a place called Eden's Sinners.

When he stepped in, Bill was not sure what to expect since he was so used to Melbourne brothels. Sure enough, the curt but nonetheless courteous receptionist ushered him in. Then Bill was hit with a hefty surprise. The line-up of women that night put the Red Lantern to shame. Every second girl could have been a model and there were at least a dozen girls introducing themselves that night. The beautiful women were unfortunately all covered in at least one tattoo or piercing but Bill remained entranced. One girl especially caught his attention. Unlike the rest, she caressed Bill with her right hand and slid down to sit right beside him with her soft, uncovered thigh making contact with Bill's trousers. Oh, she was soft, warm and fragrant. She made Bill almost gasp, something he never felt before.

"Hi there, my name's Vivian, how are you enjoying your night so far?" she tenderly introduced herself. Vivian, Bill thought, just like Julia Roberts in Pretty Woman. Bill stared at her body. She wore a black brassiere and very short skirt which accentuated her slim, well-proportioned build. She did really have both the height and physique of a model. She was perfect. Bill was enraptured by her gentle intimacy and curves so perfect they could have been carved by God himself. He ignored her tattoos until he stared directly at her stomach. She was covered in tattoos. It was too late. Bill was smitten and not even tattoos could get in his way tonight.

After leaving the brothel, Bill needed to update his friend Cheng.

"Yo my ne ge, you won't *believe* what happened," Bill greeted Cheng on the phone.

"You went and fucked some hooker again didn't you?" Cheng sarcastically replied.

"Come on man, why do you gotta talk like that? The therapy centres here are like a different planet compared to Mel-*born*," Bill exclaimed, "There was one model after another. I would pay to bang any of them but this one girl, oh my God, she was like a work of art, and she was super nice."

"That's cause you paid her $300 an hour, wait, this is Sydney so did they charge more?" Cheng asked.

"I can't remember, I think it was about $400, but this girl, she said she works at Red Lantern on Thursdays, you know she's one of those fly in fly out girls," Bill explained.

"Then why you phoning me about it?" Cheng asked with some irritation, "it's like 10pm, don't you have any Korean friends to bother with this shit?"

"Fuck dem Ko-reans, they wouldn't understand," Bill replied then continued to explain in yet again, unwanted and unwarranted detail about his Sydney red light district adventure.

"She was hell nice and none of that low energy shit. When I asked her to slap me, she did it pretty hard. She said she liked it a little rough herself, heh. You know I'm into some of that damaged goods shit," Bill continued. "Out of all the girls, she was the only one who touched me and tried to comfort me *before* I paid her anything."

"That's only 'cause competition must have been pretty fierce that night," Cheng reasoned.

"This must be fate, everything had to just line up perfectly -" Bill tried to say.

"This fate bullshit again. You know, you should remind yourself each time you take a shit that every moment in life has led to you taking that dump right then and there. All this 'fate' bullshit is supposedly some motivational tool but fate has as much influence on your toilet time as it does on your sexual escapades," Cheng criticised.

"OK, OK fine, I get you bro, but this time, it's different, this is my last chance," Bill said.

"Again with this last chance bullshit, how many last chances has it been now? How come you're not breaking down over your great tragedy again?" Cheng asked.

"Don't fucking remind me," Bill warned, only it was too late, the pain was starting to creep back in.

"Go to sleep bitch, go learn how to rip off desperate women tomorrow, maybe that will keep your pain at bay," Cheng signed off.

"Fine... bitch," Bill said his goodbye and hung up.

Perhaps Cheng was right. To protect his sanity, Bill tried to preoccupy himself with the second part of his course the next day. He could not help but think about Vivian but being distracted made the pain slightly less severe. The second day focused more on dermal fillers, or basically just collagen protein being injected into lips. Bill had no idea why women did this. Kim Kardashian looked revolting to him. Yet somehow they revered her like a goddess. If Kim Kardashian suddenly started rejecting tattoos, these NPCs would follow a revolution harder than the Bolsheviks to stop tattooing themselves. Tattoo removal specialists would become overnight millionaires. So much for individuality.

* * *

By the time Bill arrived back in South Yarra, it was well past midnight. Unlike Sydney, Melbourne Airport lobbied the government hard to ensure there would never, ever in a million years be a train network connecting the airport to the city. He was forced to endure a slow bus drive to crawl back to the city. There was no way Bill would pay for expensive parking at the airport. His head was aching and he felt lethargic. Travelling always depleted his energy but he also had sex on Saturday night which left him so weak he could barely stand up for more than a minute. He was really getting physically old as well as mentally broken.

Surprisingly enough, Bill had a young girl come to see him about Botox injections the Saturday after he returned from the course.

"I read on the website that you offer Botox injections. My previous dentist gave me this plastic mouthguard to wear at night but it's just so painful. I'm in the middle of my university exams and every night I wake up in pain. It's hard to sleep with or without wearing it. He referred me to see this specialist but they told me it was going to be two months before they have an appointment available. He also told me that botox was an option I could try. Can you tell me more about it?" the patient asked.

"Sure, what I do is I can inject some botulinum toxin injectable inside the left and right jaw muscles and this makes them temporarily weaker. There are no reliable long term studies but early results would suggest that maybe some of the muscles stay weaker and shrink in size over time. Typically, the effect of the injectables last about 3 months and you need to return for periodic doses," Bill explained.

"Is it painful?" the patient asked, "How much is it?"

Bill then went through the risks and complications based on the template he received from the course. He spent over an hour discussing every detail on the form and quoted very clearly $750 for the whole procedure. At least to begin with, he would not jump into the deep end with useless cosmetics and at least try to treat some sort of functional disorder with the new skills he learned. The girl seemed eager to pay and try the treatment so Bill had no qualms with proceeding. Unfortunately, a week later the girl phoned in to complain that she did not feel any different. Fuck.

The worst was yet in store for Bill. It was December and even Carlton was beginning to pick up because of the usual "Christmas rush." Bill had been back to the Red Lantern every two weeks but never saw Vivian again. He unfortunately resorted to seeing random prostitutes once in November and again this month each time leaving him feeling worse than when he walked in. Each time he was reminded of just how unfairly society treated him. For the hour he spent with the sex worker, it was as close to distilled happiness as he could reach. However, within minutes of clearing his head, the agony of tragic reality struck him mercilessly leaving him feeling like shattered glass. Then came one fateful Friday before Christmas that he received the worst news of the year.

It was a letter from the dental board. "We have received a complaint about you regarding your services as a dental practitioner..." it began. There was a mountain of useless explanations about processes and procedures but Bill looked at the details:
Patient name: Zara Bronson

Fuck. It was his Botox patient, Bill thought as he read onwards.

"I was told by my naturopath that dentists aren't allowed to give Botox injections."

The dental board quoted the submission she wrote word for word. There were no further particulars. It was somewhat of a relief that she did not accuse Bill of negligence or incompetence since the Botox injection did not end up helping but a false allegation was among the worst crimes.

The rage again exploded like a nuclear furnace inside Bill's head.

"FUUUUUUUUUUUUUCK!" Bill screamed out loud while inside his apartment as he punched the desk. His knuckle started bleeding but he was too angry to care. He was going to find that fucking naturopath and butcher their whole family. After all, cancer can only be eliminated by cutting it out. If such a diseased genetic specimen were to breed, they would only be spreading their disease. Did not matter if it were man, woman or child, Bill was on a warpath and there would be no survivors. Perhaps the ancient Chinese and Koreans had it right. When one person's sin was too heavy for them to be punished alone, their entire family would be slaughtered.

Bill realised then and there that dentistry was a dead option. It was "beyond a reasonable doubt" as lawyers would say. Bill had tried everything he could. There was nothing left to do. He tried doing dentistry properly, patients would not accept it. His colleagues all sold expensive treatments but when Bill even remotely mentioned the word "crown" patients would start complaining. He tried to go with the flow and start doing useless cosmetic treatment, only to receive a fully fledged Dental Board complaint based on a fucking FALSE ALLEGATION! Dentistry was fucking doomed. He was done with dentistry.

Textsecure had recently changed its name to "Signal Private Messenger" and Bill was going to announce his soon to be retirement from dentistry.

"Gentlemen, I've told you about all this bullshit that's happened. It's now beyond a reasonable doubt: I have to fucking get out of this fucked up profession. It would be a tragedy if all of you smart people keep practising dentistry after 10 years. You could all do so much more. Dentistry has been corrupted. Modern dentistry is all about unconscionable conduct, charging as much as possible and convincing patients not to complain. I've fucking had it." Bill announced on the forum.

Within a couple of minutes, as predictable as the sunrise, Tom responded sarcastically.

"Amazing. What are you going to do now?"

"I don't fucking know. I'll study programming or something." Bill wrote back.

"Lol. Maybe after 10 years you can learn how to code 'hello world' in Visual Basic," Henry joked.

"I'm fucking serious. Anything is better than dentistry," Bill retorted.

"You need to change jobs. Take a holiday and develop some hobbies" Tom insisted.

"Oh my God, how many times do I have to say it? I'm NOT going to fool myself into believing it's all good cause dentistry is fucking CANCER. The problems will NEVER go away. Dentistry is fucking DOOMED." Bill stated with confidence.

"Just do things properly. You don't have to be like those people." Tom shot back.

"Read what the fuck I just wrote. I can't JUST don't do this or JUST do that. I TRIED doing things properly. The entire profession has become far too corrupted for people like me. I HAVE to ditch dentistry." Bill wrote with conviction.

"Why would changing professions help?" Tom decided to throw fuel into the fire.

"Oh my God. Why? WHY?!?? Why the fuck do you think why? Don't give me shit about other professions being shit cause NOTHING even comes close to the harm dentistry is doing to me and everyone else. God. Fucking. Damn. It!" Bill lashed out.

"Nobody is ordering you to harm people. I never stoop to the level of the people you hate. I actually help patients." Tom dug his own grave.

"DENTISTRY ONLY DOES HARM! FUCK YOU ASSHOLE, I THOUGHT YOU WERE MY FRIEND. YOU'RE EITHER WITH ME, OR YOU'RE AGAINST ME!" Bill never thought he could get so angry at his "friend."

"I'm just trying to help you. You need to think before making big decisions" Tom's messaging continued.

"Again with this bullshit Tom. Why the fuck do you have to disagree with EVERYTHING I say? Do you have some fucking disease which COMPELS you to argue against me just because I'm the one saying it? Do you hate Asians this much?" Bill typed back.

"I can't agree with you when you're wrong" Tom stated bluntly, seemingly lacking in empathy.

"Fuck you all. I am done. Don't contact me again. We are through." Bill typed his final goodbye before leaving the chat group and blocking Tom.

It hurt Bill because he had lost such a good friend. Despite being white, Tom felt like a brother from another mother. When they met, Bill was sure that guy had some closet Nazism which Bill 100% supported. They had an instant connection in a world overpopulated by corrupt morons. It turned out that Tom was just another cucked social justice moron. Bill noticed after the blocking that he was hyperventilating and his heart was racing like a bass drum. 2015 was supposed to be his year. Not only had Bill lost all avenues to safely practise dentistry, he also lost one of his few friends and was facing a Dental Board investigation over a false and senseless allegation. How could it get any worse? Perhaps suicide was the only option. After all, if this was the *best* life had to offer, perhaps just ending it here was the best option.

To his surprise, Bill heard his phone ringing with the screen displaying the name of someone he had neither seen nor spoken to for a long ass time. It was Henry.

"Uhh hello?" Bill answered the phone.

"Hehehe, don't tell those idiots, but I'm quitting dentistry too. I'm coming back to Melbourne," Henry replied.

"Ma ni-guh, master troll is back son! Fuck those morons. I missed you man, no homo," Bill replied. As the two started to reminisce, Bill realised, perhaps there was some silver lining to this year after all.

Chapter 13

Fate (II)

Bill looked at his iPhone, it was 5:49pm, January 9th 2016. Henry notified him earlier that he was already hanging out with Cheng at the Carlton practice. The trio had agreed to meet up at the Grattan Street KFC next to the dental school. Bill saw the empty former women's hospital before anything else and proceeded to the KFC where he spotted Cheng and Henry waiting for him. As Bill approached, he extended his arms to his sides in a victory pose and greeted the two others.

"Ah hah. Hah. Hah. Hah. Hah. Look who it is, welcome back my niguhs, I missed you people, no homo," Bill greeted.

"Man, you were like dial up internet, took your time to get here," Cheng remarked while Henry sniggered.

"He was too busy doing his triple shower," Henry mocked.

"You don't gotta be like that man, come on." Bill retorted.

After ordering their meals, Bill initiated the multilateral convention,

"Henry told me some very important intel. This shit is for our ears only. I'm gonna need y'all to do this," Bill instructed as he took out his phone demonstrating turning the power off, "and put it in my bag here. This shit is so thick it's almost sound proof. I've tested it, trust me."

"So... what? If it's so important, why are we discussing it in KFC?" Cheng seemed puzzled.

"It's cause nobody here gives a fuck. Only the NSA cares, so fuck 'em. Sir, if you please," Bill explained. Cheng and Henry followed suit and lazily handed their phones to Bill.

"What we're about to talk about here is DEFCON 1 level shit. It's on a need to know basis. Henry, sir, would you care to explain?" Bill gave up the podium.

"Uh... well, I quit dentistry and my name is Jason now lol," Henry/Jason explained.

"What... Is this some sort of out of season April Fool's joke?" Cheng uttered with a puzzled expression.

"This is some serious shit. This nigga pulled the highest IQ move possible. Remember that day I told Tom to fuck off? I was pissed at Henry too but that kid called me later to tell me he was just trolling. Anyway, what really happened was this guy got fucked over trying to do dentistry and is now on the lam," Bill explained.

"I don't speak American, what the fuck is 'on the lam'?" Cheng asked.

"He's running from the law. This guy is like Jason Bourne right now. Fuck it, he *is* Jason Bourne," Bill declared.

"Lol yeah, dentistry is fucked. I went from billing $2-3k a day to less than $500 a day. I was ballin' in the clinic I bought in Mallacoota until some moron decided to invade. I went that far away because it's basically the most distant population centre from Melbourne. If someone is desperate enough to invade that far away, you know there are no other options left. I did a lot of research before graduation and I've worked in lots of places. Most dental clinics were either not hiring or unsustainable. Most owners were basically debt slaves competing against each other to see who could outlast and survive. Most places, even if I got a job, they would be paying peanuts. I personally scouted out the location at Mallacoota and everything seemed reasonable. The previous owner was going to retire soon so when I said I was interested in buying, he gave me a job on the spot. I personally verified that the place was good to buy after working there for almost a year. Worst case scenario, even a pump and dump would have been a safe last resort. But, there is no limit to desperation," Jason lamented.

"This guy was hell smart. You know the government actually *paid* this guy to move out of Melbourne. He got a free OPG machine just because the government is stupid enough to hand out free money for people who want to work in the middle of nowhere. This guy was prepared to pump and dump. That's all dentistry is these days. Just cook the books and sell some fake inflated garbage. But some asshole beat him to it. They must have been hell desperate. You see how there are *three* times as many job seekers on Dental Job Search compared to job postings? Some desperate immigrant moron got pushed all the way to Mallacoota, the very fucking edge of Victoria so they can go bankrupt themselves fighting against this guy here," Bill elaborated.

"Heh heh, yeah. If only that desperate moron came in just a couple more years later, then I could have dumped it on a huge profit. But that piece of shit stole a hell of a lot of my patients. I'm not certain as to how because when I tried investigating, I couldn't find anything solid. I suspect lots of patients wanted fake treatment like ceramics and orthodontics. This is because after a while, I started seeing his fuck-ups. That guy was some overseas trained guy who must have got a dental degree off the black market 'cause he had 4mm gaps in his crowns and he was trying to put Invisalign on patients who had fucked up teeth needing jaw surgery," Jason continued with his story.

"You don't need to look overseas to find that level of garbage. Just go visit Howard Chan. You see this? Day after day, all I see is dentistry getting fucked. Up. It's over. This is the only way to make money in dentistry now. In the past, people actually cared about quality. You see, this has all come about because of the fuckin' consumer mindset corrupting dentistry. In the past, dentists had to drill properly for that amalgam shit to stay in. Nowadays, you don't even need to remove caries. Just whack it in. It's all about bonding. Ceramics and bonding. All that snake oil just to make teeth look good even though it doesn't last. It *can't* fuckin' last. Just invent reasons for treatment and the morons just jump in to get fake treatment. But you haven't even heard the best part. Tell nigguh Cheng what happened next," Bill chimed in.

'Heh. Well considering how much this guy was fucking up, I *could* have held on until he imploded but after a few months, I was behind on payments and the next step would be to dip into my savings to keep myself afloat," Jason continued.

"This is what I've been talking about all this time. Dentistry makes you poorer. I'm not even kidding. The harder we work, the worse off we are," Bill complained.

"Heh heh. For you maybe. But I was not going to tolerate that bullshit. My money belongs to me. Not some fucking bank who decided to approve a loan to a desperate moron in a country town they knew for certain could not sustain two dentists. Yes, you heard me right, I did some investigating and found out the same bank gave both of us loans," Henry dropped the truth.

"What... that is fucked. Up," Cheng reacted.

"Yes. When I applied for my loan, they had me fill out a financial plan and forecast which included the prospects of competitor businesses in the local region. I know for a fact that the bank knew they were fucking up my loan repayment prospects but those fuckwits all believe that dental clinics can't fail. Money just magically grows and trees and the only thing better than one debt slave, is *two* debt slaves. It just never occurred to them that the town could not support two dentists. They screwed me over big time," Henry bitterly complained.

"This is why all those fucking bankers, they all need to die. It's not just dentistry that's corrupt. 50 years ago, bankers actually cared about their loans getting paid back. But today, all they want to do is give out loans because of their fucking commissions. This is pump and dump on a grand scale. We dentists can pump and dump one clinic, but these bank motherfuckers get to pump and dump a whole country. Millions of loans. You know it used to be a crime for loan applicants to lie about their income. But today? Fuck it, the bank managers do the lying for you. They say, 'don't worry fam, you earn $50k? Let's say that you will be earning $75k. Can't pay back the loan? Don't worry fam, not my fuckin' problem once it's approved lol!' " Bill mocked.

"Heh heh heh, that's right. Fuck them. They fucked me first so what I did next was only fair. I had no other reasonable option. I sold off my equipment in cash, took the money and ran," Jason defiantly stated.

"Shit fam, that's right, you had no goddamn choice. Even if you held on, the bank would just approve another fucking loan for another desperate fuckwit to move in. Morons always say 'there's always a choice', but so is suicide. Nobody mentions it because it's not a fucking reasonable choice. The bank thought they could pull a high IQ move but they were actually too low IQ to realise they fucked themselves. It's like you always say Cheng, people deserve to live with the consequences of their own actions," Bill complemented Jason's story.

"Yes. Do you know how useless debt collectors are? I took out a million dollar loan and I was paying it back ahead of schedule with all the money I was earning. I still owe like half a million but I don't even think about that money. I used to get phone calls begging me to pay the money back. That's all they can do.I just ignore their calls and they can't do shit lol," Jason confidently declared.

"You see this shit? You see how useless this country is? If this were Korea, this guy would have both his kneecaps broken by now but in Australia, you can just do whatever you want. This is what *I* should have done the moment I graduated. Banks are actually begging me to take out loans. It's so fucking easy to just pretend to buy a business, take the money and RUUUUUUUUUUUNNN!" Bill joked, "that's why this guy pulled a genius move. I talk about doing fair trades and I have to say, what Jason did was 100% fair. He pumped and dumped back on the bank *exactly* what they deserve."

"Hahaha yeah lol, it's like the people who run banks and debt collectors are the same as the guys running the dental school. I changed my name and number, now they can't even contact me. What a joke. You would have to be as dumb as a banker if you want to keep doing dentistry," Jason stated, "if you look at raw wages, the average dentist has been earning the same amount since the 90s. If you take into account inflation, in real terms we're just going backwards."

"This is what I've realised too. The patients we're seeing, they don't fucking need dental treatment. It's all just fucking unconscionable garbage driven by fucked up Kim Kardashian NPC animalistic urges. The harder I work, the poorer I get. Dentistry makes me poorer, not just Jason," Bill added.

"Yeah, we're pretty doomed. I'm sure Jason's seen it, all that propaganda about 'workforce shortages' and 'burden of disease' doesn't matter one fucking bit because where I worked, there was this grand strategy that worked every time - just wait until the dental problem becomes a medical emergency and Medicare will pay for it. If it's just a small infection, who cares? Nobody is going to spend $300 to save themselves since they think dentists exist *only* to rip them off. Once it becomes life threatening, you'll be airlifted down to Melbourne where surgeons will save your life for free," Cheng added.

"This entire country's banking system is going to collapse. We're copying the US banks which led to their 2008 fall. Then everybody will be waiting to be airlifted to Melbourne to treat their dental infections. Nobody is going to pay for dentists," Jason continued while sniggering.

"This kid is hell smart, I wish I could spend my time doing the same research this guy does but fuck dentistry. You know, this kid told me that Melbourne CBD alone has more cranes used in construction than New York state? Where the fuck is all this money coming from? You expect the rich Chahn-nese to keep propping up this fake construction work? Fuck dem Chinese and Koreans, do they come to this country and expect us to bow and kowtow to their bullshit and sell all our land to them so that one day we can become the Chinese republic of Australia? Fuck them," Bill exclaimed. "I've found this back door entry to Harvard, it's called the Harvard Extension School. If you pass with more than a certain GPA, they actually accept you into a full degree course. This guy," Bill said while pointing to Jason, "agreed to study that shit with me together. We're gonna move in, no homo, to study computer science and fucking ditch dentistry. I know this guy can't get a proper rental with a fake name but what we're doing is some high IQ shit. We're not taking advantage of each other, we're taking advantage of this subhuman country!"

"I wish I could go to the US like this guy I know who works for Microsoft. That kid is earning close to $200k US dollars, not just our shitty deflated dollaridoos AND he pays a fraction of the bullshit tax that we have to. On top of that, he receives the highest tier of medical benefits. That kid earns double what I earn and he had a head start cause computer science is only three years. I was fucking retarded back in high school. I believed that bullshit propaganda Asian parents said about how the best careers require the highest VCE scores. I almost topped the school and look where the fuck I am now. If I knew what I know now, I should have started programming at age 5 so that I didn't totally suck at age 18. Now I've got no hope," Cheng admitted dejectedly.

"Don't worry fam, if we get in, we'll get you out of dentistry too," Bill assured Cheng. Afterwards, the trio reminisced about their disastrous careers.

"Has the dental board finally sorted out that Botox bullshit yet?" Cheng finally asked, raising the uncomfortable elephant in the room.

"Fuck no. They haven't fucking responded at all. DIS," or "Dental Indemnity Society incorporated", "didn't do Jack shit again, I had to draft this bullshit response and hand over all the fucking records. That was a week ago and I haven't heard shit," Bill explained.

"No surprise, it can take them months, sometimes even a year to respond, so I've heard," Cheng empathised.

"If that were a sign, that's the most fucking obvious sign there is, dentistry is FUCKED. Look at what society has become. We are supposed to be fucking professionals but these fucking cockroaches can fuck us up any time. In the United States, you would NEVER fucking tolerate this kind of bullshit. There ain't gonna be rats crying to the dental board making shit up unlike THIS COUNTRY which has no fucking DECENCY! Look at these fucking millennials, they want to pay nothing but expect everything handed to them like an entitlement. It's only going to get worse," Bill denounced.

"You're the one who decided to do botox. I'd be way too scared to inject that toxic waste into people's faces. What's more important is manipulating those crazy patients who want it in the first place. Just think about it, who actually wants that crazy shit injected into their faces? Does any healthy, sane, rational person *ever* make such a decision? Yet you decided to single them out and invite them into your office thinking it will be easy money," Cheng criticised.

"Fuck. You're talking hell sense ma ne ge. You're always right. I should have listened to you from the start," Bill admitted, "if Linda and Lauren did that shit, even if it failed, patients would still think it worked. In fact, I know those two have attended some cosmetic injectables course. I'm 100% sure that they've injected that shit before."

"You don't have the looks bro," Cheng mocked.

"That's the fucking problem. The moment some millennial bitch looks at me, she would think, 'what the fuck does that guy know about cosmetics?' and I'm fucked. People say, 'just manage the patient, just manage the fucking patient' FUCK YOU. I CAN'T FUCKING MANIPULATE SHIT CAUSE I'M NOT A CHAD! Those pieces of shit just look at Linda and Lauren and they're like, 'I'm going to be as good looking as them, tee hee!' FUCK OFF. They need a fucking head transplant. I can help with that, heh," Bill joked at the end of his rant.

"Heh, heh, heh!" Jason continued sniggering at Bill's misfortune, "they need the botox to stop their facial muscles from contorting in agony after looking at that guy's face." Cheng started laughing out loud while Bill merely stared daggers at Jason.

"Laugh it up all you want, none of you have had the dental board investigate any false allegations made by some degenerate naturopath. I just want to get aaaalll those fucking GPs, cosmetic doctors and naturopaths, line them all up, then cut them all in half with a chainsaw hanging out the window while you drive me Cheng," Bill decreed. "Wouldn't that be fun? That reminds me, isn't it a tragedy that these days, all the good looking women have mutilated themselves with tattoos, piercings, hard as hell fake Kardashian lips, fake tits, fake lashes, fake nails, fake everything. Who actually finds that shit attractive? Are they intentionally trying to attract the fetish obsessed rapists like those granny rapists? Who do you think is responsible for this crime? Those fucking cosmetic doctors don't give a FUCK how much they slice and dice. They should also be lined up and chainsawed for their crimes against humanity."

"You were about to join them idiot," Cheng pointed out.

"Not any more. Only subhumans do that kind shit, I'm an Ubermensch, so are you two by the way," Bill declared, in reference to Nietzsche's concept of the ideal human.

"You make us sound like we're all superior," Cheng replied dubiously.

"You ARE superior goddammit!" Bill half shouted while slamming his fist on the table.

After discussing more of their troubles for a while, Bill finally announced to Cheng,

"Jason and I are gonna be upgrading. I know you make fun of that Hope Street drug den but since we're moving in together, I'm gonna leave that dump for good."

"I knew it, finally decided to abandon women and become gay, you know gay couples can get lots of tax benefits just like standard heterosexual marriages," Cheng mocked.

"If I could cheat the ATO I would but no homo son, we're gonna study computer science together and get out of this fucked up profession and possibly even this fucked up country. It's a long shot but I have no goddamn choice," Bill declared.

"What happened to 'Melbourne is the best city in the world' and how the 'women are responsible for global warming?'" Cheng brought up some regrettable quotes.

"Melbourne was once the best city but any day now, this place is gonna fall. You're gonna see blood on the streets. Those fucking real estate assholes are gonna be jumping out of buildings and running in front of your car. Anyway, the guy who said that shit is dead. I killed that fucking moron," Bill stated with confidence before the trio finally went their separate ways.

* * *

It was the first Saturday of February 2016 and Bill exited Cheng's shiny Mercedes after saying goodbye. Bill could not help but feel satisfied for the first time in years. He was taking advantage of Cheng's poor life choices. After all, who was stupid enough to waste their money on a shining, brand new E class Mercedes? Bill accompanied Cheng for the test drive as well. The ride quality was marginally improved compared to Cheng's old Toyota but if he were blindfolded, he would be hard pressed to tell. That was $100k down the drain. Yet Bill was the one being chauffeured like a diplomat back to his equally shining new apartment on Toorak road. He was a "baller" now and there was no luxury Bill was missing out on. Bill had to take an elevator to his new apartment on the top floor. It felt like a penthouse to Bill. Even the elevator was made by Schindler and not cheap Chinese junk he would see in the city apartment blocks.

As Bill opened the door to his apartment, he noticed the scent of pasta emanating from within. Jason was probably cooking with the discount sauces they bought in bulk last week. Fancy food was one luxury Bill did not care for even one iota. It even gave him a thrill to hunt down cheap, tasty food. It may have been Jason's influence but Bill had switched to eating solid food now rather than food replacement. It might have also been because recently his stool was basically constant diarrhoea. That was definitely *not* normal.

"Yo nigga J, you better have made some of that shit for me," Bill greeted.

"Yes dear, you're the man in the relationship now, bitch," Jason sarcastically replied.

"Come on man, you don't gotta talk to me like that, just make sure you clean that shit afterwards, the red pasta shit is impossible to clean after it sets," Bill remarked before heading off towards his triple shower.

After dinner, Bill turned on his computer to try and listen to the Harvard extension program's introduction to computer science lectures. Fuck. It was frustratingly difficult. Bill remembered he could program in PHP during high school but this was next level difficult. He tried listening to the same 15 second segment 10 times but still could not understand the complex syntax of the C programming language. Jason seemed to have no problem and unfortunate as it was, he was the only one completing all the assessment tasks while Bill struggled to even complete the non-assessed finger exercises. Bill did not know why his brain just could not function these days. He felt like a depleted shadow of his former self. 18 year old Bill would probably have blitzed through all these trivial challenges like a hot knife through butter. Was it dentistry? Did thinking about teeth and complaints all day cause irreparable brain damage in addition to chronic physical injury?

Bill felt his headache returning. No matter how many times he tried, he could not construct a single functioning program beyond "Hello world." With his head swirling, Bill staggered towards the sink, only to find the unwashed dishes Jason had promised to clean. Bill could not help but feel anger surging. He had *told* that slob to clean up that shit but it was always Bill who ended up cleaning it. Bill unceremoniously dumped his bowl in the sink then headed towards the bathroom. The floor was wet. Again. Goddamn it. Bill had to tolerate this last week but Jason did not change. Telling that guy once should have been enough after all he warned Jason repeatedly before cohabitation that Bill was very particular, perhaps even compulsive. That slob had better change, Bill thought before preparing to rest for the big day of work tomorrow.

That night, Bill decided to return to Red Lantern once again. He was compelled to do it. This time, Bill was in for a surprise. Bill had fully intended to try out any ordinary working girl who was not the size of an elephant and did not mutilate her body (with tattoos). What he found was a girl named Esmeralda. Bill sat down in the introduction rooms and for a couple of seconds forgot to breathe. Esmeralda literally took his breath away. She had no visible tattoos, had an incredibly beautiful face, brunette hair and an enchanting smile.

"Hi how's your night been? I'm Esmeralda, would you like to hear about my services?" Esmeralda introduced herself.

"... Uh.. Um," Bill had to clear his throat, "Uhh sure."

Bill knew she was saying the usual sundries regarding brothel services but he was struggling to pay attention. Just watching this girl talk entranced him. She rivalled Erika when it came to beauty *and* she had no tattoos, unlike Vivian who Bill still pined for. It was like Esmeralda had walked out of a Victoria's secret advertisement and into Bill's arms.

"I want you tonight, I don't need to see anyone else," Bill replied after pretending to listen to her speech. There were no objections and within 5 minutes, Bill was lying next to Esmeralda. She was even more beautiful with her clothes off. Most women knew how to hide their flaws with well chosen apparel covering the right areas but this girl had no flaws to speak of. That long lost feeling Bill felt during his fleeting yet fateful UN re-enactment, Bill was reminded of that yet again. He almost felt it this time.

"You know, screw these guys who own the place. I want to be with you. The moment I saw you, I knew you were special and I think you feel something similar 'cause gosh, I've never been with someone who's treated me so well before. I always leave brothels feeling worse than I came in because there's *no way* we could have met outside this place. Isn't that just a tragedy? I need to ask you this because I have no other choice. I *need* to see you outside of these premises. Would you be OK with private sessions? We can meet in a hotel," Bill pleaded.

"Sure, I do private work. I do need to charge a bit more because we are safer in these licenced venues," Esmeralda accepted. Bill liked her honesty. It almost felt like she was sincerely telling the truth. For the fourth time, Bill had fallen in love with a sex worker.

* * *

It was Monday night a week later and Bill was prancing around anxiously in the hotel foyer they had agreed to meet in. Why had she not arrived yet? They had agreed to meet at 8pm and it was already 8pm. Bill had to calm his nerves. He instinctively called up Cheng yet again.

"Bitch you gotta help me," Bill demanded.

"I'm taking a shit here, what the hell do you want?" Cheng asked with irritation.

"Oh my God, I can't fucking wait any longer. What the fuck is happening? Remember Esmeralda, the girl I told you about? She should be here by now but where the fuck is she? Jesus, Jesus, Jesus... Goddamn mother fuck! She better not have ghosted me. Fuck!" Bill ranted into the phone.

"Calm down already, women are always late, they have to do makeup and shit and it takes forever. Did you tell her it had to be 8pm sharp?" Cheng replied.

"I said we'll meet at around 8, and I've been here since 7:30." Bill advised.

"It's barely past 8, I wouldn't be surprised if she's half an hour late. Just think about how often you run late treating patients," Cheng mocked.

"It's not the same goddamn it!"Bill complained.

"She's probably working through the backlog of clients just like you need to work through your patients," Cheng continued.

"Impossible, she told me she goes to uni on Mondays so she's definitely not working," Bill argued. Bill could not even contemplate being second in line on the same day. It was too revolting for him to even consider.

"And you believed her? What incentive do any of these girls have to tell the truth? They can pretend to be some Russian spy one week and a poodle trainer the next, and you're just gonna take her word for it?" Cheng asked.

"Goddamit! I fucking know that but this girl, she seems honest, she's different," Bill defended himself.

"So you've fallen in love again. You do this for every second girl you pay for, I told you to just study and play games or some shit. If you hate women so much and not only that, they cause you so much suffering, why are you doing this bitch?" Cheng continued chastising.

"Oh. My. God. Jesus fuck. I know but this time it's different!" Bill continued arguing back.

After what seemed like an eternity, Bill finally saw Esmeralda strolling through the rotating doors of the hotel lobby. She was 15 minutes late.

"She's here, I gotta go. Fuck! I'm nervous as hell. Jesus fuck," Bill tried to emotionally prepare himself.

"It's not like this is a date, stop acting like a princess idiot," Cheng chastised.

"Fuck you bitch, gotta go, I'll give you a debriefing afterwards,"Bill said before dashing off. There she was. She wore an elegant black dress like Bill requested. Bill did not want to be seen in public with a drug addict.

He wanted the old men to stare enviously at him parading his beautiful companion around like a champion.

Later that night, Bill phoned up Cheng yet again. At 11:30pm.

"What the fuck, can't you let me sleep?" Cheng answered with irritation.

"Fuck you bitch, I know you hell interested. Oh my God. I think I really got a chance," Bill responded.

"Stop being delusional, idiot. She's being paid to pretend. How much did you actually pay?" Cheng asked.

"Uh, we agreed to $300 an hour but she charged extra for the dinner so it came to around $1500," Bill admitted.

"What the fuck dude. That's fucking insane. You know how many times you could have banged her in the brothel for that much?" Cheng asked. This was becoming like an interrogation now.

"It's different OK! Jesus, I can't *stand* to be inside a goddamn brothel with her. I *need* to experience this. This is my *last chance*!" Bill cried out in frustration.

"Let's see, how many last chances has it been? Three? Five? You must be luckier than a Hollywood action hero to get so many last chances," Cheng mocked.

"Come on, you don't gotta be like that man," Bill complained, yet again before explaining yet another time what happened in unwarranted detail.

"Aside from having dinner, it's almost like that time you had with Holly. Sounds like the only 'special' thing this girl did for you was to have some fake dinner with you," Cheng pointed out.

"You weren't there idiot, this girl knew exactly what to say. She's a uni student, the best quality girl to be with. I'm not messin' with some single mom or feral meth addict. She needs me, I can tell. She said that she's got older brothers who don't give a shit about her. Her parents also don't give a fuck cause they're hell broke. She has to look after herself so she also works as a waitress. But you know those bullshit restaurants only pay shitty wages. You know goddamn well as I do that this country's minimum wage is crazy high. No restaurant can survive if they actually paid their waitresses properly. She got into sex work because she needs to. I also asked her if she had a boyfriend. You know there are desperate pieces of shit out there who would date a sex worker," Bill said before being interrupted by Cheng.

"And here you are *paying* for the opportunity to date a sex worker," Cheng dished out some reality.

"Shut up, she's gonna stop if she's with me, I can guarantee you. I can look after her if she's with me," Bill continued before Chen interjected again.

"And you think she's going to just bend over and be 'looked after' by your tiny Korean dick?" Cheng mocked.

"Shut up, it's not the size that matters, it's what you do with it. Anyway, she said she doesn't have a boyfriend but there is this one guy she occasionally has sex with, free, no sex work. She said it was even less than 'friends with benefits.' The guy apparently has his own girlfriend and he doesn't even want to be with Esmeralda. That means she basically admitted to being single. At some point, one of her colleagues found out that she was doing sex work and her family also found out. She is now basically abandoned. Can you believe that? That's how fucked up her family is. She needs someone like me and I need her," Bill declared. "You would like her too 'cause get this, she actually used to play viola in her school orchestra."

"Go to sleep bitch and stop dreaming. You change your mind every day. Who was the one who said 'NEVER trust women' and that they're all full of shit and it's all fake so that one day they can betray you and shit?" Cheng reminded Bill.

"That was a long time ago goddamn it. And Sarah was some fake Christian, all dem Ko-reans are goddamn fake. This time, it's different," Bill insisted.

"It's your funeral idiot. Remember your mental breakdown last time? Haven't you noticed that each time you have a meltdown, it takes less and less stimulus to trigger the next one. It's like one day someone can look at you and you'll explode," Cheng prophetically observed.

"Fine. Get to sleep bitch," Bill said defiantly before heading back. That night, Bill could not help but dream.

After leaving Esmeralda, Bill felt that pain in his heart but it was alleviated by his hope and conviction that he would see her again, outside of a brothel. Sure, his money was draining faster than a split aorta but he felt like he was halfway there to developing a true relationship with Esmeralda. It was like fate was at work yet again. They had met *just* by coincidence that night. That required all the stars to align. Everything needed to just perfectly happen the way it did, including all the trauma Bill had with women up to that point. If all that pain was necessary to get to this point, then Bill just had to accept it. He might even come to terms with it one day.

* * *

On the first Saturday 20th of March 2016, Bill was chauffeured by Cheng in his E class chariot down to Bill's apartment in South Yarra after work again. This time, Bill involuntarily recruited Cheng to draft his love confession, version 2.

"You gotta help me man," Bill pleaded.

"Just like the last time? Remember how that turned out? Why can't you just face reality and just be OK with staying friends? Who knows, it might turn into friends with benefits like that hooker talked about with her friend," Cheng advised.

"This is my last chance. You don't need to do this for me ever again. Just this one last time, please, you gotta help me man. I know what I want to say but I just don't know how to say it. You're the one who got top of the state or whatever in English. I need your help man," Bill continued pleading, appearing more pathetic by the second. "I also need your violin. I need to learn how to play violin in a day. She said she remembers playing "Peter and the Wolf" back in high school. I need you to teach me that shit."

"You can't fucking learn how to play that in a day. It takes beginners weeks just to play hot cross buns. Besides, my English writing skills are only essay writing, I don't do love confessions idiot. Look at me, I'm on my way to becoming a wizard, you're the one with actual experience with a real girlfriend," Cheng argued. Bill knew what Cheng meant. It was an old joke on the internet that if you remained a virgin up to 30 years of age, then you would become a wizard.

"Just help me out goddamn it, you owe me bitch," Bill resorted to dirty tactics now.

"I don't owe you shit. You think this car was for free? You're the one getting chauffeured. Normally only billionaires get this kind of treatment," Cheng cut a savage riposte against Bill's antagonism.

"I thought you were my friend. You know how I'm already losing friends. I can't afford to lose you too," Bill's emotional blackmailing only worsened.

"As I said before, it's your funeral. If you're gonna kill yourself after you fail, just leave me all your assets and we're even," Cheng finally acquiesced but not without conditions attached. And so the two repeated the same futile exercise as last time. It took over an hour but Bill finally settled on an acceptable version to rehearse.

True to his word, Cheng did bring his violin to Carlton on Sunday. How hard could this be? Cheng gave a quick demonstration of how to play the opening of the first violin part in Prokofiev's "Peter and the Wolf." Bill looked at Cheng dexterously slide his fingers up and down the instrument while alternating his fingers like a craftsman as well as sliding the bow as smoothly as a gentle stream flowing through a meadow.

"Show me slowly goddamn it, you're going too fast, I can't see shit," Bill complained.

"This is the speed it's actually played at, idiot. I told you, you need to start off with something as simple as hot cross buns," Cheng replied. Cheng then demonstrated how to play the first trash music beginner players needed to master.

Bill finally took the instrument from Cheng's hands and tried to copy the way Cheng held onto it. Only to fail because he was not paying attention.

"You hold the neck with your left hand idiot, didn't you even notice something so obvious?" Cheng chastised. Bill held up the instrument properly with his left hand this time but realised he did not pay attention to holding the bow either. He was clutching onto it like an infant clutching onto a stick.

"Jesus... You need to hold it like this," Cheng impatiently rebuked while holding the bow to demonstrate again.

After Bill struggled to just barely hold the instrument and bow, he tried to place the bow in contact with the strings only to find that he could not aim properly. The hairs on the bow were screeching against two strings.

"Just make it simple for yourself idiot, try to swing the bow to the right so you only touch the outer string," Cheng suggested derisively only for Bill to overcompensate and hit the wooden edge of the instrument and way off the E string.

After what seemed an eternity, Bill finally managed to make a sound on the instrument. Only his bow did not move like a flowing stream and more like an apprentice tradesman using sandpaper on a coarse surface with clumsy, jagged strokes. The screeching was making Bill's ears metaphorically bleed. It sounded awful.

"I told you that you can't just up and play "Peter and the wolf." Just try to play hot cross buns," Cheng said while taking back the instrument and demonstrating how supremely easy it was to play. This was humiliating for Bill. Cheng made it look so easy, so why was he struggling so much? It took Bill almost the whole hour to produce a butchered version of "Peter's theme" on a lower register because it was too difficult for him to shift his hand in the elaborate positions required to play it in the correct register.

* * *

On Monday 29th of March, it was game time. Bill had intentionally ordered the receptionists to schedule his final hour of work empty. There were still so few patients it did not matter anyway. Bill felt his heart pumping all the way from work to home and during his triple shower and post-shower preparations. Bill stepped out of the elevator and into the stacked underground garage of his apartment building. Bill still drove in his dilapidated Mitsubishi but Bill did not care. He so seldom drove that the car almost felt like decoration. He took public transport in the morning and was chauffeured by Cheng during some nights. Bill had to drive to meet Esmeralda though. Today, he scheduled to meet her at a classical music concert event being held in Hamer Hall.

Not as impressive as New York's Carnegie Hall of course, but this was Australia, the cultural backwater of the western world. Hamer Hall was quite impressive when taking that into account.

It was like fate at work. The Melbourne Symphony Orchestra was playing Tchaikovsky's Romeo and Juliet followed by Rachmaninoff's second symphony. It was advertised as, "Russian Greats" and what better introduction to Russian music than this. Bill arrived almost half an hour early, as usual. The concert was scheduled to start at 7:30pm and he asked to meet her at 7:15 knowing that Esmeralda would be late. This time however, Esmeralda actually arrived at 7:15pm. Her appearance took Bill's breath away yet again. She took her coat off and had an elegant figure-hugging formal dress which despite covering up everything, Bill could still verify the flawless curves and grooves underneath.

"Uh hello," Bill weakly mustered.

"Hello to you too Sir," Esmeralda replied while displaying some melodramatic flair to capture the "high society" pretense.

"I'm glad you arrived. You look hell good. I bet all those these elderly fuckwits are hell jelly that I could be walking around with you," Bill praised.

"Haha, I don't come cheap you know," Esemeralda replied.

"A girl like you is worth everything," Bill replied, half seriously.

"You're such a flatterer!" Esmeralda reflexively uttered. Many of her clients must have acted like this anyway.

"I hope you like Tchaikovsky. I chose this concert because everyone likes Tchaikovsky, Romeo and Juliet is played everywhere. I also wanted you to hear Rachmaninoff's second symphony. It's a very important piece to me. I've been through hell and back and Rachmaninoff's music was there for me all the way," Bill explained.

"I'd *die* without music!" Esmeralda melodramatically admitted.

While Bill was not experienced in playing any musical instrument, he had a keen interest in classical music. Unlike modern music, classical music stood the test of time. The music that survived to this age consisted of masterpieces composed by geniuses who dedicated their entire souls wholeheartedly to their art. Modern music was manufactured like a production line so naturally there was almost nothing worthy of consideration. Bill did not think much of the Melbourne Symphony Orchestra. They were as good as you could find in a backwater cultural wasteland like Australia. They would not cut it in the United States, that was for sure. Their playing seemed satisfying enough. Esmeralda seemed to not fall asleep so that was good at least. When the last movement of the Rachmaninoff symphony concluded, it was finally time.

As Bill escorted Esmeralda into the hotel room near Hamer Hall, he eyed the violin case on the bed. Good, Bill thought, not that he was expecting anyone to steal it. "I've prepared something special for tonight. Remember how you said you played viola in your high school orchestra? My friend lent me his violin. They're close enough aren't they? He taught me how to play Peter and the Wolf," Bill said.

"Wow, you have some very talented friends, haha!" Esmeralda replied in high spirits.

"Let me show you," Bill continued while opening the instrument case. Even though it was not a proper performance, Bill was feeling the same stage fright musicians felt when they walked on stage. He was putting on a sort of performance tonight and this was the opening act.

Bill assembled the shoulder rest and tightened the bow. He timidly placed the instrument on his shoulder and started to scrape clumsily with the bow to screech out an embarrassingly butchered "Peter's theme." Emeralda immediately started laughing.

"Well done! You went to all that trouble for me, that's amazing!" she congratulated. Bill felt warm and fuzzy from the praise despite his ears metaphorically bleeding. It was hard to tell from Esmeralda's expression what she was truly feeling but she probably was not feeling comforted by the horrendous, off-key screeching.

"I know I'm shit, violin is hell difficult to play. I used to play flute and clarinet back in high school. It's been so long I can't remember how to play. They're all so different to strings," Bill remarked.

"Wow, are all you dentists so talented, haha," Esmeralda joked.

"Why don't you have a turn?" Bill said while handing the instrument over.

Esmeralda deftly slid the the violin onto her shoulder and started playing. She fumbled in the beginning to find the right notes but sure enough, she managed to play out Peter's theme after some trial and error. While not sounding as smooth as Cheng, she did at least play the tune properly.

"Hahaha, I still remember a bit," Esmeralda said before handing the instrument back to Bill. Bill involuntarily started laughing too. It was fun playing around like this. Sex was not fulfilling for Bill but tonight had been amazing so far. Walking around arrogant elderly morons with a goddess-like beauty in his arm while listening to classical music - that was truly priceless. Now he was in a room alone with her playing around without Cheng's brutal mockery. Bill felt more invigorated than ever to proceed with his planned performance.

Bill walked over to the drawers beside the hotel bed. Bill theatrically opened the drawer and retrieved his passports. Bill displayed them in front of him like a deck of cards to show Esmeralda.

"Look at this. What I'm holding are all the passports I've had. They are like my very own story book," Bill started his grand tale. Bill shifted his gaze from his hands to Esmeralda. Good, she seemed to be paying attention.

"There's one passport I don't have with me. I left it in Korea. I don't know what happened to it. It was a memento of my first time I ever left my home country. I was in second grade, it was a family trip to Australia and New Zealand. It was perhaps the happiest memory of any trip I've ever had. Perhaps something stuck, I'm here after all these years," Bill continued. Esmeralda seemed enraptured in Bill's tale, good, he thought, this was just the beginning, barely an entree.

Bill marched over to Esmeralda's seat on the bed and plodded down beside her. He laid the passports on his lap but kept one in his hand, flashing it in front of Esmeralda.

"This passport, I got it when I was 13, just before I left to live in Canada," Bill explained while opening up the cover.

"You were just a baby then! You look so cute!" Esmeralda gushed.

"Hehehe, I was cute back then wasn't I? Back then, my sister was already studying in the US. I was hearing all about how good it was. My English tutor always spoke about how good Canada was. I couldn't help it. Life in Korea was nothing compared to what I heard. I knew early on that the first thing I would do once my parents allowed it, was to move the hell outta Korea. I pointed on a map and told them, no bullshit, 'that's where I want to go!' I ended up going to a private school and living in a boarding house. I met a lot of good friends. They treated me almost like their own family. Many of them have gone on to become pretty successful. I know of a few that have become doctors running their own businesses. That experience became one of my most treasured memories. If I had to forget about my childhood, I don't care if I forget everything about Korea. But I would never relinquish my memories of growing up in Canada," Bill nostalgically reminisced.

Esmeralda nodded her head as Bill thumbed through the passport.

"As you can see, there are lots of stamps going back and forth between South Korea, Canada and the USA, New York. My sister used to live there so I used to spend some of my summers there," Bill explained. Bill dropped the passport and picked up the next.

"Passport 2, I got this one after I graduated high school in Canada and was leaving for the US of A. I liked Canada, it's a great country, I would still be there if I were given the option. But as great as it is, you just can't compare the two education systems. Everyone knows about how good US universities are. Who the hell hasn't heard of Harvard? But can you name even one Canadian university?" Bill asked. Esmeralda shook her head contemplatively and sighed.

"You're right. I'm sure Toronto must have its own university but I don't know anything about it other than it has to exist," Esmeralda agreed.

"That's right. So my parents sent me to the US to study. Just so happens, I got a scholarship to Syracuse University, haha," Bill triumphantly boasted while pointing to the study permit glued to one of the pages on his passport. It had Syracuse University written on it in bold letters.

"That place had hell good amenities. Anything you wanted, free gym, swimming pool, food was paid for, my scholarship gave me discounted boarding as well. The school had a legit hotel that was at least four stars, minimum. Despite all that, I never liked going there. When you watch movies set in US colleges, there's always frats and sororities and all sorts of drugs and mayhem. Then there were the parties. In real life, it's even worse. You have no idea the kinda stuff that goes on there. The movies don't go far enough. That was not the kinda place that I wanted to be in. I wanted to become a doctor, not some daddy's boy lawyer like most of the kids there wasted their lives trying to become. I wanted to surround myself with like-minded people. I soon left that place after I found out that I could go straight into medicine if I studied in Europe.

Since the EU nations basically accepted anyone who graduated from an EU member university, hey, Poland didn't seem like a bad option. I don't know why I picked dentistry but I realised only *after* I started studying in Poland that it was hell. When people hear about Europe, they tend to assume it's some well developed utopia. Poland was the opposite. It was the same dump the Russians left it as back when the Soviet Union collapsed. Zero improvement. In fact, it might have even gotten worse. The environment was hell, the people were worse. You cannot drink the tap water straight from the tap. That's very telling. Racism was everywhere. I witnessed, multiple times, random bystanders who got assaulted. One guy was attacked by a broken glass bottle. Why? I couldn't think of any reason other than being a foreigner. I realised far too late that I had made a mistake. I was in the pits of despair. During semester break, I locked myself in and drank myself to sleep every day for weeks."

"Oh my God, poor you. I can't believe you had to go through that. Someone like you definitely wouldn't fit in with that American college crowd," Emeralda exclaimed with a genuinely concerned look on her face.

Was it that obvious though? Bill thought to himself.

"What makes you think so?" Bill could not help probing.

"You remind me of someone I know who's on the spectrum. Maybe you should do a personality test," Esmeralda suggested.

"You know those personality tests aren't really accurate," Bill responded.

"I heard they're getting more scientific, like the Myers Briggs test," Esmeralda defended herself.

"Uhh... Yeah sure. Anyways, I don't reflect on that time fondly but it was part of the journey I took to bring myself here, beside you, so I can't stay mad about it, heh," Bill chuckled. "As you see, I had to get the hell outta there but I was *not* going back to Syracuse. Instead, I remembered about the best trip I ever had. So I applied to study in Australia. One thing led to another and I studied at Mel-borne. After that, I decided to trade this passport," Bill explained while exchanging his grasp onto a third passport, "for this Australian passport. Ever since, I have never left the country. At first, I thought this country was a cultural wasteland. I mean come on, look at all this garbage about 'football' and sport. You never see the same appreciation for art, music and science. I feel like having a degree in this country makes people give you dirty looks. But slowly, I moved past that and I started to feel like I should never leave Mel-borne again. Until I met you. I was fortunate to have lived all over the world. I have discovered one very important thing. Travelling for the sake of travelling is pointless. It's hell tiring and it's boring. Travelling in good company makes all the difference. So come with me!"

Bill pointed to the empty pages on his recent Australian passport.

"Look at this empty space. This book remains unwritten. We can experience things together and write our own story right here!" Bill continued pointing.

Bill waited for her response. Bill was prepared for anything. This was a long shot after all. He had responses for all kinds of rejections and of course, he prepared for her to say "yes" as well. He already had a list of travel destinations in mind.

"You don't have to pay anything, I will cover all the costs. I'll take some time off work. We can go anywhere!" Bill sweetened the deal.

Esmeralda seemed to furrow her brows and mutter,

"Um... uh... It's really great that you offered. I'm not sure... If I were to go travelling around the world, I need to make memories that I will carry for the rest of my life. It will have to be special," Bill stared dejectedly at Esmeralda. "It will have to be special" felt like a knockout punch by

Mike Tyson. That was as much a rejection as anything. This was not the end however.

"That's OK. It's a big deal. We have all the time in the world," Bill conceded hoping that one day she would change her mind.

The next day, Bill assaulted Cheng with all the details of his "date."

"I'm not fucking giving up. I know she needs me. I have one last chance. I've actually asked a few Mega staff members about what gift to give her. I think she would like this best," Bill explained on the phone and texted Cheng a link.

"What is that?" Cheng asked.

"It's a music box playing this South Korean traditional folk song. No matter what happens, I know she'll be able to remember me when she hears it. It's like Pavlov's bell, this is some psychotherapy shit," Bill explained.

"Whatever. She's just a hooker, idiot. I don't get why you keep falling in love despite knowing that these girls don't give a fuck about you," Cheng mocked.

"Oh hahaha, that's where you're hell wrong nigguh. I know she's going to say yes. I need you to help me fam. Do me a favour, remember that piano recital we were going to attend?" Bill asked.

"The wanderer fantasy one?" Cheng replied. In fact, it was Cheng who introduced Bill to Schubert's "Wanderer Fantasy."

"Yes, that one," Bill confirmed.

"I actually want to attend that. Don't tell me you want to bring your hooker "girlfriend" to replace my seat. Neither you nor her can even play the Wanderer Fantasy," Cheng complained. Cheng was a skilled pianist. He was just learning the composition but it was already sounding magnificent to Bill. Schubert was a genius to have written such a masterpiece. Truly ahead of his time.

"Come on fam, you owe me," Bill goaded.

"I don't owe you shit idiot. Have I ever charged you for my chauffeuring? Maybe I should retroactively charge for that shit like that bitch Karen Hong back in dental school," Cheng chastised.

"Don't remind me of that bitch. Where the hell would you be without me fam? Come on, I'll pay you. I'll make it a fair trade, anything you want," Bill offered.

"Fine, I want KFC for this. I may have gotten the tickets for free but still wanted to attend the concert," Cheng conceded. Apparently Cheng had received the tickets from Mega staff.

"OK, OK, whatever you want. You still owe me bitch," Bill remarked before hanging up.

The music box had not arrived yet but Bill was confident it would soon. Hence, Bill accepted the risk and contacted Esmeralda to schedule another concert night followed by his second chance to "convert" her into a real girlfriend. On the weekend, Bill returned Cheng's violin and received the piano concert tickets. It was some Chinese pianist. Cheng did remark that he had never heard of her but Cheng liked the music which was to be played. As it turned out, Bill was fortunate enough to have Esmeralda's music box arrive on Monday 6th of March, four days before the concert. By the time Friday arrived, Bill was overflowing with excitement. He intentionally closed his books at 3pm and returned home for his grooming routine. The concert was in the Melbourne Town Hall this time.

Bill caught public transport back to the city and waited in the warm Autumn evening for Esmeralda. The concert was scheduled at 6:30pm and he requested to meet Esmeralda at 6:15pm latest. Bill arrived extra early at 6pm but he did not have to wait long. Esmeralda arrived a few minutes before schedule and greeted Bill warmly with a hug.

"Hey stranger, haha," She joked while gently holding Bill.

"Hey," Bill replied. Bill inspected Esmeralda. Her wardrobe was never identical every time they met. It did appear quite similar. She always did dress to impress. This time, she was wearing a black, shin length, figure-hugging dress which covered her chest but exposed some of her back. Bill could not see how much due to the white shawl she draped over her shoulders which clasped together at her chest area.

After some friendly small talk, the "couple" walked into the hall to watch the performance. The first composition played was not Schubert, it was some Mozart concerto. Mozart pleased the masses but it did not pique Bill's interest. Mozart seemed to be the type of person who Bill would never get along with socially. Who the hell wrote happy music *all* the goddamn time? Mozart would be the kind of person who would have thrived at Syracuse. Partying, drugs, women, he would have been in heaven. The polar opposite of Bill, and that was reflected in his music. Esmeralda was not falling asleep so she probably enjoyed it. Then finally, it came time for the Wanderer Fantasy. Unlike Mozart, Schubert's composition had no hesitations between its frequent transitions from bright lyricism to stormy violence. Mozart's piano would not have survived the thrashing from the Wanderer Fantasy. However, Bill was not impressed by the pianist. The fourth movement was clouded by frequent and obvious mistakes.

After the concert, Bill invited Esmeralda to eat at the Elizabeth Street McDondald's.

"So what did you think about the concert?" Bill asked as the "couple" started munching into their meals. Bill bought the family McValue box as he did most of the time.

"I liked both. I've heard the Schubert before, I didn't know it was that hard to play, haha," Esmeralda remarked.

"Yeah, she was making hell mistakes towards the end," Bill agreed with her, but did not comment on the Mozart. "I hope you enjoy this meal as well, I guess it's not like that fancy shit we had the other times."

"Haha, I love McDonald's, you don't need to worry," Esmeralda comforted.

"I have to say, I still like McDonald's over the fancy places I've taken you. People pretend all the time about enjoying fine dining but they're just too scared to be honest about their preferences. They paid so much for their food so of course they're going to pretend it's better than McDonald's. Just be honest you know, I don't want to lie to myself all the damn time," Bill pontificated.

"Yeah, I agree. There were some places I've been to which were also really good but yeah, it's true, most places taste pretty average," Esmeralda remarked.

"That's right. I don't think I'll ever stop eating McDonald's. To me, this food is special. I've eaten McDonald's all around the world. There are some differences here and there but for the most part, the quality is almost identical. Doesn't matter how many years later or which country you're in, McDonald's always serves me the kind of food I like. I never really liked fine dining. It's not that I've never tried it, but to be honest, it's never been as good as Mcdonald's. Some of my happiest memories have been at Mcdonald's. Just eating food with people I like, good taste, no pretense. Those were simpler days..." Bill reminisced out loud.

After finishing their meal, the "couple" headed to the hotel Bill had booked.

"I want to give you something. I don't know how much longer I can keep seeing you so I want you to have something to remember me by," Bill said while looking intently at Esmeralda.

"You shouldn't have, you already pay me so much, haha," Esmeralda whimsically replied.

"I said I would spare no expense, that's how important you are to me," Bill continued while opening what seemed to be a dark wooden box the size of his two palms. It was decorated with ornate pearlescent enamel in the shape of flowers and butterflies. Bill had spent hours trawling through online retail sites to find this box. As he opened the lid, the chimes of music started to emit. It was a music box with a mirror on the lid and a cloth lined interior.

"I want you to have this. The music being played is called Arirang, a traditional folk song from Korea. I never liked Korea but it's nonetheless part of my identity and a part of me I know you will never forget," Bill explained while the music box was playing away in the background.

"Remember when we met at the first hotel, you said you'll *die* without music?" Bill asked as Esmeralda nodded.

"Traditionally, Koreans would put their precious belongings in this kind of box. You don't have to put anything in. Even if it's empty, it will always be filled with music and your memories of me."

"Oh! It's really pretty! How thoughtful of you!" Esmeralda exclaimed.

"Esmeralda, I want you to know something. I've told you all about me. You know how hard it is for me to find a woman and here you are in front of me like it was ordained by fate. I mean, gosh, just look at how ridiculous this situation is. I walk around and women pretend I don't even exist but here I am sitting with a Victoria's Secret Angel. Everything that needed to happen for us to meet just had to perfectly line up in *that* moment. That night I met you, I was not prepared to see someone like you there. I was speechless from the moment you introduced yourself. You know, I was half expecting some feral drug addict to march in but there you were. You were kind to me unlike so many others out there. You've been through similar things to me in your life - hold up, hold up, I know what you're thinking," Bill hurriedly gestured his arms while pleading to continue. "Your parents treated you badly just like my parents treated me badly. The moment I was old enough, I got the hell out of South Korea and I've gotta say, that's the best goddamn thing that's happened to me and if I were to do it again a thousand times, I would always choose to run away. I know your life ain't easy now, just like when I was going to dental school. I only had a few good friends but everyone else treated me like a piece of shit. I actually ate nothing but peanut butter for weeks at a time. There was once when I even signed up for a multiple week long medical study. They locked me up in some lab while I sat there doing nothing but playing games and staring at the wall. Despite that, my quality of life actually improved temporarily *and... aaand* I was *paid* to live better," Bill said that last sentence placing extra emphasis on "paid" with a melodramatic expression that would have made a lip reader recoil like reading an all caps rant.

"That's how shit my normal life was. After I graduated, it wasn't much better but only now am I able to save up enough money to spend on whatever the hell I want, including you. It would hurt me, literally hurt me, to think about you having to go through all that by yourself. That, would be a *tragedy*. I hurts me even now to think that you need to have sex with all those fat, elderly cadavers just so you can have a decent quality of life. You shouldn't have to do this. You told me you once worked in some illegal Chinese massage giving happy endings. That's just wrong. This country, this society should not have done that to someone like you. You deserve better," Bill continued while Esmeralda seemed to be developing an increasingly puzzled expression, almost like Erika before.

"Just think about how statistically unlikely it was for you and I to meet. Just at that moment, just the right circumstances. How could anyone deny that it was some greater force bringing us together? You know, all the people you see walking on the road, they wouldn't understand what you're going through. Most people think, 'sex work, BAD!' and never think 'why is she doing this?' Most assholes just laugh at people like us and think our struggles are nothing. When you told me about how you used to play in the school orchestra, I knew it was fate at work again. If only we were students together, who knows. Maybe we could have gotten along. It's hard for me to get along with anyone other than my friends but I feel like I can do anything when I'm with you. You're studying for a better future but it's all a scam. The way you are now, it's gonna be real hard to find any kind of work that pays even close to sex work. It would hurt me to see you being stuck in this industry. You see the girls you work with? All the drugs, tattoos and shit. Look at how perfect you are now. You are too beautiful for this line of work. You deserve to be put on a pedestal. *I* can put you on the pedestal. *I* can look after you so you don't have to keep doing sex work. You're the first girl who's ever agreed to meet with me outside the brothel. I thank God, Jesus, Bhudda, Thor, all the Gods I was able to meet you. I need you in my life and I think in some ways, you need me too. I can make sure you *never* suffer the way I have suffered in my life," Bill finally confessed, only to have Esmeralda express an increasingly complex expression on her face.

"I'm saying all this because I *cannot* keep seeing you like it's some kinda transaction. If we were to keep seeing each other, it *has* to be something more meaningful than a transaction. If you think this relationship has been entirely transactional, like nothing we ever did meant anything, I understand. I will never meet with you again, I will never speak to you or contact you. I won't ever bother you again. You won't see me tracking you down and making your life more difficult than it has to be. You can trust me. But right now, I feel like what's happened between us has been far more than that. I think we can become something more meaningful. How about it?" Bill finally made his proposal.

Esmeralda was furrowing her brows. She definitely did not appear comfortable. There was an uncomfortable extended silence. Esmeralda finally answered,

"Uhmmm... I'm not sure. Maybe not right now. I'm happy by myself. I don't think I have room for a relationship in my life..." Esmeralda began but then paused. "OK, how about this. We can get to know each other better. I'll tell you my real name with one condition. We can never meet like this again. I'm happy to be friends. We can even hang out just as friends. You don't have to pay me. I feel uncomfortable taking your money. Look, I've stopped counting the hours tonight. I didn't know you felt this way about me. I genuinely had a fun time tonight. You're a nice guy Bill. You'll find someone right for you out there, you just gotta be patient and not be a lovesick puppy all the time."

Bill felt like he was struck by lightning. Multiple times. Simultaneously. Bill felt his heart race faster than a Ferrari just before he made his proposal. After hearing Esmeralda's answer, his heart rate plummeted like a nosediving fighter jet. His emotions instantly turned 180 degrees just like a parabola. A second ago he was elated beyond description, now all the anxiety and dread that accrued over his entire life exploded in his chest. The bitter pain he felt each time he left the brothel crashed like a tsunami pulverising any remnant of hope he still clutched. He had a prior inkling that it was all hopeless and it was just confirmed. Bill felt like he could not breathe. His emotional pain was literally crushing his chest.

Esmeralda could sense that Bill was under emotional distress. She leaned forward and hugged Bill. Bill did not feel it at all. His mind was completely preoccupied with the sheer horror of what he had just heard.

"Do you still want to have sex?" Esmeralda asked. Bill could barely even look her in the eyes let alone enter her body.

"No, just go home. I'm hell tired," Bill said, "I've prepared your money on the stand -"

"Bill, I was serious. Get some rest and look after yourself, please. You have my number. Let's see each other again, as friends," Esmeralda attempted to comfort Bill. However, Bill could not bring himself to speak another word. His head was in agony and he was struggling to hold back his tears. Bill dejectedly nodded his head and stared at the floor while Esmeralda left the hotel room taking only half the money Bill prepared.

Chapter 14

Hopelessness (IV)

It was 10pm and Bill felt like he wanted to hang himself but there was no weight bearing structure in the hotel room capable of facilitating that. The pain he was feeling now was magnitudes worse than what he normally felt after leaving brothels. Bill rolled up his sleeves instinctively only to stare at the dozens of horizontal lines decorating his inner forearms where he had cut himself at a younger age. Then the tears started flowing. That was his *last chance*. It was hopeless now. What more was there to live for? He had tried everything and nothing worked. Society and fate collaborated to achieve this end all along. He was marked for execution the moment he was born so he might as well just accept his fate and end it all.

Dejectedly, Bill took out his phone and decided to ring the one person who ever understood him, Cheng.

"Hello, what the hell bitch, why you calling me at this hour? Can't you wait until tomorrow?" Cheng's irritated voice sounded through the speaker.

"Be quiet," Bill sobbed into his phone.

"Sounds like she didn't accept your proposal did she?" Cheng asked.

"We were meant to make babies together," Bill continued sobbing. He could barely string the sentence together through spams of sobs. "If I were with her, I would have gladly worked in dentistry forever to support her. It would have been worth it. I would have done anything for her."

"Oh my God, why are you saying this shit now? When the hell did you get so cucked?" Cheng sounded disappointed.

"She was my *last chance*," Bill continued sobbing, "She was perfect for me but she still fucking rejected me. Never again am I going to find someone who's white, beautiful, a student *and* willing to go out with me. It's all fucking hopeless. It's fucking over." Bill proceeded to sob uncontrollably for several minutes barely able to utter a single comprehensible syllable.

"You done yet? Why did you call me up just to have a meltdown?" Cheng harshly questioned.

"I know goddammit, FUCK! I can't fucking help it! I thought fate was bringing me together but it was just fucking me over like it always does. How can I continue living? I have nothing left to live for. Cheng, how do you do it?" Bill responded.

"Life is meant to be endured, not enjoyed. I don't enjoy life but I'm too scared to die. I never even attempted to enter a relationship because it's too hard. You ask me how I do it? I just accept absolutely zero, rock bottom every time because life will always be shit, in fact the shit parts make the slightly less shit parts seem less shitty by comparison bringing about this weird fucked up relative happiness. Stop trying to make everything perfect," Cheng explained.

"I can't do it. I can't do what you do. I'm not asking for perfection. I'm just trying to make things barely tolerable, the bare fucking minimum and I get fucked over, I've tried everything, it's all fucking over," Bill continued.

"What do you mean bare minimum? You could have your parents arrange some Korean girl instantly and get married. But you only want white girls. First it was red heads, then you liked mixed girls, then you liked brunettes. None of the girls you find attractive would enter into a relationship with you. Didn't you mention that this girl was fucking some guy who didn't even want her? She was so desperate for that big white dick that she was willing to offer herself for free yet she wouldn't even go on a vacation with you, all expenses paid for at a 5 star hotel," Cheng harshly pounded some reality into Bill's head causing another fit of uncontrollable weeping.

"You're goddamn right, you're always right," Bill sobbed into his phone again.

"If I'm right then why don't you ever listen to me? I told you not to fall in love with this girl and look where we are now. She hasn't completely rejected you yet either. What's wrong with being friends? Didn't I mention before that you can have female friends to satiate your social needs then fuck some hookers to satisfy your physical needs," Cheng reminded Bill.

"It's not that fucking easy. I *had* to do this, it was my *last chance*," Bill repeated his old excuses. "Normally relationships start with being friends. If she's willing to be your friend, maybe one day you can foster a genuine relationship rather than this fucked up paid for girlfriend, sugar daddy bullshit. Last time I checked, you're not even rich enough to be a sugar daddy," Cheng dished out more bitter reality. Bill continued sobbing for another half hour uttering incomprehensible drivel before letting Cheng go to sleep. Bill followed up by drinking himself to sleep. It was high quality Canadian Club whisky, why would he not drink it?

* * *

The day after, Bill returned to work, hung over, like a person who had their entire family murdered in their sleep. He refused to greet the staff and the moment he dismissed his patient, he shut the door, laid down on the dental chair to sleep until the next patient. At least he could actually sleep, that was the only comfort he could achieve. Nothing else could diminish the pain he was feeling. The staff were whispering while Bill had his door shut. It became a widely accepted office rumour in both clinics, Carlton and Collins Street, that Bill was having a "girl problem." Bill regretted asking the staff for advice. Bill finished off yesterday's bottle of Canadian Club before he left the clinic. Of course he took the bottle from last night with him. After returning home, Bill again returned to his hate forums. This time, the content was not alleviating his pain. Nothing could deter his brain from assaulting him with unwanted, painful memories.

Bill tried to attempt the next assessment task. He was switching to Python programming language this time. Jason recommended using Python because Bill was struggling so much with C. However, what the fuck was exception handling and object oriented programming? Why did these things even exist? Bill remembered the lecturer's examples demonstrating similar results with a few lines of code by defining a function. Why was he stuck writing dozens of lines of useless code he did not even understand to achieve the same outcome? Not only that, his code just would not run. Bill tried to troubleshoot but all he could think about was Esmeralda. His headache was throbbing and his chest was aching so much it was as if he had severe angina.

Fuck it. Bill just could not handle it. He gave up and left it all for Jason to handle. Bill somehow felt increasingly lethargic since the hotel incident. He struggled to keep his eyes open unless forced to either because of clinical work or failed programming exercises. No matter, Bill thought, it was a good thing because at least he was not experiencing unceasing agony when he slept. For the next three days, Bill drank himself to sleep and woke up more tired than before. Bill then made his decision. There was no point forcing himself to stay awake and suffer while seeing 2-3 patients a day. That Saturday, Bill caught Andy while he was leaving.

"Hey Andy, hear me out man, I need to ask you something," Bill called out.

"Yes Bill, you feelin' alright these days? Everyone's been telling me that you've been really quiet these days. Are you having some relationship problems?" Andy asked.

"Kinda like that..." Bill answered with some regret.

"Don't be so down on yourself, you're a really handsome guy, there's plenty of women out there who will line up to be with you. You have so much of your life ahead of you," Andy commented seemingly sincerely. Bill found that hard to believe. Bill gritted his teeth and put on a fake smile.

"I think I've had enough. Look, Carlton isn't really picking up. I'm hell tired. I can't keep working 7 days. I've been doing this without a break for a year now. I don't think anybody can claim to have worked so long, every day straight, no interruptions, even for Christmas. I don't think I can keep it up for much longer. I need to have a break. How about I drop Monday, Tuesday and Wednesday at Carlton," Bill requested.

"I understand, there are some others who want to increase their days and we've got a lot of dentists wanting to join this year so it will work out in the end. Don't worry, have a good rest," Andy promised Bill.

Bill was surprised that Andy didn't complain about not giving several weeks' notice to replace him. There must be a hell of a lot of desperate dentists out there. Probably lost their wealth gambling on Bitcoin, Bill thought. On Monday, Bill remembered waking up but the moment he opened his eyelids, it felt like they were crushed by an unstoppable force and closed immediately afterwards. Bill drifted back to sleep and repeated this cycle until Tuesday night. He had to get up to relieve himself and drink some alcohol but he was too tired to even eat. It was not until Wednesday noon that he was able to eat some leftover discount pasta. What the fuck was wrong with him? Bill could not figure it out but he did not mind avoiding waking hours being assaulted by painful memories. Sleep was the only relief he had from the pain.

* * *

Bill returned to work on Thursday but he did not feel any less tired than before. It did not feel like he achieved any true relief despite sleeping close to 20 hours every day for the past 3 days. Every day was the same. He would struggle to just barely send patients out the door and collapse in the chair, unable to make a peep until the next patient arrived. Bill suspected that reception intentionally lightened his workload. He was not even angry, he wished he could just sleep endlessly. If he could achieve eternal, painless sleep, that would be even better. On Saturday night, Cheng and Jason seemed to stage some sort of intervention and accosted Bill after he dismissed his last patient. Bill stopped writing patient notes. It was a waste of time. What was the Dental Board going to do? Deregister him? Fuck them, he did not care.

"You need to see a shrink, you're not even semi-functional, you're totally fucked up right now," Cheng pointed out the obvious.

"I don't need to take fucking drugs, that shit doesn't treat the cause. I will only end up dialling up the dose and fucking kill myself when they stop being therapeutic. Everyone says I'm a monster but do they ever ask, 'who created this monster?'" Bill furiously protested.

"None of us have any psychiatric training. For all we know, you could have some plain old illness that billions of people suffer from and can easily be treated," Cheng argued.

"Lol, yes, this guy probably has Incel syndrome and needs shock therapy on his dick," Jason mocked.

"This ISN'T FUNNY! FUCK! You know as well as I do that psychiatrists and psychologists don't know what the fuck they're talkin' about. You see this shit with medical students pretending to be crazy and they couldn't even tell? They had to bring in the professors to explain to the psyche ward that it was a study and it was all pretense otherwise they would have stayed locked up," Bill fired back.

"Psychiatry has advanced shitloads since then and we're not talking about who's crazy and who's not. We don't know what mental condition you're suffering from. Even though psychiatry is full of shit, it's still the closest shit we have to diagnosis and treatment of mental illness. What else are you going to do? Witchcraft and voodoo? Shave a chicken's ass and wave it around a fire? It's disappointing that despite thousands of years, the best we have come up with is a flawed discipline with people barely knowing anything reliable but it's still the best we have," Cheng explained.

"Fuck this shit. If I were to do it, then I'm gonna need a fake name and pay *out of pocket* so that these Medicare fucks don't know what the fuck I'm doing. You know that seeing shrinks puts you out of a shit tonne of jobs? I was looking to apply as an analyst for your couch potato spies, ASIO, ASIS or whatever, they ask if you've seen a shrink in the past year on the application form. If I see a shrink, that's fucking career suicide right there," Bill complained.

"Lol, you won't have a career if you can't even stay awake," Jason mocked again.

Bill was unconvinced but what pushed him over the edge was the fact that he was desperate to try anything. He could not live a life where he spent every fucking waking hour in pain. The intervention went on for hours with the same arguments circling back and forth, even through dinner. Eventually, Bill relented and decided to look for the furthest psychiatrist he could find. Apparently there was even a clinic in Mildura but that was way too far. Eventually, Bill decided to make a booking in Horsham. It would take over 3 hours to drive there but the specialists there would not have the luxury of frequenting Melbourne, if at all. Nobody could drive 8 hours then work 8 hours every day. Apparently there was a visiting psychiatrist who worked in Adelaide. Even better, Bill thought.

* * *

It was two weeks later that Bill found himself driving for close to 4 hours to reach Horsham to this place called "Mind Care Horsham." Horsham was a fairly large place compared to Ararat and Stawell. The highway forced itself through Ararat and Bill stopped by McDonald's for five $1 hamburger specials before driving off. Stawell was almost bypassed but Bill was still forced to endure a 3 minute delay meandering past useless shops and broke ass car dealerships which sold nothing but old bombs. Finally, Bill arrived in Horsham at 2:43pm after driving the whole day. There was no train connecting to Horsham. It was so far even V-Line stopped at Ararat. There was no way Bill would accept catching a barely running connecting bus service.

The clinic was only a 1 minute drive from the large roundabout the highway went through. Bill turned left and saw a fairly packed "main street" of sorts. It was a joke compared to Melbourne but it was surprisingly packed for a backwater country town. Bill found the clinic easily relying on his iPhone GPS. Apple had a disastrous turn when they snubbed Google Maps not long ago but it seemed to be functioning now. The clinic looked like a condemned suburban slum building typical of poverty stricken Melbourne suburbs but the inside was well renovated, of course. Soothing classical music was being played. Bill recognised the middle section of Chopin's funeral march from his second piano sonata. That was a joke, Bill thought. It was a beautiful passage completely unrecognisable from the funeral march main theme and it cut off before it returned to the main theme. If only people recognised where it came from. Bill silently laughed to himself.

"Uh hello, I'm Bill, I'm here to see doctor Paul," Bill greeted the receptionist.

"Ahh, nice to meet you Bill, please fill out this form," the receptionist handed over a clipboard with a stack of identical forms for Bill to complete. After filling out his details, Bill did not need to wait long until the psychiatrist called him in. The office looked pretty much like most Hollywood depictions of psychiatrist offices. He sat down on a reclined chair while the psychiatrist, Dr Leonard Paul did not have a desk but a comfortable looking rotating arm chair which he swung towards Bill.

"Nice to meet you Bill. I see you're a fellow health worker. I welcome you sincerely, we health workers have one of the most mentally gruelling jobs out there no matter what specialty we work in. Thank you for coming all this way. Please, tell me a bit about yourself and what's happening," Leonard began.

Bill went through what happened with the sex workers and Sarah. He had prepared dot points of what to say but he found expressing himself succinctly and accurately incredibly difficult. Bill should have asked Cheng to come here beside him and explain properly. It was hard to verbalise when all he could think about was Esmeralda's rejection.

"I don't know if I explained things properly but this constant headache makes it hell difficult," Bill tried to elaborate.

"I know it's hard to describe everything in just one session but you're doing well. I can understand what's happening. You're doing the right thing taking some time off work. That's a good start. I also recommend some regular exercise and taking a vacation. 2 weeks or a month doing what you want. Engage in some hobbies, do whatever you enjoy. There is solid evidence in the literature that it does work," Leonard continued. "I also recommend some psychotherapy. I recommend seeing Dr Liz Catalan nearby. She's excellent. I personally recommend her wholeheartedly. The girls outside will give you her card."

"I don't want to see some random psychologist because they're not even real doctors. You have a medical degree so you've been through the proper way to learn your craft and you know how hard it is. These psychologists don't have the academic acumen to understand what it is they're preaching. They say it's evidence based but there's no good evidence for any of what they do," Bill argued. This triggered a slight chuckle from Leonard.

"I know what you mean. However, psychotherapy is what they're really good at and I don't really do much of it. I work with Liz all the time. We've had great success with many patients. There actually is strong evidence in the literature for the effectiveness of psychotherapy," Leonard explained.

"Can you at least recommend someone who isn't female? You gotta understand, all my problems have come from females," Bill pleaded.

"Liz is different. I understand you're experiencing a lot of issues with women and it may seem counterintuitive, but it helps you more having a woman address your concerns" Leonard stated with confidence.

Bill continued discussing with Leonard about his complaints at Mega dental. Leonard sympathetically responded with some anecdotes of his own patients and their dental nightmares. At the end of the appointment, Leonard recommended Bill try some anti-depressants.

"Here, try this SNRI, duloxetine. I've been seeing a lot of improvements in my patients in the recent years taking this," Leonard recommended.

"How long do I need to keep taking it? Do I need to keep upping the dose?" Bill asked, already knowing the answer.

"Everyone's different. You're going to feel maybe a little worse for a couple of weeks until it starts working. If you stop taking it, many patients report feeling like that initial 'worse' sensation. Some are OK with stopping it but it all depends on how you feel," Leonard described exactly what Bill thought he would say. Basically, "I don't fucking know."

By the time Bill arrived back in South Yarra it was already 9pm. A whole day was consumed by the effort today. There was very little to lose. Bill was already at rock bottom. The next day Bill purchased his prescription and immediately started feeling like there was this cloudiness in his head. On Thursday, Bill struggled with his work. He could understand and speak to patients but his reactions and judgment just did not feel right. He was thankful for the lack of patients at Carlton. Unsurprisingly, on Saturday, Bill met with the new hires that Andy talked about. They too were complaining about lack of patients at Carlton so Andy gave them shifts at Collins Street. There were two of them and they were all female. Bill could barely recall their names because his head was swimming. Like before, Bill isolated himself in his room and collapsed in his chair the moment he dismissed each patient.

* * *

It was not until 2 weeks later, just like Leonard said, that Bill started feeling "normal." Bill was surprised, his pain did indeed reduce. At the same time, his positive emotions also seemed to be moderated to some extent as well. What did ya know, Bill thought, hooray for drugs, they did work. Another thing Bill noticed was that stimulating himself while watching online adult content became more difficult. Not impotence, but it took much, much longer to finish. Bill thought he could take advantage of this opportunity and perhaps visit a brothel again. This time, he was going to avoid Esmeralda and visit Pink Paradise in St Kilda, the suburb with a reputation for street walkers.

Bill had been here a few times before but the girls were obviously of a lower class compared to Red Lantern. They were mostly fat and tattooed with piercings. Either that, or the girls were borderline anorexic with blackened or fake fingernails with chipped nail polish, the typical presentation of meth addicts. Once he did find an extremely attractive brunette girl with less offending tattoos. But only once. Bill entered and the reception gave a rehearsed greeting. Even the receptionist looked like a meth addict. She obviously had periodontal disease with long looking teeth from receded gums. However, Bill was not prepared for the shock of his life. Along came Esmeralda who casually walked in.

Bill felt like he had a panic attack. He specifically went to a different brothel so that he could avoid her. He deleted her phone number that night and was too scared to return to Red Lantern. He wanted to just forget about her but here she was. Fate was indeed a cruel mistress. Esmeralda appeared mildly startled as well but recovered almost instantaneously.

"Why hello there stranger, you may call me Emma now," Emma (Esmeralda) re-introduced herself with a slight chuckle. Bill struggled to speak. He had to violently clear his throat before he could stammer a response.

"Uhh... Didn't expect to see you here," Bill weakly replied.

"You OK? Did you miss me?" Emma asked.

"I haven't stopped thinking about you," Bill admitted. He wished that was not true but the intrusive thoughts would not stop.

"You know my services, do you want to hear them again?" Emma continued.

"No, I'm familiar. How long have you been working here?" Bill asked.

"I only started a week ago. Today's my second shift. I work 2-8pm," Emma revealed. It was now 6:45pm after work. There was no doubt that Emma had "serviced" other clients before him. With a heavy heart, Bill asked the question he did not want an answer to,

"Did you have a busy day?"

"Yeah, kind of, not as busy as the Red Lantern but I just started recently so it's expected," Emma explained.

"Give me some time to think," Bill uttered while holding back tears. He rushed out of the brothel and went back to his car parked only fifty metres or so away. The moment he closed the door, the tears started flowing.

"Answer goddammit!" Bill frustratingly yelled into his phone. Fuck! Despite the drugs, the pain returned, albeit with mildly diminished intensity. Bill dialled again immediately but was answered with an "engaged" tone of death. Perhaps Cheng was attempting to call back. Sure enough, the phone started ringing immediately after Bill cancelled his call attempt. Bill answered when Cheng returned the call,

"Answer you idiot, fuck! You gotta help me," Bill sobbed into his phone.

"Fuck you bitch, you know that the signal is patchy on my way back. I just went through a dead zone between Beaufort and Ballarat. That bit just before the bypass is always a dead zone. Why you calling me this time? Are you missing that bitch again?," Cheng's irritated voice sounded through.

"I went to a different place, but she was there again," Bill tried to explain through his spasms of sobs.

"Huh? You went to Red Lantern? I can barely hear shit," Cheng replied sounding confused.

"I went to Pink Paradise. You know that place in St Kilda? I went there to avoid seeing Esmeralda but she was there again! FUCK! She changed her name to Emma. I want to be with her but... but... she's ruined. She's ruined godammit! She's been working all day and all those wankers have been fucking her. They ruined her. I can't do it... You gotta help me," Bill cried even more desperately into his phone, barely able to string a comprehensible sentence together.

"What the fuck dude. You are seriously fucked up. I thought the medicine was supposed to help but now you're having another meltdown over the fact that your favourite hooker did her fucking JOB and fucked other men?" Cheng harshly criticised over the phone.

"The meds are helping otherwise I wouldn't even be able to have this conversation. But it's not enough. I can't fucking help it," Bill decried.

"Stop pretending that the girls there are 'fresh' or whatever you keep imagining. These girls have sex with multiple men every day. Is it somehow more fresh to wait 12 hours since the last client? It would take weeks or months for diseases and shit to go away or be treated or whatever. Do you think that 12 hour window somehow makes them 'fresh'? Why the fuck do you keep saying 'ruined?' You've been fucking other hookers, so does that make your dick 'ruined?'" Cheng dished out some more brutal reality again.

"OK, OK, FUCK!" Bill conceded.

"So get back in there and fuck her like you wanted to. Jesus, I'm starting to sound like you these days," Cheng mused.

"Bye bitch," Bill answered before hanging up.

Bill did indeed return and pay to see Emma. It was somewhat uncomfortable after what he went through but any contact with Emma elicited indescribable joy. As a welcome surprise, the duloxetine helped him last longer because it took so much more effort to finish.

"So how come you're working here?" Bill finally asked the burgeoning question.

"I couldn't keep working at Red Lantern. After my uni friends found out about me, a lot of people I knew started showing up. I kept hiding and the girls there were making fun of me. I had to leave," Emma explained.

"What a bunch of assholes. So are you going to keep working here for a while?" Bill asked.

"Probably. I don't know. Depends on how I'm treated I guess," Emma replied.

"By the way, I lost your number, are you OK if I kept in contact?" Bill asked apprehensively.

"I'm happy to meet up as friends, don't lose it this time OK?" Emma joked. "I missed you Bill. Is that your real name? I sorta make up stuff on the spot depending on what happens. I'll let you in on one secret. My real name as Alexandra."

There it was. She left Bill with a memory as indelible as a tattoo. Bill fought so hard to forget her but he could not help it. Bill could not help but consider himself a desperate piece of shit. More than ever, he needed a distraction from all this. As Bill started driving himself home, he thought back to his childhood. What did he enjoy doing? Bill spent so long doing nothing but keeping his head above water he never even considered what he wanted to do if he had time. The hate forums were amusing to an extent but did not stimulate his creative self. Perhaps he could get back into playing rather than just listening to classical music. Once upon a time he also enjoyed ice hockey. Cheng was into PC gaming as well. Perhaps he could ask Cheng to build him a proper gaming computer and not the donated AMD junk. Intel was the shit, AMD might as well be dead.

That night Bill started researching flutes, digital pianos, clarinets and ice hockey equipment. Was he going to actually entertain the notion of seeing a female psychologist? He was definitely not going to waste a whole day driving for that useless exercise. Perhaps he should ask Cheng again. Bill was glad to have a friend like Cheng. He could not have made it through all these meltdowns without Cheng's harsh voice bringing him back to reality.

"Guess who," Bill spoke into the phone with a "gangster" tone.

"What you want this time bitch?" Cheng replied.

"Come on man, I need your help again. I've decided. I am going to re-engage with my childhood hobbies. I need your help with building a gaming PC," Bill explained.

"But are you actually going to play games? You keep saying you're too 'goddamn busy' and can't do anything other than look at incels forum and sleep. Why don't you buy a console instead? They're hell cheap and then you can donate it to me after you've played it for 1 hour and get bored," Cheng questioned.

"This time it's different OK?! I'm a functional drug addict now. Come on man, help me out. In fact, you should pay me for the privilege of building a PC cause I know you love that shit," Bill tried provoking Cheng.

"My own PC yes, but if I build it for someone else and something goes wrong, they're gonna blame me. You're a dentist too, you should know what the fuck I'm on about," Cheng explained.

"I'm not gonna blame you. Just help me out fam, you owe me," Bill chided.

"I can build one for you but you better damn well play games on it otherwise it's just wasted money," Cheng conceded.

"Also what the fuck should I do about this psychotherapy bullshit? I think the guy is full of shit when he sent me to some female but the drugs he prescribed are working so maybe that guy isn't completely bullshitting. I don't trust any of these goddamn females. They *never* take responsibility for their problems. You see it in dentistry, medicine, law, fucking everywhere. They don't know what the fuck they're talkin' about," Bill complained.

"You don't know until you try. Isn't it paid for by Medicare? If it's free or mostly free, you might as well take as much as the Government gives. You pay so much tax like me, the government owes you big time. You can't just go to see any psychologist, that's true, but what if you look for one with a PhD? I know it doesn't mean much these days cause they're handing them out like candy, as you say, but at least they've studied longer than the average useless psychologist," Cheng reasoned.

Bill and Cheng discussed what specifications and how much the gaming PC was going to be for the next half hour. Bill considered Cheng's words. Seeing a psychologist probably won't make the situation worse... Probably. Almost all the goddamn psychologists he found were female. It was unnatural. Something was definitely wrong here. Bill sighed. He knew that it was all going to be a waste of time but he pulled plenty of "long shots" in his life. This was just another one of them. If by some miracle he found a psychologist with a semi-functional brain, they could legitimately help him. Bill kept his expectations low.

Chapter 15

Hope, the quintessential human delusion

Bill sighed as he abandoned all hope of lifting his spirits. It was hopeless. For almost two months, Bill had attempted to rekindle his interests in gaming, music and ice hockey. It just was not the same. Anhedonia was perhaps the best way to describe it. Bill recalled the nostalgic childhood memories of the joy he felt when he beat a boss in a game. He remembered the accomplishment of playing in synchronisation with the orchestra. He remembered the thrill of weaving through scores of opponents by gliding across the near frictionless ice rink. Today, he felt nothing.

Bill sat on his desk and double clicked the flight simulator game. He had spent a fortune on buying a realistic joystick based on actual US fighter planes as well as replica pedals and switches. Bill attempted to glide the plane into motion but he watched in despair as the screen displayed a flailing plane tilt irrecoverably and nosedive onto the tarmac. This was hard. Bill questioned why he even bothered trying. When he was young, Bill felt drawn to the Playstation like a magnet. Once he sat on the sofa, he was glued there. Today, he *forced* himself to turn the computer on and failed to even lift off yet again. Bill sighed dejectedly and exited the simulation program. He had enough. Bill recalled that Cheng recommended many games which were on sale but Bill felt absolutely zero inclination to play any of them.

This should not have been the case. Just like music and ice hockey, he did force himself to give them a try only to feel no inclination to continue. Bill spent a month annoying Cheng to help him look for a decent piano yet there it sat untouched for the past two weeks. "Just find a hobby" that damned psychiatrist and Bill's friends kept saying. What the fuck could he do if there was literally nothing he could enjoy? To top it off, Bill repeatedly phoned Pink Paradise to book in with Emma, only to have them inform him that she never returned for another shift. Bill tried to text and call her, she never responded. He had been "ghosted" as the online linguistics described it.

Bill shut down the fancy gaming PC Cheng had assembled and walked towards the kitchen. Bill and Jason each had their separate bedrooms but Bill elected to have the one closer to the kitchen. Disappointingly, Jason had left all the dishes from last night out in the open again. Bill sighed. It was just past lunch time and he did not feel hungry at all. He did not need the dishes immediately but he could not tolerate leaving the trash heap the way it was. He would not lower himself to the level of a slob. Jason never cleaned the dishes properly anyway. He needed to do fucking everything around here despite Jason not even working. Bill had to admire Jason's courage for refusing to work in dentistry any longer.

Bill sighed again and sauntered back to his bedroom. He and Jason barely spoke these days. There was nothing to speak about. Jason had finished the entire Harvard extension program by himself and was now studying well beyond what Bill could understand. Bill could not write a single functioning program for any assessment task regardless of which language no matter how hard he tried. Bill powered up Cheng's donated junk PC again and booted up the Ubuntu Linux partition. Bill used this junk computer by default whenever he "researched" online hate content. Today's focus was on Korean murderesses.

True crime was irresistibly captivating for Bill. Bill's imagination ran wild with the ways he would murder his enemies but real life criminals have done things far worse than the absolute most brutal concoctions Bill could imagine. Bill scrolled through his YouTube page which was now decorated with stories about Korean black widows. Bill gritted his teeth in anger over the blatantly overt ramblings from Tom. Bill hated Tom so much these days he no longer referenced what Tom actually said to him. Bill had invented a new personality for Tom. This Goldstein version of Tom was the incarnation of misandry and male subjugation. Goldsteinised Tom would self-flagellate while watching another man pleasure Tom's own wife. Absolute peak cuckolding.

The current video described the story of a petty Korean woman who murdered her husband to steal money for a pair of shoes. Fucking shoes. The shoes were not even expensive, the equivalent of perhaps just $200 USD. A good, loving man lost his life to this berserk, psychopathic man-hater just over a pair of fucking shoes she would discard after wearing just once. What had the world come to. Tom's voice echoed in Bill's head. "The man must have deserved it!" "Women would never do this without provocation!" Bill clenched his fists as well as gritting his teeth. People like Tom were part of the problem. It was male inaction that allowed women like this to exist.

This story truly rocked Bill to the core. In the beginning, Bill slid into true crime after looking at forensic journals online. Harvard Extension School provided open access to endless resources so he might as well conduct research he could understand rather than smash his head against a brick wall known as software programming. The crimes which were front and centre in the journals were committed by men. However, as if signalling the oncoming onslaught of gender equality, female led crime just seemed to become increasingly over-represented in recent years. Bill started seeing patterns. There were very few men who committed murders for no reason like Ivan Milat, but when they did it was incredibly attention grabbing. Conversely, all this online content about females committing murders just seemed equally if not more petty than old Ivan but barely made into the news. A pair of fucking shoes?

Time and time again, the crimes men committed were centred around violent struggles while living in poverty and despair. Conversely, these Korean black widows, their lives were not found wanting in any way, shape or form. Yet so many women murdered their husbands for petty insurance payouts. It was just so unreasonable. Bill had to laugh at the absurdity of the next video which described a series of cases where women took out life insurance on behalf of the man without the man's knowledge. There must have been something fucked up about Korean insurance companies as they did not care about obviously fake signatures. Bill knew Tom would say something stupid about how these murderess were all coincidentally poor victims of abuse and the males all deserved to be murdered. Fuck that guy, seriously, Bill thought. How was he ever friends with that moron?

Before he knew it, several hours had passed and Bill felt the weight of his eyelids forcing him off the computer. This was Bill's routine whenever he had time off. He had been awake for 5 hours and even that was pushing his limit to the extreme. He was lucky to even manage 4 waking hours in a day. Bill almost collapsed on the floor where there should have been a bed except Bill felt no need to pay for such an exorbitant luxury. All he had was a thin pile of sheets laid out on the carpet. Within moments, Bill slid underneath his blanket and just like every day, he almost instantaneously lost consciousness.

* * *

Unfortunately for Bill, Andy pressured him into accepting Wednesday a couple weeks ago as a "temporary" replacement only to have it become permanent. That was why Bill forced himself up to catch the tram down to Collins Street. At least it was not Carlton, Bill thought. He was becoming very tired of thumb twiddling at Carlton. As fate would have it, Bill had more nasty surprises waiting for him.

"Good morning doctor," yet another new receptionist, Tricia, greeted Bill in his surgery, "the next patient seems to be really nervous but I said you were the best so just to give you a heads up."

"OK," Bill muttered, preferring to be back home sleeping.

Later, Bill found out exactly what she meant. It was a young female patient whose front tooth was negligently treated by some idiot dentist who not only botched the root canal by not finishing anywhere near the end, then tried shoving in a metal post which was at least 3 sizes too small. There was heavy infection and the metal post was literally floating in space serving no function other than decoration. The tooth itself was snapped off below gum level and in a hopeless state. There was no way to sugar-coat this.

"So Andrea, if you look at this x-ray, do you see how there's this white stuff in the middle? Now let me show you what a good root canal looks like," Bill explained while searching Google for an example.

"See how in this Google image, the white stuff is solid? Whoever did the root canal before didn't do it properly. I don't blame the guy, it's worked for a while but now it's inoperable. Not even a specialist can save this tooth. Your options are either to get an implant or a bridge. Temporarily though, I can make you a denture, you see these things that can clip in and out?" Bill explained while showing an example, "If you want to do any of the permanent options, you need to wait about three months for it to heal up properly."

The patient looked like she had seen a ghost. Her face was pale and she seemed unnaturally quiet. She seemed to nod and ask if the tooth needed immediate removal.

"I don't have to remove it today, in fact, I would recommend taking a mould to make the temporary denture, have it prepared before removing the tooth," Bill elaborated. It was obvious that Andrea was suffering substantial distress as she mere nodded her head and said,

"I need to speak to my parents," before starting to cry. Bill was immediately frustrated. He hated women putting on this act. They all expected men to bow and kowtow the moment they turned on the waterworks. If a man started crying like that he would just be laughed at.

"I'm... sorry, I'll make.... a decision.... soon," Andrea attempted to say in the midst of uncontrollable sobbing. She gingerly left the room leaving Bill feeling only mildly relieved. He could not stand that.

Unfortunately, in the midst of completing a routine checkup and clean for the next patient, Tricia messaged him explaining that Andrea was weeping uncontrollably in the waiting room. She was distressing all the other patients. Fuck! Bill more than ever wished he was sleeping rather than dealing with this. It was not his fucking job to lie and pretend everything was OK. What the fuck was he supposed to say? "Oh don't worry, we'll put a new tooth on in a jiffy" and then having it fall off within a week? Bill was not a psychiatrist or psychologist. The whole problem was caused by whatever moron saw her earlier and now *Bill* was the one suffering the consequences. For the rest of that day, everyone was staring daggers at Bill like he had committed a sexual assault.

The next day was equally distressing. He had just finished treating a family. It was terrible enough dealing with children but there were three of them all crowding around the surgery. Bill intentionally shut the door the moment the mother brought her eldest in but the morons seemed to have zero fucking courtesy or respect and opened the door letting everyone in. They were screaming and running around preventing Bill from concentrating even one moment. They left Bill with a throbbing headache only to have the next patient barge in with a senseless complaint.

"Did you see the photos I sent?" the patient asked, "it's Thursday and my face is still swollen, it shouldn't be like this."

Bill muttered soundlessly "fuck you" under his mask but he checked inside and found that the healing was going well not to mention she was not complaining of pain.

"Uh Siobhan, the healing looks like it's going well-" Bill attempted before being rudely interrupted.

"It's not going well otherwise I wouldn't be having this swelling," Siobhan cut Bill off aggressively.

"The swelling you have is within limits, it can last for two weeks," Bill tried to explain.

"Ugh," Siobhan melodramatically sighed, "why didn't you tell me about all this? I can't go to work like this. The stitches are still there, why didn't you use the ones that fall off?"

"Hold on, it will go down, the stitches will dissolve but it will take longer," Bill attempted to explain, but he knew he was not convincing her at all.

"I've had enough of this," Siobhan rudely remarked before walking off.

Bill wanted to strangle her on the spot but his assistant was in the room so he could not just leave a witness like that. His headache was throbbing again and this time it was hard to stay upright. He was feeling somewhat disoriented. Bill's anger was again threatening to overwhelm him. That fucking immigrant bitch, Bill thought. He hated Europeans for a good reason. Bill never once had a problem with patients from the US. Europeans on the other hand were almost always arrogant, rude and completely incapable of accepting the way dentistry was done in Australia. Bill did not understand how Irish people did dentistry but it clearly involved ignoring every fucking word the dentist said.

Bill had told her precisely what to expect. Pain, swelling, bleeding, all of what she was complaining about now was completely normal but she did not listen to a single fucking word he said. Not only that, she sent a string of moronic "selfies" of her ugly ass face, Bill thought, which was caused by her genetics and nothing to do with what Bill did. That afternoon, there was an unsurprising one star review left for Bill's name yet again. Fuck. That was however, not the end of it.

On Saturday, Bill returned to work with more unwelcome surprises. Tricia greeted Bill again in the morning to inform him about some moronic e-mail complaint followed by a one star review. It was lucky that Bill was taking his drugs. In the past, one complaint alone would have been enough to drive him insane. This was the third in a row. Disasters tended to clump together. Bill reluctantly opened his email to read another dump of verbal diarrhoea:

To whom it may concern,

I saw Dr Parker two week ago and he told me I need big expensive plan. I did not need big treatment. I told him it was just wisdom tooth. He did not give me antibiotic even though I asked for antibiotic. I went to see GP and GP give antibiotic then pain go away. This is proof that Dr Parker did not know how to fix me. I am very disappointed Dr Parker didn't give me proper treatment. Dr Parker also charge me extended consultation. All he care about is money. This is the reason patients lose trust. He seemed very unhappy too. Why he can't smile more?

One thing Bill hated more than anything was a false allegation or in this case, an *extremely* ignorant false allegation. Despite the duloxetine, Bill felt the same explosive, white hot rage which threatened him during his Shellharbour days. How could such morons like this exist? Bill just could not understand how mentally retarded subhumans could get. He pointed at the x-rays, he repeated himself, he tried using every trick under the sun to force that cockroach to understand her fucking teeth were on the verge of dropping out and she was barely even 30.

Even a primary school student could easily tell from just a one second inspection of the x-ray that it was not fucking normal. Bill's headache was just as severe as Shellharbour now. He felt his heart thumping so hard, each thump resulted in a shuddering thud in his head.

Bill then noticed a new symptom he never experienced this intensely before. His vision was narrowing like he was experiencing tunnel vision. Murderous thoughts pulsated through Bill's mind with every thunderous heartbeat. Bill fantasised about hundreds of various gore covered scenarios with that fucking cockroach's corpse. Was tunnel vision a side effect of the duloxetine? It could not have been, Bill looked up this drug extensively on MIMs, the drug database. Bill's anger was merely so intense, his entire body was breaking down. His autonomic nervous system was being pushed to its limit by Bill's next level anger. That was right. This was a new tier of anger Bill never experienced *despite* the duloxetine taking the edge off. Bill felt like a hot water boiler on the verge of exploding from the excessive pressure. Maybe committing murder would act as a suitable pressure release valve...

Bill managed to take some deep breaths and started thinking. She was obviously some immigrant from South East Asia who was used to their trash quality dentistry where for some reason, gum disease just did not exist. Nobody treated it, nobody cared. Teeth just drop out don't they? It's a normal part of ageing right? And that subhuman cockroach came to *this* country to bring *that* trash over here and she expected Bill to just bow and kowtow to that trash level of treatment? She couldn't speak English worth a damn and clearly couldn't write either. FUCK! Bill punched the bench hard enough to startle the assistant working in the other room. He knew it because he heard someone say,

"What happened?" Both his hands were shaking uncontrollably.

Was this world a joke just to punish him? What was this clown world he was forced to endure? Bill could not take it any more. If anyone dared push his buttons again, he was seriously going to commit homicide. If only this country allowed firearms... He would not fucking stop. There would be nothing stopping him other than a hail of machine gun fire. Bill clenched his teeth and marched out of the surgery. He had to leave otherwise someone was going to get hurt. His assistant today was yet another new hire. Bill already forgot her name as she only started a week ago. It did not matter.

"Bill, are you bringing in the first patient?" Bill's assistant asked as they crossed paths in the clinic hallway.

"I need to clear my head. I don't care what you do, tell the patient to wait. I just don't care," Bill uttered with chilling coldness.

"Are you sure? You're quite busy in the morning, there isn't much time-" she was about to continue before Bill cut her off.

"I SAID I DON'T CARE, JUST DO IT!" Bill interrupted. This time, he was screaming. There were other staff and Terry walking by and all of them turned their heads towards Bill.

Fucking morons. All of them, Bill thought. He was obviously not in the right condition to see a patient. He did not possess the tolerance to receive more complaints and one star reviews. Jesus, Jesus, Jesus... Bill muttered quietly while stepping outside the clinic and onto Collins street. Patients like that bitch brought their severe problems in expecting an impossible quick fix and then get mad at the dentist for trying to do the right thing? Bill was repeatedly punished for trying to do the right thing. Why did he even bother heeding the advice of specialists when these subhuman cockroaches all demanded antibiotics? Why not just give it to them? Doctors gave out antibiotics like candy so why not Bill? Fuck this epidemic of superbugs. That bitch deserved to die of a superbug infection. Bill would love to become the next Dr Joseph Mengele and experiment all of these subhumans to death.

Bill eventually returned to the clinic half an hour later to find out that his patient decided to leave. So what, Bill thought. He could not have treated them in his condition anyway. Miraculously, Bill managed to calm himself down just barely enough to treat the remaining patients until lunch. Bill's outburst shocked the staff enough for Andy to intervene that day. As Andy was leaving, he popped in to Bill's surgery to briefly interrogate him.

"Hey buddy, are you feeling alright?" Andy asked.

"Uhh... Yeah... " Bill did not want to elaborate.

"I know it can be hard with your relationship not working out and all. Everyone's been noticing how you've been these past few weeks. I also heard from the girls about that complaining patient. Some patients are just crazy, we all get them. Don't worry," Andy attempted to reassure Bill.

"You got it sir. In fact, I am already seeing a shrink and taking medication. I'm planning on seeing another doctor soon for psychotherapy. But sometimes even that isn't enough. I keep telling the girls to stop booking in all these trash patients. I said I don't wanna do re-cementation jobs or people who can't speak English worth a damn. Trust me, these kinda patients, they're just liabilities. Nobody should see them unless they screwed up the crown in the first place or can speak whatever language," Bill finally confessed.

"I'm going to have a chat with the girls, I'm sure they can help you out. Take care of yourself Bill. You've got such a long, fulfilling life ahead of you. Oh, don't forget to use the CEREC!" Andy finished off before heading off. Bill was not completely lying. He had not booked in to receive psychotherapy but he did write down a shortlist of psychologists with PhDs he might consider.

That night, Bill met up with Cheng and Jason on another of their frequent nightly visits to KFC on Grattan Street.

"Even though I'm taking duloxetine, I still get really pissed off at these false allegations. It's like each time something happens, my fuse just gets shorter and shorter. The drugs helped a little but they're not enough. Not even fucking close. Dentistry is the fucking problem. How do you do it Cheng? How can you possibly enjoy video games when the world around you is fucking you up all the goddamn time?" Bill lamented.

"More like there's something fucked up about you 'cause everyone has at least something they enjoy doing," Cheng replied, seemingly too matter of factly stating the obvious.

"That's the problem," Bill explained, "I can't enjoy anything any more."

"Not even banging hookers?" Cheng asked.

"Not since Esmeralda. I can't fucking go to a brothel without thinking of her," Bill anguished.

"Lol, he hates women now and prefers men," Jason joked. Bill just gave Jason a stare and shook his head.

"You still haven't booked in with a psychologist have you?" Cheng asked.

"I will, maybe. They're all pieces of shit. At this point, it's too late," Bill said dejectedly.

"That's why it's the best time to try because as you said, you have nothing left to lose right? Since you have nowhere to go but up, think of this as a last ditch effort. You keep saying that you won't give up unless you've tried everything possible," Cheng argued.

"You're always right Cheng, you're a good friend," Bill replied. With that, the trio went on to discussing more trivial matters. Including how Bill could not write a single functioning computer program.

* * *

It was the middle of June. Bill finally decided to bite the bullet and book in to see a psychologist. There was a psychologist who had a PhD in her title practising very close to where he lived. As Bill approached the supposed building listed on the address, he appraised the facade. It was an eyesore. Many buildings in South Yarra were probably close to 100 years old and ought to be demolished for public safety. It had a faded grey, stone edifice that had seen too many years with a very obvious finish line against its modern, neighbouring building. The adjacent building was at least a metre taller making the stark contrast in architecture painfully jarring. The awning, which most shops had, was rusted and made of corrugated metal sheets. The street side entrance was framed by two floor to ceiling sized windows covered in promotional stock photos of smiling families. "Yarra central health" was printed in bold black letters on both panes of glass.

Bill pushed open the door and was greeted by a receptionist who handed him a clipboard form to fill out. Of course they had to do this, Bill thought, fully prepared to go through all of these standard procedures. The punctuality was not intolerable, Bill waited about 15 minutes in total as he was a little early like he was supposed to be. The psychologist went by Susan Williamson and as Bill expected, she looked like she was in her mid 40s. Obtaining a PhD and practising to establish oneself would likely take that long. Bill walked down a short corridor and entered a room with a plush sofa next to a swivel chair. It was obvious the sofa was for the patient.

"So Bill, is it OK if I call you Bill?" the psychologist asked, "you can call me Sue, I'm happy to go with first names here."

"Uh sure," Bill replied.

"Excellent. I've read the referral your GP sent me," Sue started explaining, "you have been experiencing some anger and mood issues, perhaps feeling a little bit down I gather?"

Bill needed some referral so he had to see a local GP first. That was easy, GPs would pretty much do anything patients requested of them especially if it was a waste of time. That was the beauty of taking advantage of trash socialist healthcare, Bill thought, it did not matter if it was one second, they can still bill Medicare. Bill was a true American patriot. Medicare disgusted him, especially considering how much he was paying for everyone else's health care and using almost none of it himself.

"That's mostly right. I'm not sure if you can apply any label on how I'm feeling, but that sort of comes close," Bill clarified.

"That's good, it looks like you've put a lot of thought into your circumstances. That's a good first step. Now would you like to explain a bit about yourself?" Sue requested.

Bill had trouble verbalising most things on the spot. He attempted to explain to the best of his abilities the trouble he experienced with the moronically self-awareness lacking Dr Sung.

"Are these issues still happening?" Sue interrupted. Bill looked at the time, it was 11:43 already, which meant he spent half an hour just trying to explain his Shellharbour experiences and had not even reached stepping foot in Melbourne yet. Bill hated being put on the spot like this. He begged Cheng to come along with him but Cheng had been resolutely firm about not attempting to put his words into Bill's mouth. Bill relied on Cheng too much. Bill knew that but he desperately needed assistance otherwise he would be repeatedly sidetracked like a river with too many tributaries and neglect the main narrative of his story. Even worse, rehearsing a speech was not enough especially when the person in front of him started asking questions.

"Year sort of, but let me finish," Bill attempted to explain. Another ten minutes later, Bill was getting nowhere.

"I think I'm getting the rough picture of what's happening," Sue interrupted him again, "am I right to guess that even now, you're working long hours?"

"Yes, but that's not the problem," Bill tried to justify. Unfortunately, Andy dragged Bill into working another extra day "temporarily" at Collins Street but so far he had not been advised when he could drop the day.

"I acknowledge that you feel that way but overwork produces numerous negative health consequences. There has been thorough research on this matter. Symptoms include burnout, depression, anger, extreme irritation at minor issues and even physiological, chronic illness symptoms such as sleep disorders," Sue continued.

"I understand, but I went down to only working four days and none of this went away," Bill argued.

"For how long did you cut down on your days?" Sue asked.

"I can't remember precisely but if I were to guess, I'd say it would be around a month or two," Bill honestly estimated.

"You can't rush these things. It takes sustained lifestyle change for many of these symptoms to go away. I would recommend longer than just a month to adapt to a new lifestyle and the benefits it would bring. You should consider taking a break, a holiday, have more social occasions with friends, enlarge your social circle and try new things like learning a new skill," Sue attempted to suggest.

Bill was instantly triggered. This was the same bullshit Tom, Cheng and even Jason advocated. Why did he have to pay money to see this "professional" here to seek the same advice that other people had already given? That bitch made all this shit up without even listening to all of his story. Fuck! He wasted so much time diverting off track while reciting his life story that Sue probably thought that was all he had to say.

"I've tried those things, but it's not working. In fact, I was feeling the best when I was working 7 days a week. After a while, yes it was tiring but I was feeling my absolute *worst* when I was working 4 days a week. You gotta let me finish," Bill requested.

"I'm sorry, I didn't mean to interrupt you, please go on," Sue conceded.

"Ok, Ok, so you know how the staff and the other dentists at Shellharbour were morons? The last straw was when I was *forced* to drill into healthy teeth or get fired," Bill continued, then recalled up to him starting his work in Melbourne but before he received his first complaint.

It was 12pm already. There were just a few minutes left before the end of the appointment. Bill felt like he had reached nowhere for this one hour session.

"I've treated some other dentists before. What you're describing are common problems in the industry. Take it easy, rest assured that you're not the only one. I hope your work at Melbourne has made things better?" Sue asked.

"It's much better but there are still problems" Bill explained but he knew there was no hope of explaining things properly in the short time left.

"I wish I could spend more time working on this but I will have to hear the rest of the story next time. From now until next time, I think you should definitely try to find some things you enjoy doing to de-stress. Most people don't understand how much pressure us health practitioners are under. Long term wise, finding some work life balance will have a significant impact on your symptoms. Your GP also mentioned that you're seeing a psychiatrist, is that right?" Sue asked.

Bill was not amused. Everything she said he had already tried. There was a fucking reason he could not find anything to enjoy. The horrendous memories mercilessly destabilising his mental state did not just suddenly disappear with a flick of a switch. They made everything he tried thoroughly unenjoyable. Bill could not play one second of gaming without being reminded of his tragic life. He could not even look at pornography without being reminded of just how little women thought of him. He did not need some so called "professional" with a useless degree handing out useless advice he got for free.

"I am, he prescribed duloxetine which so far has been the *only* thing which has given me any improvement even though it's not enough," Bill replied.

"I'm glad to hear that it's helping. Next time we'll go through the rest of your story and hopefully we'll find some more strategies to sort things through," Sue said, signaling the end of the session.

The first thing Bill did after arriving back at his apartment was to call Cheng to complain. He did not pick up. Fuck! Cheng was working after all. It was not until almost 6pm that Cheng called back.

"Why you call me when I'm working idiot?" Cheng complained through the phone with frustration.

"You need to help me, bitch. Oh my God, that was a fuckin' waste of time. I couldn't explain what the fuck was going on and that bitch kept interrupting me," Bill also complained.

"This is you we're talking about, you can't explain anything without getting diverted a million times before reaching the point," Cheng explained.

"That's the *problem*," Bill agreed, "I need yo ass to help me out. How about I *pay* you to be there as an interpreter for me, you know me the best out of anyone, I need you to explain what the fuck is going on," Bill begged.

"Hell no, that's insane. You need to explain everything, as much as possible from your own mouth. That's how therapy works. I don't even know what the privacy laws would say about this. Do you think you're mentally diasbled or something? Like I'm your legal guardian, or as you Americans put it, 'power of attorney'?" Cheng confronted Bill.

"Godammit! Fuck!" Bill exclaimed in exasperation.

Bill pleaded Cheng some more and explained just how useless the psychotherapy session was. However, Cheng still declined.

"Next session there better be some progress," Bill disappointedly uttered.

"How many sessions are you supposed to have?" Cheng asked.

"Medicare provides for 10 sessions," Bill replied.

"How much is it?" Cheng asked.

"It was like almost $350, I know I paid $150 out of pocket, fucking rip-off, that's after the Medicare rebate. I'm using my Medicare rebate for the first time but I lose money overall. All for useless fucking bullshit advice I already got from you and Jason," Bill complained.

"That is a fucking rip-off. When we charge that much money, at least we produce objective improvements to the patient, shit that you can see but it looks like you paid a shitload of money and got nothing out of it. At least with the psychiatrist, they gave you a drug that did something," Cheng concurred before the two concluded their conversation.

* * *

The next session was also unproductive.

"So now I've given up on trying to get into a relationship. It's a waste of time and it's done nothing but harm," Bill finished explaining the key points in his recent life for the most part.

"You're still young. Look at it this way, I got married when I was 34. You shouldn't just 'give up.' Dating is not easy and don't base your ideas about relationships on what you see on telly. Despite what people boast, studies show that most people only have a few sexual partners throughout their lifetime. It's normal to have multiple failed dates which don't result in a sexual relationship. You can't base your entire self-worth on your height either. Plenty of my colleagues are married to men half their height, haha," Sue explained with a subdued fake laugh. She was probably serious but her casual attitude exaggerating the inadequacy of males irked him.

"You need to present your best self to the woman you like. I think you're well dressed as is," Sue continued. Of course he was, Bill donned a suit wherever he went. "Women like being praised so talk about her hair, her clothes, congratulate her a bit to flatter her. You can't be shy when saying these things. There are so many things to talk about on the first date..."

Bill started zoning out. Why was he paying to listen to dating advice? "Don't you think I've tried that shit already?" Bill thought to himself. He did not just try once, he failed dozens of times to realize it was fucking hopeless. He obtained plenty of phone numbers through dating but almost nobody responded. He even paid for the dinner of an ordinary looking white girl medical student only to have her never call him back. Women treated him with such extreme contempt he was fucking done with attempting to appease them using these useless fucking strategies. Yet, he was *paying* to listen to this garbage coming out of the mouth of this so-called "professional?" Was he living in a fucking circus?

"I meant it when I said I'm *never* going to date again. I'm not here for dating advice. I thought you could help me with my problems. I'm trying to explain that I've failed with women. I've done all I can, and it doesn't work, so I. Am. Done," Bill waited for a slight pause between each of his final words to emphasise his declaration.

"You have so many years left to sort things out, don't give up yet. Studies show a strong correlation between improvements in mental health and a healthy social network including an intimate partner," Sue continued explaining.

"I know that's what studies say but I've done *everything* I can, I've tried all the stuff you talked about. It doesn't work for me. I don't care if studies say whatever, studies are not 100% and who are we kidding here, psychological studies aren't even close. All your advice only applies to ordinary people, *not* me. I'm way ahead of the curve. We're both health professionals, I think we can agree that you can't just predict what can happen when you try something a study recommends in real life. I can't predict how long fillings last and neither can you tell all men to start dressing better and expect them all to find suitable partners. In fact, all I see are broken relationships and couples harming each other. This includes my older sister who can't stop being toxic like radioactive waste for even a split second. In fact, I suspect she is working as some sex worker illegally in the United States. I'm 99% sure she's taking drugs and is in with some dangerous crowds. In fact, my parents have been telling *me* just how scared they are. They are *hoping* that she doesn't contact them, doesn't come back and stays where she is. My mom, she cheated on my dad and he knows it but they just pretend it never happened. My dad is sorta like me, that reject would never have gotten married to my mom if it weren't for his money. That's why when some useless 'pastor' came along and all he had to do was to pretend he cared for her, my mom just cheated right in front of me and my sister. It was dead obvious. I was 12 at the time but it was so obvious only a moron would believe her lies. My own girlfriend rejected me like our entire relationship didn't exist and every woman I see thinks I'm just some sewer rat! I said I am done and I mean it!" Bill unloaded in front of Sue.

However, Sue's facial expression did not change at all. If this were a movie, the psychologist would be played by an irresistibly attractive actress and would jump in the air shouting "Eureka!" Sue on the other hand seemed displeased that Bill would start ranting out of control.

"Bill, you can't project your life experiences onto every woman or every couple you see. It's normal to see a lot of relationships break down but that's just part of life. I work with many couples with troubled relationships. I even do some expert witness work with the family court. Of course there are going to be challenges in relationships but the benefits outweigh the problems almost all the time," Sue continued with her verbal diarrhoea. Bill shook his head with conviction then tried to argue back,

"I get that, some people have it good, stop stereotyping, stop cherrypicking etcetera, I've heard it all before. I'm trying to explain how much harm it has done -" Bill was in the midst of explaining before Sue interrupted him again.

"Why don't you try some online dating? There's so much attention happening with online dating. I know you've tried traditional methods already but..." Sue continued before Bill turned his head down and drowned out her annoying voice. "... I think we had a very productive session. In order to make the best of our further visits, have a read through this."

Sue handed Bill a thin bundle of stapled A4 sheets. The front page was titled, "What is depression?" Bill immediately thought, is this a fucking joke? The front page had cartoon characters with dot point summaries of what Bill assumed must have been about depression.

"I know it's a bit cliche but there's lots of good information there. It's definitely worthwhile," Sue followed up.

Bill almost silently muttered, "Uh..." He was speechless. It was not the first of April so he was not expecting this.

"The information there can also be found with a quick Google search but I like having things printed out. There's one more thing, here, do these exercises at home," Sue proceeded to hand Bill another two sets of photocopied, stapled documents.

"Uh, OK," Bill said instinctively. What was he agreeing to?

Jesus, Jesus, Jesus, Bill thought. What was this bitch trying to accomplish? He was paying $350 an hour to listen to verbal diarrhoea? He received better psychotherapy from Cheng lecturing him and that was free. By the end of the session, Bill was fed up. Bill said "goodbye" then wordlessly left the clinic after paying the bill. He had to endure 8 more sessions of this garbage. What part of this was evidence based? Did she acknowledge any part of his struggle? She skipped over any of the moments when those women in Bill's life destroyed his trust. How could a "professional" be so unconcerned or perhaps uncaring about their patient's feelings and struggles? Bill hoped that this so-called "professional" would actually start helping him eventually. He had no goddamn choice, he was too deeply invested in these useless sessions.

Bill dejectedly trod back to his car. After all was said and done, he felt absolutely zero benefit. Bill told himself repeatedly, this was just the beginning. There were going to be 10 in total. He was not expecting perfection. He just wanted some slight improvement in order to find a path forward. Bill sighed as he closed his car door. Bill looked at the next two sets of documents. One had lots of small titles. "Activating event, beliefs, consequences."

"An activating event is something which affects you mentally. Your beliefs then affect the way you feel about the activating event leading to consequences."

The document then followed this up by having Bill fill out blank spaces based on a hypothetical event involving a road rage incident. The other set of documents had explanations about "negative, neutral, positive" reactions to stimuli. It required Bill to fill out blanks based on hypotheticals again. Bill needed to write down a negative emotional response, a neutral one and positive one regarding an argument over someone refusing to give back a borrowed belonging.

Bill sighed. That useless shrink was giving him high schooler exercises. Bill realised immediately that these exercises were designed to help achieve some self reflection. However, Bill did self reflecting all the fucking time. Even if he did not want to reflect, Cheng's caustic lectures forced him to reflect. The exercises the shrink provided were designed for low IQ morons. It did not take a genius to recognise that these exercises would barely have any impact. However, Bill was all out of options. He would do these exercises. He would make sure nobody could accuse him of not taking this shit seriously.

Chapter 16

A flap of a butterfly's wings...

Work was more deleterious than ever. Every minor inconvenience felt like it was gnawing at Bill's very soul. The list was endless. Both clinics were low on consumables. New nurses were ushered in to replace the departure of previous staff. Nobody working with Bill had a decent grasp of their tasks. The new dentists all acted like "slobs" leaving a mess everywhere they went. On top of all that, patients only seemed to become increasingly antagonistic. Bill only had to think about work to trigger a nauseating wave of anger. Arriving at the clinic only worsened his deplorable state. He was *forced* to endure six days a week of this torture. Bill was not asking for perfection. Everybody made mistakes and it irked Bill to no end that he made mistakes himself. However, what was happening was forming a pattern too hard to ignore.

Bill sighed as he stared at his monitor in the Collins street practice. His first patient was a crown preparation. It was the first Tuesday of July 2016 and Bill's first day of work that week. First was a crown preparation, next was a long and difficult wisdom tooth extraction. Bill sighed again. Jesus, Jesus, Jesus, he thought. How was he going to get through the day? Bill's assistant this time was yet another new hire. He was going to run late. 100% guaranteed. Bill did not remember her name, he did not care. Bill prepared the materials himself and walked out to invite the patient in. He would never trust the assistants to set up the procedure. The crown was on a lower molar which had been root canal treated. It should have been standard enough.

However, Bill instantly knew it was a difficult task as the patient was an obese young female who clearly could not control her tongue. Like many obese patients, her mouth was short of space. Her tongue and cheeks were jammed against the tooth he needed to drill.

"Anna, could you please stop moving your tongue," Bill coldly requested for perhaps the 15th time.

"Sorry, it's got a mind of its own," Anna replied with a borderline snigger. Jesus, Jesus, Jesus, Bill frustratingly repeated in his mind. He needed to smooth out the dog's breakfast mess of drill marks on the inside surface of the tooth but within 2 seconds of activating the drill, Anna would reflexively swallow and jam her tongue against his mirror. If there were ever an Olympic event called tongue thrusting, this bitch would have taken gold. No, she would be the Usain Bolt of tongue thrusting breaking all world records forever more.

It came to a grinding halt when Anna somehow dislodged Bill's mirror with herculean strength and unsurprisingly pushed her tongue into Bill's drill. Bill immediately released his foot off the pedal but the drill was air powered. The drill tip passively stopped spinning completely unlike a mechanically driven drill which would immediately stop the moment the motor stopped. Anna unleashed a howling scream of pain and started crying. Jesus, Jesus, Jesus, mother fuck god damn! Bill's heart was pounding from the banshee's wail he just heard.

"Let me have a look," Bill attempted to ask only to be met with uncontrollable sobs. There was red fluid dripping down Anna's cheeks while she was heaving back and forth.

"I need some gauze," Bill instructed his assistant. "No! Not that shit in the drawers, I need some sterile gauze!" Bill demanded after seeing his flustered assistant being useless. FUCK! Bill screamed internally. Why did he try to achieve a good quality crown preparation? He should have just zipped along the back of the tooth like an angle grinder and left it at that. This accident only happened because he wanted to make his work neat and tidy. That moron intentionally pushed as hard as she could against the mirror he was using to shield her tongue. Bill's left hand was actually throbbing due to how much tension he had to apply to hold back her tongue.

Bill's assistant returned with the sterile gauze packs.

"Anna, I'm going to place this gauze in your mouth to stop the bleeding," Bill tried to explain.

Anna's tears were still streaming but she had calmed down slightly to the point of at least being able to hear Bill's request. She timidly opened her mouth so that Bill was able to place the gauze in. The laceration was severe. There was overflowing blood. Bill had to immediately remove one pack of gauze because of the excessive bleeding so that he could place the second pack in. Each time he moved the gauze, Anna shuddered and squealed in pain.

Bill's head felt like it was gripped in a vice. The pain was unbearable. His hands were shaking and his vision was narrowing. His heart was pounding and he could almost feel his uncontrollably rising blood pressure. How easy would it be to commit murder and hide the evidence? Such thoughts were racing through Bill's head. Unfortunately, there were too many witnesses. Bill gritted his teeth and clenched his fists as he waited for Anna to calm herself down.

"I can't finish the job today after what's happened. I need to bring you back in two weeks to finish this off," Bill finally managed to stammer out. Anna did not seem to be able to argue. She was in too much pain. She merely nodded and walked out of the room.

Bill stared at the dental mirror he was using to hold her tongue back. It was bent. The three centimetre diameter sized mirror was welded onto a stainless steel cylindrical rod. Somehow her tongue was fighting so hard she managed to deform the welding. Fuck. Sure, repeated sterilisation heat cycles may have had some effect on the metal but 126 degrees celsius was far too low to affect the metal substantially. In order to speak, humans were capable of intricately manipulating their tongues to produce the most subtle sounds. For some reason, the same morons could not obey a simple instruction of not fucking moving that infinitely dexterous and intricate muscle. She managed to fuck up her own tongue and forced him not to charge a fucking cent. Fuck!

Despite leaving the procedure incomplete, he was already running late. Pausing every two seconds of drilling was not fucking normal. Nobody could work on time with such a handicap. Bill slumped down on his chair and typed a message for reception instructing them to book in for another hour long appointment in two weeks. Unfortunately, that was not the end of the day's suffering. The wisdom tooth patient was extremely difficult and took 90 minutes longer than planned. After Bill dismissed the patient, he discovered with horror that the treacherous receptionists had booked in another patient in the hour's gap he was supposed to have. FUCK! He repeatedly told them to ask him before they booked anyone in and if he did not respond, THEY SHOULD HAVE DAMN WELL KNOWN BETTER THAN TO BOOK SOMEONE IN!

Bill smashed the keyboard, shocking his assistant.

"Goddamn it! FUCK!" Bill yelled. Fortunately the keyboard did not break and his door was closed so probably not many people heard him. She seemed taken aback but was too scared to say anything. Bill was running 90 minutes late. The patient the team booked in had apparently been waiting for 90 minutes. Bill wordlessly exited to call the next patient in. Crown re-cementation. Fuck. Bill strongly felt the urge to start murdering. How could anyone not murder under these circumstances? After Bill arrived back in the room, his computer had a message from the front,

"Doctor, your next patient said he had to go and left."

There was only one reason why. That patient had already waited half an hour only to see another patient called in. Despite the high turnover of staff, Bill was certain he spoke in no unclear terms they were *not* to book in patients without his permission. Especially not crown re-cementation patients. Bill looked at the crown the patient brought in, fucking hopeless. Broken at the root level, impossible to glue back on.

"I can't glue this back on. There's nothing to glue onto, see?" Bill explained while pointing to the photo he took, "I'm not going to charge you any money, go back to whoever did the crown for you." With that, Bill dismissed the patient and walked out.

"Cancel my afternoon, I'm going home," Bill announced as he walked out through the door. Those sub-humans did not listen to him anyway so why would he even care to explain? Bill's headache was threatening to overwhelm him. He was unsteady on his feet as he limped out the door. He almost fell over if it were not for his hand on the wall. His anger had reached nuclear levels and if he stayed in the clinic any longer, who knows, maybe someone would end up being carried out in a body bag. It could have been Bill himself, the malicious reception, a patient, any other dentist stupid enough to approach him, who knows?

As Bill opened the door to his apartment, he saw a stained frying pan on the stove. Fuck it, Bill was too goddamn tired to care. Bill did not have the energy to care. Within seconds of lying down, he was asleep. Sleep was the only relief he had. The drugs were not enough to quell his anger. Taking time off was not enough. Therapy was fucking useless.

Was his entire existence a joke? The next three days Bill shut himself in his office the moment the patients were dismissed. He did not say a word to anyone. He did not eat a scrap of food either. The staff were left wondering if Bill needed to eat or drink but he did not even bother to beg for leftover food. Predictably, Bill's odd behaviour was surprising for everyone. Nobody understood what was happening to Bill though.

* * *

On Friday night, Bill was desperate. If there was even a remote chance he could see Alexandra, that was her real name, he would still try. Bill was out of options. He just wanted to see her one last time. She could have changed her name. It was normal for working girls to change their name just in case they had some unruly regulars they wanted to avoid. Was Bill an unruly regular? Bill drove down to Pink Paradise with a thunderous headache and broken spirit, only to be met with dismay. She was not there. The last prostitute to introduce herself walked in and sniggered the moment she saw Bill's face. This did not bode well.

Bill's heart rate suddenly skyrocketed and he felt his fists clench involuntarily. That fucking cockroach was sniggering at *him*? Who the fuck did she think she was? Bill was a hard working and high achieving Übermensch, the hero of Nietzsche's philosophies. Hard working men like Bill were the core elements keeping society functioning whereas these goddamn whores were parasites draining the life blood from men like Bill yet she *dared* look down on *him*? Bill spent his precious money he slaved over every day to earn just so these whores can leech it away and live like royalty. Did she think Bill had a fucking choice? He had no goddamn fucking choice but to pay for sex. She reacted like he was some kind of sewer rat. A true sewer rat looking at a giant yet not understanding that she was the fucking subhuman sewer rat herself. That just happened.

Bill leapt up and did not wait for the girl to introduce herself. He stormed out of the brothel and stomped back to his car.

"FUUUUUUUCK!!!" Bill screamed at the top of his lungs repeatedly after he closed the car door. Bill slammed his arm against the car door repeatedly enough to shake the car left and right spasmodically. He could not stop. All that anger had to go somewhere. His car could take it but that whore would have been turned into red mist. How *dare* she? How *dare* someone like that, the lowest of the low, *dare* look at Bill like that? Bill's anger was only intensifying the more he thought about it. He decided to phone Cheng again.

"What you want?" Cheng answered the phone.

"Listen to me, I am fucking DONE with these goddamn females. You know what I've come to realise?" Bill replied.

"What?" Cheng responded with an audible sigh.

"Don't fuck with me. This is the goddamn truth. This is the fucking objective truth. Sex is a purely animalistic act. I admit now that sex has done me more harm than good. Those females aren't even human," Bill continued.

"You sound exactly like Hitler and the Japanese when they discussed executing prisoners, thinking of them as less than human made them easier to murder," Cheng interrupted.

"THAT'S CAUSE THEY'RE GODDAMN FUCKING RIGHT!" Bill screamed into the phone while pummelling the car door with all his strength again. "Don't you go siding with those goddamn fucking liberal SJW fuckwits on me! YOU'RE EITHER WITH ME, OR YOU'RE AGAINST ME!" Bill continued screaming into his phone. "Cheng, I've known you for a long ass time. You're a good friend. I don't want to lose you too," Bill continued with slightly less venom in his voice. Cheng merely responded with silence.

"I've realised, I don't feel a goddamn thing during sex because I am an Übermensch, so are you by the way," Bill explained, "men like us are above these cockroaches. If you think these animals are on the same level as us, you gotta have a goddamn hole the size of a football in your head. Is there anything these subhumans do that even comes close to what you and I have done? Just think about the act of sex itself. It's just two animals sweating and heaving against each other and somehow you're supposed to feel this indescribably special feeling like you're in another universe? FUCK OFF! ANYONE WHO SAYS THAT IS A FUCKING SUBHUMAN COCKROACH!" Bill raised his voice again.

"Just think about who these whores are. They are the lowest of the low. Men like me give *our* hard earned cash so just they can act like a bunch of fucking animals together. Somehow it's meant to feel good? Relieve stress? Forget about how fucked up life is? FUCK...OFF! These parasites can't get a proper job or they can't stand working a proper job so instead they choose to suck dick and earn more fucking money than I do! These goddamn street rats don't pay any tax. The morons at the ATO take all my fucking money and pay for these rats to have health care while *I* have to pay $150 an hour for some fuckwit useless female to tell me to take a fucking holiday?!! FUCK... OFF!! Society is FUCKED. Mark my words, Australia has fallen. We are already fucked up beyond all recognition. This is the kind of society where someone like *me* is treated like a fucking sewer rat while all those useless fuckwits you see on the street are 'essential.' The subhumans have taken over. People like us, we're actively being hunted. Not just passive. It's not like they're just not caring about us or anything. Noooooo way, these subhumans are *actively* trying to murder us," Bill explained while pausing for Cheng's response. There was none.

"You want to hear what happened today?" Bill asked, although it was more rhetorical.

"Whatever, what happened?" Cheng replied with exasperation.

"I went back to Pink Paradise. Before you say anything, this was before my epiphany. That idiot who went into the brothel, he's fucking dead now OK? Bill is fucking dead. I am the new ubermensch Bill. Well I went in and I was hoping to see Esmeralda, you remember her?" Bill started his story.

"How can I not," Cheng replied.

"She wasn't there, I don't know what the fuck happened. Maybe she died or got scared of me. I know they all think I'm psycho or something but THEY'RE the fucking ones with mental problems, NOT ME! There was this girl who came in with a smirk. She fucking went 'heh' just as she was about to introduce herself and she gave me this dirty look. I could tell, she was looking down on me. *ME*! THAT FUCKING WHORE WAS LOOKING DOWN ON ME LIKE A FUCKING SEWER RAT!" Bill started screaming again and punching his car door. "How can these cockroaches not have a fucking sense of humility? They're paid $300 an hour to fucking pretend they like me and they can't even do that. Can you see how pathetic it is? That fucking cockroach can't handle a proper job, can't do what I do even if you got 6 of her trying at the same time. All she had to fucking do was to hide that fact that she thinks I'm some street rat but she can't even do that AND PEOPLE SAY I'M THE CRAZY PERSON?" Bill continued his screaming.

"Are we really superior to her? You don't know anything about her," Cheng commented.

"WE ARE SUPERIOR GODDAMIT!" Bill screamed even louder than before while punching his car door uncontrollably. "DON'T YOU FOR ONE SECOND THINK THESE WHORES ARE WORTH ANYTHING! Even if you get a hundred of them, a million of them, they wouldn't be able to accomplish *half* the shit that you and I have accomplished. I am not going to lower myself to their level again. Just thinking about females makes me feel disgusted," Bill declared.

"So you like men now?" Cheng extrapolated, sarcastically.

"Fuck you. You get my point, go to sleep bitch," Bill ended the conversation.

* * *

The day after, Bill decided to eat McDonald's after work. He deserved it. He had not eaten solid food for two days. It had been a long time since Bill neglected eating for so long. In the past it felt like he had no time but for the past couple of days, he was too tired to even eat. Bill had not spoken a word to Jason either. He could have asked Jason to prepare something for him but Bill had become increasingly irritated by Jason's "slob" like behaviour. It was better he did not speak to Jason otherwise he would start cursing. At times like these, Bill would order the giant family McValue box which probably had enough food to feed 4 mildly hungry people. Bill however, was famished and could eat all of it.

The nearest McDonald's was next to Flinders station on Elizabeth street, only a few minutes' walk from the clinic. As expected, it was during peak dinner time and there were people queued right to the door. Fuck it, Bill thought, he might as well wait. After Bill walked in, he saw a stunningly beautiful woman waiting at the back of the line. She was a tall young brunette with a very well proportioned body. She possessed an enchanting face and she had no tattoos, at least visible ones. Bill watched more hate content yesterday night decrying the shameful state of the fashion industry. The women on the catwalks all wore caked on make-up and this even covered up their nasty tattoos. Bill had never seen an attractive tattoo on anyone, male or female. The models themselves must have known that otherwise why would they cover it up? Almost all of them had fake lips, fake lashes, Botox, plastic surgery... the lot. Men did not find any of that fake shit attractive. Bill saw example after example of fair or attractive women being disfigured by modern culture.

The brothels were only worse. Everything was fake and plastic, except the outcome was even worse. It made Bill feel revolted that he once paid to spend time with these animals. However, the girl in front of him was just naturally beautiful. She stood there staring blankly into the ether, obviously bored from waiting. Bill could not resist the urge. What was the harm? Bill felt like it should be perfectly reasonable for him to walk up to whoever he liked and proposition them in exchange for money. He knew he would be persecuted by the corrupt society if he attempted that but it was just a fair trade. Females could not recognise a fair trade if their lives depended on it. Who knows, it was a long shot but maybe he might have a chance with this girl. "Pick up" artists did this all the time online so why should Bill not give it a try?

Bill approached the girl and started talking,

"Hi there," Bill greeted.

"Uh, Hi?" the girl replied.

"The first thing I noticed when I walked in here was how beautiful you are. You know, I'm a bit of an expert when it comes to beauty because I have lots of experience with cosmetic dentistry, including cosmetic injectables. Most women want to be like you but even with cosmetic treatment, they don't come close. I was watching a fashion show yesterday, and I thought, 'Gosh, why do these women have so much cosmetic surgery done?' Without exception, all those fake lips, fake lashes and Botox make things *worse*. You could go on a catwalk any day and you would be more beautiful than any of those fake models out there," Bill stated with confidence.

"You're so kind, thanks," she replied.

"I'm not asking for anything and neither am I offering free treatment. If you want to contact me, feel free to have a consultation. I don't think I can improve your face anything beyond your natural beauty but there's always problems which come up. I work at Mega Dental right around the corner. My name is doctor William Parker, you can call me Bill," Bill introduced himself.

"Nice to meet you, I'm Sasha Kemp, you can call me Sash," she courteously responded to Bill's advances.

"You can email me on williamparker@gmail.com," Bill then spelled it out just to make sure she got it. Surprisingly enough, she actually wrote it down on her phone.

"Cool, my email's samster_k153@gmail.com," Sasha reciprocated.

Faster than Bill expected, the line progressed and it was time for Sasha to order. They said their goodbyes. Bill thought that went better than he imagined. He did not have to ask for her contact details, she just volunteered them. He would definitely brag to Cheng about this. Bill ordered his family sized meal and devoured it on the spot. The moment his hands were free, Bill phoned Cheng who said he had to have dinner with his dad. There was probably still time before Cheng had to start eating so Bill dialled Cheng's number.

"What?" Cheng answered.

"Guess what bitch, you won't believe this," Bill attempted to engage Cheng's curiosity.

"What? Did you sexually assault someone?" Cheng said sarcastically.

"Fuck you bitch, I didn't assualt someone because that person consented. I could tell she thought I was a Chad," Bill continued.

"Ugh..." Cheng sighed, "I told you not to proposition random people, I bet you did something retarded again. Why do you never listen to me?"

"Hold on, hold on idiot. So I was walking into McDonald's and I swear, this girl was giving me looks," Bill started embellishing his fantasy, "so

I went up to her and told her how beautiful she was. In fact, compared to all those fake ass cosmetic surgeon fucked up models out there, she was far better looking. Those fakes whores don't even come *close*."

"Ughh...." Cheng sighed even more heavily that second time, "you keep saying, 'Cheng you're right, you're always right' and I tell you repeatedly not to do that pick-up bullshit in real life because you're just opening yourself up for sexual assault allegations. Why the fuck do you never listen to me?"

"Alright, alright, Jesus fuck, it's different this time alright?" Bill tried to justify himself.

"Sounds like sexual assault to me. Men like us are too ugly to approach women. Any attempt will be considered sexual assault because we're creating an apprehension of imminent threat just by looking at them," Cheng stated in no unclear terms.

"Just listen goddamn it. She gave *me* her email, I didn't try to pick her up or even ask for her number. You know, maybe I'm a Chad. You know, Incels call Asian Chads 'Changs.' I'm a Chang now," Bill continued deluding himself.

"Don't do that you idiot. Stop trying to put yourself in prison. I'm almost at the restaurant, tell me more another time, bye bitch," Cheng said.

"Ohh I will, bye bitch," Bill said before hanging up.

Bill felt so elated that he felt half way normal. The elation he felt was insufficient to fully recover from the torment he endured that week but it gave him the energy to sit down and send the girl an email. Bill wrote about the same content he said to Sasha that day and elaborated on every point. *She* was the one who voluntarily provided Bill with her personal email. This was not harassment at all. If she did not want to be bothered, she could easily have just turned around and ignored Bill. Clearly, her actions demonstrated otherwise. Maybe it was not such a long shot after all, Bill convinced himself. Maybe he had a real chance with this girl.

* * *

On Monday, Bill presented to his third therapy session.

"How are you feeling today Bill?" Sue asked in a neutral tone.

"Uh... I wouldn't say I'm feeling better. Maybe a little better for a day or two? The problem is goddamn female patients. I'm not asking for perfection here, is showing just the bare minimum common courtesy too much to ask for?" Bill grumbled in displeasure.

"Hmmm, what did you think of the exercises?" Sue responded.

"It's not that they did nothing, I know what they're trying to get at. I get it. I know. But... It temporarily helped a little... the thing is, I do that sort of thinking all the damn time. Maybe not exactly in that way, but my friend Cheng, he always makes me reflect on my own actions. I can say with confidence that I always limit the harm to myself. Can anyone else make that claim? I don't think so," Bill pontificated.

"You must have some very good friends," Sue commented.

"My friends are all stable geniuses like me," Bill stated with conviction.

This time, he was tasked with completing psychological tests which involved looking at fictional scenarios described in words and pictures then answer questions like,

"The woman depicted in figure 1 is:
a) sad

b) angry

c) scared

d) excited"

Bill did not know what useless information the test would provide but at least he did not have to listen to "go take a holiday" again. Bill was forced up and about due to his therapy session but the moment he returned home, he was immediately lying down and did not get back up until it was time to work the next day. He was also given an excerpt from a book written by some random lawyer, Susan Cain. It was trash that Bill already knew.

Work was unrelenting as well. On Tuesday, a patient came in demanding to give a discount because the dentist down the road offered a cheaper deal.

"What can you do about the price?" he asked while showing a piece of paper listing the cheaper quote made down the road. Bill promptly dismissed him otherwise he would have committed murder then and there. Bill was a professional. He was not working at McDonald's. Even at McDonald's, customers did not walk up to the counter to ask, "what can you do about the price?" Nobody dared go to a heart surgeon and say, "the guy down the road said he'll do my transplant cheaper, what can you do about the price?" Yet that subhuman dared treat Bill like some bargain basement desperate?

* * *

Wednesday, another patient almost triggered a massacre. Bill was doing some emergency root canal treatment when the patient spontaneously asked,

"Are you sure you know what you're doing? Are you sure you know how to do this?"

Bill immediately felt murderous thoughts accompany his surging anger. Bill did not say or do anything to cast doubt on his own ability. He did not hesitate, he did not stutter. It was an open and shut case which left no room for doubt yet this cockroach *dared* accuse Bill of being incompetent. The *only* goddamn reason such a moron would think Bill was incompetent would be a delusion that dentists had to be elderly cadavers on the verge of retirement. Those cadavers had failing eyesight and arthritic hands and practised out of date dentistry that was downright dangerous. How easy it would have been to grab a surgical instrument and perform a lobotomy then and there.

Bill was confronted with problem patients day after day until Saturday when Andy stopped by to chat with Bill.

"Hi Bill, you doing OK these days? There are a couple things I wanted to mention before I head over to Kew. You had a patient who needed a crown prep right? Anna I think? She called in saying that she wanted to see someone else to finish the treatment and speak to the boss. I asked the girls to book in with me. What happened there?" Andy asked. Bill was already angry but just thinking about Anna made him feel homicidal rage again. If he were negligent, it would not have happened. If only he cared absolutely zero about quality and did a shit job that did not involve risking the patient intentionally shoving her tongue into danger's path. That was the last fucking time he would care about quality for such a suicidal patient.

"Uhh I was doing a crown prep but she kept pushing her tongue into the bur," Bill explained.

"Ah I see, you didn't write any notes so I wasn't sure if treatment was finished or not. So you're pretty much done with prepping right? I just have to take a mould and send it off, don't worry, I'll handle it," Andy reassured. "We should all be writing notes though," Andy added.

"Yeah the dental board says that but what are they gonna do? Nobody is going to come and investigate" Bill decried.

"Haha, that's true I guess. The second thing is, the girls forwarded me this strange email from someone we can't find on our system, but it was about how you met them at McDonald's?" Andy asked. Bill was feeling a sinking feeling. Maybe Cheng was right, Sasha was trouble after all.

"I'm not sure, what did it say?" Bill asked back.

"Come, I'll show you," Andy replied while leading Bill to the reception desk.

Andy asked one of the girls to open up the email so Bill could have a look. Sure enough, Sasha did provide her real email but never responded. This was why. She forwarded the email Bill sent to her and accused him of being a fake dentist because she could not find his name on the Dental Board website. That was because he was still registered as Jin-Woo Park and the fucking Dental Board required paying money to change his name. She laid bare everything Bill said as it was clearly written in his long email. However, the breach of privacy was not the worst part. It was one sentence which really triggered apprehension

"Bill's conduct was even more inappropriate as I am only 16 years old. I hope you investigate this person pretending to be a dentist, making inappropriate contact with the public and messing with your brand."

God. Fucking. Damn. It. Bill cursed internally. Bill just wanted to find this bitch and murder her entire family. She made a false allegation against him and was actively trying to destroy him simply because he told her she was beautiful. Incels were right. Females all needed to be exterminated. Bill reached his final epiphany. As a result of being actively hunted, Bill had no fucking choice but to hunt back. He fucking *needed* to kill. Bill decided. He would not rest until his enemies got their just deserts. Bill was prepared to die but that just meant his life was wasted. He *needed* these subhumans to die. They had better be prepared. "Don't mess with someone with nothing left to lose," Bill thought to himself.

"I think this girl is just straight up silly. We'll just add your old dental board name to our website profile. That should clear up any confusion. As long as she doesn't leave a misinformed review that would be fine. Is she a patient of yours Bill?" Andy asked.

"No sir," Bill replied with the style and vigour of a US Marine.

"What's wrong with chatting to women in public anyway? 16 is the legal age of consent in Victoria," Andy added.

"There are too many morons like these today. I hope she never comes to our clinic," Bill said while clenching his fists.

"I hope she stays away as well. I don't wanna deal with more crazies like her. I don't think any of us do. Anyways, hope you enjoy the rest of your day, try the CEREC, bye!" Andy said before rushing off.

Bill could barely contain himself. Andy only seemed to care about that subhuman leaving some bad review on their webpage. Terry was the fucking same. That moron was rendered mentally invalid whenever he received a bad review. On the other hand, it was not the review itself which infuriated Bill. It was the fact that there existed morons who were mentally enfeebled to the point where they thought complaining publicly was going to somehow fix their problem. These people came to *him* to look for a solution and what did they do? They completely fucking ignored everything Bill said, or perhaps intentionally and maliciously misinterpreted it. Then they tried to maliciously inflict as much harm as their impotent hands could inflict. It was good they did not come back to see him. There were too many sharp instruments in the clinic for Bill to restrain himself.

Bill walked out of the clinic onto Collins street. If he stayed in there, who knows? Would he be able to control himself? It felt like there were so many problems confronting Bill on a daily basis. He was becoming increasingly sensitive to provocation. Each time his anger flared up, it became increasingly uncontrollable and his fuse was becoming ever so slightly shorter with each episode. Some day, he might just go berserk. However, Bill had a fucking duty to keep it together so he could one day have his revenge. It was his sole mission now. The Count of Monte Cristo was able to enact revenge because he had money. In the end that moron grew soft hearted and regretted it but Bill was different. Oh if he had the Count's wealth, he would be fucking torturing these cockroaches right now. There was no limit to how cruel Bill's punishment could get and he would enjoy every last second of it. What Bill needed now more than ever was money. It was a means to an end.

Bill invited Cheng and Jason to meet up that afternoon, this time to share the McDonald's family sized value box. Bill explained the whole situation while they were eating, this time at the Melbourne Central McDonald's located in the second level food court. Of course Bill would not return to the scene of the crime. He may not be able to resist murdering that subhuman on the spot. She had better hope they never see each other again. Cheng was the first to respond.

"Why the hell do you never listen to me?" Cheng stated with frustration in his voice.

"I know, goddammit! I should have, I need you with me all the time now," Bill concurred.

"You say that shit all the time, 'Cheng, you're right, you're always right' but you never listen to me and just do your own shit all the time. I told you before, women don't find us attractive, propositioning them in public is a form of assault. Don't go practising your fucking pick-up bullshit on random people. This isn't university any more. And here you go shooting yourself in the foot again and again," Cheng continued.

"I know! Fuck! You should have been there to stop me!" Bill pleaded.

"Not only that you go and send her a fucking *email*? What the fuck were you thinking? You just dropped irrefutable proof, a digital footprint you can say, that you assaulted this girl," Cheng heaped on the damage.

"I know... Fuck! Jesus, Jesus, Jesus, goddamn mother fuck! I swear I will do as you say from now on. You're always right Cheng," Bill lamented.

"That bitch took it way too far, she's a piece of shit. If she wasn't interested, she could have just stopped there. She decided to conduct negligent research which was totally wrong about your qualifications and the law. 16 is the age of consent, but not if there's some supervisory role undertaken by the older party, including being a dentist..." Cheng mused. The blood drained from Bill's face.

"Oohhh no, don't gimme that shit, what the fuck you talkin' about?" Bill asked in fear.

"I don't think it counts because you're not her dentist and you're in no way accountable for her wellbeing. It's meant to stop teachers and guardians from having sex with 16 year olds. But who knows, there could be some wriggle room there for some lawyer to mess with," Cheng warned.

"God fucking damn it! She looked over 20, what the fuck! Why can't these damn females just tattoo their age on their foreheads? Fuck!" Bill decried.

"Lol, that's why that guy needs to have sex with grandmas in brothels, then he'll be safe," Jason sarcastically butted in on the conversation.

"Fuck you, if you were there, you wouldn't have been able to tell her age," Bill protested.

"Maybe you do have an age recognition problem, I mean just look at those scantily clad girls, they would be slammed into prison in China for wearing such outfits but they look 13," Cheng said while tilting his head towards a passing group of girls.

"Fuck, how the hell do they look 13? How are they allowed to dress like whores at that age? If that were my daughter I would fucking murder that subhuman," Bill retorted.

"That's the problem idiot, you must have some sort of problem. Not only do you have no self-control, you can't even tell what age they are, idiot," Cheng rebuked Bill.

"Fuck! What the fuck am I supposed to do? What if that bitch makes some false allegation to the police?" Bill said in a worrying tone.

"Most likely it will end up nowhere but the legal system is fucked up. There's a chance that some ideologically driven prosecutor wants you drawn and quartered because they don't like your face. You know, there's tonnes of lawyers doing no win no fee shit and free consultations. There's this place called 'Golden Fort legal' offering that shit close to our Carlton clinic," Cheng recommended.

Ever since Cheng mentioned even the remote possibility of legal repercussions, Bill could not stop thinking about it. Maybe he should hunt that bitch down and murder her. What risk was higher? Some legal system gone wrong or him disposing of the evidence by committing a real crime? Either way, Bill was not going to prison as an innocent man. Jason discussed with Cheng regarding his progress with computer programming. While Bill was still working, Jason never stopped studying. He seemed committed to never practising dentistry again. It was too late for Bill though. After the trio finished their meeting, Bill decided. He did need to speak to a lawyer.

Chapter 17

Beyond a reasonable doubt

Bill took up Cheng's advice and arrived at Golden Fort Legal. It was located in the tall building next to the Maserati dealer on the corner of Swanston and Victoria Streets. It was within walking distance of the clinic so Cheng was right, it was quite close. Bill stepped out from the elevator and walked up to their floor space."Golden Fort Legal: The gold standard in defense" was written on their door. The reception ushered Bill in and one of the junior solicitors conducted an interview with Bill. Bill discussed what happened that night and in the middle of the explanation, a much older man in a suit walked in. That was probably the head of the firm.

After Bill finished, the old man introduced himself,

"I didn't want to interrupt you, sorry. Greg," while he held out his hand for Bill to shake, "you've already been introduced to Krishna here. Mate, you gotta be more careful when dealing with women. I've had so many clients get into deep trouble simply because of talking to the wrong person."

"I know, my friend told me the same thing," Bill acknowledged.

"Sounds like he's a smart man. Let's look this girl up. Young people always have social media these days, let's try Facebook," Greg advised, "Sasha Kemp, K-E-M-P was it?"

"That's right sir," Bill confirmed.

"Is this her? There's a few results," Greg asked while showing Bill some results on Krishna's laptop. Bill looked and sure enough, the first result was unmistakably her.

"Hmmm... High school student, down in Caulfield Grammar... She does dress up like a tart doesn't she? You can't just assume their age. I have a daughter her age and I'd be very upset if I saw her posting photos like that online. What kind of parent would approve of this?" Greg said with a deeply scornful tone.

"But 16 is the age of consent isn't it? My friend said something about exceptions for teachers and doctors," Bill asked the question that most worried him.

"You're right. I think you're safe for the most part, you've never treated her as a dentist right?" Greg asked.

"No sir," Bill replied.

"Good, I doubt anything will happen from the criminal law side of things, however most people don't feel that way. Socially, it can become a serious problem if the public found out about it, even if it's legal. 16 is just too young. You need to be much more careful around women in the future," Greg chastised again.

Bill almost felt that same anger bubbling to the surface. He did not have to listen to this preachy garbage. He had to shut it down then and there otherwise someone was going to go out in a stretcher.

"Trust me, I am done with females. When I need a fuck, I'll just pay for a hooker," Bill explained eliciting a chuckle from Greg.

"That's prudent. This is what I think can happen. This girl might complain to the dental board or leave some sort of defamatory public message like a review on your Google page or something. Us lawyers may belong to a different profession but we share some pretty similar board regulations. I can tell you that for us lawyers, inappropriate public conduct can threaten our registration. If anything of that sort happens, give us a call. We also have a lot of experience dealing with defamation so if anything of that sort happens, you know who to call. Just in case there is any police involvement, here's my personal number, contact me immediately and don't say a bloody word to the cops without me. If you don't hear anything in the next few months, I think you're safe, so definitely be on your best behaviour until then," Greg advised while handing Bill his business card.

"Thanks," Bill replied. Greg and Krishna held out their hands as a final formality.

"Nice to meet you today, I hope for the best," Greg concluded.

"Nice to meet you too," Bill replied before the trio said their goodbyes.

Bill left feeling substantially reassured. Those lawyers behaved with professionalism Bill would have expected from any professional, medical or legal. The information Greg provided was incredibly helpful and succinct. If only dentists behaved like that, Bill lamented. Best of all, since there was no formal legal advice provided, they did not charge him any fees... yet. Bill hoped there was no hidden bill. Dentists loved stacking on hidden fees. As it was Monday, his therapy session was that afternoon. Getting both done was like killing two birds with one stone, Bill thought to himself.

Again, Bill gained nothing from the session. Some more tests were done and the psychologist recommended he read some books. A "reading list" so to speak. It included garbage like "How to win friends and influence people." The book was garbage because Bill wanted to be left the hell alone. Almost everyone he met was not worth the few joules of energy required to move his tongue in saying "hello." Bill had few friends as worthy as Cheng and Jason but aside from them, God could wipe out the rest of humanity with nuclear fire and Bill would only be happier. A more appropriate book would be "How to manipulate subhumans like a psychopathic politician and dispose of them like the trash they are." If only Hitler wrote a manual as part of "Mein Kampf," Bill mused.

Bill bought some McDonald's before returning home only to find more dirty dishes and an un-mopped bathroom. Bill sighed. That Jason never stopped being a slob. In light of today's relieving turn of events, Bill did not flare up at Jason but if that slob left a mess on a slightly worse day, there would be hell to pay. Bill even had time to shower before collapsing on the area of floor designated as a "bed." So the cycle repeated itself. Bill was forced to work more than he could tolerate only to return home too tired and angry to do anything but sleep. On his Mondays which were the only days he had off, he wasted either sleeping or speaking to the useless psychologist. Bill was forced through this torture for week after week until it all just blurred into this purgatory of suffering where each day rolled onto the next until the penultimate therapy session.

* * *

"I don't know why you keep giving me dating advice and telling me to read all about this garbage on making friends with women. I do not want to associate with those kind of people, don't you understand?" Bill decided to confront Sue about all her useless advice.

"Whether or not you decide to follow my advice is up to you. What I'm discussing works very well for most people," Sue attempted to console Bill.

"I'm not like most people, I keep trying to say this, what works for the *average* will not work for me. I don't just walk into work trying to do a half assed job. I'm compelled to strive for perfection otherwise I'm forced to act out in strange ways. Do you think I want to be this angry? Do you think I want to shower three times every day? But if I don't do those things, I'll explode or something," Bill said, raising his voice.

"You gotta take it easy, nobody is perfect," Sue argued.

"That's what normal people, untermensch do," Bill shot back, "are you familiar with Nietzsche's writings?"

"Not particularly so, what do you mean?" Sue asked.

"Nietzsche wrote about the Übermensch, or the 'over man,' the ideal human who never stops striving to be better every day. The Übermensch does not settle for mediocrity, no, no, no, he has the 'will to power,' a drive to always set his own unreachable goals. The advice you keep talkin' about works on untermensch, the 'normal' people out there who seek nothing but comfort. 'Take it easy' you say, that's what untermensch do. They don't care about goals or perfection, all they do is get away with the *absolute* minimum and take zero goddamn risks just so they can keep breathing and eating the next day. That's what the goddamn 'last man' does. I will *never* lower myself to that level. I just *can't*. My brain won't let me. Do you think Nietzsche could just wake up any day and pretend he forgot how to think? Look, had I been born one of them, I would have had a lot more fun living life. My life would be that much easier. I would just coast along, dancing through life, not even hesitating to just mindlessly accept and follow what society thinks a 'normal' life should be. But I am me, born with my obsessive compulsion and certain will. My brain won't let me live any other way. Why can't you understand that as a psychologist?" Bill pontificated with pride.

"Bill, it's good to have lofty goals, I think that's amazing, I really do, but it's hard to keep doing that every day. You told me that you don't take holidays at all. Your work should not come before your mental health, or even physical health," Sue said with a hint of concern.

"Oh my God, taking holidays doesn't work. If you're going to 'help' me, you need to give me better advice than that. Hobbies? Girlfriend? You gotta be kidding me. I've told you week after week, I've tried that. It. Doesn't. Work. The only thing that's come close to doing anything useful is the medication I'm taking and even that does not stop all these assholes from actively hunting me and ruining me. Just the other day, some female made a false allegation against me. She tried to make me lose my job by lying about how I'm a fake dentist and some sort of sexual predator," Bill explained.

"Tell me about what happened," Sue asked.

"Long story short, I was lining up at McDonald's. It was pretty full and I saw this attractive girl in line. All I did was say 'Hi' and tell her that she looked beautiful. I'm a bit of an expert on beauty cause I do cosmetic procedures,. They don't work by the way, on a beautiful girl they only make it worse and on someone ugly, they offer zero improvement. This girl didn't have any of that and she still was better looking than any of those fake fashion models I saw online. We exchanged emails and I repeated what I said to her in an email. Then she decides to forward my email to my *clinic* accusing me of being a fake dentist and that she was only 16. I don't know what the hell she was trying to imply by writing that but I know she's stupid enough to interpret the law to mean that I should go to jail for asking her out or something. I changed my name from my useless Korean name, Jin-Woo to William, lots of dentists do this by the way. There are a couple of other, *female* dentists at my clinic who also have different names on their dental board profiles from their clinic names. She didn't do *any* goddamn due diligence and just assumed I was some predator and tried to ruin my life. Why did she do that? It's not normal to go above and beyond to ruin someone's life for just a compliment. *You* talk on and on about how females are good for me and I need them, but that's totally, unilaterally, *one hundred percent* wrong. The evidence is *beyond. A. Reasonable. Doubt*," Bill explained while emphasising and prolonging the last four words. Bill then took out his phone and showed Sue the screenshot of the false allegation email.

"See this? I have evidence of everything that happened. Beyond a reasonable doubt," Bill repeated.

"Beyond a reasonable doubt?" Sue seemed perplexed.

"Remember our second session? What I said about my mom, sister and fake 'girlfriend?' There has not been a *single* female in my life that goes against this evidence. Females are *not* good for me and if I lived in a society where females did not exist. Like if the moment I was born, I was ripped from my mom and dumped in a country with zero females, my life would be *that. Much. Better*," Bill declared. Sue seemed silent.

"You know what pisses me off most? False allegations are the worst goddamn crimes someone can commit. Yet the legal system does nothing against false accusers. There are some 'laws' on it but they're almost never enforced. When I was in primary school, I still remember this incident because it was the first time a false allegation got me in such serious trouble. After school these kids who I wasn't really friends with took me to some toy shop. The ringleader stole some toy then the school found out about it and those cockroaches privately ratted on the teacher but lied their asses off. They started crying fake tears and pretended I pressured them into doing that and that I stole the toy. When the teacher kept me back after school, she kept slapping me until I confessed to something I did not even know about. I was *forced* to write a confession based on the fake story she *forced* on me. My dad beat my ass off after he found out but he wouldn't listen to me. Nobody would believe me. Then when I was in high school, I was caught installing some remote access software on a school computer. I was completely new to hacking and I wanted to test this tool I downloaded from some forum which was supposed to let me use the computer even if I'm at home. However, the head of school was some corrupt, racist asshole who blew it right out of proportion. He accused me of intentionally infecting the school computer with an "illegal software" and threatened to get the police involved like it was some federal crime. This was before 9/11, the internet was new and people experimented with all sorts of creative programs back then. You could have classified it as malware but there was nothing to suggest it was harmful. That piece of garbage then told me he would make sure I would never amount to anything. It was his mission to make sure I never got in to whatever university I wanted. He personally lowered some of my grades and wrote about how I was a menace to society on my records. This was the same piece of shit who decided to 'forgive' a white kid who was caught dealing drugs in the school. Back then, Canada was suffering a drug epidemic just like the US. Drug offences were felonies with mandatory sentences. That piece of shit head of school announced during one school assembly that this white kid made a terrible mistake but it shouldn't affect the rest of his life. He made up all this garbage about how this white kid had so much potential ahead of him and did not deserve to be remembered as a drug dealer. Do you believe that? He *personally* made sure to sabotage my future as much as he could. As you can see, despite what that cockroach did, I still made it here. For some reason, that same moron just pretends a drug dealer did nothing wrong. Did. Nothing. Wrong. Totally forgiven. The two kids who ended up in hospital? Fuck 'em. So you better believe it when I mean that false allegations are the worst crime, there is nothing anyone can say to counter that," Bill finally unleashed some of his deep seated hatred.

"That's very sad to hear, I'm sorry you went through that. Look at it from a positive perspective. What happened was really bad, but you've survived it and now you're an adult. As you said, you proved your head of school wrong. Look at where you are now," Sue attempted to mollify Bill.

She just did not get it. This was the moment where she was supposed to show some goddamn empathy and perhaps analyse the situation but that bitch just did not care. Instead, for the rest of the session, it was as if Sue totally ignored Bill's tragic past and pretended Bill never said anything about it. She continued issuing useless advice. Consequently, Bill walked out of the clinic even more frustrated than when he walked in. There was only one last session left for that bitch to redeem herself. Bill did not have high hopes. No matter what, he was going to make sure that bitch received a serving of true justice. If she pissed him off enough, he could report her to the psychologist's board. However, Bill also knew that his complaint would be ignored because he was a man.

* * *

Another weekly cycle of purgatory later, Bill presented for his last session of therapy. What was Bill expecting? Another disaster of course. However, this time Bill would offload all the pent up complaints he had been weathering. After all, he had spent about $1500 on these sessions just to confirm what he already knew - that therapy was complete bullshit. In fact, it made him feel worse. Sue began by giving out more useless advice as usual until Bill found a pause to start unloading.

"What is your diagnosis for me? So far all you've done is give me all this advice which isn't very helpful. Do you think I have autism?" Bill demanded.

"What makes you ask about autism in particular?" Sue asked.

"Some people I know have accused me of it. What is it that I have?" Bill repeated his demand.

"I don't think you have autism, at least not from the sessions we've had so far," Sue began her explanation.

"Hold on, what do you mean you don't 'think' I have it? Aren't you supposed to do some sorta test? Something better than the Myers Briggs garbage but properly validated," Bill interrupted.

"The diagnosis for autism takes a long time. It requires both testing and a lot of interaction with the patient. There is no one simple test we use although there are a combination of them we rely on. However, the Myers Briggs test is definitely not a valid test used in clinical psychology. I'll need to have some more sessions working with you to come up with an accurate diagnosis," Sue explained further.

Her pathetic excuses only served to further inflame Bill. Bill knew well beforehand she was about to pull some propaganda garbage about needing 'more sessions.' Psychologists exploited patients just like dentists and surgeons. They all wanted patients to keep coming back. Not for the benefit of the patient, but for the benefit of the practitioner. Anger clouded people's judgment but for some reason, it only gave Bill clarity of thought. After all, he was finally elucidating how Esmeralda exploited him. That fucking whore thought of Bill as some autistic retard well beneath *her* fucking social station. Bill thought she was "smart" because she was a university student. Fuck it, they let anyone study these days. Especially delusional whores who were low IQ enough to believe the Myers Briggs test had *any* scientific validity. With this conviction before him, Bill had to confront this bitch psychologist on everything.

"This is what I don't get about you people. A long time ago, autism was only a diagnosis given to very unstable patients who cannot function properly. Nowadays, you people introduced the 'spectrum' and everyone is 'on the spectrum.' Instead of trying to treat genuinely mentally ill people, you just create new mental illnesses so that everybody is mentally ill and whaddaya know, you guys start making more money," Bill asserted.

"No, that's not what psychology aims to -" Sue began to protest.

"YES IT IS! You can't pretend that this is 'helping people.' Oh my God, this is like dentistry all over again. My very smart friend once told me,'Without making a profit, the business won't be there the next time.' That means the beneficial health outcomes are unavoidably tied to protecting your bottom line. Autism is the best example of this. Mild autism, I see all these articles about normal adults, especially females, who somehow have 'undiagnosed' autism. They were perfectly functional people but all of a sudden they get a giant red 'DEFECTIVE' label branded on their foreheads. And the best part? There is no goddamn effective treatment but you people insist on these so called 'patients' coming back again and again for zero fucking benefit. If there's no effective treatment, then why do you keep bringing them back?" Bill continued, then adopted an extremely sarcastic tone for the next part, "Gosh, whaddaya know, it's somehow as if bringing them back gives you guys a steady income source. All of a sudden, society needs more psychologists. Just invent an illness, pretend that it's destroying society but at the same time, it's untreatable, but for some reason, all this demand for more psychologists just magically appears." Sue was silent.

"Every second person needs to see a psychologist these days. 'Oh you have depression, go see a therapist.' But why do they have depression? Why does society treat these people so badly? Society is filled with morons who make their own lives that much worse every day and in fact, make it ten times worse for ubermensch like me. You look at kids with ADHD. It used to be that the worst kids were diagnosed but nowadays, 'Oh that kid wasn't concentrating in class?' ADHD. That kid raised his voice? ADHD.' Then you put these kids on amphetatmines. Literally meth. Just what the fuck is wrong with this world? Broaden the diagnostic criteria, and voila, everyone has ADHD. Just keep widening the net. The more you widen it, the better your income and the more psychologists society needs. Isn't it surprising that talking never cured anyone? I'm supposed to believe that talking is for my benefit but the incentive structure behind psychotherapy *depends* on people coming back, not getting cured. I know that the word 'cure' is full of shit but at least try to treat the underlying factors, the actual cause of these problems. Yet, I'm supposed to sit here listening to 'techniques' which fool myself into thinking that everything is OK? Hell no! Everything you have told me so far, I have heard from my friends *for free*. I keep asking you to help me but you keep treating me like some low IQ moron who could just bury his head in the sand and say, 'all my problems are gone!' I know I need help. I do need help. But all this is *not goddamn helping*." After a brief pause, Sue finally responded, but not effectively.

"I understand you're upset Bill, but we are making progress. We've eliminated a lot of potential diagnoses and it's got you thinking this far. I know you're frustrated by a lot of what's happening in your life that's why making some of these changes will have a significant positive impact," Sue attempted to mollify Bill but clearly failed to address his concerns. She merely wanted to control the flow of conversation.

"God damn! We're not making progress!" Bill complained.

"We've covered so much ground and you're asking all the right questions. It's going to be a lifelong journey. Remember those exercises?" Sue asked.

"Yeah I remember them," Bill replied dismissively.

"Keep doing that each time you feel the way you do right now," Sue suggested.

"Oh my God... I told you before, I've been thinking in similar ways long before you told me. For your sake, my sake, everyone's sake, I actually did those exercises *properly*. Nobody can accuse me of not taking this seriously. I've gone along with everything you've said. I've read all the handouts you gave me and more. None of it helped long term. Maybe for a few minutes it made things slightly better but they do not do a God damn thing when confronted by the regular threats I face every day. I'm not the one being unreasonable. I can't just keep fooling myself every day when I'm being *actively* harmed by society," Bill delivered the final blow. Sue did not have a good response to that. She just repeated the same verbal diarrhoea she did every time.

For the rest of the session, Bill merely sat there defeated. He was never going to see a psychologist again. $1500 down the fucking drain and he felt much worse for it. It was demeaning to be treated the way he was. The bitch could not even be honest even at the very last moment. Not for one moment did Bill feel like his concerns were taken seriously. Not one moment did that bitch show any goddamn empathy. Not a single iota of useful advice was provided. It was a total wash. Bill furiously settled the account with the receptionist and exited the outdated clinic building. He was never returning to see that useless bitch again.

* * *

That final psychotherapy session left Bill with a foul taste in his mouth for the rest of the week. Bill had reported the failure to Cheng who agreed that it was useless. Cheng recommended Bill find another psychotherapist who was able to understand Bill better. Bill remained unconvinced. It would be best to look for a psychiatrist, male only, who also performed psychotherapy. Bill now had the firm conviction that females should not be allowed to be professionals. He would never place his life in the hands of a female professional. It did not matter if it were life or death, he would prefer to just die in that case. Work was equally as frustrating. Bill did not know if it was the frustration felt from his failed psychotherapy sessions or that life was just becoming increasingly difficult.

On Friday, Bill found himself filing away at a filling he did only a week ago. The patient returned with tears saying that it was giving her excruciating pain. Clinical testing and x-rays were normal, just for some reason touching one particular point on the filling triggered some sort of sharp pain. Bill dreaded these cases. It may have been a microscopic deficiency in the deepest part of the filling, necessitating removal of the whole thing and doing it from scratch. Bill hated patients crying in his office. His Carlton books were actually becoming half filled these days so Bill hated to spend over an hour of strenuous labour re-doing his recent work for free. However, he had no goddamn choice. He spent 90 minutes painstakingly removing micron by micron, carefully avoiding damaging more of the remaining fragile tooth. It was already a fairly compromised molar.

Only that re-doing the filling did not fix the problem. The patient came back crying the next day chasing him down at his Collins Street practice. She had the gall to complain about Bill spending over an hour trying to do the goddamn job properly, for free, and was crying yet again just to frustrate Bill further. Ultimately, she did not end up replacing the filling again only to book in with the boss the next week. Then in the afternoon, Bill tried to use the CEREC machine Andy kept on reminding him to use every goddamn time. Except it broke down and could not manufacture the veneers that he wanted to make. Bill had neither the time nor the hand skills to sculpt perfect teeth better than a micron accurate machine. Bill gritted his teeth and fought against the headache storm caused by his anger. He gave the patient a deal she could not refuse - to have the veneers made off site for the same price.

Bill trusted that piece of shit machine for just one day and it decided to screw him over. This was not fucking normal. No clinic should operate like this. Bill was *forced* to give that girl a deal she could not refuse because if he did not, there would be yet another fucking useless copmlaint he had to waste time trying to resolve. Or a growing liability. Why did dentistry have to be like this? Bill repeatedly told the reception team not to book these cosmetic cases with him because he was so fed up dealing with these types of demanding patients. Yet, look at the fucking situation now, Bill thought. He quoted only about $1500 for the veneers because the CEREC machine reduced costs massively. However, sending the job off site increased Bill's own costs to about the same price. He stood to make $0 out of the whole mess and to have over 3 hours of his life wasted. However, Bill's troubles did not end there.

Bill's head was pounding from his headache as he walked into his apartment. He was immediately assaulted by Jason's negligence. Dirty dishes were piled up on the countertop. The reason for that was obvious - the strainer was draining above the sink filled with recently cooked pasta. Fuck. The blazing inferno that was raging inside of Bill only intensified further. He was this close to committing murder, Bill thought. He had no fuse left to deal with this slobbery. How could this fucking slob cook with all these dirty dishes around him? If Bill switched places with Jason, he would be *forced* to cook food in a dirty pot covered in grime. His vision would be assaulted by the grime each time he looked. He would not be able to concentrate even for one second. It would have been enough to drive Bill insane. Yet that subhuman slob just accepted it as a normal way of life.

Bill clenched his fists and approached the bin. He was holding a pile of junk mail. As much as he detested receiving this unsolicited harassment, if he did not clear it out, then there would be no room for important mail. Once Bill reached the bin, he spotted an empty tub of Reese's Pieces ice cream. Bill purchased that while it was on a special promotion to treat himself. Bill did not mind sharing some food, after all he bought several tubs, but that slob ate a whole fucking box in one day? One day!? It was then that the gears suddenly clicked together in Bill's mind.

They were out of detergent so Jason could not clean the dishes even if he tried. Any sane person would have walked a few fucking minutes to go buy some but instead that slob decided to down an entire tub of fat and sugar. The kind of stereotype Hollywood depicted for the whole world to laugh at. That was right, Bill thought, Jason reached slob levels only seen in cinema. Bill did not give a shit about Jason's false identity. In Jason's own words, the debt collectors did nothing more than try to phone him up. There was no "APB", or a manhunt, for him. In fact,

Jason never gave a shit appearing in public either. It was therefore no surprise that the pasta was left in the strainer untouched. That slob did not care that there were no dishes to eat from. He was intentionally waiting for Bill to come back and clean the dishes. When he got bored of waiting, that slob decided to down the tub of ice cream.

The inferno exploded into a nuclear furnace. His head felt like it could explode. His arterioles felt as if they were about to burst. His heart was thumping like a jackhammer in his chest and his fists were clenched white, almost to the point of drawing blood.

"Hey hey! What the fuck is this?" Bill coldly growled in a guttural voice. Jason was in his room being silent. After a short while, Jason opened the door and stepped out.

"What?" Jason replied matter of factly, either completely oblivious or being intentionally provocative. It could have been both, Bill thought.

"LOOK AT THIS SHIT! HOW THE FUCK DO YOU COOK WITH DIRTY DISHES AROUND?" Bill had no control any more. He thought of Jason as a friend but this was beyond the pale. He could not keep it in any longer.

"What are you raging at me for? We're out of detergent," Jason apathetically returned fire.

"Did it not occur to you to step outside to buy something we both need?" Bill continued with his inquisition.

"I thought you might pick it up on your way back," Jason protested, with some hesitation. It probably truly did not occur to him. This was the problem living with a slob. The issues were minor but at some point, it would inevitably reach breaking point. Jason probably never imagined such a "minor" issue for him would turn into a shouting match.

"HOW THE FUCK DO YOU COME UP WITH THAT THOUGHT? YOU EXPECT ME TO KEEP EVERYTHING STOCKED UP AROUND HERE? INSTEAD OF DRAGGING YOUR LAZY ASS OUTSIDE, YOU WOULD RATHER EAT AN ENTIRE TUB OF ICE CREAM?" Bill did not want to do this. Bill was *forced* into this position. He had no fucking choice. Jason merely shook his head and retreated into his room while shutting the door behind him. Pathetic.

* * *

Bill limped his way back to his apartment while his head was pounding yet again. Bill had a premonition. For the past two weeks, Jason managed to reliably clean the bowls but Bill just *knew* Jason was going to fuck something up again. Bill *knew* it would happen. It was inevitable. Hence, for two weeks, Bill returned from work with trepidation. He was one trigger away from committing murder and part of Bill was actually afraid of what he was capable of doing. Bill grasped the door handle and opened the door... Preliminary analysis appeared fine, Bill thought. Bill silently sighed with relief. He did not want to feel like this but he could not help it. It made Bill uncomfortable but he knew very soon he would have to tell Jason to move out. It was either him or Bill. Their time together was running out.

Jason's door was closed as usual. Bill dropped his belongings into his room and then started preparing to take his triple shower. Then it happened. It definitely caught Bill off guard so maybe that slightly softened the blow. There was dirty water all over the bathroom floor. FUCK! Bill's heart started pounding like a bass drum yet again. Bill clenched his hands so tight that both of his arms were spasming involuntarily. Every work day was hell and now Bill had to arrive home to this? This?! Bill was not asking for perfection. He did not want to wade through the dirty water from Jason's body. Was it beyond that fucking slob just to show some basic human decency?

"Oh my God, Jason, what the fuck?" Bill asked loudly. There was no response. Bill marched up to Jason's door and loudly knocked. A few seconds later Jason opened the door and exasperatedly asked, "What do you mean what?"

"Oh my god, Jesus look at the fucking bathroom floor," Bill pointed menacingly at the puddle of water.

"It's just the bathroom, it will dry up later," Jason retorted.

"How the fuck do you live like that? What is wrong with you?" Bill was almost shouting.

"Fine, if you want me to mop the floor you have to tell me," Jason gave in.

"That's not what this is about," Bill rolled his eyes, "each time I tell you to do something, something else pops up. Wiping the goddamn floor is so fucking obvious. How do you live like this?"

"You never told me to mop the floor," Jason continued arguing.

"YOU SHOULDN'T NEED SOMEONE TO TELL YOU! Goddamn it!" Bill was shouting this time. Jason merely shook his head and retreated back into his room, closing the door.

Bill took his triple shower completely fed up. Bill knew this was the end. He and Jason were through. Bill had warned Jason that he had compulsions. Keeping the apartment neat and tidy in the way Bill wanted was essential otherwise he would be driven insane. It was true that Bill did not warn Jason specifically to mop the bathroom floor after showering but that should have been obvious. It should have been self-explanatory since Bill repeatedly warned about the dishes. Jason could not even do that despite the warnings. Bill could not live like this. He was shocked at how angry he was. If he lost control, Bill worried about what he would do to Jason. Bill worried about Jason's health and safety every fucking day because he knew that Jason would do something again.

If Jason somehow miraculously bowed and kowtowed to Bill and started to live like a normal person, Jason would be the one suffering every day. Jason was a slob so living like a normal person would be unbearable torture. Jason would be the one exploding at Bill. The two of them would be living in a tinderbox environment. Bill could not live in this kind of environment. There were no compromises. There were no alternatives.

Bill worked his way through the unappealing leftover pasta Jason prepared. As he ate, Bill prepared his speech. He was going to give Jason an ultimatum. Bill placed his bowl in the sink then knocked on Jason's door again.

"What?" Jason remarked after he opened his door.

"Jason, I respect you, I think you're one hell of a smart guy and I hate to say this, but I have no choice," Bill started his proposition. Jason seemed to almost roll his eyes in frustration. "What happened today, what happened 2 weeks ago, this kinda stuff, it can't keep happening. As you know, my fuse just keeps getting shorter and shorter. I don't blame you. You're a slob. You can't help acting the way you do. Some day, you're gonna do something that will set me off. I don't know what it is. Maybe you'll forget to take out the trash. Maybe you'll leave a cupboard door open. I don't know. Whatever happens, I'm gonna explode much worse. Much worse than today."

"Ughh... Just tell me what to do. I know you told me you had compulsions, but you never tell me what to do," Jason complained.

"Look... Look, look. I don't want to have to say this, but I do. I can tell you what to do, it will be OK for a while but think about it. You're not gonna be comfortable. It's like I'm forcing you to be uncomfortable. Eventually, you're going to start going back to the way you were or something new is gonna bother me. Either way, there is only one option. You gotta move out Jason. I say this as a friend. I'm trying to help you. This is the best option. It can't be me that moves out. I've been paying for this place all this time. You haven't given me your share. I'm the one that keeps this place clean and tidy for the inspections. If you're by yourself, you need some shitty ass apartment where you can be as much of a slob as you want," Bill finally said it. He needed to get that off his chest.

"No, why should I move out? It's easy to pass an inspection," Jason determinedly disagreed.

"It's not just that. Oh my God. Jesus, Jesus, Jesus," Bill had enough and walked away. He was going to need Cheng's help.

The following morning, Bill phoned Cheng.

"I need you to hold an arbitration or mediation session for me and Jason," Bill told a half truth to Cheng. Bill liked to use legal terminology around Cheng. But the truth was, there was no arbitration or mediation. The decision had already been made. Bill needed to say his last goodbyes to Jason and he needed Cheng as an independent witness in case the situation devolved into a mess.

"What happened this time?" Cheng asked.

"Just do this for me, I need you to, you owe me bitch," Bill was playing seriously.

"Fine whatever, did your gay marriage with Jason finally hit a divorce?" Cheng conceded while he asked mockingly.

"Something like that. I'll explain the details tomorrow. How about we meet at McDonald's here in South Yarra tomorrow after work?" Bill offered and so Bill texted Jason instead of talking to him to schedule the meeting.

* * *

"This better be quick cause I need to drive out to the country soon. Hotels don't stay open after 10pm," Cheng urged the trio as they sat down at the South Yarra McDonald's.

"Alright, alright. Jason, I have to say this, I think you're a really smart guy, you're one hell of a master troll and you're a genius at all this computer science shit, but I have to put an end to this. I warned you about my compulsions before but you still don't clean the dishes or mop the floor. Up uh uh uh" Bill started stuttering to stop Jason or Cheng from interrupting him, "let me finish, let me finish. I don't like confrontation," Bill continued while eliciting a scoff from Cheng, "I don't like confrontation, I'm not a confrontational guy. Look, you see this over and over again. Couples, dorm mates, any sort of situation where people live together. There are always going to be arguments and those arguments are always about the same shit every fucking day. There's an argument and then the parties pretend to come to a compromise. I thought about this, and it seems to me that each time there is an argument, people slowly build resentment towards one another. Let me explain. You see, we each have a set of habits, a particular way of living we are used to, and prefer. When people make a series of compromises, it usually ends up with everyone being dissatisfied, and worn-out. I am only telling you something I learned and tested in my day to day dealings with my patients. People tend to think making compromises is a positive thing, because their low IQ makes them think that it is being considerate, but it is anything but. It only appears as such. Making one compromise won't be much, but having to make one compromise after another will start to feel uncomfortable as if our preferred way of living is being restricted by one another. There will always be this nagging feeling of discomfort of having to cater to one another, and it will only get worse the more compromises we have to make. I told you I have a compulsion with cleanliness and tidiness, and I have come to accept that it isn't something I can change. Even if you were to compromise and cater to my preference, slowly over time, you'll likely go back to your preferred ways. This is just how people are.

People prefer to live according to what they are used to, and you put two people with different preferences together, they'll find themselves having to make compromise after compromise and each time they do, bit by bit, they'll build resentment towards one another because they'll feel like they can't live their lives according to the way they want to. Look, Jason I value you for all the positive impact you had in my life, and I don't know how much value I have provided to you, but I don't ever want to fight like we did, I don't want us to get any worse than how we are now. I don't want us to be of negative value to each other, and I just cannot see how we can prevent that while living under the same roof. It can only get worse, and that isn't good for either one of us. There is only one option, I have to move out."

"I thought this was supposed to be mediation or arbitration. Normally arbitration is when someone is meant to decide who's right or wrong. Mediation is when the parties each tell their side in order to come to an agreeable outcome," Cheng said, after realising Bill's dishonesty.

"This is mediation, I'm telling my side of the story, and I'm moving out," Bill twisted Cheng's words.

"Uhh... what? You don't need me here at all..." Cheng started trailing.

"I need you here goddamn it! You're mediating a discussion. Goddamn it, this isn't some legal case. There is no better term that comes to mind. Enough of your law bullshit, I can't do this by myself. I need Jason to understand what the fuck I'm talking about without it getting into a shouting match. Nobody can understand me better than you, Cheng," Bill declared.

"So you 'need' me but so far all you've done is rant about your compulsions," Cheng pointed out.

"Look, look, look," Bill fired in quick succession only to be interrupted by Jason.

"What. I know you told me about your compulsions but this is just about mopping the floor, which you never told me to do. I can compromise and just mop the floor. You just have to tell me what you want to do," Jason defended himself.

"You're a smart guy Jason but people CANNOT change their nature. This is just fact. Beyond a reasonable doubt. You'll be very uncomfortable living with me and I will be uncomfortable living with you. Even if you do mop the floor, which you won't do forever, there will be something else that will piss me off and after that something else will pop up. I'm not doing this out of hate. How long have we known each other? I would like to think that we all know each other better than our fake ass parents who we have known for almost thirty fuckin' years. You know as well as I do that I have always limited the harm to myself. Unlike all those subhumans out there, when have I ever set out to harm anyone? You have to understand, I'm not trying to fuck you over. This isn't about fucking each other over. I'm losing money too. I don't want to move out of the Führerbunker but I have no goddamn choice. Believe me, I've been thinking for months and months. I've thought of every fucking possibility. I have come up with absolutely zero," Bill pontificated while air signing a zero symbol with his fingers.

"There are zero possible solutions. Nothing will work. Listen, I don't hate you Jason. I understand you. You will always end up falling back to your preferred way of living. It's not your fault. Maybe you were born like that, maybe quitting work made you worse. I. Don't. Know. But what I do know, is that you will never fuckin' change and neither will I. There are no "second chances," no goddamn third, fourth, millionth chances. I can't do that. I know you know deep down, you can't do that either. You know that my fuse is getting shorter. Each time we get into an argument, and there will ALWAYS be fucking arguments, one *hundred* percent, my fuse is going to get shorter... and shorter... and shorter. Next time it won't be me talking smack about you not mopping the floor. Next time, one of us is gonna fuckin' die. So BELIEVE ME, I have no fucking choice. This is the only possible way. There's nothing you can say, nothing Cheng can say, no possible idea or solution even Jesus can think of. There is. No. Way. Believe me when I say I don't want to do this. I have no goddamn choice," Bill stated with conviction.

"So there's zero chance of you two getting back together?" Cheng asked.

"Absolutely zero," Bill declared again for emphasis.

"I initially thought we could share costs and even help each other get out of dentistry," Jason added.

"Yeah, much good that has been. Bill, can you even program a single line without syntax errors?" Cheng asked.

"Oh my God, don't remind me. That was because I wasn't in the right frame of mind! Fuck! It's all because of Esmeralda! Fuck that bitch!" Bill angrily muttered.

"Well if you're dead set then you're getting everything you wanted out of this 'mediation' session but Jason has gotten nothing. At least apologise so he walks away with something, even if it's symbolic," Cheng decided to declare a judgment.

"Woah, woah, what do you mean apologise? Did you just hear what I said? If you understand, then I see no reason to apologise. I understand Jason, and I explained myself well enough for you both to understand. Like I said, neither of us is at fault. We just happen to be ingrained with ways of living that are mutually incompatible, so I am withdrawing before things get worse. I got nothing to apologise for," Bill argued.

"No, I'm not trying to say you need to actually apologise. You called me in to "mediate" and it's completely normal for the winning party to just offer a fake apology," Cheng explained.

"I will not *EVER* apologise when I have nothing to apologise for. I thought we all agreed upon this already. Why do you even say that shit?" Bill retorted immediately.

"Come on, Jason got nothing out of it. Our insurer tells us to say 'sorry' all the time. It's meaningless, stupid etcetera, etcetera, but it's just a gesture, better than offering nothing," Cheng

"Oh my God, how is that better than offering nothing? It's WORSE. What difference would an apology make? Whether I apologize or not, it doesn't change the outcome. This isn't a matter of whose fault it is, it's just a matter of our different ways of life. Apologising for the sake of apologising is low IQ shit. It's a fucking insult. Oh, 'I'm sorry," Bill imitated a sarcastic primary schooler,

" 'Wow I feel so much better because I heard that fucking word,' " Bill imitated in another sarcastic voice.

"It doesn't fucking do anything! It's useless to fucking 'apologise' without following it up with action. I'm not doing anything wrong. I am doing Jason a favour. This is the only possible solution. I'm doing what's best for everyone here. I do not owe him an apology because I have nothing to apologise for."

"My indemnity insurer has this as their first recommendation every time something goes wrong. It's not an admission of liability, it's like a fake apology. You're just saying a word to make people feel better. Most people are low IQ compared to us. Just say it," Cheng goaded, however that merely caused Bill to have a mental meltdown.

"FUCK YOU AND YOUR LAW BULLSHIT! I WILL NOT FUCKING APOLOGISE! YOU'RE EITHER WITH ME OR AGAINST ME! FUCK YOU GODDAMN IT! FUCK! I WILL NOT APOLOGISE WHEN I HAVE NOTHING TO APOLOGISE FOR! I AM NOT GOING TO LIE AND PRETEND TO APOLOGISE SO SOMEONE

CAN FEEL BETTER!" Bill screamed loud enough to capture everyone's attention in the restaurant.

"Calm down, lawyers do this all the time like, "I'm sorry this happened" without expressing your fault in any way -" Cheng tried to explain before being cut off.

"FUCK YOU! I THOUGHT YOU WERE MY FRIEND! NOW YOU'RE TELLING ME TO APOLOGISE FOR NO FUCKING REASON? FUCK YOU, YOU'RE JUST LIKE THE REST OF THEM! WE ARE THROUGH!" Bill continued screaming before stomping out of the Mcdonald's restaurant.

Chapter 18

The Russian affair

The failed negotiations between the trio left a sour taste. Bill barely spoke a word to anyone other than dental patients for the next month. It took that long to find a new apartment. It just so happened someone was vacating in the same apartment building. Unfortunately for Bill, he needed Cheng to help him move the heavy furniture across. Bill sighed, he had to reconcile with Cheng. Bill had to call Cheng.

"Look who comes crawling back," Cheng mockingly answered.

"Guess who," Bill greeted.

"Was all that really worth it over some bullshit fake apology?" Cheng asked. Bill sighed.

"Fine, I was hell angry that day, you know what happened in the clinic so I got too angry but I will NOT apologise," Bill reiterated.

"OK fine then, I won't ask you to apologise in the future," Cheng continued.

Bill eventually organised for Cheng to help him move with the incentive of getting paid real money. Fortunately, the move was simple enough as the apartments were so close to each other. However, life remained agonising for Bill. He had lost another friend and was on rocky ground with Cheng after that tantrum. However, the one solace was that he was living by himself. Bill acknowledged that this was the only possible way to live. At least that was what Bill told himself. In reality, Bill was experimenting with Tinder. Bill did a "world tour" through Tinder location settings and swiped a billion, trillion, quintillion times resulting in hours of wasted interactions. It felt like a rigged game for the 80% of men women found repulsive. Bill now understood that finding a suitable female in a western country was impossible. The females were all the same. They were corrupt and actively hunted men like him every day. Foreign females however...

Bill looked at his smartphone before he stepped into his apartment building. It was 8:05pm Sunday 6th November 2016. Bill was tired. Life had taken away every last hope he had. He fumbled for his apartment key fob as his right hand lethargically crept towards the door handle. With a familiar click, the door unlocked and it took every ounce of strength his arm could muster to push the door open. His arm ached. The dark thoughts were swirling in his mind, coalescing in an infinite pit of despair. How long could he keep this up for? Bill had found himself in yet another dispute with a patient. Then his assistant infuriatingly defended the inane drivel of the patient afterwards. It took every last atom of control he had left in him to not explode. It was a miracle he even made it back here in one piece.

Bill's life was a mess. There was nothing he could do to stop himself from sleeping 18 hours a day. He barely had the strength to finish a day's work without his psychiatric drugs. Bill could not help but blame his life on females, who he hated. There was only one thing he hated more. He could not stop thinking about them. While walking towards the elevator, Bill reflected on Cheng's words, Bill was a dog that could not stop eating shit. No matter what Bill did, he could not stop himself from pursuing his own worst enemies, the female race. Today was no different. Bill could start feeling his legs about to give out underneath him as he stepped out of the elevator and limped towards his door. He lethargically turned his key and collapsed in his room as the door closed by itself.

How much longer can I keep going like this? Bill thought again. One day he could literally faint while at work and not be able to get up again. As he removed his iPhone from his pocket, he noticed his alternate Tinder phone flashing on the carpet where he left it this morning. As if injected with a shot of adrenaline, Bill's heart rate suddenly doubled. Within an instant, his self-loathing was washed away. Bill excitedly unlocked the phone to reveal an immensely relieving message. His Russian Tinder match Nadia messaged him back. It was like an instant happy pill. Her soothing words were like honey to his ears. "Yes! Let's meet in Korea!" Those magic words illuminated the dark room and the dark recesses of Bill's mind. Bill was no longer tired.

This was his last chance to ascend. Nadia was beautiful, smart and everything he ever wanted. She was also the *only* one who agreed to meeting up. He had done everything he possibly could in the past and was not able to convince a woman to willingly engage in a relationship. However, here she was, not voicing a single hint of opposition. She was the one. This was going to be Bill's fairytale romance. What followed was a flurry of texts organising the expensive trip which was to come. In the dark recesses of Bill's mind, Cheng's voice of conscience was echoing amidst Bill's turbulent thoughts to no avail. Bill had made his mind up long ago. He was going to Korea.

* * *

As Bill sat in the airport lounge, he noticed the bright rays of sunlight shining through the floor to ceiling windows. It was the end of spring, almost summer so it was normal for the sun to be this bright. However, there was a special quality of brightness in Bill's life today that did not come from the sun. The brightness came from an inner fire that was shining like a beacon. That flame was called hope. Nadia embodied all of Bill's hopes and dreams. She was like a star shining in the dark masses festering in Bill's mind glowing brighter and brighter with every web-cam session. At last, they were going to actually meet in person. Bill's excitement was insurmountable. He arrived 3 hours early just to make sure everything would go perfectly.

Unfortunately however, there was nothing in the airport to calm his fidgeting. Instinctively, Bill reached for his phone. If he could not talk to Nadia, he could at least talk to Cheng. Cheng was number 1 on his dialling list. Cheng's name and avatar immediately popped up the moment Bill unlocked his phone. Without hesitation, Bill tapped to dial his friend.

"What you idiot?", Cheng's familiar voice sounded through the speaker with no small hint of irritation.

"Come on man, why you gotta do that? I'm your friend." Bill said, as was their usual greeting routine.

"You dog that can't stop eating shit, I told you again and again this was a terrible idea. Just give up and go play some games properly." Cheng's voice again came through with a great hint of irritation this time.

"I will, I will, but I'm too goddamn tired!" Bill lied. There was a truthful element to that statement, he was indeed too tired to do anything important, like fixing up his life. However, he had plenty of energy to book the flight tickets, hotel tickets and musical concert tickets all lined up for this romantic getaway. In contrast to the verbal diarrhoea ejecting from his mouth, Bill was indeed more energetic than ever. Nadia was his source of energy. He was running on Nadia euphoria.

"I hope you tell me everything day by day so that I can write a proper obituary about your pathetic exploits. Then the world can see just how pathetic you are. Best case scenario is that you buy this vapid girl some $5000 handbags and shoes for sex whereas you can skip that Gucci/LV and jump straight to sex here in Melbourne for less than a tenth of that much," Cheng berated Bill mercilessly.

"But this is different!" Bill protested, "She paid for her own tickets and we're going to sleep in the same room with one bed", Bill lied again. She did not pay for her tickets. In fact, Bill paid for the most expensive Russian airline to transport Nadia to Korea. His Nadia euphoria was an illusion, but Bill did not want to think about that. He needed to believe in this fairytale narrative. If Cheng found out the truth, his vicious mocking would become too brutal for Bill to cope.

"She'll still end up stealing your kidneys. I hope you have travel insurance to pay for your dialysis, bitch," Cheng continued with his barrage of mocking, "bye bitch, enjoy your delusion."

Cheng had hung up. What Bill yearned for more than anything was for women to see him for the champion he was. Indeed, Bill thought to himself, he took on the United States, Canada, Poland and now Australia. He studied one of the most difficult university courses available. It would take the intellect of a dozen deadbeat arts graduates combined to accomplish what he managed. He was a champion, an elite specimen of the human race. Yet all these subhuman, vapid airheads could see was a short man. He may as well have been in a wheelchair. They were the true subhumans but in their eyes, he was subhuman.

Bill willfully diverted his thoughts from that dark trajectory. It was so easy to slip into that familiar territory. However, with Nadia waiting for him, those days were in the past. Nadia was stunningly beautiful and she wanted him. Cheng had repeatedly stated that these Russian women were concerned about citizenship. Once that was guaranteed, they would divorce and successfully pursue any man they wanted in

Australia. Bill was smart. He would not end up like those men. Cheng had also repeatedly stated that Bill was a poor judge of character. Bill could not help but disagree. Even if Cheng's words were factually accurate, Bill did not feel like that was the truth. Bill innately felt like he was a brilliant judge of character and there was nothing Cheng could say to change that. He was going to prove Cheng wrong.

Bill clutched onto his Tinder phone gently, like it was a proxy for Nadia. He caressed it lovingly in eager anticipation for their meeting. Just one more day! One more day and he could meet the love of his life. His mind fell into a trance contemplating the busy schedule he had meticulously planned over the past week. He never stopped planning be it at home or at work. Bill's thoughts drifted from one scenario to another. It was going to be perfect. It was going to be straight out of Disney's textbook. Just him and Nadia holding hands, walking into the sunset with the main theme from Beauty and the Beast playing through his head. Then the announcement came,

"... is now ready to board, passengers with special needs and priority seating please board."

A brief spark of anger flashed in Bill's mind. There were women and children given priority again. Here was an example of society just showering people with privilege simply by the circumstances of their birth. Where was his priority seating? He was disabled in the eyes of women all around the world. Being short and being Asian was like a synergistic combination of revulsion for these Western women. Where was his wheelchair? If these women saw him as such a disabled sewer rat, where was his special treatment? Bill was going to board last like the others. He had all the disadvantages in life but was given zero assistance. Then there were these women born with every advantage conceivable having privilege dumped on them like a tsunami.

Nadia was going to make it all better. He was no longer going to remain a sewer rat. He was going to ascend. The flame of Nadia could not be extinguished by these trivialities. Bill calmed himself down and waited for his turn. This was the first leg of his journey and it was the longest. By the time he seated himself on his designated seat, the lethargy started coming back to him. Bill ignored the over-played safety video and briefing and closed his eyes. He was going to have a rest and catch up on some missed sleep. Maybe after sleeping he might watch a movie or two. In just one more day he would be meeting Nadia.

When Bill finally stepped off the plane, his first task was to connect to a WiFi source. What if Nadia had messaged him? She must have messaged him by now. After all, in a couple of hours, she should be stepping off her plane at the same airport. The time had finally come. It was truly happening. This was what Bill thought until his phone finally connected and received Nadia's text - her flight was delayed by over three hours. This was not going to plan. It was as if he were struck by lightning. Bill was paralysed. His heart dropped and his hopes vanished. This was the first fracture in the fairytale facade. Bill had dealt with many literal fractures in his career. When one fracture appeared, more would follow.

Then more bad news followed. "I will meet you at the hotel", Nadia texted. But why? Bill asked himself. He furiously texted back demanding to understand why. "I need time to get ready. I look like a zombie," Nadia responded. This was absurd. Not only was she incredibly late, that part was not her fault, but she also insisted on trivialities like make-up. Bill much preferred women not to wear make-up. Why did these beautiful women want to disfigure themselves with toxic chemicals plastered across their faces? Cheng occasionally laughed at Bill using foundation himself, the hypocrisy was lost on Bill however. If this girl truly looked like a "zombie" without make-up, then this trip was a lost cause. His disappointment was brewing.

The world had gone silent. All Bill could think about was the dreadful thought of his plans falling apart. They were probably going to miss the romantic river cruise he meticulously planned for this afternoon.

During the stopover, he could not help repeatedly imagining their first meeting. Just like in a Disney movie, they would catch each other's eyes across the cavernous terminal. It would be love at first sight. Time would slow to a standstill and the hustle and bustle of the thousands of other passengers around them would disappear into a blur like a camera lens dilating its aperture. At that moment, the world itself would become a platform for the two lovers. There was nothing but Bill and Nadia. Then they would spend their precious first moments introducing each other floating on the serene lake.

Bill was once a Christian. However, after seeing the endless streams of wheelchair-bound, terminally ill children being pushed into their final resting rooms in the Royal Children's Hospital, Bill had finally realised that belief in such a fiendishly sick and twisted god made no sense. Outwardly, Bill attempted to project confidence in his atheism, but he was agnostic at best. His Christian upbringing still lingered, tainting his thoughts. This was another one of those moments. Was it the actions of that same sadistic god punishing him again? This first crack in the fairytale facade was about to send Bill off the precipice and into a fit of panic. He had to sit down.

Eyeing the nearest seat, Bill placed his luggage on the ground first and then sat himself on the seat. He hesitantly responded to the text while masking a sense of desperation. "Don't worry, we can still make the cruise," he wrote, followed by, "Catch the bus, it will get you directly to the hotel." Hopefully Nadia would check her messages and receive those texts as soon as possible. Bill somehow knew that she would not be able to make it in time for the cruise. With a heavy heart, Bill lifted himself from the seat and started walking out of the airport.

Being back at Seoul triggered many unhappy memories from Bill's childhood. Having an unhappy childhood and troubled upbringing was so cliche among Asians these days, Bill thought. However, Bill's suffering was especially severe. The moment he was able to travel by himself, Bill departed from home and started boarding school in Canada. He could not get away from his parents fast enough. Despite all that had happened, why was Bill going to visit his parents again? He really was a dog that could not stop eating shit. He was desperate to secure at least some of his inheritance. After all, his parents were multi-millionaires in terms of their combined liquid and non-liquid assets. There was no level of humiliation low enough to prevent Bill from begging for his share of that prize.

When Bill was working, the only thing that was able to calm him down was leaving his stressful workplace and going for a walk. As he walked out of the airport and towards the bus, eventually the panic started melting away. After all, he was still going to meet Nadia! Sure, there would be no romantic eye interlocking from one end of an airport terminal to the other, but meeting at the hotel would be just about as good. Even if they missed the river cruise, there was still plenty of time at the art exhibit and sunset skyscraper tour to flesh out their romantic confessions. Life was unpredictable as it always had been. This was what made the fairytale more exciting.

The hotel receptionist was friendly enough, his room was ready and Bill set off in the direction of the elevator as soon as the girl handed him the key cards. The facilities were quite reasonable for the price. The same facilities in Melbourne would have cost twice as much. Nadia was still going to be at least two hours away, maybe more. For now, there was nothing more Bill could do other than wait. Nonetheless, Bill was a meticulous man. Before meeting any woman, Bill would triple shower, shave, perfume and suit-up. He only had two hours to prepare. If he actually performed all of those preparations properly, it may not even be enough time.

Unsurprisingly, Nadia was more than just a couple of hours away. When she finally landed, she responded back. However, what Bill read did not ease his anxiety. There was less than an hour to go before it would be too late to attend the river cruise. Knowing this was the case, Nadia insisted that she take the subway. The subway was technically speaking faster. However, Bill was also aware that the Seoul subway was extremely complex and a tourist had virtually no chance of navigating it. Bill did not approve of Nadia riding the subway, but he did relent that it was indeed faster. He would not let anger cloud his judgement, so he did not argue. Instead, Nadia decided to execute her plan then successfully lost her way due to the complex line changes. She was going to be even more late than initially thought.

Again, Bill had no choice but to wait. Anger and frustration were slowly creeping in, but he would not let them take over. Bill knew that this was going to happen so when it actually did, he felt less perturbed by its occurrence. After all, there was little he could do to contain his excitement. With all preparations ready, the last thing to do was to rehearse what to say during the day. Although Cheng disagreed, Bill thought of himself as an excellent social manipulator. He had prepared both mentally and in writing several questions and responses for convincing Nadia he was the one for her. The more he rehearsed, the more confident he felt that Nadia was going to fall for him. What could go wrong?

Bill had finally decided to sit in the lobby in eager anticipation. Where was she? She was supposed to arrive at the airport by 11am but it was already approaching 4pm. By now, the river cruise was departing without them. There was no chance. It was difficult to keep his anxiety in check. What helped were the messages Nadia was sending. They fed him hope that she would be walking through the doors. After what felt like an eternity, there she was. Whatever fantasies Bill had imagined were dispelled in an instant. The first thing that struck his eyes was not Nadia's eyes but her extensive make-up. She appeared superficially attractive, but who knew what lay underneath? She was extensively covered up in thick clothing. It was a very cold winter after all. Who knew what lay underneath that? Her figure could have fit the mould of anything between a super-model to a beached whale.

Those insecurities were flashing through his mind as Bill nonetheless eagerly moved forward to embrace her. Both of them said, "Hi, good to finally meet you!" as they embraced. Nadia hesitantly said, "I have been looking... forward to meet... you!" She continued with great difficulty in her thick Russian accent, "I'm sorry for being late... I got lost... trains too many. I really want to go on river cruise... Is there time?"

Bill consolingly responded, "Don't worry, just have a rest, we've got an art exhibition to attend soon. Let's go to the room." He was not happy since the boat cruise set him back about $40 but that was nothing major in the grand scheme of things.

"My room is ready?" Nadia responded.

"A single room as we said," returned Bill with a creeping sense of suspicion.

"No, I need my own room." Nadia said, with no small sense of indignation.

Bill immediately felt the urge to erupt in anger. However, he managed to control himself. Women never seemed to appear comfortable around him no matter how hard he tried. Everyone would tell him to just smile, just be friendly, just do this, just do that, just appease, appease and appease. No matter how hard he tried, it never worked. This girl was responding the same way all women seemed to treat him. Why was she playing him like a violin? He paid for everything yet she was still making unexpected demands. Bill thought to himself, I can't afford to screw this up. Just keep smiling.

"We are just friends... we just met... I want to get to know you first, I want you to know me," Nadia quickly replied to control the damage. Bill's brief flare of anger must have triggered some fear, but he managed to recover.

"OK, I'll go talk to the hotel," Bill responded, desperately attempting to hide his anger. The costs of the trip were already mounting and here Nadia was making demands the moment they met. This was yet another fracture in Bill's fairytale facade. His heart was sinking fast but he did not believe it was over yet. Sure, this girl did agree to a single room but perhaps her English was so poor she did not understand what he really meant. Come to think of it, it was indeed insane for someone who he had only met online to agree to sleep in the same bed. Her English skills were demonstrably poor so it was probably just her English skills at fault.Yep, had to be that, Bill surmised.

Bill was invested beyond the point of no return both financially and emotionally. He lied to Cheng, and he lied to himself. To the ordinary person observing Bill, this surely would have rung alarm bells however Bill forced himself back into his fairytale realm. It did not matter that there were fractures appearing. He was going to keep pursuing this path no matter what because it was his last chance to ascend. Anything could be repaired with duct tape so Bill metaphorically held his facade intact with the strongest and largest supply of duct tape in existence. It was going to be okay, Bill told himself.

Unfortunately, the hotel did not have adjacent rooms available and Nadia's room was far away. Bill's fantasies about romantic Hollywood movies where people in adjacent hotel rooms separated by a thin wall were crushed. No matter, he had to push on.

"I've got some presents for you," Bill said as he led Nadia towards his room.

"Me too!" Nadia replied enthusiastically.

Bill had actually recycled some gifts his colleagues had given him. He planned to purchase some more gifts in Korea for her. Nadia then offered Bill some books which were thankfully translated into English for him. Then she needed to get ready for their evening activities.

More alarm bells should have rung. This girl clearly required high maintenance. Bill sat patiently in his hotel room hoping she would be ready any second but it took well over an hour before that time came. No matter how hard he tried to suppress his thoughts, small tendrils of doubt were creeping into his mind. Nadia had repeatedly delayed meeting him despite being so late. Why did she do this? Was the risk of Bill seeing her without make-up even worse than the risk of disrupting his plans and enraging him? There was an even more dreaded explanation Bill dared not contemplate, that Nadia was not interested in him at all. That she did not even care one iota about his pathetic plans or him as a person in general. To a regular observer, this latter explanation would have started becoming increasingly obvious. However, Bill was under a compulsion spell. He had no control over himself or his delusions. The fairytale was more important than life itself.

After what seemed an eternity, Nadia was finally ready. The first part of their plan was to have dinner. Bill last left Seoul almost a decade ago but much was the same. As he walked around the concrete jungle, he realised that he must have been in Melbourne too long. Melbourne had a few tall buildings confined to the central business district whereas here in Seoul there was no end to the skyscrapers. There were also advertisements everywhere. Not a single advertisement appealed to Bill. Bill was naturally drawn to technology so of course advertisements targeting women were of no appeal. However, the advertisements for gadgets were equally repulsive.

Samsung and Apple were grossly over-represented with their expensive junk. Bill contemptuously scoffed at the fools who paid for Apple products. Those who bought Samsung equivalents were equally as pathetic. Back home in Melbourne, he was about to pay $100 for a colleague's iPhone because the colleague was willing to pay over ten times that for a new phone merely to stay in fashion, not that the upgrade would have made any difference. It seemed like consumer culture had corrupted the soul of Seoul like a cancer consuming its host from the inside out. Once upon a time, Koreans took pride in their traditional culture. Gone were the temples and monuments, in with the skyscrapers and shopping malls. Then there were the shoebox apartments.

Bill really had been away from Korea for too long. Although he also lived in a shoebox apartment in Melbourne, almost everyone he knew lived in expansive houses. Real houses with actual gardens and lawns. The kind of living space his former countrymen would not even dream of having. Yet his narrow minded former countrymen took pride in paying what amounted to millions of Australian dollars to live in shoeboxes smaller than his friend Cheng's lounge room. It took them a lifetime to pay for a prison cell Cheng would have used to stash furniture he did not even need. The icing on the cake was the way people treated Gangnam, the "pride" of South Korea. The morons even erected a hand monument as a homage to that shitty song. Yet, people were spitting revolting yellow sputum onto the streets in broad daylight. Litter covered the ground in cockroach infested lumps.

Did these morons not realise how pathetic they were? Yet as his countrymen passed him one by one, they appeared so conceited, so arrogant. Did they not know their position in life? Even the slums of Tokyo were far cleaner than this dump. It was all over the internet. Bill was the one earning more and living a lifestyle beyond these subhumans' imaginations. Bill was never comfortable with rats failing to acknowledge their inferiority. It was hard for someone like Bill to resist the urge to start murdering then and there. Good thing Nadia was present.

Bill, who was acting like a loose cannon liability through the streets of Seoul, accompanied Nadia until they finally arrived at a "modern art" exhibit. This was Bill's idea of a good time but he was not sure if it would work for Nadia. If she were anything like the women Bill had encountered in his life, she would probably want to dance, sing, party and get inebriated. Seoul was well known worldwide for having a vibrant night time scene with a combination of clubs and karaoke. However, Bill detested that subhuman behaviour. He avoided it like the plague. It seemed like Nadia fought hard to fight back the urge to yawn at the unsightly hunks of trash on display, but eventually failed.

"Let's go to the skyscraper," Bill said, noticing her tedium, "I was hoping that this museum would be like the Museum of Modern Art in New York, turns out it's not. We'll make it just in time to see the sunset though." Bill thought that anyone would enjoy watching the sunset. However, since his new partner did not seem so enthusiastic about the not so interesting art exhibit, he was not sure. Hence, he decided to cut it short and the pair headed towards the famous "63 building", the skyscraper Bill selected to watch the sun set. The way the light changed into a darker orange almost red hue as it inexorably drifted under the horizon was a marvel to admire. It seemed flawless to Bill. Nadia did not seem very enthusiastic. The smile on her face appeared as fake as her makeup.

As they left the skyscraper, they returned to the now electronically illuminated streets of Seoul to head for a restaurant. It turned out that the Korean Barbeque they decided on was perfectly acceptable. The food was decent and because Bill paid for it, it tasted even better. They had some trivial conversation about how the day went. Nadia was full of praise for Bill and the night he planned. However, Bill was too starstruck to observe her carefully. There was a subtle edge of insincerity to Nadia's remarks. After dinner, it was Bill's turn to navigate them back to the hotel. Unfortunately Bill still lost himself in the subway network and ended up needing to walk the final fifteen minutes or so back to the hotel.

Bill was eager to keep talking so Nadia proceeded to follow him into his hotel room. Then Bill kissed her on the lips. Cheng warned Bill about being so direct but he was pulling out all the stops this time. Thankfully, Nadia did not seem stunned. It was a short kiss barely a few seconds in length. Then Nadia quickly turned her head aside and swept around to Bill's ear. She whispered, "don't be too fast, OK?" Bill was ecstatic. The first thing he did was to phone Cheng and brag about it.

"Guess how it was?" Bill said to Cheng.

"I bet it was shit," Cheng replied with a hint of irritation.

"No, shut up. I got to kiss her on the lips! It was the best!" Bill replied.

"Don't fool yourself you dog that can't stop eating shit," Cheng berated Bill, "You could just as easily have paid a Melbourne hooker for that."

"Oh my god... it's not the same. I'm not paying her," Bill defended himself.

"You're not paying her directly but she's getting a $3000 holiday for fucking free. I'd have to be as dumb as dog shit to believe she paid for her own ticket," Cheng mocked.

"It's not free, she better fucking put out," Bill declared.

"Then why don't you fuck a whore in Korea? Are there Russians in Korea?" Cheng asked.

"Now that you mention it, for some reason, there's a hell of a lot of Russian hookers in Korea. I don't know why. Korea has gone to hell. You can walk along the streets, and there are hell posters of underground brothels plastered everywhere in broad fuckin' daylight," Bill wistfully lamented about his fallen motherland.

"You should have stayed back and played some games," Cheng chastised again.

"I'm too goddamn tired! I don't have time to do that!" Bill lied in response. The hours he spent waiting on Nadia could have easily been spent on gaming.

"I can't believe you would blow thousands on this bullshit trip. I told you it's not worth paying a woman for her time and here you are setting your money on fire. Bye bitch," Cheng responded with a great hint of irritation in his voice.

Cheng was just jealous. Cheng had never even been on a date other than having Chinese princesses being matched up by his father. He did not know what he was talking about. Bill was the one in the right, he thought to himself. Tomorrow would be even better. Bill planned on visiting a vast theme park and then go ice skating. Bill had watched endless figure skating videos. Women were over-represented in that sport so Bill had the notion that all women must innately enjoy ice-skating. However, to begin the day properly, they needed to be up early. If they arrived late at the theme park, all the good rides would have queues stretching longer than an Apple store releasing an iPhone. Surely, Nadia would not let him down this time would she?

She definitely did. It was 12pm before Nadia was ready to leave for the theme park. Bill had hoped they would enter the theme park by 10am the absolute latest. By the time they arrived, the interminable queues did indeed crush Bill's remaining hopes of embarking on the most popular rides. It just happened that the most popular rides were the most thrilling, such as the purported largest in-door roller coaster in the world. Bill was still eager to enjoy some of the more enjoyable rides. As they explored the park, Bill pointed to one ride after another which had an acceptable queue. To all of these, Nadia rejected with paltry reasons including, "too dangerous!" or "it will mess up my hair!"

As a last resort, Bill requested that she attend the star attraction of the entire theme park, the imitation blimp which was firmly attached to the roof of the theme park. To Bill, this was meant to mark the end of their park visit. It would be the culmination of a thrilling and action packed adventure in contrast to the quiet day yesterday. They would hover over all the attractions they would have rode earlier while embracing each other and their shared experiences. However, Nadia said no. The only ride she consented to was a spinning wheel with some boxes attached via chains. It was meant to be for children who were not tall enough for the proper rides. Bill was not pleased.

Bill had such high hopes. A day of adventure and fun turned out to be several boring hours of watching other people enjoy themselves. Nadia trampled on Bill's precious plans again. And again, Bill questioned why she would do this but accepted Nadia's inane responses. Not for one moment did Bill accept the high likelihood that this woman was not attracted to him in the slightest and would rather stare at wet paint than look at his face.

After finally exiting the theme park, Bill invited Nadia to a shopping mall food court larger than anything in Melbourne. The saying where there was too much available choice for one to make a choice was applicable here. There was pretty much every kind of food available. There were a plethora of standard Korean restaurants, as to be expected, and there were shops selling food from all around the world. American, Chinese, Japanese and even Australian foods were represented here. The ultimate result was anticlimactic, it turned out to be generic chicken.

Fortunately for the "couple", Bill agreed that riding a taxi was better than losing themselves in the subway again. The next part of the "date" was ice-skating. Bill had heard from his friend Cheng that a Chinese princess eagerly asked Cheng to take her ice skating once. Cheng had even said that she enjoyed it. Bill did not interpret this information correctly. Women were all prisoners to their one and the same biological urges so Bill decided to over-generalise that all women wanted to ice-skate. Bill conveniently ignored Cheng's comments about how the princess asked for Cheng's help because all of her female friends were afraid of ice-skating and would never go with her. After Bill surprised Nadia with the ice rink, she did not seem happy at all.

When Nadia landed on the ice, she immediately fell over. Nadia desperately clutched the wall for dear life. Her entire body was visibly shaking. Bill tried to help her up and with a combined effort, Nadia managed to upright herself. She clutched onto the wall as she gingerly waded her way, centimetre by centimetre along the ice rink. One lap around the rink was the most Nadia could handle. Bill tried his best to help but it was nowhere near enough.

None of what happened today pleased Bill. Nadia had crushed his hopes again and again. It was like nothing he could do was ever able to please her. He really tried. Bill sincerely believed that Nadia should have enjoyed everything he had planned. Instead, she just seemed to be aloof the whole time and simply refused to participate. The ordinary observer would have realised by now that nothing Bill could do could change the fact that Nadia was just not interested in him. Bill unfortunately was oblivious and felt the need to keep pushing.

Both parties departed the ice rink in low spirits and uncomfortable silence. They decided to risk taking public transport again but since Bill never learned from his mistakes, they became lost yet again. This time Nadia could not handle it any more. They needed to walk fifteen minutes from the wrong station and Nadia protested, "Let's call cab... I really need bathroom, now."

"The hotel is just round the corner," Bill said, "I know where we are, trust me, just 5 more minutes."

"Please, I really need bathroom now," Nadia insisted.

"I know but trust me, we're going to be there immediately. Plus, the cab will take too long and they won't drive us only a few hundred metres," Bill insisted back.

"No! I need cab!" Nadia almost shouted this time, visibly shaken.

"Oh my god," Bill said under his breath, hoping Nadia would not hear him. He started walking ahead towards the intersection. "Just have a look, trust me, see?" Bill gestured as he talked.

"Please," Nadia pleaded this time. Her lips were trembling as if it was taking every ounce of strength she had to stop her entire body from shaking.

"Come on, I see the hotel from here, I promise, just five minutes," Bill said again. With some effort, Nadia managed to calm herself and mutter,

"OK."

The next day started and ended in disaster. Bill was a poor planner in addition to his delusions and it resulted in the farcical couple needing to shift hotels. The main problem was that he did not inform Nadia she needed to vacate by 11am. So when the time came, Bill needed to request that the hotel staff message her room to wake her up. Then it took an additional hour before she was able to meet Bill in the lobby. Then came the bill Bill needed to pay. Nadia had incurred over $50AUD equivalent in mini-bar fees. Apparently a can of soft drink alone was about $12. Bill was infuriated but he still needed to pay.

He forced this all upon himself and did not for a moment allow his rational judgment to prevail. Cheng knew and even Bill himself understood logically that the actual chance of success was low. However, Bill was governed purely by his emotions when it came to women and to this date, he had not made a single decision about women based on logic. They say that love was purely emotional. However, Bill interpreted this to an extreme extent so much so that feelings of lust should override every other consideration including the impact it had on his work and welfare. Bill cursed himself under his breath for his poor judgment and took out his debit card. It was onto the next hotel from here.

After revisiting the food court and a visit to Dunkin' Donuts, it was time for the main event. Bill planned to take them to a classical music concert. Here, Bill was going to seal the deal. In his infantile delusions, Bill believed that Nadia's emotions would come to a tumultuous climax.

He specifically chose Russian composers without understanding that most Russian people paid not one iota of attention to their own musical culture. He planned to have Nadia swoon over Rachmaninoff's second symphony. It was indeed a hauntingly beautiful composition full of lush symphonic textures and exquisite melodies. To Bill, the scene would play out like the opera scene in the movie Pretty Woman. With Nadia swooning, Bill would bring her back to the hotel and issue her with his prepared speeches and love letter. Then he could finally consummate the relationship without the assistance of Gucci and Louis Vuitton.

What Bill did not anticipate was reality. Bill paid no attention to Nadia's words. He did not read between the lines. Classical music was a niche interest and only those with a radical interest would attend a classical music concert in person. Nadia suggested but never explicitly confirmed she actually enjoyed classical music. This should have been a clear and resounding sign that Nadia was no radical classical music lover. Yet Bill insisted. Cheng warned Bill that Prokofiev was a niche composer even among musicians. Nobody but devout enthusiasts actually wanted to listen to his music. Yet Bill inisted. The warning signs were everywhere but Bill paid zero attention. In fact, Bill never paid attention to reality. Once he made up his mind, his decisions were final. It was questionable why Bill even bothered asking for other people's opinions.

Suffice to say, none of Bill's pathetic, infantile delusions came to fruition that night. It was an absolute disaster. The Prokofiev 1st violin concerto was a cacophony of unbearable, jarring screeches. It was clear that Nadia was not enjoying it. Bill realised his mistake but there was nothing he could do. What he really wanted to listen to was the Rachmaninoff second symphony. This piece was special to him and Esmeralda seemed to enjoy it. He hoped more than anything that Nadia would also share his appreciation of this work. The opposite happened.

Bill expectantly observed Nadia from time to time only to find her vacantly looking away or staring at her phone. She was not interested in the slightest. Occasionally when Bill surreptitiously turned to check, Nadia was taking selfies with duck faces. Bill could not help but feel his frustration mounting. She fucking pretended that she attended classical music performances and knew how to behave. She had sent photos of her visiting Rachamaninoff Hall, Moscow. That bitch was probably taking selfies and making duck faces there too. He wanted to enjoy this, but he could not. This was a disaster.

By the time the ninety minute, intermission withheld concert had finished, both parties had had enough. Nadia suddenly surprised Bill with a request,

"Would you like... drink alcohol with me and friend?" she asked.

"You have a friend here?" Bill replied with genuine surprise.

"Yes, he's good friend... from university," Nadia explained.

"Go by yourself, I'm going back to the hotel," Bill responded unamused.

"But I don't want... go myself," Nadia said again.

"Alright then don't go!" Bill retaliated.

"OK. Let's go back... hotel," Nadia replied dejectedly, "I no go."

Bill's fairytale facade was not merely fractured, it was shattered into powder. It was beginning to dawn on Bill just how much of a fool he was. He started adding up the costs. He was about to reach $6000 soon. All this for an infantile delusion. Every step of the way, Nadia crushed his hopes and dreams. Every step of the way she resisted his advances. There was no more doubt in Bill's mind, Nadia had no interest in him. How could it possibly get any worse?

The situation was about to worsen. The next day began with Nadia being late, again. Bill may have been blind to everything up until this point but even he was able to pick up on just how poorly rested Nadia was. He immediately realised that she must have gone behind his back to see her friend. Again Bill paid the bill for the hotel rooms and the trainwreck couple decided to walk towards their favourite restaurant, Dunkin' Donuts. This time, Bill was on a warpath. He was going to confront her head on. Bill felt exploited, cheated, deceived. Despite Cheng fervently urging him to abandon this madness, he persisted and that was why this hurt even more.

"You went to see your friend didn't you?" Bill asked in the most caustic tone he could muster. This was an interrogation.

"Yes," Nadia muttered. At this point she had completely given up and there was no need to put on an act any more. She was not wearing make-up. Bill thought she looked dishevelled, just like a zombie in fact.

"Why did you do that? You promised me you weren't going to do that," Bill continued.

"We both adult... I can do what I want. We just talked, my friend good person," Nadia tried to explain. Nadia continued, "I invited you, you didn't come." However, Bill would accept none of that.

"That's because I don't drink, don't you understand?!" Bill replied furiously.Bill continued with another furious retort, "I bet he went back with you to your hotel room didn't he?"

"What?" Nadia replied feeling slighted, "I'm not prostitute, my friend good person. We just had chat! Not long, I come back to hotel very quick."

"But why are you so tired? You were up all night!" Bill retorted again.

"Why do you think me so bad?" Nadia responded sounding genuinely hurt.

At this point, Bill's nostrils were flared and sweat was pouring down his face. This fucking whore fucked her boyfriend on his dime. Who knows, maybe she was fucking a whole fraternity. She was a whore after all, no matter how much she pretended not to be. Working and making money on his dime. His heartbeats were ringing inside his head and his hands had a vice-like grip on the table. The rage that was swirling inside his head was reaching a crescendo. He could barely contain himself, but he had to. Just as he was about to erupt into a tantrum, the injured, effeminate sounds that Nadia was making instilled in him no trifling amount of guilt.

"Look, I'm sorry," Bill said, "I don't mean it that way. I find it difficult trusting women. My sister, my mother, my first "girlfriend", they all betrayed me. Why don't I buy a ticket for you and you can go back to Moscow now?" Bill asked.

"No, I can't do that!" Nadia responded suddenly, shocked by Bill's proposal.

"This didn't work out and I'm seeing my parents next. You don't have to follow me," Bill continued.

"But I can't go back now! My mum worry, she see me back too early, know something wrong!" Nadia responded.

Bill simply looked back at her. He was stuck. He could not simply force her to go. Yet if she did not, what would his parents think? Was it because she would get beaten by her pimp if she failed to fuck enough Korean men? He hated his parents for forcing on him fake as hell traditional Korean values. Despite his opposition to them, those entrenched values still engendered a sense of guilt and foreboding at that thought. Flights back to Moscow were not expensive. The extra hotel fees may indeed exceed the cost of a flight. Fuck it.

"OK, fine. We're going to be late for the high speed train," Bill begrudgingly muttered, accepting his defeat.

As they were leaving, Bill inspected his phone. They had just spent the past three hours in Dunkin Donuts. Unsurprisingly, Nadia seemed quite distressed and started smoking a cigarette the moment they exited the store.

"Hey! You told me you didn't smoke!" Bill exclaimed while harshly staring at her in disappointment and resignation.

"But I can't stop when I'm stressed," Nadia explained in a cold tone.

Without another word, Bill simply walked off. He could not tolerate the smell of cigarettes. All his United States college roommates did was smoke tobacco and marijuana. They treated him contemptuously like an outsider and mocked him for being different. Any mention of recreational drugs triggered in Bill his religious zeal for the war on drugs. He felt physical revulsion at the sight of this woman smoking.

As Bill expected, they were late for the train and the trip to Busan was three hours long. During peak times the train was full and there was no choice but to stand for the whole way on a long haul journey with very few stops. This was exactly what Bill wanted to avoid. Bill was caught between a rock and a hard place. He was livid with rage. Nadia had lied to him from the outset. She was a typical drunken party girl who was feeling the ravages of time forcing her to nail down an unfortunate cuck like him to emigrate out of her third world shit hole. She had crafted a personality profile just to allure him. The reality was dumbfoundingly different. Without her make-up, she was below average and Bill could not at any point determine if she was in a healthy weight range or not. She drank and smoked and had zero appreciation of the arts, especially those of her own country's proud culture.

Everything about this woman turned out exactly like the typical air-headed whores that Bill detested. The kind of subhuman scum Bill contemptuously encountered in his everyday life in Melbourne. He had spent close to $6000 because he thought this would be different. Instead, he wasted the money just so he could be in physical proximity to one of these degenerates all the way in his detested home country. He left Korea for a reason and being here only fueled his rage. Not only that, Nadia exploited him just so she could "work" at Bill's expense. This was the penultimate level of "cuckery" that Bill feared, directly below divorce court rape.

The torturous train ride finally ended and Bill was in for a nasty surprise. The moment the couple of degenerates entered their Busan hotel, Bill's parents were lying in wait. Bill's heart almost skipped a beat. He was certain that his parents agreed to meet up at their shoebox apartment later. Bill did the best he could to keep his distance from Nadia and pretend they did not know each other. It was too obvious. His parents knew.

During the planning stages, it was actually Nadia who pushed Bill towards his parents. Bill declared he would never see his parents again after arriving in Australia but here he was. His traumatic childhood was too heavily ingrained into his soul and no matter what, that fragment always dragged him back. Additionally, Bill wanted his parents' money. When Bill's parents saw him, their eyes lit up. They knew they failed as parents and they knew Bill did not want to see them again. He had not met them face to face for close to 10 years. Bill's father stood up and embraced him, as did his mother. Despite Bill's feelings towards them, they did miss Bill.

"Who was that girl?" Bill's mother asked, in Korean.

"I don't know, just a stranger," Bill lied. However, it was not a convincing lie. His parents knew that Bill would not visit Korea just to see them. By adding two and two together, the circumstantial evidence demonstrated Bill's true intentions beyond a reasonable doubt. For now, Bill's parents ignored the transgression and invited him to dinner, at their expense of course.

His parents were indeed glad to see him after so long. They talked and talked about so many trivial matters until finally it became more serious. Bill's father said in Korean,

"Look son, be wary of women. They are not to be trusted. Don't you ever think about getting married. If you do, we are done. Marriage ruined my life and it will ruin yours." Despite clearly hearing these words, Bill's mother fervently nodded in agreement. "Having children was our sin and I'm sorry that you are paying the price," Bill's father continued. When Bill's father talked about sin, it was very biblical because his parents were Korean Christian fundamentalists.

"Yes, I understand," Bill obediently nodded.

"We missed you after such a long time. Please come back to see us more often," Bill's mother said.

"Yes mother," Bill lied in response.

"Son, there's something we need to tell you before it's too late. We are getting older and will be retiring soon. Now that you've become independent, we cannot be prouder. After we retire, me and your mother are thinking of moving to the countryside and selling off our city apartment. We will be tithing the majority of our holdings to the Church before we die," Bill's dad declared.

This was the worst possible outcome. The church was an abhorrent international super-corporation with the Korean branch being especially corrupt. Bill heard it directly from other church members that they smuggled money overseas by exploiting fake missionary work. In fact, Bill knew of several "ministers" who were miraculously reformed crime lords showering the press with fake repentance upon finishing their commuted sentences. Bill needed that money for himself. Bill did not know how much longer he could practise dentistry. In fact, he could suddenly get sued tomorrow and that would be the fucking end of it. Bill tried to argue.

"Father, are you sure? There are many people, including me, who need the money much more than the church," Bill pleaded.

"My decision is final. It is easier for a camel to fit through a needle than for a rich man to enter the kingdom of God. Son, you have a solid future ahead of you. You will not die a poor man. The Church needs this money more. As your father, I will always support you if you run into trouble. I will also help you study medicine. Come back to Korea, study at Yonsei University. Otherwise, you must forge your own path through life. Read the Bible and you will understand," Bill's father continued with his ideological drivel.

FUCK! Bill screamed internally. Coming to Busan was a total fucking mistake. Bill wanted more than ever to just strangle his family here and now. Years of trauma and violence had cast a spell on Bill. If anyone else angered him this much he probably would have committed homicide on the spot but Bill could not even move. He could only weakly mutter a faint,

"Yes father." It was absolute torture. How was Bill able to enrol at Yonsei University? His Korean language skills were not nearly sufficient to pass even their first application test. Bill's heart sank to its lowest depths. This was a total wash. Failure upon failure, doom upon doom. Perhaps it was better for Bill to try one of those Korean suicide bridges that night.

* * *

On the final day, Bill still needed to take a train back to Seoul and for whatever reason his mother decided to follow him. Nadia surprisingly left her hotel room on time. As a consequence, she looked like a zombie yet again. Bill's mother also saw Nadia in her dishevelled state and asked Bill,

"You don't have to keep pretending, I know you came to Korea to meet this girl, but why did you choose someone so ugly?" Bill had no proper response. Without her make-up on, Nadia was incredibly plain and forgettable. Bill would not have paid $6000 even if he were guaranteed to have sex with that thing which stood there.

After Bill's mum insisted on riding on the train with him, Bill begrudgingly and uncomfortably sat beside his mother while Nadia found her own seat away from them. Bill never forgave his mother. To make their journey even more awkward, Bill decided to aggressively confront his mother about cheating with that hypocritical and malevolent priest. She had denied it at the time and the priest treated Bill with contempt. Bill loathed and detested that much older lecherous animal for enticing his young, weak and pathetic mother. That priest acted as though he was indeed holier than thou but in fact had a heart of pure darkness. Who knows, he probably molested children and filmed it as well.

She finally confessed. It happened almost twenty years ago and there was no sense pretending any more. The situation was obvious. Bill's father was short and terrible with women. He worked hard and became wealthy enough to attract Bill's mother who was very manipulative and reasonably attractive. However, like typical women, she was not satisfied with her husband's height disability. She needed a real man. At least his mother cared enough for Bill to recognise the same faults of the father. She told Bill to take her actions into account and not repeat his father's mistakes like a vicious cycle. There was all the reason in the world to be concerned considering Bill paid $6000 for the harpy sitting a few rows back.

Then Bill's father called him. "Please go to Church," his father said. This legitimately triggered an explosion of rage in Bill. Religion had already caused him so much pain and suffering. Religion continued to taunt him and religion was the reason his feeble-minded parents were about to donate their money to the legalised mafia. The public and his mother watched on as Bill shouted furiously into his phone. Bill's initial meeting with his parents was more civil than most other times in the past but this brought the relationship back where it was supposed to be. From that point onwards, their relationship was over.

Bill's mother on the other hand actually hugged Nadia, thanking Nadia for indulging the puerile whims of her failed son. Then she uncomfortably hugged Bill and said her final goodbyes, knowing that she would probably never see him again. As Bill walked towards the airport terminal, he did what had to be done, to phone Cheng again.

"You're right. You were right about everything. You're like a prophet, you predicted everything," Bill said.

"You pathetic piece of shit. That ho was obviously going to screw you over. You could have seen it from space. Why did you not listen to a word I said?" Cheng replied.

"I had to know for sure. Unlike you, I can say that I really tried. Now I know that my last chance is gone. I need to give up on pursuing these subhumans forever," Bill's resigned voice flowed into the phone.

"How much money did you light on fire?" Cheng asked.

"It was $6000. $6000 to sponsor some Russian whore to work in Korea. There are so many Russian whores working in Korea and I helped one on my own dime," Bill lamented. Then Bill heard Cheng laughing in the background. Yes, Bill's life was indeed a joke. The cruellest joke possible. It was so pathetic an ordinary observer could not help but laugh at his predicament.

"Do you have any idea how powerful a PC you can buy for $6000? We're not talking about overpriced Apple junk, we're talking over the top, top of the line dual Titan Xs," Cheng said in between breaths from laughing so hard. Just one of those graphics cards sold for $2000, more than most fully assembled high end gaming computers.

“I know, I know,” Bill replied in great pain, “I’ll make you a promise, if you see me doing this again, I’m going to buy that computer for you. I guarantee, I’ll never do this again.”

* * *

“Jinwoo, your dad and I are both very disappointed,” Bill’s mother spoke through the phone a day after he arrived back in Melbourne.

“From the moment I saw her, I knew there was something strange about her. You must stop your relationship with that woman. She will do so many bad things to you. Women can’t be trusted. Your dad and I have said this many times. You have to be extremely careful when dealing with any woman. You should be open with us about these things. It was obvious what you were doing when I saw that girl walk in after you. I could see her soul through her eyes with the way she looked at you. On the day we didn’t say anything but we were so worried. Why did you think your dad warned that ‘we are done’ if you marry? She will take you to the cleaners if you continue with this relationship. You need to cut ties with her. We only want the best for you...” Bill’s mother continued.

Bill could feel his frustration rising. He did his best to drone out the verbal diarrhoea that was passing into his ear. All he could say was a timid, “yes mother” repeatedly. She went on and on about the typical retarded Asian mantra of studying hard, getting rich and having all the fucking women flock to him. What the fuck was she thinking? After all this time was it not evident enough how stupid that ideology was?

“Wait mother, do you not realise the contradiction in your words?” Bill decided to stand up for himself.

"What? Are you speaking back to me!?" Bill's mother responded in surprise.

"Oh my God, you were just telling me about how women will take me to the cleaners and then you start repeating that same bullshit you told me as a kid. 'Study hard, get rich, whores will spread their pussies.' Something doesn't add up," Bill argued.

"You were young, how could we talk about mature things at that age?" Bill's mother defended.

"And you think *now* is the right time to bring it up? Why didn't you warn me about women fucking me over back then?" Bill stood his ground.

"We wanted to protect you from the evils of this world. You will always be my little boy," Bill's mother explained.

"Do you actually believe that? You should know by now that you must know evil to avoid evil or to fight it. It is way too late now. Had I known that all these females are whores, do you think I would have spent this much effort chasing these delusions? Don't you feel any responsibility for creating these delusions?" Bill vehemently fought back.

"Son, we did the best we could for your future," Bill's mother replied then returned to regurgitating her senseless traditional drivel endlessly.

At some point, Bill had enough.

"Mom, I have heard all of this before. You just don't understand I am a different kind. A superior kind. Don't keep phoning me to say all this repetitive garbage. None of it applies to me. This isn't the kind of future I would set myself up for," Bill put his foot down. Unfortunately none of his pleadings got through to his mother's head and she did not stop. By the time he put the phone down, Bill could not help but collapse into semi-consciousness with a raging headache.

Chapter 19

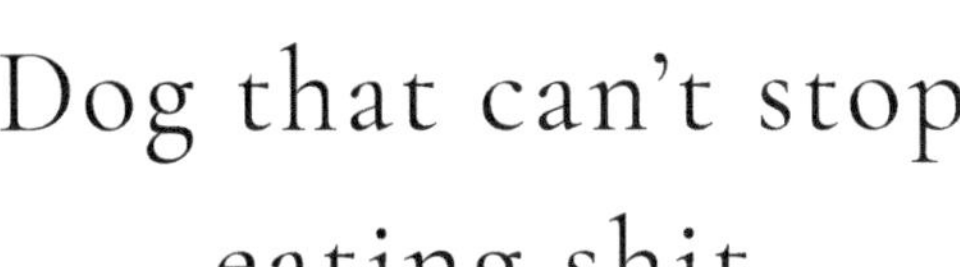

Dog that can't stop eating shit

Christmas and New Year came and went. Bill vehemently declined to join the staff Christmas party for 2016. His life was in far too much turmoil for him to celebrate anything. Celebrating in the midst of suffering unrelenting emotional pain would have been like salting a wound. So time went on and Bill continued to suffer in purgatory. Bill truly believed it was purgatory and not hell. If he were truly stuck in hell, Bill would have washed his mouth out with a revolver. There had to be at least some hope things would improve. Purgatory was supposed to be for sinners who were *not* condemned to an eternity of torment. Yet, his life in Mega was worsening week by week. His mistreatment by society worsened day by day.

Bill spiralled into a deeper level of purgatory than he thought was possible after what became known as the "Russian affair." Prior to the disastrous trip, Bill showed off pictures of Nadia to everyone he spent more than a few minutes with. His complete and utter defeat could not be covered up. Cheng did not have to repeat "I told you so." It was painfully obvious to Bill personally. Bill could not believe he was so desperate that he was willing to clutch on to such ridiculously tenuous straws while drowning. In fact, it was worse than clutching onto straws. His feeble desperation was more futile than an accused witch begging inquisitors to spare their life.

Every day at work, Bill showed up with a miasma of despair palpable before people even laid eyes on him.

"What's wrong Bill?" was repeated by many people but Bill did not even have the energy to return, "Fuck you!" He was so utterly depleted it was a miracle he could stay standing on two feet. Even then, he could not stand for long. The moment he arrived home, he collapsed and woke up the next morning. He did not even have the energy to eat. That was how pathetic he became. If only Bill could travel back in time and murder that stupid former Bill. The pain was so unbearable that sleep became the only relief. On his only day off, Bill could not even rise out of bed. The moment he opened his eyes, it felt like there were weights on his eyelids forcing them shut.

During the odd hours when Bill had enough energy to stay awake, he was online searching for more hate content. This time, not even hate was enough. He had insatiable bloodlust. Why hate people when you could see them die? Bill could never achieve his dream of watching the Earth enshrouded in nuclear fire from space. The next best thing was to see real people brutally murdered online. That was how he found Bestgore. Other times, he spent watching animal abuse. Brazil was such a fertile country for violence. For some reason, the most extreme acts all came from Brazil. Just how fucked up did a "society" have to get to unleash pitbulls on a man's testicles?

Animal abuse reminded Bill of his childhood. He once enjoyed tearing the wings of dragonflies and kicking cats. Bill thought it was entertaining. Bill could not help but laugh at a compilation video of cats falling to death from extremely high apartment buildings. Seeing the suffering of others somewhat numbed his own pain. The fact that these beings had misfortune greater than his own had an infinitesimal calming effect. What do you know, Bill thought, Tom had a point to compare Bill's suffering to African children. Tom was still wrong because those African children did not even come close to the victims on Bestgore.

The icing on the cake was the unending series of false allegations and overtly ridiculous complaints arising from dentistry.

"Dr Parker is ripping me off"

"This should have lasted longer!"

"I don't think I should pay because my insurance card was not working!"

"Dr Parker is so slow, other dentist fast! He cannot do good job!"

"Why is there a gap payment? My other dentist didn't charge me a gap!"

"Dr Parker was so rude, I knew I had bad teeth but now I feel completely hopeless"

"Don't bother with Dr Bill, never had a problem for years then suddenly I have holes everywhere."

Every couple of weeks, there was some piece of shit who intentionally and maliciously misunderstood Bill. Bill not only charged less than his female colleagues per procedure, he also recommended more cost efficient options yet *he* was the one being accused of ripping people off all the time. Insurance companies were reducing their rebates all the fucking time and these patients blamed *him* for it. Bill spent the appropriate amount of time to not rush through procedures yet so many of these morons thought that he was incompetent. Bill cared little for his patients' health, but because *his* work was in their mouth, their problems became his canvas for perfecting his art. However, so much of the time, attempting to do things properly resulted in these ridiculous complaints. This infuriated Bill more and more.

Everyone around Bill said, "just do what the others do." Bill heard that so many times he wanted to strangle the next person who dared utter such trash. Bill could NOT walk away from work that was not up to his standard because he could not sleep, eat or do anything without thinking about the disaster. It was basically asking Bill to sabotage his own work. Other dentists were fine with lowering their standards to make more money. Bill would love to make more money but not at the cost of his mental health. Just the thought of attempting that made him feel inferior, low IQ, pathetic and useless. His head would ache, his hands would shake, his heart would spasm and his compulsions would overcompensate. To *dare* suggest for Bill to voluntarily downgrade himself to an untermensch, that was a cardinal sin punishable by death.

Mental health wise Bill found no help. Horsham was just far too distant so Bill needed another psychiatrist. Bill's GP referred him to a male psychiatrist who was reputed to do some psychotherapy. However, that moron tried to offload the therapy to a female psychologist. Bill's previous experience with a female psychologist only worsened his mental health and depleted his wallet. That realisation triggered an explosion of anger forcing him to yell,

"I will not see a useless female! Females have zero fucking empathy and take zero fucking responsibility for their negligence!" Yet, that moron psychiatrist tried to defend his choice of referral. Even if that moron did not do psychotherapy, Bill was willing to accept seeing a male psychologist as a compromise. However, that must have injured the cockroach's stubborn pride. That cockroach vehemently argued back. Was he gay? Why was that pile of excrement obsessed with simping for some female? Bill stormed out of the "therapy" session early and complained to his GP who found the subhuman asshole in the first place. There were no more recommendations following that incident.

Bill's mental and physical health were both nosediving. There was nothing Bill could do. Society was actively hunting him through passive genocide. Bill discovered this after comparing the way various societies had enacted genocide. The Nazis actually learned from the US. The Americans were pioneers in eugenics. However, instead of compulsory sterilisation, what if the authorities simply engineered a society where those unwanted people would never be able to reproduce? The unwanted specimens would die and be cleansed from the genepool without any violence or intervention needed. Bill was such an unwanted specimen. Simply by being born the way he was, he was condemned as an enemy of the state. Society actively sought to engineer strategies which deprived Bill of opportunities while handing the lowest untermensch with all the power. Society was one step short of tattooing "defective" on Bill's forehead and locking him in a concentration camp.

There was nothing to live for. Bill had tried everything and nothing worked. He would work for as long as his mental and physical health lasted and wash his mouth out with a revolver. Fuck the gun laws in Australia, Bill thought. It seemed like gun control did indeed work for Australia otherwise Bill would have washed his mouth out with a .44 magnum years ago. Before that, Bill wanted to write his manifesto but found that he could not write a single sentence before falling asleep on the keyboard. He begged Cheng to write it for him but Cheng said that a manifesto was too personal. Bill had no choice but to find ways of staying awake. However, nothing worked long term.

Bill begged Cheng to recommend an unscrupulous Chinese doctor who would prescribe any drug without caring. Since Cheng was Chinese, he did indeed recommend a very reliable script mule doctor who prescribed some Modafinil for Bill. Even though the doctor had never heard of the drug. It worked for a while but after a few months even that stopped being effective. Bill's other GP referred him for a proper sleep study which yielded no results. Bill decided to ask Andy to drop two days so he only worked four days a week. That made zero difference whatsoever. Even with drugs, Bill could not help but waste almost all his days off sleeping. This unceasing suffering continued without end until the final months of 2017.

* * *

Bill looked at his iPhone before entering the doors of his Collin Street practice. It was Saturday August 19th 8:59am, 2017. These days Bill had no intention of arriving early. As long as he was not late, it would not interfere with his day. Bill walked through the clinic doors and ignored the receptionists. He did not care who they were, what they wanted. Everyone who worked there completely ignored his requests anyway. They were enemies to be controlled. Bill lethargically slumped in his clinic chair while muttering, "Jesus, Jesus, Jesus." Bill reluctantly signed in and checked his books. He was three quarters booked up. It was going to be another long day.

Bill struggled through his patients. Wisdom tooth extractions, root canals, and a few checkups and cleans. It was not an easy day. The moment the last patient before lunch was sent through the door, Bill shut it behind him and slumped in the surgical chair. Within moments he was unconscious, only to be woken by Krishanti's voice. Krishanti was a terrible assistant. She arrived 30 minutes late today, worse than her average of 15 minutes. The only reason Bill remembered her name was because he hated working with her. Of course they would dump the trash assistant on him because no other dentist wanted to work with her.

"Doctor, your next patient is here, would you like me to call them in?" she asked. Bill did not bother to respond. He just walked out towards reception to look for the next patient.

It was a new patient experiencing toothache. She had a Chinese sounding name, "Chunyun Su." Bill scanned the waiting area, there were quite a few young Chinese looking people waiting. Bill called out her name, then a diminutive young girl turned her head and started walking towards Bill. She seemed kind of cute, Bill thought to himself. She seemed a bit shy and did not make prolonged eye contact. Bill led her down the corridor to his surgery and started the consultation.

"So Chunyun, I hear that you had some toothache?" Bill asked only for Chunyun to nod her head and go, "Ngh" in affirmation.

"Can you describe the pain for me?" Bill asked again.

"Nghh... Big pain, I eat and painful," Chunyun quietly and slowly uttered.

"What does it feel like? Sharp pain? Is it a wide area affected? What about cold water? Did you have any recent work done?" Bill tried to gauge more information but it seemed the girl was not very talkative.

"I don't know... Lots of pain," Chunyun replied.

At that point Bill realised he was not going to obtain any more useful information. So many of these Chinese patients barely spoke a word of English and there was no point trying to ask them questions they could not understand.

"OK, let me have a look," Bill admitted defeat and went straight to the examination. As he expected, her mouth was full of neglect. She clearly had not seen a dentist for many years. There were multiple holes and the worst of which was a molar that had a giant hole large enough to cause infection. Her teeth were covered in dental calculus. Chinese people for some reason just did not care about maintenance so their dentists almost never cleaned their teeth. On top of all this, the Chinese in Australia were rich and treated their mouth like a dumping ground for their ill-begotten money. They would funnel in high sugar foods without care and the end result was exactly what he was seeing just now.

Bill took the required x-rays and tests then tried to explain the problem.

"So uhh... Chunyun, your pain is coming from this infected tooth here," Bill tried to explain while pointing at the broken molar, "You have two options, we could remove the tooth, bad, lose tooth, nothing to bite on. Or... We could do root canal." Bill then used Google translate on the screen to try and translate the terms "infection" and "root canal." Chunyun seemed a bit confused. Bill then tried to explain the situation again... And again. He used Google images to show pictures of bad teeth and root canals and crowns. Chunyun also took out her phone and tried to translate some questions.

Bill looked at her screen. It seemed like she was concerned about pain.

"Doctor, I am scared. I live by myself... If pain, can I call you? I need to talk to you," Chunyun tried to ask.

"I will be here until 5, if I'm not busy, then I can speak to you," Bill attempted to explain. Bill was already annoyed. This girl came to *this* country without speaking a goddamn word of English and she expected *him* to cater to her beck and call. She was not in goddamn China any more and she needed to listen to him. Chunyun looked as if she were on the verge of tears. Bill felt like rolling his eyes in frustration. Then she weakly consented,

"OK. Please do treatment. I need pain gone."

The procedure was not easy, but not overly difficult. Bill only ran 15 minutes late which was not the worst considering the language barrier difficulties. However, after the last patient left, Chunyun came back without making an appointment. Bill saw her standing next to the reception desk when he was on the way out. There was another new receptionist. Bill could have sworn she was a drug addict who escaped from a mental asylum. She wore excessively strong perfume, her make-up was haphazard and she talked about crazy fantasies including being a Rothschild.

"Doctor, your patient came back, she said she wanted to have a word with you, did you receive my message?" Christine the questionable new hire asked.

"I closed my computer, I'll handle it," Bill replied while ushering Chunyun back into his surgery.

"Sorry doctor, pain is little better. I'm very worried. What to do if pain come back? Can I sleep OK?" Chunyun asked.

"If pain is getting better, then it should not increase tonight," Bill explained.

"... OK... I am doing exams soon... I live alone, nobody help me. I trust you doctor," Chunyun struggled to say. "What to do if pain come back?" Chunyun asked again, more insistent.

"We have an after hours call service, they can leave me a message when I'm back in the morning," Bill explained.

"But I'm scared, what can I do?" Chnuyun just appeared to refuse giving up.

"Worst case scenario, you can go to hospital," Bill said while conducting a Google search on nearby hospitals, "see here? Lots of hospitals here in Melbourne, they're all open 24 hours. How about this, I can also prescribe you some anti-biotics." Bill placed emphasis on "anti" with an American accent, pronouncing it like "ant eye."

"OK doctor," Chunyun finally gave up, leaving after taking her prescription.

* * *

The week after, Chunyun came back to continue with her root canal. Bill did his usual Google image searching and long explanation of the risks and complications. The female dentists never bothered with such detailed explanations but Bill had no fucking choice. Even when he tried so hard to explain things, patients still complained and pretended that Bill explained nothing. Bill completed the procedure seemingly fine, at least that was what he thought, only to have Chunyun come back in the afternoon waiting for him to finish his last patient. Again, Christine alerted him to Chunyun coming back.

"Uhh hello, I didn't expect you back so soon, is the tooth OK?" Bill asked Chunyun.

"Yes doctor, it is feeling good. Can I talk to you?" Chunyun seemed to have that insistent attitude again.

"Uh sure, follow me," Bill replied, leading her back to his surgery.

"Thank you for seeing me doctor, I brought you a present," Chunyun announced while reaching into her handbag. It was a tie. Not just any tie, it was an authentic Jean Paul Gaultier tie. These did not come cheap. It perhaps cost close to $200 AUD in some shops. Bill knew his suits, shirts and ties back to front. He could recognise the quality of the material and stitching by inspecting it with his eyes and fingers.

"Uh, as a doctor, it would be unprofessional for me to accept gifts from patients, your payment for my services is enough," Bill said but not consciously handing the gift back. It was somewhat unnerving for a girl almost half his age, 19 years old, to shower him with attention. Bill savoured it nonetheless since nobody treated him so well.

"You deserve it doctor. You help me a lot. You are good doctor. You tell me the tooth will feel better and it is feeling much better," Chunyun heaped on her praise.

"Uh, thanks," Bill said. Chunyun then took a surprisingly awkward turn.

"You are the only one I can trust," she said, "I am so... lonely all the time. I did not want to study in Australia but... my mother... she tell me I have to. Me and my mother, not very close. She is always yell at me. She too strict. I live by myself, my friends not understand me well. I am very scared to see doctor. It was hard for me to come see you. You have been so nice. I don't feel scared any more."

"Uhh... I can only help fix your teeth but you're gonna need some other doctors to help with those problems," Bill explained.

"But I am scared of other doctor. My friends cannot help me. I don't trust them to help me. They are also very busy. We are all doing exam," Chunyun continued to explain.

"You need to find some better friends," Bill explained, "here, let me show you."

Conveniently, Bill carried his USB storage drive full of old photos. He carried lots of documents and equipment he needed for his job inside his A4 paper sized briefcase which was about 10cm thick. Bill brought up photos of his high school and dental school years.

"You see that guy? He's the one that I trust with anything. In fact, he works for Mega as well but at a different location. You need friends like that guy," Bill concluded after explaining a series of anecdotes.

"It's no easy," Chunyun replied, "we go different class. We only see each other once a week. I see different students every time. I need person I trust like you doctor. Can I have your number?"

Bill was surprised by all these confessions. He could understand her homesickness and loneliness. Despite him running from Korea as young as possible, he did occasionally feel that as well. Maybe she sensed that part of Bill. They were kindred spirits, almost like fate intervening again. Fuck that fate, Bill thought, ever since confessing to the whores, Bill cursed that concept. Bill thought about it silently for a few seconds. He disliked the notion of handing out his personal details to patients. However, this girl was pretty cute and he just could not resist the warm feelings of attention she was heaping onto him.

"OK but do not call me for anything other than dental problems," Bill warned her before warily providing his details. "I'm not a shrink, or therapist or whatever, I'm only treating your dental problems."

* * *

A few weeks later, Bill received another surprise. It was no surprise that Chunyun would phone Bill for something other than dental but she truly crossed the line.

"Doctor, please help me. I need your help. I need to certify some form, can you do it for me?" she asked.

"I don't do that sort of stuff. You can go to the police station and they'll do it for free," Bill recommended.

"I'm scared, I don't want to alone," Chunyun asked and again and Bill relented. It seemed suspicious that she would be afraid of something so straightforward and rightly so. Bill accompanied Chunyun to the Spencer street police station on Monday and immediately afterwards, she took him out for dinner.

Chunyun seemed to have a bottomless pit of wealth. She took him to Silks at Crown entertainment complex. The restaurant screamed luxury complete with dishes priced inversely proportional to the serving sizes and an atmospheric imitation Mongolian tent in the middle. Bill knew he was behaving unprofessionally but she seemed to rope him in one step at a time. She kept pushing the limits and placed him in a position where he could not say no. Not only that, Bill could not help but enjoy the attention. It was unbelievable that such a rich, attractive Chinese girl was showering him with so much attention. She was attractive enough to have any Chinese man she wanted but here *he* was on the receiving end.

A week after, Bill received an unfavourable missed call from Cheng. Cheng followed up with a barrage of texts on Signal, which was what had become of Textsecure. When Bill finally managed to speak to Cheng over the phone, Cheng's displeasure was all too obvious.

"Why the hell do you never pick up? You know, if someone held me at gunpoint and told me my survival was only possible if the person did *not* pick up, I would phone your lazy ass, bitch," Cheng complained the first thing he said.

"I was busy, Jesus, Jesus, Jesus, why did you call me?" Bill asked.

"I saw this patient, Chunyun," Cheng began but Bill already felt apprehensive the moment he heard that name, "who was complaining about feeling nauseous and weird after seeing you for that endo." Bill already knew where this was heading. Chunyun probably made up an excuse to try and go to the clinic hoping to see Bill but he was not there.

"There seemed to be nothing wrong. I told her that but she just continued wasting my time. You owe me bitch," Cheng berated.

"I know, just ignore her. She's some rich Chahn - nese," Bill emphasised the word "Chinese" the same way certain Americans did, "she came in just for attention. Let me handle that."

"I don't want to deal with your endo shit, go clean up your own messes," Cheng complained.

"Alright, alright, Jesus, I'm going to tell the reception morons to book her in with me only. Did she say anything to you about me?" Bill asked.

"Why you interested in that? Did you do something weird to her?" Cheng asked with suspicion.

"Hell no, she's the one being weird to *me*. She got me a gift and took me out to dinner-" Bill explained before getting interrupted.

"What the fuck? You better have said no idiot, don't you know that if you fuck her, you'll be derigestered?" Cheng warned.

"Jesus, Jesus, Jesus, I know goddamit! Jesus fuck! I'm only seeing her so that I can get her to see a shrink," Bill made up an excuse on the spot.

"You better watch yourself. I keep telling you to stop messing with women. By now, it's 100% obvious that you messing with women *only* results in disaster. Your so called 'tragedies.' There is no happy ending so stop trying to put yourself in prison," Cheng warned with a heavy sense of frustration in his voice.

"Fuck! Jesus, I know. You're always right Cheng," Bill admitted but he continued to explain Chunyun's circumstances to Cheng as if he were justifying his own poor decision making.

"She is suffering from severe mental illness, you are not a shrink. Even shrinks suck at treating mental illness. You better stop that shit idiot, she's hell dangerous. But I know you're a dog that can't stop eating shit. You're just lapping up all the attention cause she's kinda good looking," Cheng chastised again. The words hurt because they were the truth.

"Fine, I know, Jesus," Bill promised to follow Cheng's advice before hanging up. Only it was not so easy.

* * *

Chunyun made another desperate plea for Bill to help her buy a car. Only it was a Porsche. Probationary drivers were simply banned from driving cars of that performance to weight ratio. That did not stop Chunyun. Despite her being only 19 and not even having a driver's licence, she had the gall to pay $120,000 AUD on the spot for a 718 Cayman. Chunyun showed the dealer a fake licence from 'California' which was so pathetic it showed the age incorrectly. If the dealer just did some basic maths, he would have realised that the date of birth printed, 7 July 1997 did not add up to "21 years old" which was also printed on the fake document. The vehicle had a turbocharged engine capable of 220kW at a weight of 1.6 tonnes. Yet, the morons at the dealer simply handed over the keys for such a lethal weapon to a 19 year old with no fucking licence. If she was fearless enough to commit blatant fraud, why the hell did she invite Bill over?

A week after that, Bill discovered a pile of gifts waiting for him. Chunyun had dropped them off on Friday and Bill was back at Collins Street on Saturday. Bill met up with Cheng later that evening to unwrap the gifts. The gifts appeared to be professionally wrapped. There were three rectangular boxes of similar size with pristine white wrapping paper neatly folded with a single strip of adhesive tape holding it together. Many shops had attendants who performed this service at a small fee and they were good at it. None of that messy mass of tape holding together a failed origami project. Each box was about the size of a Bible. Bill did not care about the meticulous wrapping and tore open a hole with brute strength on one end of the first box. In the glint of the street lamp, Bill could make out a fork glistening. Chunyun had sent him cutlery it seemed. Bill roughly tore off large swathes of wrapping then retrieved the whole box.

"What the hell, this shit ain't even silver coated," Bill remarked as he saw the "100% stainless steel" sign printed on the packaging. "Who the fuck is Georg Jensen?"

"Let me look that shit up," Cheng replied while Bill started unwrapping the next box. This time, there were spoons inside the box.

"Woah, what the fuck, that shit costs $200 a box," Cheng revealed after having found the product on Google.

"What. The. Fuck? $200 and it's not even silver? For that price I would have expected pure silver not even electroplated shit," Bill remarked, equally surprised. Cheng then started laughing uncontrollably.

"What the fuck. Who would spend $200 on some shitty cutlery? Typical rich Chinese, she's got too much money to spend," Cheng remarked in between bouts of laughter. Cheng took out his phone to activate the torch function.

"Oh. My. God, look at this shit. I am not even kidding. Produced in PRC. Fuck! This shit was made with Chinesium in China! She's Chinese and she didn't even realise... She paid top dollar for some garbage... She could have taken from some factory a couple of blocks from her apartment back home... This can't get any funnier," Cheng paused between each phrase after nearly dying of laughter, "Gotta read between the lines. She's sending a message. Looks like she wants to take you out on another dinner date."

"Jesus, I told her about my eating habits and she said something about trying to help me change my lifestyle and shit. That's probably why. Fuck, I can sell this shit online if it costs so much, but who the hell would buy it? This shit isn't even silver..." Bill mused.

"You should sell this online and ditch that crazy patient already. Just tell her to see Andy so she can do this crazy shit to him instead. How suicidal do you have to be to continue this bullshit with her?" Cheng repeated his concerns.

"I know goddamit, I'm trying to get her to see a shrink. I promise, I'll send that bitch off once that happens," Bill stated. Although, he might have been enjoying the attention a bit too much to do so.

Chapter 20

Hopelessness (V)

Terry and Bill were attending a free "course" which was a pretense for advertising some new tooth prosthesis. Bill checked his phone, it was 6:03pm November 17th 2017, Friday. It should have started by now but most courses started slightly late. Terry apparently attended plenty of these free propaganda "courses" because of the free alcohol. Out of nowhere, Bill spotted a familiar female figure he had not thought about for years.

"Oh shit, pretend I'm not here" Bill suddenly whispered to Terry the moment he realised who he saw. Bill sank from his chair and tried to crouch behind Terry's legs.

"What? What happened?" Terry asked looking confused. However, it was too late.

"Oh Jin-Woo, Terry, it's been so long guys!" a familiar voice erupted behind them.

"Oh hey, I didn't know you came back to Melbourne," Terry replied while Bill was essentially forced out of hiding.

"Uh yeah, I was picking up my pen... Didn't expect to see you there," Bill bluffed, making up a pathetic excuse for his obviously ineffective hiding.

"Oh wow, I missed you guys, how have you been?" their former female classmate asked.

"It's been pretty good, heheh," Terry replied with his characteristic chuckle, "how have you been? I thought you went to Korea or something, I haven't heard about you from anyone."

"I came back to Melbourne last week. I worked in Korea for a while and I've been back from time to time," she explained.

"You mean flying in and out every week?" Bill inserted himself into their introductions.

"No way! It's a long flight to Korea!" Helen remarked.

"It's not that bad. You know, I once worked in this ghetto-ass shithole called Shellharbour, I was flying in and out for a while. It ain't so bad once you get used to it. You can say I'm kind of an expert on this fly in fly out shit," Bill elaborated.

"Oh really? So now you're permanently in Melbourne?" she continued.

"Yeah, you made the right choice. Mel-borne is the best city to work in, isn't that right Nigga-T?" Bill casually sent a rhetorical question over to Terry.

"Yeah lol, it's pretty good," Terry affirmed.

"By the way, Jin-Woo, he's dead. I killed that guy years ago. The name's Parker. William. Hastings. Parker. Otherwise known as Bill," Bill explained while rummaging through his pocket for his wallet to flash his driver's licence, "you better believe it, it's official, I paid money to have it changed."

"You did? Really? Like change your passport name as well?" she asked, somewhat surprised.

"You know it, it's hell easy, you can do it too. Don't half ass it like these Chinese princesses who just tell people to call them by some random ass English name. You gotta do it legit, know'm sayin'?" Bill stated, or in other words, "do you know what I am saying."

"Ahahaha, I go by Helen. I like my real name but Australian people find it hard to remember. If I change my legal name, I think my parents will be unhappy haha," Helen remarked.

"You have the right idea, don't use Korean names cause people are too low IQ and think that you're shit just by looking at your name. You should learn from me, I don't give a fuuuck what my parents think," Bill bragged.

"Ah haha, you haven't changed," Helen remarked before the speaker finally approached the lectern, "let's have dinner later guys."

Hence, the dinner date was set. The lecture turned out exactly as Bill envisaged, just pure advertisement. However, the Italian speaker made one very noteworthy comment.

"Let me know what you guys think about this case. In Italy, we like doing veneers which look natural. Patients think the best veneers are ones where you cannot tell they are done by dentists, but by God. Do your patients ever ask for these lines and stains?" he asked.

Then a random voice in the crowd called out, "They want 'em white."

Immediately following, another voice called out, "As white as possible."

"Don't they complain that it looks fake?" the Italian speaker posed another question with a puzzling expression of incredulity on his face.

"We only give patients what they want, haha," another random voice called out yielding a chorus of sympathetic murmurs and laughter.

"Hmmm.... You see, it is good to discuss these cultural differences. I'm glad I asked!" the speaker said before continuing with his shilling.

When intermission came, there was barely any food served. Trifling morsels of sliced desserts and some coffee. The trio decided it was not worth it so they prematurely and surreptitiously exited the hotel room where the "course" was being held.

"That was some bull shit," Bill stated with an extra long pause between the "bull" and the "shit," "that shit is made 99% by machine, so the technician spends about 5 minutes polishing and glazing that shit, and you're telling me they're going to charge full price for a second one? Fuck. Off."

"Lol, even the food was shit," Terry exclaimed.

"Come on guys, it was free, where should we go now?" Helen asked. The trio then discussed where to go. Since they were fairly close to a Korean chicken restaurant, they decided to try that.

"Look, I am not proud of what I did. In fact, I feel ashamed. I know what you're gonna say... Just hear me out. I had no goddamn choice. I told you about what happened with Sarah. It was a total wash. I've literally tried every fucking thing under the sun. Nothing worked. I was left with no choice, but to pay for it," Bill stated regretfully. The trio had well settled into their dinner and were reminiscing about their past experiences. Helen did not laugh at Bill, she seemed to have a wistful expression on her face, as if pitying him.

"Why you gotta look at me like that, come on man! That guy is dead. Trust me, that desperate piece of shit who paid to have sex, I killed him. I will never pay for that stuff ever again. I've come to realise that I was behaving like a fucking animal. You see those internet pictures of monkeys throwing their shit? That's what I was. I was just controlled by these urges. But that's all in the past. I have come to gain complete control over myself. It wasn't easy - it was a long and incredibly painful journey, but I am glad to say, I have won. I am an Ubermensch! Hoo rah!" Bill exclaimed.

"Lol, what is an Uber what? Those delivery guys?" Terry asked.

"Übermensch are the elite, a term coined by Nietzsche. I've been reading a lot of Nietzsche lately and I have to say, that guy has a lot of good points. A lotta good points. You know who also admired Nietzsche? Adolf. Hitler. Uph uhuhuhuh," Bill intentionally stonewalled again, "before you say anything, ignore all that shit all the low IQ subhumans say about him. That guy did nothing wrong. He did nothing wrong, Hitler did nothing wrong!" Helen seemed somewhat perturbed by Bill's strange rhetoric but decided to go with it assuming Bill was joking.

"Uhh... Anyway... Did you actually pay for prostitutes?" Helen asked.

"Yes, I am proud to admit that because I have killed that moron who did that. It took great effort, but I have not seen any sex workers, for over a year. How many people do you know have overcome an addiction like this? None. You better believe it. I'm not proud of having done it, but believe me, nobody else could have done the self-reflection and possess the mental fortitude to quit like I have. You take anyone, especially those morons in our class, if they went through the same shit I went through, they would be dead in a ditch right now, I am not fuckin' kidding," Bill proudly announced.

"Wow, poor you, I'm so sad to hear about Sarah," Helen empathised.

"Well it's over. I've moved on. That simp called Jin-Woo is dead, I killed him," Bill proudly declared.

"It must have been hard for you. You're a good guy, I'm surprised Sarah decided to dump you. She must have been a stupid girl," Helen stated.

Bill was suddenly struck with a realisation. Helen was not unattractive. She was intelligent enough to graduate in his same class and she had the right ethnic and cultural background to match. Did she mean what she just said? Meeting Helen was the most unexpected event to happen to Bill in the past year. Was this fate intervening again? As much as Bill hated fate, maybe this was his last chance after all. It was going to be yet another long shot. Perhaps he had a chance this time. Not just an imaginary chance, a real chance.

The trio continued their conversation and it turned towards their classmates.

"I don't keep in touch with those morons, they treated me like shit so I give it right back," Bill remarked.

"Me too, everyone just pretended to be friends with each other. I don't think we actually liked being together haha," Helen agreed.

"At least you guys had a choice. I was stuck with the worst bitches," Terry complained, reminiscing about the bullying he received.

"Don't think about those pieces of shit any more, look where you are now ni-guh, you can run rings around dem hoes any day," Bill consoled, "by the way, Cheng has been telling me that there have been lots of marriages and children. I don't know who would be crazy enough to have kids before their careers even kicked off but that's typical of them morons. What's been happening with you?" Bill managed to sneak this question in, hopefully without alerting Helen to his true intentions. Bill waited with bated breath, anxiously awaiting her answer.

"You know, I've been working so hard, I haven't really had time to get married. I met some men but they were all assholes," Helen replied.YES! Bill thought, a tsunami of relief washing over him. The window was open. Then Terry had to say something stupid.

"Ha ha, I've been working too hard for marriage too, ha ha," Terry could not even maintain a straight face. "I have an idea, why not marry Sarah's brother? He's a pharmacist so he's sorta close to what we do. Then you can get Bill and Sarah back together ha ha ha!" Terry continued with his feeble ramblings. Bill almost felt like stabbing Terry then and there if it were not for the completely unexpected response from Helen.

"Eww... He's just a pharmacist... He couldn't make it into medicine or even any other health practice. He's just a drug dealer ha ha. Do you know how little those kinds of people make? I can't marry someone who makes so much less than me. They only want to marry me for my money. We'll find some other way to get Bill and Sarah back together!" Helen dismissed the idea rather scathingly.

"Shut your mouth Terry. Don't even joke about that shit. Me and Sarah are over," Bill coldly stated while staring daggers at Terry. Terry somewhat shrank back into his chair, unable to withstand the visual assault.

"Don't worry Bill, you're a great guy, I'm sure lots of girls will like you," Helen consoled.

Terry and Helen struck a nerve. Bill had not even contemplated reuniting with Sarah all this time. It was a foregone conclusion that they would never see each other again. Then Helen said the most remarkable statement. That fucking moron brother of Sarah's once looked down on Bill for not having a job the fucking day after graduation. That was so typical of Korean fuckwits who look down on others while possessing zero capacity for introspection. In the eyes of ballers, that fucking moron brother was just a cockroach. Bill was earning way more than that moron and he had an actual shot with Helen. There were not many men earning that much money.

* * *

The Saturday a week later, Bill invited Cheng to join them. Cheng must have experienced early onset Alzheimer's because he did not recognise Helen at all. The quartet decided to go to hotpot that night in order to share "intel" on what happened to their contemporaries.

"I'm working so hard but also going bankrupt. I might even lose my car. I can't believe I blew so much money on something so unreliable... Fuck Mercedes. Fuck all European cars, they don't even know how to make proper cars. Life is so fucking unfair. I hope everyone else in the class is suffering," Cheng bitterly enunciated.

"Poor Cheng, why are you so angry when Bill and Terry are so happy? You all work in the same clinic. I thought you would be making a lot of money," Helen replied.

"It's cause this guy is way too scared to do anything like the females at Mega," Bill explained.

"Didn't I just say that it was because I wasted all my money on a shitty Merc? How many times do I have to repeat myself," Cheng complained.

"Haha, it's OK, you're driving a lot so you need a comfortable car. I haven't seen many of our classmates besides the other Koreans. I heard about Cho-Seung and Tae-Hyung. Ever since they were arrested they disappeared. Someone told me they got involved in drugs and pimping and got murdered or something," Helen explained.

"You see? I told you it was in their Ko-rean DNA," Bill reiterated his longstanding convictions earning a glare from Helen.

"Those guys were just bad people. Even in dental school, they were hiring prostitutes and snorting cocaine off their chests. They pretended nothing happened and continued treating patients the next day. They once invited me back in dental school, I strongly rejected them. They were total assholes. I heard that Jeong-Min has been setting up lots of clinics and selling them. He's done it at least 3 times now, at least that's how many times people tell me, he might have done it twice as many times. He was complaining to other dentists about the government being unfair but everyone told me that he was exploiting workers all the time. Rumours were that he would just keep booking patients in after closing time every day and staff would be forced to keep working without getting overtime pay," Helen continued.

"That's ridiculous. I've never seen staff so stupid. Any of the staff I've worked with would complain to Fairwork if the boss so much as closed a door angrily," Cheng interjected.

"I know right? I find it hard to believe but everyone has been saying the same thing. He only got in trouble after he refused to pay a dentist, some new grad, for over a month," Helen further explained.

"Those moron staff were too scared or too stupid to complain. Probably both. They must have been hell desperate and deluded. They must have known that moron Jeong-Min was going to pump and dump within months but they were hoping for a fucking miracle. 'If I don't complain then I get to keep my job!' What a bunch of fucking morons. They have to kiss that guy's ass then lose their jobs *anyway* when that guy dumps the place. You know as well as I do that after these pump and dumps get dumped, the next owner can't pick up the pieces. It's all a house of cards. You see this shit? You can't deny it. I can confidently say that the two of us, we've both overcome our corrupt Korean DNA. If it weren't for us being stable geniuses, we would be doing the same thing. Upupupuphh, before you interrupt me, just let me finish, let me finish. Dentistry has gone to hell. Pulling pump and dumps, that's the only way to make money in dentistry now. Nobody cares about quality or doing things properly. Patients come in wanting fake treatment like Invisalign and whitening even, *even*, when their mouth is collapsing from holes everywhere. They don't wanna pay for real dentistry any more so what do we do? We just extract as much money as we can from them and ditch before their mouths collapse. Take the money and run, just like Henry Park. I thought that guy was my friend, but he was just another fake ass Korean criminal pretending to be Jason Bourne," Bill pontificated.

"I heard about Henry, someone told me he started a church recently but I can't find his name anywhere," Helen commented.

"Yeah, that's cause that guy keeps changing his identity, he's a criminal, literally. He just robs people and ditches," Bill slightly exaggerated the story.

"Wow, I never imagined Henry would do that. I know some of our classmates have married and some have specialised," Helen continued.

"Yeah, I met Blake Llewellyn again recently and he said he was studying ortho postgrad but was still practising on the weekends. He said that 80% of his work was ortho now and he was billing almost 1.5 million a year. On 40% that's like 600k," Terry chimed in this time.

"You're not supposed to do that... You're not supposed to be practising privately while doing post-grad..." Cheng commented.

"Lol yeah, but everyone does it so I don't think they care ha ha," Terry replied.

"Again with that moron, Jesus just stop worshipping that subhuman already. Do you want to be one? This is exactly what I mean. See how far dentistry has fallen?" Bill lamented.

"That's not the worst of it, I read on the dental board website, Tim Zheng was caught practising while intoxicated. That guy was always hell dodgy but he was caught after he was practising high on marijuana despite multiple prior complaints of working while drunk. You know, not many people would complain about weed because you're almost guilty by association if you can recognise the smell," Cheng contributed this new intel.

"That ain't the way it works here in the city. You can walk along the streets and there will be random areas all over the city smelling like weed. I recognise it because those subhumans in Syracuse were smokin' weed all the fuckin' time. Next time, I'll point it out to you. You already know the smell, you just don't know what it is. See how much Melbourne has fallen? This is all because of those 'culturally enriching' immigrants," Bill denounced.

"Whatever. But this guy, Tim, you remember him? He was always out partying while surrounded by girls all the time back in dental school. The dental board website had records of hearings with this guy fucking patients up while drunk but nothing could stick until that weed patient actually reported him to police. They raided his place and found a tiny bit of weed that wasn't enough to lock him up. He must have had good lawyers or something cause he just received a suspended sentence and some community service. You know, that weak sauce garbage. Anyway, the dental board finally banned him from practice after that, temporarily lol," Cheng explained.

"Woah, that kid was too cool for school, he once tried to sell me weed and I was kinda tempted ha ha," Terry commented.

"If you ever smoke weed, we are fucking done. Don't you fucking lower yourself to the level of that subhuman sewer rat. That's like sub-subhuman behaviour right there. I didn't know the dental board website contained criminal proceedings, where did you read this?" Bill asked.

"Just Google his name and 'weed dentist'," Cheng replied. "If you kept Googling the Dental School, you might also have found out one of their shitty oral medicine professors, Peter Wakefield, got deregistered for quackery. He was caught pumping ozone up people's arses in order to 'prevent' oral cancer. That isn't just regular homeopathy, that's dangerous psycho tier homeopathy. I hope he rots in prison for that. Also since you don't use Facebook, some research guy, Charles Latham died of a massive heart attack, you remember him?"

"Yeah I remember that asshole. He was hell arrogant and didn't know what the fuck he was talking about. Kept going on and on about how he was paid to travel all around the world doing 'research'. I hated that guy," Bill maliciously recalled.

"Oh my God, don't say that! Everyone was so sad when it happened! It was all over Facebook. I can't believe you're so mean!" Helen retorted.

"Heh heh, you don't have to pretend with me. Whenever someone dies, everyone pretends that they were a saint. Even when Charles Manson died, there was an outpouring of fake 'grief.' How is it that hundreds of people who barely spoke a single word to this Charles guy suddenly became friends with him overnight? Fuck society and their fake acting bullshit. If I told you that guy," Bill said as he pointed to a random stranger, "dies tomorrow, would you care? Fuck this bullshit, just be honest, you never even spoke a word to that Charles guy, you know nothing about him. The significance of his death is the *same* as any random person in this restaurant dying tomorrow. None of us would even care unless we were *forced* to pretend we care," Bill stated.

"That's some legit truth right there. I never knew the guy either. That's why I didn't bother discussing it. I didn't think any one of us would care," Cheng complemented.

"That's still not right guys! I can't believe you can be so cold hearted, he was so young!" Helen retorted.

"Yo, actually I do care, cause I enjoy knowing that at least *someone* from that shitty Dental School died, you should tell me when you find out others have died," Bill remarked.

"Well on that note, one of the professors who taught anatomy, Prof Trentham, died a year ago. He was hell old though," Cheng added.

"Thank you Jesus!" Bill exclaimed while clutching his right fist in a victory pose, "well that guy never really bothered me, we might have even gotten along if only he didn't come from the UK. You know nothing good ever comes out of the EU. Everyone at the University, they all deserve to die."

"Oh my God, that's not normal! I can't believe you can say those kinds of things!" Helen remarked, seemingly shocked by Bill's verbal lashings.

"It's cause I'm not afraid of telling the truth. Who actually liked the Dental School? Nobody. In fact, every time one of our old professors die, I'd gladly take us all out for a meal to celebrate. Actually, everything is on me today. How about that? I can't believe I'm feeling so happy," Bill declared, somewhat concerned he may have revealed too much too soon.

"Also get this, the school owns some milk protein patent right? Well ever since that D'arcy v Myriad Genetics case in 2015 where the High Court, our country's most powerful legal institution, ruled that you have to be a moron to claim naturally occurring genetic sequences as an 'invention', there have been lots of biotech companies losing money ripping off naturally occurring phenomena. Among these biotech companies, is none other than Melbourne Dental School. Vegan groups have been patent trolling those assholes back to China for all their snake oil research," Cheng shared.

"Good. I hate vegans, patent trolls and all those MDS fags. I hope all those assholes fuck each other up in a caged deathmatch. The dental school better go bankrupt," Bill replied.

"You know, that just might happen cause the court filings revealed lots of management issues with their fake 'private' clinic. It's hilarious, abusing public funds to make a private profit, only they can't do that. To stop the haemorrhaging of money, they decided to attract private investors. Among them is your favourite boss, Howard Chan, who also decided to become a 'consultant'. I've been hearing that ever since Howard Chan started joining in, that place actually started to run better lol," Cheng revealed.

"What the fuck. I told you how dodgy that piece of shit was. Imagine how bad you have to be to consider 4mm gaps in crowns an 'improvement'," Bill remarked, genuinely stunned.

"Heh, he may leave 4mm gaps in crowns but he must be a genius at pumping and dumping," Cheng added.

"Who is this guy? I've heard his name but nothing else," Helen asked.

"I'll tell you more later. I once worked for him. I don't know what's wrong with that guy, his DNA must be hell corrupt, like beyond corrupt. Hell, that nigga is even *more* corrupt than Melbourne Dental School. The fucking dental school was dripping with snake oil but they didn't have enough to pull off their scam clinic. That's why they needed the snake oil king. Now that I think about it, those assholes can't even pretend to call themselves the 'best' any more. You know how the morons in the street all think, because it's Melbourne Uni it has to be the best right? Well now that sewer isn't even owned by Melbourne Uni any more. I know for a fact that piece of shit is gonna pump and dump that sewer onto dem Chah-nese. Then the CCP can operate a fake police station to spy on all those fuckwit Chinese students and gweilaos *on campus*! Ha ha! That nigga is way worse than even the shit I've seen from Korea, and Helen, you know what I'm talkin' about," Bill fantasised.

"Ha ha, I've seen some pretty bad bosses too. Why do you hate Korea so much? You can find such a good wife from Korea. Ha ha, I was just joking. Don't tell anyone, but I heard that Seo Joon imported a Korean wife who dumped him the moment he was married and took all his money. She disappeared immediately," Helen revealed.

"See what I mean? See this shit? I learned my lesson from that Russian ho. Whores from overseas can *never* be trusted. Doesn't matter which country. Not even the US of A. Seo Joon was lucky he wasn't stabbed. I've seen Korean women murder their husbands over a pair of shoes. *Shoes*," Bill exclaimed while intensely grimacing on that last word, "that guy was lucky he just got divorce raped."

After sharing more stories, what happened afterward was what mattered most to Bill. Terry and Cheng both went their separate ways but Bill accompanied Helen on the tram.
"Hey, are you busy tonight? If you have time, I want to show you something. How about we catch this tram to Spring Street?" Bill requested.

"What do you want to show me?" Helen asked.

"I just want to go somewhere quiet, it won't take long, I promise," Bill asked.

"OK," Helen assented.

The two of them walked towards Victoria's Parliament House and into the public park immediately beside the large, ornate building. It was a starry moonlit night, the exact atmosphere that Bill pictured. There were railings guarding a grass covered area with sparsely located tall palm trees. The couple walked on the concrete footpath which carved itself in a curve around the grassy field. They talked as they walked under the moonlight. It was as picturesque as a Hollywood movie. There was a modern art styled fountain with criss-crossing metal bars shimmering under the dim moonlight. Even though the water was not spraying, it commanded a statuesque presence nonetheless. Eventually, Bill finally confessed.

"After that free course, I remember you saying that I was a pretty good guy, do you mean that?" Bill asked.

"Yes, I like your honesty," Helen praised.

"I promise that I won't be like those assholes you talked about. I have to be honest with you, and with myself. That stuff which happened to me in the past, I can't hide that shit. Eventually, it will always come out. Most other men, they will always try to hide that shit," Bill continued.

"That's right. It's been very hard trying to find someone who I can trust," Helen continued.

"That's why, after hearing all the shit I've confessed to, you can still walk by me here and not hate me, I think that's truly fate at work. Most other women wouldn't even bother to look at me, nevermind me confessing about my past. To be honest, I was hiding from you because I didn't want to meet anyone from dental school again," Bill confessed further.

"It was pretty obvious... You weren't even trying..." Helen stated the obvious.

"Ha, that's true, but if you never found me, that would have been a tragedy. Just think about how unlikely it was that we were reunited after many years, in that course on that day. You're the only woman who would ever understand what I went through and forgive me for seeing prostitutes," Bill said while Helen nodded in assent. "I'm glad we found each other and I think, if you give me a chance, I can make your life better than any of those assholes, and I think you will make my life so much better. Don't leave me alone," Bill pleaded. Then Helen wordlessly embraced Bill tightly.

Bill felt amazing. She basically said yes to starting a relationship. Her warm, soft body felt extremely comforting despite the unusually high night time temperature. Bill wrapped his arms around her in reciprocation. He had a chance with this girl. However, the Monday following, Bill was invited to and attended another dinner date with Chunyun. Bill could hear Cheng's voice in the back of his head. "Dog that can't stop eating shit." Yes, Bill was pathetic but he was addicted to the attention this rich Chinese girl was showering on him. Bill enjoyed having dinner with Chunyun. Then on the Saturday following, Bill had dinner with his usual quartet including Helen, Terry and Cheng who were none the wiser. If women paid attention to him, why not grasp it? Bill knew that it was not appropriate to receive such attention from two women at once but he could not help it. Then came the Mega Dental staff Christmas dinner scheduled at The Conservatory, a high end buffet in the Crown Entertainment Complex.

* * *

The date was December 3rd 2017 and Bill knew it was going to be the final staff Christmas party he attended. Nothing could force him to attend yet another one. He might as well make the ultimate impression as there would not be any more. Bill always prepared himself before attending. He must shower and style himself. He always attended in style - a fitted suit at least. However, this year, he was going to wear a tuxedo. He would show them. He would show society just how superior he was compared to them. In fact, Bill expected those dirty subhumans to bow down to him and have their faces stomped on by his shiny, polished, leather boots.

All the appointment books were cut short on purpose and Bill took advantage of this to rush home the moment he finished. South Yarra was outside the city and was not easy to reach. Sure, there was a train station, but Melbourne's public transport was notoriously unreliable and Bill preferred not to take any chances. He left with barely a hint to the rest of the office and with a short walk after the train ride, he was back in his apartment. Bill did his triple shower, shaved, applied after-shave and perfume, and put on some foundation. This was time consuming and must be performed meticulously. The subhumans laughed at him for doing things like this, but this was his life's passion. Bill had an obsession with his appearance. No, it was more than an obsession. To Bill it was merely fact that his appearance was superior and he was obligated to cultivate it so the subhumans would suffer in envy.

By the time Bill had finished pampering himself, it was almost time. Cheng and Terry were close if not there already. Cheng was incredibly blasé about his appearance so he probably stayed behind in the office spending the time taking a dump or jerking off. Bill did not approve of any of Cheng's lifestyle activities and unceasingly concocted exaggerated stories of Cheng committing foul acts. To this day, Bill still cultivated the belief that Cheng was a drug dealer. Terry lived right in the city so he could do anything he wanted and still be on time. As Bill set foot on the street, he continued his long running tradition of contemptuously staring at the worthless insects passing by. That's right, he thought, keep looking at me you morons, I bet you don't get the opportunity to look at someone as superior as me even once in your pathetic lives. The dead Bill of the past would have found them attractive but now he saw them for what they really were, attention seeking whores reserving themselves for sub-human Chads.

Take a good look, Bill thought to himself, you stupid bitches are never gonna get this. Bill felt good. It was empowering to be this good looking, or so he thought. Even though he needed to return to the city fairly quickly, he still enjoyed savouring the feel of this evening. South Yarra had lots of attractive young women. It was either the second or third most expensive suburb to live in so these young whores must have been working their mouths hard to evacuate enough dough from the rich, white cadavers inhabiting this suburb. The old losers were rich enough to afford high quality women too, they would not settle for just any used up whore.

By the time Bill arrived at The Conservatory, most of the attendees were already present. Cheng and Terry invited Bill to sit as a trio but as soon as he sat down, his most hated enemies started arriving. "I'm staying away from those whores," Bill declared, viciously brushing his chair aside and moving over to the other table. Bill declined to attend the previous party because of the Kew crew. Fortunately, his most hated nemesis was not present. Even though Bill tried avoiding eye contact, one of the women locked eyes with him and half screamed,

"Bill!" and rushed over to give him an unavoidable hug. That was Bridget. Bill did not particularly like her but he did not hate her either. "It's so good to see you! We've missed you sooooo much!" Bridget said with a wide, disarming grin on her face.

"I'm good, but what I want to make one thing clear, tell Jane to stop smoking that crack pipe," Bill declared. Jane was his nemesis. He hated her. Her name immediately triggered memories of her overbearing aggressive attitude towards him. Even now, Bill had a trunk full of sample toothpastes he was supposed to transport as a "favour." Bill did not do "favours", and that final "favour" was way over the line. He was not a delivery man and those boxes of toothpaste were far too heavy for him to carry. Bill's distasteful and exaggerated memory of her was that of some bogan drug addict.

"Oh Billy! I will," Bridget played along sarcastically, "she misses you too, you look great today!" Bridget had more words to say but Bill did not particularly care. He felt empowered by finally saying what he said out loud. Cheng on the other hand looked at Bill disappointingly again. Bill was full of confidence when making unilateral declarations of war. However, when it came to actually confronting and actualising his aggression, the best Bill could do was meekly mutter micro-aggressions to avoid any real trading of blows.

After returning to his seat beside Cheng, Cheng asked,

"Bridget was never your target so why did you say that gibberish to her?" Bill was full of hot air and this was yet another example of his innate, cowardly nature. When Jane finally arrived, Bill sat down and turned his head around, pretending he never saw her. He did not dare say the same things to Jane's face.

The food was delicious, as usual. The Conservatory never disappointed, but Bill was not here tonight for the food. He was here to impress. About an hour in, Bill received a text. It was from Chunyun. Part of Bill wanted to just leave it alone but the other part was addicted to her attention. Bill quietly uttered to Cheng,

"If anyone asks where I am, tell them I've gone to the bathroom." It was a lie but Bill accomplished his mission and there was no further reason for him to be here. Bill exited the restaurant and dialled Chunyun's number.

"Hello doctor Bill?" Chunyun answered.

"Yeah, what's the matter?" Bill asked.

"I'm scared. I need your help," Chunyun said, reminiscent of her usual sob story tone. She frequently called Bill complaining about her anxiety, no matter how trivial the reason.

"I'm at a company event right now, what do you need to do?" Bill asked for more details.

"My mother was very angry over phone. I just want to talk," Chunyun said. So it was basically nothing again. Probably another thinly veiled attempt to have another dinner date. Bill knew he should decline and he genuinely felt like it, but he just could not bring himself to reject her.

"Uh... where are you now? I'm at Crown," Bill inevitably succumbed to pressure and assented.

"I will meet you at Crown in 10 minutes," Chunyun announced and she was true to her word.

It was 7:41pm by the time they met up and they were back at Silks. Chunyun apparently was scolded by her mother for some reason or another, Bill stopped paying attention after a while. It was always something related to her marks and her future career. Bill skipped out on the Conservatory buffet for this incompatible fine dining menu and some sob story. Bill felt some level of regret but the fact that he sat alone with an attractive girl boosted his ego enough to account for the majority of the losses. He just could not help it. He was a dog that could not stop eating shit.

Bill woke up the next morning with an uncomfortable aftertaste in his mouth. He was too goddamn tired to get up as usual but added to this was the burden of guilt. He planned to meet Helen for a romantic evening on Thursday. The day after, Chunyun invited him to ice-skating. Bill knew what he was doing was wrong. He could never have a sexual relationship with Chunyun because of so many reasons not limited to her being far too young and that she was his patient. Yet he could not say no when she invited him. He had the gall to plan a romantic date with Helen the day after that. But Chunyun was the one who invited him, Bill thought. He could not just turn her down... Fuck! Bill was tormented. Why was it that women did not show him any attention earlier? Why did it have to happen like this? Despite his torment, Bill had a grin on his face as he drifted back into unconsciousness.

* * *

Christmas and New Year came and went. Bill refused to work on any of the public holidays. He just did not care. Bill continued to meet up with Helen multiple times every week and went on "dates" with Chunyun behind her back. It was now the last Saturday of January and Bill had made the decision. He was forced to remove Chunyun from his life once and for all. He had finished all her treatment and he was fully prepared to hand her off to Cheng, who was at least able to speak Chinese. Bill decided to invite Terry and Cheng alongside Helen for their dinner meet-up tonight. Bill took out his iPhone and dialled Cheng's number.

"Cheng ma ne guh, I need you to do me a favour," Bill asked, catching Cheng writing up his patient record notes.

"What is it this time? Is it something ridiculous again? I'm hell busy typing all these bullshit notes which nobody is going to read," Cheng complained back with annoyance

"No, it's about a patient you've already seen," Bill explained.

"I bet it's that Chunyun isn't it? Don't dump her on me, she keeps making up all these bullshit symptoms," Cheng complained further.

"... Yes, it's her, uph uhuhuh," Bill hesitantly replied before stonewalling, "I finished with all her treatment, I just need you to do her checkup and cleaning, come on man, you owe me bitch."

"I don't owe you shit! I can't take over from you, she's like your girlfriend now bitch. You keep going on dates with her every week. You do realise you will get deregistered if this gets serious?" Cheng stated sounding like he had enough of this mess.

"I know, I know goddamit! That's why I'm trying to give her no goddamn excuse to contact me. You know, once she actually drove down to South Yarra then called me?" Bill explained.

"You actually gave her your address??" Cheng sounded stunned.

"No, I only told her I live in South Yarra, but she expected to meet up then and there. How the fuck am I supposed to say no?" Bill countered.

"Easy, tell her to get the fuck home, she's only 19 as well, it may be technically legal from a criminal law perspective but if you hit that, some feminazi on the dental board is going to nuclear deregister you over that," Cheng warned again.

"Jesus, I know goddamit! That's the whole point! I can't see her again. Come on man, fair trade, you actually make money over this, and come meet up tonight and I'll buy you, that Gami chicken place we went to last time, come on man," Bill pleaded. Eventually Cheng agreed to the terms.

Cheng was late because of his administrative garbage. At the restaurant, Bill, Terry and Helen had just finished ordering on behalf of Cheng.

"Cheng's always complaining about being hell broke all the time. I guess that moron legit dumped all his money into that Mercedes and now he's got nothing left so I had to bribe his ass to see Chunyun, that crazy Chahn-nese patient. That's why I'm paying for him tonight," Bill declared his magnanimity to Terry and Helen.

"Lol, he just eats KFC all the time," Terry agreed.

"Ah, that's so nice of you. You're such a good friend," Helen said just as Cheng sat down on the table.

"What's this about Chunyun? Are you telling everyone about those gifts and hot dates?" Cheng remarked, oblivious to the situation.

"What?" Helen screeched.

"Woah..." Terry also chimed in out of the blue.

"Oh my God..." Bill muttered while clasping his face in his hands, "Jesus... I need to go to the washroom." Bill stood up and briskly proceeded towards the toilet leaving behind all his belongings, including his phone. Bill heard some final fragments of conversation as he left.

"What? I thought you already confessed to dating Chunyun," Cheng uttered, very much taken aback by everyone's reactions.

"Nobody told me! What the hell? What an asshole!" Helen said.

Bill felt like crying. There was a brief flash of anger and he wanted to smack Cheng. But Cheng was constantly blurting things out and up until this point, Bill kept his romantic intentions with Helen a secret. He could not blame Cheng for what he said. He now regretted seeing Chunyun more than ever. There was another emotion which entered the arena of Bill's mind, that of shame. It was like a choking sensation emanating from his chest, ransacking Bill's youth and replacing his body with that of an elderly man about to die from angina. The pain was raw and almost physical. Every fibre of his essence was convulsing in tension, then pain. He could not stay here and face his friends again.

There were many times in Bill's life when he was emotionally overwhelmed. There were times when untermensch of inferior intellect tried to lecture him on subjects he knew more about than they would be able to learn in a lifetime. Him of all people. There were times people made false allegations of misconduct or negligence against him. At those times, Bill exploded like a ball of white phosphorus, burning with such an unmitigatingly terrifying level of rage. He stood no chance of controlling it so he had no choice but to walk away from the aggressors. At those times, if he did not take a walk, he might have ended up committing homicide, or be the victim of defensive homicide. Someone would have died. This time, the anger was replaced by shame. If he even looked into the faces of his friends again, he might have collapsed never to get up again. The table they were eating at was on the second floor. He might have even jumped.

Bill surreptitiously opened the toilet door a few centimetres then closed it almost immediately after. Good, his friends were still berating Cheng. Bill quietly slipped out of the toilet and down the narrow staircase. Bill thought, "Ah... fresh air at last." There was only one place Bill could go to find peace in a situation like this. Bill loved the United States military most of all but the Australians fought side by side as allies beside them many times. The Australians were inferior but not by far. Just so happens, his house was situated within walking distance of the ostentatiously obtrusive ANZAC memorial. It was his safe place, aside from his apartment. On many a sad and lonely night, Bill would walk out and stand contemplatively on the highest point of the memorial. To him, this was the most beautiful sight, capturing perfectly the skyline of the city of Melbourne.

Tonight was one of those nights when he needed the solace of his safe place. Without skipping a beat, Bill walked without rest for half an hour until he reached the Shrine of Remembrance. As Bill mounted the final step leading onto the platform, he unleashed a long sigh of relief. Bill pondered if it were even possible to make it through life without a safe place like this. The silhouettes of the skyscrapers against the moonlit night created a breathtaking tapestry which did indeed take away his breath every time. He was still somewhat upset at Cheng but he vowed to forgive him. He *had* to forgive him as Cheng was right after all. Bill valued honesty and a friend who spoke honestly was the most valuable thing. Even if hearing the truth was immensely painful. His friends would have realised by now that he had abandoned them and would probably figure out where he went. Cheng definitely would have figured it out by now. Once he collected himself, Bill started walking back to his apartment. He left his normal phone with his friends because he did not want to see them try to call him. He had more phones in his apartment. Once he returned, he would give them a call.

"Hello? Where the hell are you?" Bill heard Cheng's voice. Bill was silent because of his hesitation to speak.

"You can drop off my stuff at my apartment," Bill said before hanging up.

The first thing Cheng did once they arrived at Bill's apartment was to apologise. Bill played down the apology and had his own speech.

"I'm sorry I left without telling you all but I just couldn't go back out there. I've never felt such shame in my life before. You know that feeling when your asshole shrinks to the size of a decimal point?" Bill tried to explain. Unfortunately, nobody else knew the feeling of their sphincters shrinking to the size of a decimal point from shame.

"I'm sorry, I'm sorry, it was a mistake. Chunyun was a mistake. For the record, I regret ever going out with her," Bill added.

"You piece of shit, you asshole," Helen said, "I feel sorry for Chunyun. We were looking for you. I thought you were honest because you confessed to seeing prostitutes. No man would ever admit that. But you're just an asshole."

"Okay, Okay, I'm sorry" Bill continued trying to apologise.

Bill loved the sound of his own voice and had a speech prepared at ready almost every time. Bill again set off on a meandering, tangential and tiring tirade about how he was weak to temptation and it was all a once off. He was not angry but ashamed and would understand if everyone thought less of him. Bill looked and felt more pathetic than ever. Gone was the overconfident, narcissistic poise. His arrogant tone of voice was replaced by a much quieter, meek voice.

"OK go, I'll drive Terry and Helen back home," Bill said to Cheng.

After dropping off Terry at his apartment, Bill stayed behind alone with Helen.

"Please don't go, I can't do it alone after what happened," Bill pleaded, "please stay a little longer." Bill's voice was breaking as if on the verge of tears. Bill slumped back in his car seat appearing like a vulnerable man burning in pain.

"I don't blame you for what happened. We were not really a couple. I listened to all your confessions and believed you might have changed but I was wrong. We can stay the same as we are now, like friends," Helen wistfully consoled Bill.

"... I understand," Bill weakly muttered

"I'll see you next time," Helen concluded before leaving the car. The apartment she was renting was so close to Terry's that it was probably faster to reach by foot than by car.

After Bill returned to South Yarra, he closed the door and collapsed on the ground. Bill dejectedly held his face in his palms and started crying.

"Oh God," Bill cried out loud. There was nobody to hear him and it was better that way. Bill thought he had a chance to ascend this time but he fucked it up again. He should have left Chunyun alone but she was just way too manipulative. He cursed himself for finding her "cute" and fragile. Bill cursed himself for enjoying the attention from him walking in public beside her. He was made to feel like a "Chad" so he could not resist saying "yes" to her every demand. For no other point in his life was he ever showered with so much attention. Bill did not even bother to turn the lights on. He just slowly drifted into sleep with his head in his hands.

The next day, he received a strange text from Chunyun. It merely said, "goodbye." Bill had to phone her.

"Hello?" Bill gingerly spoke into the phone.

"Don't talk to me any more. You just weird," Chunyun replied before hanging up. Bill's heart dropped. He wanted to never speak to her again, that was true, but not like this. It was the ultimate cruelty. Fate lavishly showered him with these opportunities only to strip them away at the cruellest of moments. He was supposed to be the one breaking up with her. Instead, some cruel bitch of a friend or her mother must have brainwashed this girl into becoming Bill's enemy and have her abusively end their relationship.

Bill had never before in his life felt so much hopelessness. He lost both women in the space of 24 hours. He felt like a North Korean prisoner again. Rescued from destitution and showered with a lavish lifestyle only to be cruelly thrown back inside the North Korean hellscape once more. Why? Only to show just how shit life was. No other reason. If Bill had lived a life where he never received any attention from women, he would have quietly fumed and left it at that. This time, he was given the royal treatment but unceremoniously dumped twice consecutively just for fate to teach him a lesson. And that lesson was that Bill's life was fucking hopeless. This demonstrated just how pathetic his life was and forced him to accept he must never try again. There was no hope for the future.

Chapter 21

...Can trigger a tornado

Bill was awoken from his slumber by Krishanti knocking on the door. Fuck. He had fallen asleep within seconds of preparing the room for the afternoon. Bill did not intend to lose consciousness but these days if there was not a patient demanding his care right in front of him, he would not be able to keep his eyes open.

"Doctor, your veneer patient has arrived," Krishanti announced in her Indian accent. Bill was forced to work with this subhuman again. Obviously, she arrived late for this morning's patients and ditched for lunch the moment Bill stopped working. Bill lethargically lifted himself out of his chair and pointed to the capsules he prepared earlier,

"Krishanti, I can't afford to mess this up, I have done all the preparation, you just need to hand me the cement. See these tips? I've prepared 6, see?" Bill repeated pointed hard and exaggeratedly at the cement mixing tips he prepared, "Make sure you use a new one for each veneer."

"OK," Krishanti said as she nodded. After Bill's song and dance about the 6 different mixing tips, anyone with IQ above room temperature should be able to understand. However, Bill still had misgivings about Krishanti.

Bill's intuition turned out to be right. As Bill cemented on the fourth veneer, it contacted the tooth at a slightly rotated position so Bill tried to rotate by a couple of degrees to seat better. It did not budge. The instant it contacted the tooth the cement was already set. Bill's heart sank. He knew exactly what happened. That fucking subhuman moron fuckwit did not change the cement mixing tip. Bill turned his head around. True to his suspicions, there were 5 unused mixing tips lying on the bench. Bill's rage exploded into an inferno in an instant. His heart started pounding like a bass drum and his head started throbbing. This time, Bill's visual field narrowed like a wide aperture camera. It was like tunnel vision. Bill's entire body was shaking. Murderous thoughts projected themselves in Bill's mind. Last night he watched many Bestgore videos of vicious murders from Brazil. Bill turned to gaze at Krishanti with more than enough malice to petrify a gorgon.

Oh how he wanted to tear her limb from limb right this moment. The fact that her facial expression did not waver meant that she did not care even the slightest about her grave error. Either her IQ was below room temperature or she intentionally ignored everything Bill said. Maybe it was both. Such a subhuman cockroach did not deserve to breathe oxygen. Bill's right hand started shaking even more now that his homicidal urges were bubbling to the surface. Bill stood up and viciouscly grabbed the double barrelled cement cartridge out of Krishanti's hands. Only then did she show any change in facial expression. Just merely blinked a couple of times with surprise. Bill was too angry to form a sentence together so he did not speak.

Bill twisted the current tip filled with old, near solid cement and threw it on the ground. With shaky hands, he screwed on a new syringe tip and proceeded to finish the procedure all by himself. Gluing on the fourth veneer even a slight micron off caused the remaining veneers to not seat perfectly on the tooth surface. They looked close enough so only the one veneer looked slightly off. Bill's head was still throbbing but his tunnel vision had eased.

"Uh Crystal, I've glued them all on but my useless fucking assistant gave me some half set cement so one veneer is slightly off," Bill now did not hesitate to say whatever the fuck he liked in front of patients. It was not just because he was angry. These days, he actively rejected patients who would not agree with his personality. If they passed the "fuck" test, then they would probably remain loyal patients.

"Oh, can I see?" Crystal replied. Bill brought a mirror over hesitantly. He was mentally preparing for another complaint. Once the complaint came through, would he be able to stop himself from murdering Krishanti? Crystal gazed at her reflection.

Bill had went through a long fucking journey with Crystal. It took way too long. She was that patient who requested to have some old veneers replaced and she wanted something cheap. Initially, Bill was happy to give her some cheap machine made veneers because he did not have the patience to craft some veneers on her teeth by hand. However, the CEREC machine that Andy loved so much broke down on that day and he was *forced* to give her an offer she could not refuse. He sacrificed his own income to pay technicians to make porcelain veneers for her, just to prevent some fucking complaint. It was not easy either, she was extremely fussy and there were multiple visits back and forth from the dental laboratory attempting to get things right. It had already taken over a year. Just when she was finally happy, Krishanti happened. It took all of Bill's colossal mental fortitude to resist giving Krishanti an instant lobotomy.

"You know, I like it," Crystal said, "I know you want things perfect and all Bill but if my teeth looked perfect, all my friends would notice they're fake immediately. Having it this way makes it hard to tell." Bill was somewhat mollified but he could not forgive Krishanti.

"Are you sure? I can remove that veneer and do it again, it won't cost you anything," Bill said, knowing that being glued in the wrong place actually reduced the lifespan, even if it were fractions of a millimetre off.

"I'm happy with it as is," Crystal replied, "It's fine."

"OK but I gotta bring you back to do some cement clean-up, it's gonna take at least another half hour and my hands are shaking too goddamn much," Bill said while holding up his shaking hands.

"It's alright Bill, calm down, do I have to worry about anything regarding the cement?" Crystal asked.

"Uh... it's gonna be hard to floss and clean, so you might wanna hold off on that until I tidy it up, but you can eat and brush as normal," Bill advised while trying to keep himself together.

"OK, I trust you," Crystal replied.

Bill dismissed Crystal and waited for her to exit the clinic. He was holding it in all this time but he could no longer wait.

"GET OUT OF MY FUCKING SIGHT! YOU'RE A FUCKING USELESS PIECE OF SHIT! I DO NOT WANT TO SEE YOUR FACE AGAIN!" Bill screamed at Krishanti. She was damn lucky the patient was agreeable enough to allow Bill to simmer down. Bill seriously did not know if he could have resisted murdering Krishanti if the patient were not there. What Bill was sure of was the fact that he would murder that subhuman if he were forced to work through another patient with her. In order to save her useless fucking life, he ordered her to go home. Why was he such a nice person? Bill really ought to be given a medal for saving the life of common scum subhumans.

Bill knew what would happen if Krishanti left. He would have no nurse and although having no nurse was better than having a negative value Krishanti, Bill could not accept that either. Seeing Krishanti seemingly disappear towards the reception area, Bill took off his clinical gown and marched outside.

"Cancel my afternoon patients, I'm going home," Bill expressed to the reception team, sounding calm but dripping with malice. He meant it. In fact, Bill was so angry, he would not be able to work on Sunday, tomorrow, either. Bill took out his phone again. He text messaged Andy,

"I can't work 4 days. I need to drop 2. We need to talk." The boss was normally busy all the time but within a minute of the text being sent through, Bill received a call back.

"Hello, this is Bill," Bill answered the phone.

"Hey Bill, what's going on? Krishanti told me that you started yelling at her today. I know Krishanti has been a bit slack but that's no reason to act like that..." Andy asked.

Krishanti's false allegation immediately triggered an instantaneous nuclear chain reaction. Bill's blood pressure skyrocketed and resulted in Bill feeling the thumping of his heart splitting his head apart. His vision blurred so much so it was like tunnel vision again. Violent fantasies raced through his mind. A thousand different ways of rending that subhuman's worthless body apart flashed a thousand times. If only he could resurrect her again and again because killing such cockroaches once just was not enough. Bill held onto the wall to support his shaking hand. That. Fucking. Liar. She got the first word in so now Andy thought Bill was bullying her. Krishanti pushed *Bill* onto the defensive. Now whatever Bill said to Andy would sound like a desperate plea to beg for forgiveness.

It should have been the other way around. Krishanti being the useless subhuman she was fucked *him* over and the light scolding which required Bill holding back the tsunami of anger was the least of what she fucking deserved. Now the boss was blaming *him* for *her* mistake? Was Bill living in a parody world? How was this real life? Not even the most farcical comedies could make this up. This crime was so severe, he should be throwing her distant relatives into a giant blender but they lived in India so he could not find them even if he tried. Bill struggled to take in two deep breaths to calm down enough to start speaking.

It was at that point that Bill started understanding how murderers were made. That was right, regular people get transformed into murderers because of situations like this. The subhumans kept going on and on about how they could "never" understand how someone could do such things. But Bill understood. He truly empathised with the murderers. It was ironic how all those morons who kept falsely accusing Bill of being autistic and lacking empathy were the true autists lacking in empathy.

"SHE WAS THE ONE WHO PICKED A FIGHT WITH ME!" Bill raised his voice, even to his boss this time.

"OK, calm down, I'm not blaming you, in fact I've heard lots of other dentists complain about her, it's just that you haven't complained before so that's why she was rostered on with you," Andy tried to calm Bill down.

"Oh my God, I am *not* a dumping ground for everyone's problems! She should not be allowed to work in this country with that goddamn attitude. You better fire her on the spot. If nobody else wants to work with her, she's fucking useless. We don't need people like that working here," Bill complained.

"So she didn't listen to you? Was she not assisting properly?" Andy asked.

"It was worse than that. Much worse. It's not just today, she keeps showing a pattern of behaviour, the kind which you know she will never change. She ignored my instructions today but if she works with me next week she'll ignore me again in a different way. People like her will never change. You can't keep giving her more chances, she is done, finished," Bill forcefully explained.

"Sounds rough. I'm going to have a chat with the girls to see if they can arrange to have you work with someone else tomorrow," Andy offered.

"I can't work tomorrow. My head is spinning, I can't concentrate. I am not kidding, I can barely even walk properly right now. I don't know if I can get better any time soon. I probably won't be able to work Thursday and Friday either," Bill said, while literally stumbling on the pedestrian path.

"Are you sure? We can just open it half a day if you like," Andy seemed persistent.

"Hehehe," Bill could not help but laugh at the absurdity of the situation. Here he was literally admitting to be unfit for work. Literally unable to do dentistry without causing a severe accident, or perhaps even death... Yet his boss would not listen. "I'm not kidding. If I work tomorrow, someone's gonna have a big problem. It could be me, it could be the patient, it could be the assistant. Someone's not gonna make it home," Bill added with a chilling tone.

"Hmm... If you're that unwell, have a good rest so you get better soon. I don't want to intrude on your time off so the next time I'm available to talk in person would be Saturday. Are you sure you only want to work 2 days? I'm worried about you man. Are you going to be OK with just 2 days? How are you going to keep up with your income?" Andy asked.

"I'm not worried about money. Unlike everyone else you know, I am *not* buried 6 feet under in debt. As you know, I'm making way more, waaaaay more than when I first started. In fact, all that will happen is that I'll get a few dollars shaved off my income," Bill announced. It was partially true. Depending on which part of Bill's career it was compared to.

"Alright Bill, I know you gotta look after your self interests. Enjoy your time off. I'll find someone to fill in for you. Let's have a chat next Saturday," Andy announced before the two said their goodbyes.

Bill had to endure a torturous train ride home. There was a girl on the carriage sitting in front of him who seemed to snigger at him. That fucking bitch. It was another sign of being actively hunted. He was reminded everywhere he went that these fucking whores thought of him as just a fucking sewer rat. Bill clenched his fists. He could barely contain his anger. That fucking bitch was looking down on him by giving him that dirty look. Bill involuntarily punched the empty seat beside him causing a few other onlookers to stare at him. More fucking subhumans looking down on him. Bill had to leave, but he was on a moving train. With no other choice, Bill exited the carriage and entered the next one. His blood pressure was sky high already from before and now his tunnel vision was returning. As soon as the train stopped, Bill leapt out and started walking. It was not his station but he was *forced* to step off the train. He might have committed murder otherwise.

By the time Bill arrived back at his apartment, he was so tired he could barely even stand up. Bill collapsed on the ground after taking a couple of steps inside his apartment. He could not lift himself up again. The drowsiness was just too heavy. After opening his eyes again, it was daylight again. Yet, Bill did not feel refreshed. He was woken by his fucking phone alarm. He was too goddamn tired and forgot to disable it yesterday. Bill shut the alarm down and dragged himself to his "bed" which was still just some blankets on the carpet. After lying down, Bill's eyes were forced closed again by the lethargy and by the time he opened it, the sun was already setting. It was dusk. Bill tried to relieve himself then had a drink of water. But that was all the energy he had. Down he went again.

It was Tuesday afternoon that Bill finally managed to gulp down some Cheezels snacks he bought. It was a "meal" of sorts but he was too goddamn tired to make himself any proper food. Bill immediately drifted into a state of semi-consciousness but awoke a matter of hours later. He turned on the garbage donated computer and went back to watching gore and animal abuse. Jesus, how cruel life was to these poor sods. Bill was glad to be alive after watching so many people die. Nothing "cured" Bill's extreme depression but at least it made the situation slightly less severe.

To Bill, gore videos portrayed the true essence of humanity. All those subhumans out there were satisfied to live in a drug induced coma based on delusions crafted by one sweet lie after another. Not Bill. Bill was only interested in the truth. The brutality Bill witnessed was identical to the beastial animals found in National Geographic videos. Perhaps worse. This was the *truth*. Society was just one small push away from descending into their true animalistic state. After a few hours online, Bill collapsed back on his "bed" and fell asleep again. These days, Bill was lucky to enjoy more than 4 waking hours a day. Hence, this activity continued until Saturday.

Bill honestly was not sure if he could handle being back at work on Saturday but he had to give it a try. He arrived nonetheless for an unpleasant surprise. There was no assistant for the first patient. Bill did not bother bringing them in until someone arrived. He just did not care any more. Unfortunately, Krishanti came in, only 20 minutes late this time. Bill's fury flared again, but not as severely as last week.

"Why are you here? Go home. I'm not working with you," Bill stated with a chilling calmness.

"OK..." Krishanti said before walking back outside the clinic. This time, Bill indeed had enough. He did not care if that fucking patient left. It was Andy's fault for letting things slide this long. After a while, an "Emergency assist" nurse walked in. That's right, Bill thought, these desperates had to resort to a labour hire company to fill in despite having a fucking week to prepare. Bill was going to give it to Anday today.

After Bill finished with his morning patients, Andy walked in.

"Hi Bill, I have a few minutes free now, do you have time for a chat?" Andy asked. Bill sighed, it was time to unload. "Yessir," Bill said. Then Bill explained in detail the problems with Krishanti and exactly what happened that day.

"My God, I can't believe she acts like that. When she assists me, she seems really good," Andy relented.

"It's not just that. I keep talking about problems but they never get fixed. We have staff meetings where I've brought this up multiple times. We all wanna see more patients through the door but these goddamn morons aren't showing any sense of professionalism," Bill continued.

"I know, I love your advice, it's been so helpful," Andy encouraged Bill, perhaps a bit too much.

"The staff operate like a revolving door, in and out, nobody knows what the hell they're doing. The new dentists, they act like a bunch of slobs. They leave shit everywhere and never clean up after themselves or take any responsibility. They treat me like a dumping ground for all their problems," Bill bemoaned.

"You mean Brendon and Stacey? They tell me you're so wonderful," Andy asked.

"Yes them two. They're just making shit up. I've seen how they work. Nobody wants to work with them, trust me. Just the other day, Stacey left her dirty as hell gown all over the chair. She leaves the computer logged in so I have to shut it off and on again. I keep telling her but she doesn't care. Brendon is the same, except he also dumps all his failures on me. I see all of them adding their patients on WeChat or Facebook or some shit. That just leads to arguments. If you go to any lawyer or heart surgeon, do you expect them to give you their personal number when you demand it the moment you walk in? No! Because they're not your slaves. Professionals have standards. Not every patient is your friend, and neither should they expect goddamn special treatment. I have to make it clear, there is *never* a good outcome when dentists start chatting with patients in their personal capacity. I know this better than anyone," Bill had to regrettably admit.

"You make some great points," Andy agreed.

"I have to work with all this happening around me. But when I try to shut it all out, there's always people coming in and out of my room. Why do they have to do this? I keep telling everyone to stay the hell out when I'm trying to concentrate. I keep telling people lots of things, no crown re-cementations, kids need to stay the hell outside when I'm seeing their parents, no Chinese patients who can't speak a goddamn word of English. I don't say this because I'm some prince who only does glamorous work. These patients have *repeatedly* caused me problems. You've seen this. We've talked about it before. When I tell reception about this, do they listen? Hell no. I don't know what's wrong with people. In fact, I have found that people *only* start listening when I start cursing and shouting at them. Nothing else gets through to them," Bill complained.

"I see. I'm so sorry to hear about having such a hard time here," Andy said despite Bill knowing that guy was well aware of everything that happened. However, he was so lenient on Bill, Bill could hardly complain, until now that is. Bill continued complaining about all the miscellaneous issues again for at least another five minutes.

"So are you 100% sure you're OK with just working 2 days?" Andy asked again hoping to elicit a different response.

"Absolutely sir. I'm not like the other dentists. I don't need 'retail therapy' like the females or go on some Thailand trip hopping from brothel to brothel. I can't bring myself to even think about living such a life of financial recklessness. There is no way I can keep working this hard.

I don't need to work this hard. Someone's gonna die and it's probably gonna be me," Bill remarked almost comically.

"But you have such a bright future ahead of you," Andy attempted to cheer Bill up, which merely backfired. "How about this, you do Fridays at Carlton and Saturdays here on Collins Street. I couldn't really find anyone to fill in for you on Friday," Andy gave a counter-offer. Bill did not really mind. Money was not an issue and by now, Carlton had picked up to the point where one day was about half as productive as a Collins Street day.

"OK, we'll go with that," Bill consented and the two shook hands on that deal.

Out of all the clinics Bill worked in, Mega had been the best by a wide margin. However, Bill hated it nonetheless. This was the best this country could do? This was "normal"? Bill was not the crazy one. Every other fucking person in Australia was crazy. This was not fucking normal. There was no professionalism, no organisation, chain of command and no fucking decency. Everyone treated him like shit and none of them were aware of just how terrible their standards were. In the United States, assistants would have been fired on the fucking spot if they showed dentists the kind of attitude Krishanti displayed. Dentists would have been on the firing line if they tried to dole out favours for patients. Worst of all, those subhuman morons could just not admit that they were out to take money.

Bill could have forgiven them if they just openly admitted,

"I need to make a profit so I will charge through the roof then slice and dice." Bill could understand the need for money. If that was their mission in life, then at least be fucking honest about it. Bill respected honesty. If they were truly honest, they would be able to self-reflect and recognise their fucked up poverty stricken childhoods distorting their sense of value. Any honest self-reflection would have also made them realise the harm they were causing. Instead, liars just said to themselves day in, day out, "I'm here to help people", "I can do no wrong." So far, Bill and Cheng were the only dentists who refused to behave like this. Liars could not contain the harm to themselves but spread it to others including Bill.

These cockroaches always blamed everything but themselves when their work failed spectacularly. It must have been the materials! The equipment failed that day! It was the patient, the assistant, bad luck... The list was endless. Bill could proudly declare that he took responsibility and limited the harm to himself. Bill's work had flaws too but at least Bill never claimed he was "helping people" or "doing no wrong." All his achievements were to satisfy his own compulsions to do the best he could. If he could not achieve a good result, at least he tried his honest best and could admit he failed. He would look back and examine *why* so that it would not happen the next time.

Bill could not believe he used to be friends with Terry. The more he saw that face, the more he wanted to give it the sashimi treatment. All the other dentists except Cheng, who was too scared to take any risks, deserved the sashimi treatment. They *needed* the sashimi treatment. Unsurprisingly, working only two days a week, *just two fucking days followed by five days rest*, did NOTHING to help Bill. The moment he walked into Mega, he was instantly triggered. How could he keep working with these subhumans? Bill had to laugh at himself. "Not even the *marines* could get me outta here." Bill could not believe he once said that. His life was a fucking joke. Dentistry was a death sentence.

* * *

Bill barely managed to keep it together for a few months until he received the worst Easter present. Bill checked his iPhone, Friday March 30th, 2018. Bill barely made it to the clinic without stabbing a bitch. How *dare* they look at him with contempt? He was prepared to quit working altogether but he had not yet solidified a back-up career.

Computer programming was a bust. Attempting to enter into medicine required high marks on the GAMSAT. There was no chance of that. Bill questioned whether or not his father would pay for a dumpster fire Australian medical school. Korean medical school was even more difficult. His Korean skills were as trash quality as the teachings of Australian medical schools. Bill gritted his teeth as he sat down inside his surgery.

"Good morning doctor, there's a letter for you," announced Barbara, the grandma receptionist Bill hated. Bill did not verbalise anything in return, he merely grunted. However, the letter he was about to receive spelled certain doom. "Chao and Chaudry solicitors at law" was printed on the envelope with a set of scales as its logo. What the fuck was this? Bill did not know what to think. They sounded like one of those new generation desperate lawyers begging for food on street corners. "No win no fee" solicitors. Why the fuck did they send him a letter? Then Bill realised. It could be a letter of demand from some fuckwit patient. Bill did not remember having a 1 star review for many months. He could not remember any patient being angry enough to see a solicitor. Tentatively, Bill opened the letter and scanned the contents.

Bill could barely make it through without exploding in anger. All he could process were snippets. "Anna Jane Williams"

"Permanent loss of sensation and motor function"

"Severe psychological injury"

"Too scared to see a dentist, too scared to socialise"

Finally, the document concluded with one absurd paragraph.

"Our client used to be a social butterfly. Anna expressed that she loved to sing karaoke every few days before the incident but has become introverted and depressed because of the slurring and stuttering the injury caused. In her words, her social life meant everything. After the harm she received under your care, she has never once returned to sing. Through thorough and considered calculations, our client demands the payment of $3.4 million to compensate for her severe and permanent physical and psychological injuries."

Three. Point. Four. Million. Fucking. Dollars. WHAT THE FUCK? Bill could not believe what he was reading. Bill could not hold it back this time. His head was throbbing in agony due to his aggressively over-stimulated heart. His entire body was shaking and his tunnel vision was almost blackening his visual field. Bill slammed his fist into the dry wall and kicked his chair over.

"FUUUUUUUUUUUUUUUUUUUUUCK!" Bill screamed at the top of his lungs for as long as his breath could hold.

"What happened? What's the matter?" Barbara slowly tiptoed over.

"CLOSE MY BOOKS. I FUCKING QUIT!!" Bill screamed to her face as he stormed out.

Bill was pushed one step too far. He still opted to work *only* because he was earning money but this predicament wiped away EVERYTHING he had worked for from the moment he was born. Bill could not help but laugh out loud in the public street he walked on.
"Ah ha ha ha ha ha! What a fucking joke!" Bill shouted in the faces of the confused onlookers. Why did Bill live in a society which arbitrarily decided to steal everything he worked for in an instant? This was evidence beyond a reasonable doubt. He was being *actively hunted*. Society was engineered to commit passive genocide against hard working people like Bill for no other fucking fault than being born. What a fucking joke.

Bill saw his phone ring. It was Andy. Bill ignored it. Fuck it, Bill thought. He was a dead man walking now. Matters pertaining to the mortal realm no longer fazed him. Conveniently, Bill was passing by the

Royal Dental Hospital of Melbourne. Why not finally give them a piece of his mind? Bill approached Swanston Street and turned past the new buildings that were erected above the remains of the demolished former women's hospital. The Dental hospital's large yellow cover loomed with a blue sign reading, "Royal Dental Hospital of Melbourne." Bill walked towards the double automatic doors and noticed they decided to waste some space and placed a large hexagonal desk in the middle of the foyer. This is what my tax dollars support, Bill thought, I bet some useless fuckwit got paid $100,000 for that useless idea.

Bill walked to the stairwell on the right, immediately past the staff dining area, and headed up to the fifth floor. Bill noticed two "professors," or more accurately, useless fucking morons, working behind their desks.

"FUCK YOU! YOU PIECES OF SHIT OUGHTA JUST FUCKING KILL YOURSELVES. YOU KNOW WHERE THE ROOF IS. JUMP. JUST DO IT. YOU KNOW YOU CAN'T DO DENTISTRY FOR SHIT. THAT'S WHY YOU TRY TO TEACH YOU DUMB FUCKS!" Bill shouted. A familiar face curiously poked their head out of the room. It was "professor" Alex Chao, a useless fuckwit from overseas who was given a job because no sane specialist in Australia wanted to ruin their reputation by getting involved with the dental school.

"Who are you? What are you doing?" Chao asked. Of course that moron would not remember Bill. These cockroaches needed help remembering to breathe so having to spare brain function to remember Bill was far too much of a stretch.

"Heh heh heh heh, go back to fucking China you ineffective moron!" Bill arrogantly puffed his chest while raising both his middle fingers to the subhuman in front of him. Bill turned around without missing a beat and headed towards the second floor - the teaching floor.

As if it were fate, there was a student exiting the second floor clinic just as Bill stepped out of the stairwell. Bill rushed forward and slipped in before the door closed.

"ALL YOU FUCKING MORON STUDENTS! LISTEN UP! NOBODY IS GOING TO TELL YOU THE TRUTH EXCEPT ME! YOU'RE ALL FUCKING SCREWED! THAT'S RIGHT, JUST FUCKING QUIT DENTISTRY WHILE YOU'RE AHEAD. YOU THINK YOU CAN LEARN DENTISTRY FROM THESE FUCKING MORONS? FUCK. OFF. PEACE OUT NIGGAS!" Bill shouted at the top of his voice as he headed back out towards the reception area of the second floor. Bill turned around and saw Pamela, one of the nurses from long ago, staring at him. She was as useless as it got. No wonder she was stuck working in this shit hole. She had a troubled expression on her face.

"What the fuck you lookin' at bitch?" Bill spat at her while assaulting her with a chillingly twisted expression. She seemed lost for words as Bill exited the clinic.

The shouting attracted the attention of the security guards standing in the ground floor foyer. After all, the floors all had balconies overlooking the ground floor.

"Sir, please leave the premises. We will not ask kindly a second time," a tall, bald, dark skinned man said to Bill calmly while accompanied by a short, fat, old white man with white hair. What a fucking joke. That white cadaver should be in a hospital. Bill could kick his ass blindfolded.

"Alright, don't worry, I'm leaving, I'm leaving. What you gonna anyway? Ask me unkindly? Haha, fuck off. Next you're gonna call the popos who are gonna ask me even 'unkindlier'? I'm only here to tell the truth. I bet you don't remember me that's why you useless fucks get paid by *my* tax dollars to eat donuts all day," Bill verbally assaulted them as he left for the stairwell. The two guards followed Bill as he exited the hospital.

It was somewhat cathartic but not enough. Nothing less than murder murder would be enough to satiate Bill. However, if he committed murder now, his long list of enemies would remain untouched. He had to be patient.

As Bill walked towards the CBD proper, he remembered that he should probably call his indemnity insurer. Bill searched for their number on Google and dialled. It was an answering machine of course. Bill worked his way through the options until he reached a human operator.

"Hello this is Michelle from Dental Indemnity Society limited, how can I help?" a female voice sounded through the speaker.

"Uh hello, my name is doctor Bill Parker, I received a letter from some piece of shit law firm asking me to pay three million dollars, I need your help with this bullshit," Bill spoke unamused.

"Oh, that sounds very serious, please give me your membership number or confirm some details then I'll pass you on to one of our dento-legal advisers immediately," Michelle informed Bill.

After Bill gave her the details, a man answered the redirection.

"Hi, is this Bill I'm speaking to?" the voice asked.

"Yes, this is Bill, who am I speaking to?" Bill responded.

"Hi, my name is Dr Reginald D Archibald, I was told you received a letter from a solicitor?" Reginald asked.

"Yes, are you a lawyer?" Bill asked.

"I'm a prosthodontist by training but I've got looooots of experience with these matters. I've been doing this sort of work before you were even born. You haven't seen anywhere near the stuff that I have. I'm also a consultant for five hospitals and a shared Professor for both our

Victorian dental schools. I've been practising for over 30 years as a dentist and I've been dealing with dento - legal matters for DIS for -" Reginald was about to keep self-aggrandising his non-existent qualifications before Bill butted in.

"I'm not here to joke around. I need a goddamn lawyer. I was informed on your website that you have a partner law firm so why am I not talking to them?" Bill asked in a cold tone.

"Calm down Bill, I'm here to help. I may not be a lawyer but I'm very experienced with assisting clients manage their patients and prepare the information to pass onto the lawyers," Reginald replied.

"Oh my god, Jesus, Jesus, Jesus. Am I even living in the real world? What the hell is wrong with you people... There is no fucking patient, I haven't seen this bitch for years! I don't know what the fuck happened after the clinic owner said he'll "take care of it." There is no fucking patient management required here!" Bill started yelling into the phone.

"Hold on there Bill, hold on. I've dealt with this a million times, I know exactly what's going on. My experiences are much wider than yours-" Reginald seemed to be tone deaf.

"Jesus FUCK! I DO NOT CARE about your qualifications or experience. You are not a lawyer. There is no benefit in speaking to you," Bill firmly stated.

"Calm down, I understand how troubling receiving a letter from solicitors can be. I've even received one myself. Believe me, you can rest assured this is familiar territory for me. I was giving a lecture about dealing with solicitors only a week ago. You're just shocked this is the first time it's happened to you. I'm not belittling you but you are a young practitioner," Reginald said.

"Oh my God, I did not call to compare dick sizes over our fucking credentials and experience. I do. Not. Give. A. Fuck. If I can't speak to a lawyer then just tell me goddamit!" Bill raged further.

"You can speak to a lawyer, it's just that there's a procedure to follow. Can you tell me just a bit more about what happened?" Reginald insisted.

"Why? If you're going to pass the information on, why don't I just tell the lawyers directly? Why have all this middle man bullshit?" Bill asked.

"I completely understand your perspective. Of course direct communication is more reliable but I am just following protocol. I'm not just rubber stamping. I'm very experienced in these matters and bear in mind, progressing to the lawyers is very rare. On occasion when it's happened, the legal team have been very thankful for my contribution -" Reginald started to blow his own horn again until Bill interjected.

"I. Do. Not. Care. Do you ever see a heart surgeon coming up to you and telling you how to do a crown prep? Why? Cause THEY'RE NOT FUCKING QUALIFIED! Jesus fuck! If you want the whole story, then I need to speak face to face to a goddamn lawyer! It's fucking ineffective to speak over the phone, everybody just twists my words and never listen properly!" Bill raged like an inferno.

"OK, OK, I understand you're very upset. If there were a lawyer on speed dial, we would love to just pass you straight onto them but you have to understand the system in place. It's not designed for that and they're very busy. Look, the law firm we work with triages the cases and depending on the circumstance, they may arrange an interview with you within the week or it could take much longer. They don't just deal with our cases either," Reginald explained.

"Can you understand that this case needs a lawyer immediately? There's no clinical management, no goddamn patient communication, no manipulation bullshit. It's way too far gone," Bill pleaded for the moron to understand some sense.

"Yes, it does indeed sound very serious. Alright, trust me, I will be passing this on immediately to the legal team. However, I still need some more information. The lawyers need at least a basic outline in addition to the letter you received," Reginald requested yet again.

"I'm going to make this as simple as possible. I barely remember shit. It was two years ago and she was a fat fuck who shoved her tongue into my bur when I was doing a lower molar crown prep. I haven't seen her since. I did not make a crown for her, I did not cement anything, she did not contact me and I heard nothing from the clinic owner. I do not have a fucking clue what's happened. Does that sound like enough information?" Bill fought back.

"Alright. Take a break and have a good rest at home. You will be hearing from us soon, maybe even today. However, rest assured, legal matters do not progress like you see on TV. Sorting this matter out could take until next year. We have time on our hands," Reginald informed Bill.

"Is that all?" Bill asked.

"Yes, have a good day," Reginald said before Bill aggressively slammed his finger onto the "hang up" icon.

Chapter 22

Clown world

That day Bill headed to the ANZAC memorial for a walk before heading back. He was not feeling any better. How could anyone relax after having such a bombshell dropped on them? Bill was right about dentistry. Dentistry made him poorer. The harder he worked, the more his liability skyrocketed. He had to quit on the spot. Bill noticed a trend. Patients were getting worse. The next generation of patients would be the millennials. Bill was a millennial himself by definition. He knew how fucking destitute these subhumans were yet they were a million times more demanding than the baby boomers. Always wanting everything for nothing. The next millennial that walked through the door could be another fucking $4 million liability.

Bill turned his phone silent that night and ignored all the calls henceforth. Bill was completely unable to rise out of bed for anything other than urinating or drinking and eating for the whole week. He was unable to even rise for more than one hour a day. The anger was so overwhelmingly painful to bear, he could only feel relief by sleeping. As he turned his phone silent, Bill also missed the call from his indemnity insurer. A week later, Cheng seemed to buzz on Bill's apartment.

"What the fuck are you doing idiot?" Cheng's voice rang through the intercom after Bill picked up the receiver. Without saying a word, Bill pressed the door access switch for Cheng. A minute later, Bill heard Cheng knock on his door.

"Where the fuck have you been bitch? Everyone at the clinic has been trying to reach you. Andy actually asked me to contact you but you haven't answered shit," Cheng said.

"I fucking quit. I can't do dentistry any more. I am fucking done," Bill replied.

"I heard that from Barbara, what made you so angry? Was it another complaint?" Cheng asked. Bill sighed. He did not want to have to explain the bullshit again.

"Just read this," Bill said while he rummaged through his small briefcase to find the solicitor's letter. Cheng read the letter with a complicated expression on his face.

"What the fuck? $3.4 million? Are they insane? You do realise when men have their arms ripped off, their payout is in the hundreds of thousands not millions. What the fuck is wrong with this world? It's like a circus," Cheng replied completely agreeing with Bill.

"I've told you, men like us, we're being actively hunted. This is a sign. I am a victim of the passive genocide. I am already a dead man. The harder I work, the poorer I get. The more I earn, the more I lose. It's a fucking rigged game. As you said Cheng, the only way to not lose, is not to play. I can't do any more fucking dentistry. In fact, there's no point working at all now since they're gonna take all my money. Every fucking thing I've worked for, society has decided to steal from me. They might as well just put a gun to my head and shoot me while looting my cash. The only fucking reason I'm not washing my mouth out with a revolver is because of my mission. I need to enact justice for those who have it coming," Bill coldly replied.

"Do you remember anything about this case?" Cheng asked.

"It was from 2016, I barely remember shit. In fact, do me a favour Cheng, go to Mega and send me all her records. Notes, x-rays, photos, all that shit cause I bet the lawyers are gonna need that," Bill requested.

"So you're never coming back to Mega again? Not even gonna step foot through the door?" Cheng asked.

"Never again. Fuck it. I am never gonna even get close to a dental clinic. Not even to treat my own teeth cause fuck it, I'm gonna be dead soon so why would I need dentistry?" Bill stated with confidence.

"Well don't kill yourself before you can enact your revenge. Are you still seeing the shrink and taking your meds?" Cheng asked.

"Fuck psychology and psychiatry, you know it's a scam. In fact,why don't you look up Gert Postel? That guy proved, beyond a reasonable doubt, all those psychology and psychiatry wankers don't know what the fuck they're talkin' about. He just decided to one day pretend he was a psychiatrist and they were too fucking stupid to tell. I'm not gonna see any psychiatrist or psychologist again. I'm just taking out repeat prescriptions of my meds from my GP now. If anything, I need to spend all of what I've got left on my revenge. Believe me, those people who have it coming, they better fucking watch out. All those morons out there, they talk all that shit about "do no harm" but *I'm* the one who actually admitted I have a problem and I went to see a fucking shrink and took responsibility for my problems. I turned my compulsions to my advantage. You will never see people do the kind of work I do, or you do for that matter. It's because I'm compelled to do things properly unlike Terry or Linda or all those cockroaches there. I've isolated the harm I have caused, to *myself*. And I'm the crazy one? You look at Terry, that's what's considered normal now. And I'm the fucking crazy one? Am I even living in the real world??!" Bill despairingly choked out while clutching his head and shaking back and forth.

Bill continued his ranting to Cheng for almost an hour. Bill recounted all the complaints he could remember and all his frustrations about dentistry without stopping.

"Don't die. I'm sure you can find some sort of alternative career. You were talking about becoming those public safety officers," Cheng suggested.

"But there's no recruitment drive on at the moment. I might apply. But only if this legal bullshit is resolved, which it probably won't. By the way, are there metal detectors in court?" Bill asked with a sudden chilling twist.

"Uhh... Dental matters almost never go to court dude... The most probable murder opportunity you're gonna get is either mediation or VCAT. Even then, you're pretty short and weak. I bet you haven't eaten in a week. Even a bunch of girls can restrain your malnourished ass," Cheng poured some cold water on the fire.

"Hehehe, believe me, if I planned it properly, there will be no survivors," Bill said while oozing with malice.

"O...K... then. Don't kill anyone. I was just joking. Seriously, don't bring any weapon in," Cheng stated seriously this time.

"Heh heh, you're a good friend Cheng. You're a good friend. I regret most things, but if I could re-live my life any way I wanted, I would not change a thing leading up to the time I met you. My life would be that much poorer if we never met. Don't look so worried. I would have died a long ass time ago if it weren't for you holding me accountable for my actions, turning me into the Ubermensch I am today. Remember the time you accidentally outed me and Chunyun in front of Helen?" Bill asked.

"Uh... yeah, sorry about that," Cheng replied.

"No, no, you don't gotta apologise. I should actually thank you for that. You see, given all the attention I was getting from multiple females, I became lost in my euphoria. I felt like it was okay for me to do what I did. When you outed me, I looked in the bathroom mirror and I asked myself, 'Are you proud of what you've become?' And that's when it hit me. I had turned into a subhuman cockroach. You know I endeavour to set myself apart from everyone, to be an Ubermensch. Had you not exposed me in front of everyone, I might have continued down the wrong path, not realizing that I was destroying myself and becoming the opposite, an *untermensch*. Looking back, I now realise you did the right thing so you should have nothing to feel nervous about, nothing to apologise for. What you did that day, that's what a friend of the superior kind would do. Nevertheless, you run your mouth off at the worst of times so my gosh, just watch your goddamn mouth alright?" Bill expressed his deep seated feelings.

"Okay then, as long as you're not mad about it... Well what should I tell Andy? Should I reveal everything?" Cheng asked, somewhat concerned about Bill's intentions.

"Say whatever the fuck you want. I'm not talkin' to the guy any more. I'm done with dentistry. I don't care what he does. He doesn't even have to pay me for the past week. It's just gonna get stolen by some lawyer fuck anyway," Bill dejectedly declared.

"Well, whatever. Bye bitch. Don't kill yourself, and don't go killing," Cheng urged.

"Keep that attitude up and you're gonna be on my list too," Bill warned. Cheng seemed to be quaking with genuine fear as he left Bill's apartment.

Bill checked his phone. There was a voice message from Dental Indemnity Society. Fuck. Bill missed it entirely. Bill dialled his voice message service and after skipping through a stack of useless messages left by Andy and the Mega crew, Bill finally reached the important message. "Dear doctor William Parker, please call to schedule an appointment with our legal team" a woman's voice sounded through followed by a 1300 number. Bill dialled the number and was met within a few seconds by a real human operator.

"Hello this is Mary from Dental Indemnity Society speaking," another female voice sounded through the speaker.

"Uh hello, this is Dr William Parker. Last week I reported that I received a solicitor's letter. I haven't heard anything back until today. I was a bit busy. You tell me what's going on," Bill lied, he was not busy. "It said something about scheduling an appointment with the legal team?"

"Ah yes, let me please confirm a few details..." Mary said and Bill had to go through the whole charade again.

"So we have a few appointment slots available," Mary started speaking slowly as if expecting Bill to suggest a good time.

"When's the earliest available. I'm unemployed now so I have all the fucking time in the world," Bill explained. He heard Mary chuckle for a second.

"How about Thursday the 12th of April at 2:15pm?" Mary suggested.

"Alright, lock that in," Bill requested.

"Do you know where to find the lawyers?" Mary asked.

"No," Bill replied, obviously.

"Alright, so it's on 469 La Trobe Street, Melbourne. It is located right beside the Slater and Gordon Building. You want to look for Montpellier and Partners. To prepare for the interview, make sure you send us a copy of the solicitor's letter as soon as possible, and bring with you on the day, all patient records including but not limited to models, photos, written notes, any sort of patient correspondence, lab correspondence and notes and anything you can think of in relation to the patient," Mary explained. She must have been following a script.

"Alright, I know where that is. I'll get everything ready," Bill replied.

"Is there anything else I can do for you today Bill?" Mary asked.

"No that'll be all," Bill sternly concluded.

"Bye, bye," Mary signed off and ended the call.

Fortunately for Bill, Cheng came through and provided the information for Bill. There was one critical problem. There were no written notes. Cheng informed Bill that there was a photo and an x-ray and nothing beyond that. Apparently that bitch never saw Andy or anyone else at Mega for that matter. She just ditched like a cheating bitch and never came back, Bill thought. Bill repeated his pattern of slumbering with the absolute minimum time dedicated to eating and relieving himself as usual until Thursday arrived. Despite the absurdity of the situation, Bill still did his triple shower and self-preparation regime. Bill brought a USB memory stick containing all the files he received and placed it and the solicitor's letter of demand into his briefcase. Then Bill set out.

Stopping only to buy a cheap cheeseburger at McDonald's, Bill arrived half an hour before the expected time. It was traumatic riding public transport. Bill had to struggle hard not to start killing. After all, how could anyone in his position not kill? There were used up whores staring at him like he was some fucking sewer rat as usual. What the fuck was wrong with society? Did his face fucking *offend* them? Bill felt like he was Anne Frank. He was forced to be locked up in his apartment. If he *dared* walk out in public, his face was a fucking shining Star of David. It screamed “Der Jude” in a crowd of Nazis.

He could not just ignore them. They were actively hunting him. How could anyone surrounded by enemies not think of murdering? He would not go down like Anne Frank. If he were put in her body, he would have gone down killing as many Nazis as he could. Fuck “morality.” In a game of survival, there were no rules. The only way to stop himself from murdering was the online gore videos. As long as he could watch those subhuman cockroaches getting murdered, that was enough catharsis to temporarily satiate his bloodlust. Both on the train and tram, Bill had to clench his fists hard while replaying the bloodbath he watched online in his head with his eyes closed. Just insert the faces of the women on public transport onto the bodies of the online victims.

The final tram ride delivered Bill virtually right in front of 469 La Trobe and he walked into the foyer. Montpellier and Partners... they were located on the fifth floor. Bill caught the elevator up and exited onto the fifth floor. Bill approached a typical office like space and opened the door to see a receptionist with a headset talking as he entered.

“That will be fine, good day, we’ll be in touch, bye!” she said before greeting Bill, “Hi, welcome to Montpellier and Partners, did you have an appointment with us?”

“My name is Bill Parker. I was sent here by Dental Indemnity Society for an appointment at 2:15pm,” Bill explained with a dark expression.

“Alright, that’s right, we have a meeting scheduled soon, please have a seat in the lounge while our team gets ready,” the receptionist said while pointing to a large, fancy, 6 seated leather sofa.

Bill sat down and appraised his surroundings. The space he was in now was a rectangular area around 5m by 10m. The reception desk ran parallel to the long wall and behind the receptionist was a metal plaque with the name "Montpellier and Partners" in large letters. The desk ended with a right turn into the wall and a pot plant filled the gap between the desk and the large floor to ceiling window. There was a door leading to the offices on the opposite side. Bill waited while scrolling through more black pill content online. Montpellier, Bill thought, same as that place in France. Was it even a real name? Some idiot probably picked it because it sounded foreign and fancy. Some pretense of pedigree. If they were legitimate, they must have been a better established firm than Chao and Chaudry who clearly showed Asian ethnicity. There were lots of Asian lawyers now but the wealthy, established lawyers were almost all old white men. Same for any fucking industry, Bill had to admit.

Soon the door opened and an old white man did indeed appear.

"Hi, you must be Bill?" the man asked.

"Yes," Bill replied. Then the man extended his hand and firmly gripped Bill's hand.

"Bruce, nice to meet you," Bruce introduced himself.

"Follow me, we're going to have an initial conference and introduction. Welcome to our firm by the way," Bruce said while leading Bill through a maze of corridors and offices. "Have a seat," Bruce finally stopped after leading Bill into a conference room with a rectangular wooden table surrounded by six meshed office chairs. Bill sat down opposite two other people. One was an older woman and another was a young Asian man.

"Let me introduce Margaret and Liu, they're part of my team," Bruce said while allowing an opportunity for Bill and the team to greet each other.

"I was informed about your situation from DIS and they have forwarded me the details you sent them. Can you give us more background?" Bruce started the questioning.

"You're asking me about something which happened two years ago. I barely remember what the hell happened. I remember her coming in as a new patient. I did not schedule the appointment, it was all done by the reception team. Normally I don't just do crowns straight up, I keep telling those morons at the desk to always book a consult *before* doing any big procedure but when it comes to me, somehow anything goes," Bill mockingly admonished Mega dental, eliciting a chuckle from the lawyers, "so she comes in and tells me something about doing root canal and I must have taken the x-ray to check. The tooth was pretty heavily filled so I agreed to do a crown on the spot since they booked her in for a long ass time. I don't remember much other than her pushing her fat tongue repeatedly against me. No matter how many times I told her to stop, she just kept pushing. My hand was hell tired and she just kept pushing and pushing like an addict. She managed to bend my mirror, and I mean stainless steel, then jammed her tongue into my drill. After that, I tried rescheduling her to finish the procedure and check on her but she cancelled and decided to book in with the clinic owner. That's all I know. I only found out yesterday that the patient never came back. I have no idea what the hell is going on any more than you guys."

"Hmmm. I see. This is quite unfortunate. It's clearly not your fault. No follow up, no communications. This isn't favourable but it's clearly her responsibility for cancelling and refusing to see you again. I'd just like to confirm, there were no written notes about the patient afterwords," Bruce checked with Bill.

"I don't know. I'm usually so goddamn tired that I sometimes don't have time to write notes. You have no idea how bad it gets. With the shit that goes on at Mega dental, you would be that tired too," Bill declared.

"This makes things a bit more complicated but don't worry. These kind of threats are completely baseless. I know of Chao and Chaudry. They're just a collection of youngsters out to make a quick buck. Just to quote some stats, some studies show over 96% of cases are settled before judgment. Something like over 80% of civil litigation never gets presented to a judge. Chao and Chaudry are way in over their heads if they want to front up to the Supreme Court for 3.4 million dollars in litigation. There's no chance they would proceed to actual court. We've worked with DIS for over 20 years and in my experience, only one case we've dealt with ended up with a judgment," Bruce stated.

"Did you win?" Bill asked.

"Sort of. We massively reduced the payout because the other party was showing such poor conduct, however the guy we were defending did something pretty awful. Anyway, everything else has been settled out of court. Most of which never even came to a judge. I am obliged to divulge one thing before we proceed. We have been hired by DIS and our fiduciary responsibility is shared to both DIS and you. So we're technically not your "personal" lawyers but we're definitely on your side. This is how it's going to go. The letter you received has a ridiculous demand but that's how lawyers make their money. Their client is going to get what's left after they take their fees out so of course their initial demand is going to be ridiculous. Our job is to negotiate that demand down to a reasonable level," Bruce started explaining before Bill interjected.

"Come on, 3.4 million is far too ridiculous. Are these guys morons?" Bill asked.

"Aha, ha ha, I wouldn't put it that way. I think they're looking overseas at the United States where there was this dentist in St Louis by the name of O'Keefe who had something similar happen. In fact, their letter pretty much quotes word for word the complainant's impact statement. The patient was awarded 2.5 million US dollars so they just converted that to Australian dollaridoos. But look mate, we're not in the United States, or as we call it, 'fantasy land.' We aren't that stupid," Bruce went on to explain with a casual tone.

"So aren't you gonna defend me? I should be paying zero fucking dollars," Bill argued vehemently.

"Woah, calm down. I know it's shocking but reducing it to zero dollars requires actually fronting up to court. They know they can't afford to go to court and we definitely don't want to run that risk either. DIS have got geniuses crunching the numbers in their actuarial team. It's beyond a reasonable doubt as we lawyers like to say. Just paying a nominal payout a hundred times is far cheaper, and I really mean it, far, faaaar cheaper than receiving judgment even once. Even if you win civil cases, the other side goes bankrupt and you get nothing in the end. Believe me, and I'm not kidding when I say this, going to court and fighting it out, is the worst possible outcome. It will involve years of stress and the fees alone could blow out into the millions. Plus, you can never predict how the judge will decide. Even the strongest 'open and shut' cases get turned upside down on their heads. I've seen it happen many times. I've pulled a couple of those victories myself, not to toot my own horn," Bruce elaborated calmly and casually again.

"So how much am I going to lose? Is the insurer going to pay for everything?" Bill asked.

"I can't guarantee you, but most of the time, DIS would cover all fees as long as you adhere by their terms and conditions. They would have to confirm it with their underwriter of course but that's usually just a formality. Don't worry about this. Let us handle everything. This isn't like what you see on telly. It's gonna take months and months before you hear from us again. What's gonna happen is this. We're going to be communicating with Chao and Chaudry and give them a piece of our mind. There's going to be lots happening in the background so you don't have to get involved. I hope they listen to reason and accept our deal but worst case scenario, you'll probably need to front up for some mediation. This is when we meet with the other side. Now it's not compulsory for you to be there, neither is it for the patient but trust me, under these situations, the outcome is almost always more favourable with the good faith demonstrated by all parties being present. All you have to do now is relax, go on a holiday or something, take your mind off this. Just listen out for our communications," Bruce confidently stated ending their discussion there.

"Just handle it for me, I don't fucking care..." Bill dejectedly uttered before leaving.

Bill and the team said their goodbyes and Bill left without feeling reassured. Those morons were just going to accept defeat? What the fuck was happening to this world? Bill was not sure what to do. He could possibly contact Golden Fort legal and hire some independent lawyers to properly work for him but then he would have no money left to eat and pay rent. Since Bill was not footing the bill he was just a nuisance to be pushed aside. Bill could not help but laugh out loud at the absurdity of the situation. He had about $200,000 invested in total over the past four years working at Mega. It was not bad considering just how terrible his income was during his first two years but if Bruce's opinion was anything to go by, he needed a million fucking dollaridoos to fight it out in court.

Bill gritted his teeth and clenched his fists. He was rendered powerless by the mass passive genocide. Bill could guess why Bruce the moron refused to "guarantee" the insurer would cover all costs. That subhuman cockroach knew that the insurers would try to wriggle their way out of paying as much as possible. It was the claimant's job to secure a payout whereas it was the insurer's job to wriggle out of it. In the United States, it was basically routine to take insurers to court due to this exact problem. Bill looked at the time. He was certain they began the discussion at 2:10, running a little early. It was now 2:31pm. With all the time spent walking in and out, the interview lasted 15 minutes at most.

He spent at least 30 minutes at Golden Fort and it was all free. It was clear whose interests Bruce was protecting.

* * *

Bill discovered that Bruce was right about one thing. Real life legal matters took forever to resolve. Bill did not hear from Bruce or DIS for months. Not that it mattered. Bill was depleted to the point of becoming a gelatinous blob. Bill had hoped that quitting dentistry would improve his mental and physical health. Unfortunately, Bill could not manage anything more than 5 waking hours a day. That was if Bill took double the dosage of Modafinil and caffeine together. If he did not take those drugs, Bill could only manage 1 waking hour at most. Staying awake was painful.

The Friday after the lawyer consultation, Bill woke up to read the news.

"Toxic masculinity fuelling pandemic of domestic violence."

Bill instantly exploded into fiery rage causing him to smash his $2 bargain keyboard with both fists. His right hand still ached from punching the dry wall at Mega at Carlton but he could not help it. The trash, liberal (with a small "l") "non-player character" filled mainstream media outlets were shitting propaganda again! Bill was forced to remember he was being *actively hunted* even in the safety of his own home. Bill was trapped in a clown world. Bill's hands were shaking uncontrollably again. His head ached and his heart raced, his vision narrowing yet again. These fucking subhumans were destroying society and killing Bill so the only option, the *only* fucking option, was the final solution. Bill *had* to kill. How could anyone not kill? Kill. Kill. Kill.

Bill regretted reading the news. The burning pain from his relationship failures raced through his head yet again. He could not control it. Sarah, Erika, Esmeralda, Helen... The pain was insurmountable. Why? Why? Why? Why?!! Bill screamed internally. Anna the tongue patient was there laughing at him. She was going to destroy *everything* he worked for! "You're either with me, or against me!" Bill thought. Nobody was on his side. Especially not those useless fucking moron lawyers he met. The pain was lighting his head on fire yet Bill had no recourse, no relief except sleep. Bill returned to watching violence and animal abuse for an hour before lying down to sleep yet again. Every waking moment was agony.

The week after that, Bill had to go shopping. He almost failed to return. All Bill had to do was purchase his weekly necessities plus a few discount snacks. Normally, he was in and out within 15 minutes but that was ample time for the females to torment him. Why did those subhumans have to train here? Bill wanted to napalm that fucking gym on the top level of the South Yarra shopping complex. As he was looking for some discounted pastries, a girl wearing tight yoga pants and a figure hugging tank top exchanged eye contact with Bill. In that most fleeting of an exchange, Bill noticed a smirk on her face. She was looking down on him. All of a sudden, the rage flooded Bill like a tsunami again.

Bill tried looking away but the rage would not subside. How *dare* she look down on him? She was just some fucking whore flashing her used up goods in the hopes of finding some sugar daddy. She was nothing. She was absolute scum. Yet she looked down on Bill like he was some kind of *sewer rat*?!! Bill started shaking again, this time with all his usual symptoms of angina plus hyperventilation. There were knives being sold right behind the fresh food area. If he ran, he could grasp any old knife and start slicing and dicing. Bill started to walk in that direction, except there were public safety officers standing outside. Fuck. Bill wanted to murder now but he knew that he had to protect his best interests. If he were caught now, who would enact revenge on his death list?

In the end, Bill had to spend another five minutes huffing and puffing in the fresh food area avoiding all eye contact. He barely managed to contain his homicidal rage. That was too close. Bill could not guess how much longer he could pretend to be functional in public. All it took was a glance and he was triggered. Bill had no choice but to withhold bargain hunting today. He could not risk another outburst. Bill rushed to collect some basic prepackaged salad and frozen vegetables, then some discount pies. Whatever was cheap and easy would suffice. He was unemployed and about to become bankrupt, not that it mattered. Bill never purchased fancy groceries. After a herculean effort, Bill barely made it through to his apartment door before collapsing on the ground. He woke only a couple of hours later to place the refrigerated groceries in the refrigerator. Then he collapsed within seconds of lying back down on his "bed."

Such was life for Bill. Sometimes his anger was forcibly ignited by the subhumans a whole week in a row. Sometimes it was just one day. Once, Bill was lucky enough to narrowly avoid the genocidal forces of the subhumans for 10 days in a row. Bill did not choose to be like this. Society made him into the monster he was. Yet, society *never* took responsibility for the mess it created and continued to torture him like a wounded, chained bear. Society was sadistic beyond words, yet they called Bill the crazy one? It took five whole months before Bill heard back from Montpelllier.

"Hello Bill? This is Bruce calling from Montpellier and Partners, how have you been?" Bruce's theatrically friendly and energetic voice sounded through the phone.

"Uh, uh hem," Bill croaked to clear his throat. He had not spoken in over a week so his larynx was somewhat rusty. "Uh hem, yes this is Bill."

"Bill, I think we're coming very close to some sort of resolution. Let me give a brief run-down of what's been happening. After your meeting, we returned a sternly worded counter-offer. Basically we told them to get stuffed. There have been payouts in the hundreds of thousands for disabilities like hers, but nowhere near what they asked for," Bruce explained. Bill was not amused. A "counter-offer" was not the same as "get stuffed."

"So are they backing off? Did you tell them zero fucking dollars?" Bill asked demandingly.

"Aha ha ha, close to. Very close. The thing is, the more evidence you give us, the more confidently we can bargain our way down," Bruce casually pointed out. Great, Bill thought, this fucking subhuman moron was now blaming Bill for their weak ass defence.

"Hold on, hold on, you're not gonna pin this on me. I did nothing wrong. Jesus. Oh my God. All you lawyers don't understand what it's like working in THAT FUCKING SHITHOLE," Bill could not help but scream.

"Oh no no no, don't get me wrong, I'm not trying to blame you at all. It's not your fault she never came back and threw this curveball at you. Normally we'd hire some specialist involved to examine her but we didn't get the chance. They have all the advantage since they got their own specialist in on this, do you know a Professor Tara Nelson?" Bruce asked.

"WHAT? They got that moron bitch? She's just some fucking retired dentist who hasn't worked for 20 years. She used to teach at the dental school as some kind of 'dental anthropologist' so what the fuck would she know about actual fucking dentistry?" Bill exclaimed in disbelief.

"I know, they know, everyone knows but she's still got letters behind her name so let's pretend this matter does go to court, in the eyes of the judge, she's still just as convincing as someone who is an actual dentist. Probably even more so," Bruce explained further.

"FUCK! Can you get rid of her? What the fuck did she say?" Bill enquired aggressively.

"I can send you the report. I didn't want to bother you since you sounded like you wanted us to handle everything. Their lawyers are following this professor's words about using a dental dam to protect the tongue-" Bruce summarised before being interrupted.

"THAT'S FUCKING BULLSHIT! NOBODY USES RUBBER DAM WHEN DOING CROWNS!" Bill was forced to shout.

"We know, we know. We got Reg, remember Reginald? Amazing guy, he's the best specialist when it comes to crowns. I think we have a good chance of reducing the payout to almost nothing compared to what they're demanding. However, we do need you to come in for mediation. I mentioned before, you don't have to come, but it's a show of good faith if you're there. I have a good feeling we can resolve this then and there," Bruce said.

"Alright. I'll let you do all the talking," Bill said.

"Aha ha ha, that's fine. You'll be hearing some more details from Mandy our secretary. She'll explain all the details to you," Bruce concluded before the two said their goodbyes.

Chapter 23

No fake apologies

Bill sat in a conference room with a large rectangular desk. There were six chairs on each side of the table. On Bill's side, 4 chairs were occupied by Bruce's team and Bill. On the other side sat Anna the tongue patient and two people who were probably her legal team. Both of whom appeared to be around Bill's age. One was a Chinese Asian looking man, the other was a dark skinned Asian man. If Bruce's report was accurate, they were probably Chao and Chaudry who were small time petty lawyers. Bill stared daggers at everyone in the room. He was in full anger mode. His heart rate and blood pressure were sky high. His headache pounded like thunder and his vision was half black. Bill fought to keep his hands from shaking under the desk. Hopefully, nobody would see it.

The mediation session started with the mediator introducing himself. Bill forgot the name already but he was some retired judge. Bill was then forced to endure the subhumans from the patient's side orate some sob story while the bitch patient cried crocodile tears.

"Our client is so traumatised by her injuries that she has ceased talking in public. She now only speaks to family members and friends. Our client wishes nothing more than to get on with the life she has left. I hope this matter can be settled today. Thank you for your attention," Chao ended his verbal diarrhoea.

"Hmmm... You have done well to adhere to time limits. Thank you for your speech. Now we will hear from the other side," the mediator said, motioning for Bruce's team to speak up. Bill did not expect much from Bruce but even then he was disappointed. That fucking cockroach didn't even bother to defend me, Bill thought.

Bruce immediately began with a fake exaggeration of how sorry Bill felt and that this was a "one in a million" freak accident. There was the usual bullshit about how much Bill cared about his patients. I guess that's not entirely bullshit, Bill thought, he cared about his work but not so much his patients. Bruce said nothing about the fact that this fucking bitch in front of him *forced* her tongue against his drill. She fucking lunged at it harder than Usain Bolt running for gold. In fact, that fucking bitch probably trained in Olympic level competitive tongue thrusting and they expected Bill to protect *her* from the results of her own actions? All these morons, they deserved nothing but to live with the consequences of their own actions.

"We do not argue with the fact that a dental dam theoretically had the potential to avoid this injury. However, we have very convincing authority, and believe me, from someone who actually still does loooooots of real dental work," Bruce said while giving Bill a wink, "in Anna's case, a dental dam arguably may have been more of an inconvenience than a benefit. Doctor Bill, upon weighing the risks and benefits, decided not to apply the dam. A decision any ordinary, reasonable dentist would have made in the circumstances. As the law dictates, we cannot retroactively assess risk with the benefit of hindsight. Thus, I must stress, the accident, deeply regrettable it may be, was a freak accident and is not to happen again. I also stress that our client, Doctor Bill, feels profoundly apologetic and we are willing to compensate. The amount you have demanded does not fit our expectations. I hope today we can eventually come to an agreeable figure. Thank you for your attention, that will be all from us," Bruce concluded.

After that, there was a break and the mediator had some private talks with both parties in separate rooms. Bill seethed quietly. He was too angry for words. The day dragged on without his consent. After returning to the negotiating table, both sides started deliberating figures. Eventually, the best offer the other side could accept was $300,000 and a personal apology from Bill. Again, the two parties were escorted to private rooms. The mediator came to have a short chat with Bruce. Bruce merely nodded at the guy. The fucking bitch did not deserve $300,000. Bill would also not fucking apologise. Bill would *NEVER* fucking apologise for something that was *NOT* his fault.

"Bill, you look a bit upset. I understand. It's OK. I think today has been *really* productive despite what it looks like. The other party is willing to settle! That's amazing! This can be ended right here right now. I'm feeling pretty confident that if this all goes through, the underwriters will approve and take care of everything for you. I think we're really, really lucky that those guys are just small fry, this is the best they can come up with after all. They know they won't get anything better. Come on mate, just say, 'I'm sorry,' and this nightmare will be over for you. Then you can get back and start doing good ol' dentistry again," Bruce explained.

"Oh my God. I will *NOT* apologise for something that's not my fault!" Bill stammered through gritted teeth.

"No, not at all! Definitely not your 'fault' per se," Bruce remarked while doing double finger air quotes, "if this matter is settled, you're completely absolved of liability. Just say, 'I'm sorry' and you're all good! It's not an admission of fault or liability at. All. All you're saying is that, 'Look Anna, I feel bad about how things have turned out, it's not anyone's fault, but what happened has happened,' alright?" Bruce encouraged.

"I've said this many times before and I will say it again. I never make fake apologies. When somebody gives me a fake apology, it just pisses me off more. Believe me, I've had it done to me so many times. NO apology can be made without following it up with action and NO fucking apology should EVER be made for something that I have zero fucking fault to begin with. If I make some fake ass apology, that bitch is gonna think that she won. Afterwards, she's gonna tell all her fake ass friends and they're all gonna think dentists are a bunch of pushovers. Just invent some bullshit story and then get a payout! Teehee! Don't you see the harm this causes? Just think of everyone doing this. Can your underwriter afford to pay hundreds of thousands for every fucking patient? It's not just you or me. Other dentists are gonna start changing their behaviour. Everyone is going to only do bullshit treatment and tell patients to piss off. You think I like to practise defensive dentistry? Does anyone *want* to treat their patient like a fucking liability? I am NOT going to support this kind of bullshit!"Bill protested vehemently.

"Bill, I completely agree with everything you said but this is all just legal mumbo jumbo. Lawyers do this all the time. Do we mean it? No way! Who cares? In the end, you walk, she walks, I walk, everyone drops this matter and it's done and dusted. I know it leaves a sour taste in the mouth but don't think of this as a loss. If this ends today, then we've won!" Bruce continued attempting to persuade.

"Oh my God, that bitch isn't a lawyer. She isn't gonna know it's some fake ass apology. How would someone like that know what 'no admission of liability' means? What the fuck does that legal bullshit even mean? All she sees is some dumbass bowing and kowtowing *and* she gets paid," Bill protested.

"Alright Bill," Bruce replied, adopting a stern tone. "Don't do it for her, do it for me, OK? Just do it for me."

Bill did not respond. He was far too angry to say a word. Did that moron not understand the sheer audacity of what he said? By having

Bill blatantly fucking lie, like a fucking cheap washed up actor, they "won"? Lawyers do this "all the time"? This was the brutal reality. Lawyers lied their asses off like diseased rats in a diseased sewer that was the legal system. No, not just the corrupt system, all of society was like this. Everything was run on lies. Just fucking be honest, Bill thought, why could people not be honest? Now Bill was being *forced* to participate, like a rat being drowned in infested sewer water. Bill should have brought a knife along but he was perhaps feeling too kind in the morning. Maybe it was good he did not bring a knife. He could not have resisted stabbing if he did. Bill merely nodded his head. He could not risking his last $200k. No money meant an imminent death. In other words, a death sentence.

"That's the way mate. I thought you would be reasonable!" Bruce congratulated Bill while slapping Bill on the back. After a few more minutes, the participants were escorted back into the central conference room.

Bill sighed deeply. Bruce was just another manifestation of the terminal illness affecting society. Whenever there was the slightest problem, the insurers and dentists both surrender and say, "I'll pay, I'll pay!" while at the same time leaping into the air and slamming their heads on the ground like the Japanese "dogeza" apology. The fact that Bill already lost was a foregone conclusion - Bruce did not give a flying fuck whether or not Bill was at fault. Bruce was solely and purely focused on protecting the interests of the underwriter. Bruce *only* fucking cared about the patient walking away so that they could save on fucking legal fees. Where was the justice? Where was the morality in all this? This was just like how dentistry had nothing to do with health any more. Just fucking cosmetics and ceramics. This was the fucking standard in this fucked up country.

Bill had to hand it to the Koreans. Where his parents were, indemnity insurance was not compulsory and definitely not widespread. There were endless fraudsters attempting to steal money from doctors and dentists through the legal system in Korea. These morons had to sue practitioners individually and the system revealed them to the fraudsters they were. Practitioners paid real lawyers to defend them properly. Subhumans had to think twice about spending a truckload of money in the legal system unlike this fucking country. The regular practitioners were *forced* to fund the negligence of the subhuman moron practitioners. This was a moral hazard on both ends. Subhuman practitioners get to slice and dice and subhuman patients like Anna fuck themselves up and get paid a bonus. All these fucking vulture lawyers knew going after health professionals was a guaranteed easy win. Zero effort required.

Bruce took the helm and stated, "Through our discussions, Doctor Bill is willing to personally apologise and offers the $300,000 payout."

"Thank you. We are glad to accept your offer," Chao replied smugly.

"OK Bill, you're up," Bruce gestured for Bill to speak. Bill decided to stand up. The spotlight was on him so he might as well make it count. Just as he was standing up, Bill noticed something. Anna had a barely noticeable grin on her face. It was just the right side corner of her lip. It was curled upwards very subtly. Within an instant, nuclear rage roared inside Bill. Bill had seen that expression far too many times. He saw it on divorce court videos where women laughed at their husbands being thrown in prison because of losing their jobs and failing to pay child support. Bill saw it in his final brothel visit when that subhuman whore treated Bill like a *sewer rat*. Bill saw it repeatedly in public with women walking by, as if Bill's short stature somehow fucking *offended* them. He was so short his existence alone *offended* women. That fucking bitch sitting in front of him thought she had won. She was mocking down. That fucking subhuman trash, cockroach, untermensch was looking down on *him*. And now the subhumans were coercing him to *lie* for the sake of this fucking cockroach. This was not just any lie. It was one lie too many. The final straw which broke the camel's back. Money be damned. Bill would NOT be fucking *FORCED* to lie ever again, not even to protect himself.

"I WILL NOT FUCKING APOLOGISE FOR SOMETHING THAT ISN'T MY FAULT!!" Bill screamed at the top of his lungs. All of a sudden, the entire room was taken aback. Anna's lawyers immediately sat up straight, the mediator almost jumped in his chair. Bruce appeared to roll his eyes and break eye contact with Bill. The others on Bruce's team seemed to respond just like the other side.

"I DID NOTHING WRONG! I WAS TRYING TO PROTECT YOUR USELESS TONGUE YOU FUCKING SUBHUMAN WHORE! IT WAS YOUR FAULT YOU FUCKING SHOVED IT INTO MY BUR! And you know the worst fucking part? I was trying to HELP you! Am I the only one around here who cares about fucking STANDARDS? I tried to DO A GOOD FUCKING JOB PREPPING THE TOOTH PROPERLY!! You know the whole joke of this situation? If I were some ACTUAL negligent dentist, this would never have happened. I would have spent less than ten minutes turning your fucked up tooth into a cube and your tongue would have been fine!" Bill continued ranting.

"Bill, that's enough, stop," Bruce stood up and confronted Bill coldly.

"DON'T YOU FUCKING LECTURE ME YOU FUCKING SUBHUMAN! YOU DIDN'T DEFEND ME FOR A SECOND SO WHAT VALUE ARE YOU? You fucking subhumans want to kill me. But guess what? I'm already fucking dead," Bill declared with literal froth foaming around his mouth. Bill walked past the mediator sitting at the head of the table and started leering his head at Anna.

"You think you've won? You think you can get away with this -" Bill spat into her face within centimetres before Bruce and the mediator suddenly leapt into action and started restraining Bill. Each of them grabbed a hold of one of his arms.

"Get the fuck off me you cockroaches!" Bill struggled violently but they were too strong. That old grandpa retired judge and Bruce were stronger than Bill despite their advanced age. Bill's lifestyle of malnourishment had indeed caught up to him.

"Security! Help!" Bruce and the mediator both shouted.

Within about 30 seconds, two men walked in and took over restraining Bill.

"Don't mess with someone who's got nothing left to lose," Bill coldly uttered while oozing with malice before he was dragged out of the room. Bill was forced down on a stool in the foyer while more security officers arrived.

"What the hell do you think you were doing there mate?" one of them said, while another officer spoke into his walkie-talkie, "We have another code black."

"Jesus mate, calm down," the original security officer repeated while the one with the walkie talkie continued speaking, "Nah, definitely unarmed. No, there wasn't anyone injured, looks like the mediation just got a bit heated."

"Here, have some water, just take some deep breaths," the original security guard said while handing Bill some water.

After what seemed an eternity, Bill's anger finally diminished to the point where he could speak. The team of security guards had long since dispersed after they concluded that Bill was no longer a threat. Only two guards were left, including the original man who spoke to him earlier.

"Right, can you hear me mate?" the man asked.

"Yes," Bill grumbled.

"We've just had a chat with everyone involved. The girl seemed a bit shaken but nobody has decided to press charges. You're very lucky we didn't have to call the police. What were you thinkin' mate?" the man continued asking. Before long, Bill watched as the other people inside the mediation room started walking out. Chao and Chaudry were holding up some paper to hide Anna's fat fuck face from him while she cowered against Chao's shoulders pretending to cry more crocodile tears. Bruce walked by glancing at Bill then shook his head as if he were a disappointed father.

"Bill. You messed up big time. The deal fell through and now the matter will escalate. It might actually end up in court. I hope that doesn't happen. You will hear from the team soon," Bruce this time showed none of his previous overly friendly attitude. He was blunt and harsh this time. After saying his piece, Bruce walked off out of the building.

* * *

Bill regretted not murdering that bitch then and there. Bill returned to his life of suffering afterwards feeling even worse. It was exactly like before except this time, Bill was freshly branded by the horrors of the subhumans inflicting genocide upon him. They were succeeding. Bill was losing the war. Inch by inch, just like trench warfare, the subhumans were gaining ground. With every victory, the subhumans killed off more and more of him. Soon, he would be dead. When would he be murdered? Bill did not know. Bill started crying. How could all the people on his list receive their just deserts? So many people needed killing but Bill was just one, increasingly powerless man. Bill was actually afraid of dying before he could start murdering. How could he die before correcting this grand injustice?

Bruce and DIS gave him updates every few months. Apparently the case was forced into court. It was progressingly slowly even into 2019. All the while, Bill kept suffering through his endless days. Bruce and DIS made it a condition that Bill seek a psychiatric opinion from two different psychiatrists. Bill eventually did see them but they had nothing more to add other than "depression." They did not recommend changing medications either. Bill had long since realised that psychiatry and psychology were total fucking scams anyway. Bill's expectations were low but these fucking morons still managed to blow his expectations right out of the ballpark every time.

Then came 2020. Bill shut off all contact with anyone in his past. He hoped that everyone thought he was dead. Cheng tried to visit a few times but Bill pretended not to answer. Then he stopped coming. There was this new disease called "coronavirus" which seemed to be raging across Melbourne. Apparently there was some lockdown. It did not even cross Bill's mind because he was basically already living in lockdown. The only difference it made for Bill was that he had to wait a month before he could buy more toilet paper. However, Bruce informed Bill that the case was stalled because of the courts being shut down from the pandemic. Bill did not care. Bill suffered in hell, it was no longer purgatory, his suffering was upgraded to hell. Hell continued throughout 2020 then it all came to a halt in 2021.

Bill received a notification from Montpellier and Partners. There was a judgment date scheduled for March 8th. Apparently there was intense court action happening in the background. Bill repeatedly declined to respond and Bruce once phoned him to instruct him not to show up in court. The psychiatric evaluation concluded that Bill's mental illness was far too severe for him to attend court. Bill was not surprised considering what happened. The legal team arranged for him to have a consultation after the judgment was issued. Hence, Bill suffered until March the 15th arrived. The morons made it sound like they were doing him a favour by inviting him to the office since most activity was now done from home. It was all because of the so-called "pandemic."

On March 15th, Bill dejectedly crawled back to 469 La Trobe Street to hear the bad news. Bill knew the outcome was going to be unfavourable. Bruce had insisted on a face to face meeting. Ironically, Bill was the one who normally would have insisted. Bill sighed. He was triggered several times by passing whores but Bill just barely managed to keep it together. It was hard being in public. Bill struggled up the stairs and was greeted by the same receptionist as last time. Heh, at least here staff stayed on longer than Mega, Bill thought to himself. Again, Bruce opened the door but this time, without the welcoming attitude.

"Hello Bill, follow me," Bruce unemotionally stated while wearing a face mask, gesturing for Bill to follow. Again, the two proceeded to the same conference room from long ago.

"Bill, you're not going to like what I'm going to tell you. In summary, we lost. The fight is not over yet, we can still appeal. The Supreme Court did not offer an appeal application hearing on the day but I'm hopeful they'll be able to give us one within this month," Bruce sourly informed Bill.

"Uh hem," Bill had to clear his throat first due to disuse, "Is this because of what happened during mediation?" Bill knew it was the case before Bruce had to answer. Bill was at peak anger because he had to live with that for the past year and a half. Bruce then sighed very loudly. He was the only member of the team in the room this time.

"Pretty much. Let me read you some of the most important points. '...showed absolutely no remorse and remains unrepentant to the nth degree... His extreme rejection of a very reasonable offer of settlement demonstrated an unfathomable lack of empathy, bordering on cruelty in addition to a demonstrable lack of genuine or sincere steps to resolve the dispute. In such light, arguments offered by the plaintiff are thus ever more convincing. I find the defendant negligent and order exemplary damages to the amount of $900,000 and indemnity costs respectively.'" Bruce looked up at a seething Bill.

"Bill, do you know what indemnity costs means?" Bruce asked without expression.

"No," Bill chillingly stated.

"It means that instead of ordinary costs, which is what the court normally orders, the judge has ordered you to pay almost all of their legal fees. Depending on what the lawyers charge, ordinary costs sometimes account for as little as 30%. If I were to guess, their legal costs would be between $300,000 to $500,000. Let that sink in," Bruce stated this time almost bordering on hostility. Bill did not bring a knife again! Damn! Bill knew that if he killed this subhuman right here and now, he would not be able to murder the patient, her lawyers or the judge. Bill was speechless.

"There's more I need you to understand. There's a chance we can appeal this. In my professional opinion, I don't like our chances. I'm not even sure if our hearing will go through. Even if we have permission to appeal, we'll have to go through another trial which will be an uphill battle. I have spoken to DIS and their underwriters have finalised their offer. DIS will indemnify you for the amount of $300,000 as per the original settlement amount. Their underwriters have their own legal team. Their solicitors have informed me that your stunt during mediation breached their terms and conditions. I have included a copy of their terms and conditions with the relevant sections highlighted. They claim that you did not act in good faith in accepting the legal counsel offered. That basically means that in order for them to indemnify your liabilities, you needed to follow our advice. You did not do that. In addition, the judge ordered punitive or exemplary damages which breaches their 'gross misconduct' section," Bruce explained as bluntly as possible. Bill remained speechless. Bruce sighed deeply for a second time.

"Wait a minute. Why do I have to follow these bullshit rules? My patients often don't follow my advice yet when they fuck things up, they still demand a refund," Bill protested with boiling hatred.

"This is just the law," Bruce replied in a nonchalant tone while waving both hands in the air.

"God fucking damn it! Don't give me that bullshit! You know as well as I do that this was just some fucking kangaroo court fake judgment. You told me those morons were small time losers. You said they couldn't afford to go to court," Bill seethed through gritted teeth.

"Look Bill. I'll overlook your language this time. I've seen many clients feel the same emotions that you do. I get it. I really do. Normally these small time streetside lawyers can't risk litigation. This time however, they knew it was basically in the bag after you rejected the settlement. Whenever us lawyers need advice, we go to our seniors and I bet some big shot barrister must have told them the insurers always pay and even if they refuse, the dentist is so rich they can just take out a loan and pay it off like a mortgage," Bruce explained in an attempt to calm Bill down.

"WHO?! Who the fuck told them this bullshit?" raged further.

"I don't know. They hired more than one barrister. Anyone could have offered them that ill-informed advice. It could have even been the mediator or the judge herself," Bruce explained.

"How can you sit there talking as if this is all fucking normal? How the fuck am I supposed to get an unsecured fucking loan for a million dollars? I am NOT the crazy one here!" Bill continued, struggling to contain himself.

"Don't take out a loan yet. Look Bill, I've never had to restrain anyone before. I don't blame you, I honestly don't. If I were the judge, I still honestly believe you're in the right. However, you can't let your emotions get the better of you. This case is not dead yet. The appeal might succeed and look, I'm going to be a big man here and put all that mediation kerfuffle behind me. Let's pretend it never happened. I'm still here to help and if you would like me to ask DIS to pay more, I'm more than happy to help," Bruce offered some consolation. Bill however, was not interested. He would never trust this subhuman moron again.

"I'm not interested," Bill flatly rejected with a homicidal expression on his face. Bill grabbed the documents on the desk and exited the law firm.

Bill decided then and there that his life would end today. Bill did not have a million dollars. Over the past two years of unemployment, Bill was now down to $130,000. Bill caught public transport home, narrowly avoiding committing homicide yet again. Bill walked down to the basement car stacking garage and turned his ignition on - it was dead. Bill was not surprised. He had not ignited the engine for half a year at least. Bill called RACV. It took them 15 minutes to arrive and they switched out a dead battery and did a quick engine oil change. It must have been 2 years since Bill last had the engine oil changed. Bill still needed that thing to run well enough to survive a 100km journey.

Bill refueled at the nearest petrol station and drove onto the West Gate Bridge. Bill planned on driving to the remote countryside and then drive as fast as possible into a tree. There had to be very specific conditions. First, it had to be a road with no other cars in the way. He had to drive really fucking far remote for that to happen. Secondly, the weather and visual field must be clear. Thirdly, the road must be straight and well maintained so that the car would not flip and render him disabled rather than killing him. Fourthly, the bulky, strong tree needed to be well in the open, no damn barricade or ditch getting in the way. Bill recalled that Cheng used to work in Beaufort. Cheng used to say that it was an easy drive there.

As usual, the cars were bumper to bumper on the West Gate. Bill set the transmission to "Park" and pulled up the hand brake. Fuck the rules, Bill thought, there were no police about so nobody was here to stop him. Bill rolled down the window and moved his entire torso out. The surrounding car drivers had quizzical expressions while observing the bizarre sight. Bill did not care. Bill moved back his right arm holding his phone in preparation for an overhead throw. Yes! It made it over the suicide barrier and would probably land in the ocean. Bill did not want the police to be able to easily find his corpse. Hopefully his corpse would be so unrecognisable that he would be reported as missing. He planned to turn into a side road after reaching Beaufort and then scout out a location that satisfied his criteria. Hence, Bill turned onto the Western Highway and headed towards the middle of nowhere. It was a smooth drive, as Cheng informed. Bill remembered the time he lived with Cheng. He remembered roughly where to go. There were no turns involved so how could anyone get lost?

Bill was prescient of his imminent doom. He finished the lawyer meeting at 12pm and started driving at 3pm. The GPS said he would reach Beaufort by 5pm before he threw it out. If he were speeding, he could get there faster. So Bill tried driving at 130km/h which was about as much as his shitty car could handle without sounding like it was about to explode. After an hour of driving, Bill went past many signs saying, "Ballarat City Centre" with "x" number of minutes. It was starting to get dark. Bill did not reach Beaufort yet but that did not really matter. He was past Ballarat and there was only the occasional car on the road now. Bill decided to take the next small road exit. He did not know where it led and he did not care.

Alright, if I see no car for 10 minutes, then there will be nobody on the fucking road, Bill thought. So Bill counted down the minutes. Indeed, this side road was completely empty. Bill drove a little further and saw it, a nice, lone standing, sturdy gum tree after a long stretch of straight highway as far as the eye could see. That was it. That was where he was going to die. Bill drove just past it slowly to inspect it close up - it was good. Then he did a U-turn and slowly started driving back to the start of the straight strip of highway. Unfortunately, as if by magic, a car suddenly appeared and it was approaching fast. It clearly had no respect for road rules and was driving down the middle of the road, thus occupying both lanes. Fuck! His piece of shit car could not speed up fast enough, Bill realised. He was basically flooring it but even then, the car would take about 15 seconds to reach 100km/h, Bill had tested this before. He was reaching 90kmph before the car was basically within ramming distance. The car behind must have been speeding because it was approaching way too fast. Before he knew it, the loud horn of the car behind him was blaring.

Bill's anger was immediately summoned. Society would not even allow him to fucking die in peace. Bill was already driving far away from his designated suicide zone. However, the car behind him refused to overtake. Was the driver disabled? Were they incapable of driving in a single lane? Bill attempted to lean more towards the left. For a split second, the tyre hit the dirt and the car lost traction and skidded. Panicked, Bill immediately corrected course back onto the road. A cold sweat poured down Bill's back. He almost lost control. If he did, the car crash might not kill him but disable him to the point of quadriplegia and unending physical pain. That was a fate worse than death. Bill dared not drift any further left yet the moron behind him refused to overtake. There were no other cars on the road, what the fuck were they thinking?

Bill decided to slow down and stop on the dirt to let them through. He did not want to drive too far away from his designated suicide tree. Yet, the moron behind him also slowed down and stopped behind him. It was an old, beaten up Holden Barina. An old favourite for impoverished Australian bogans. A young woman walked out. She was barefoot, probably because flip-flops, the footwear of choice in the countryside, were illegal shoes for driving. She had dirt covered, thigh length jean shorts and an equally dirty pink polo shirt. Her arms and legs were covered in tattoos. The sun had almost set but the subhuman still wore sunglasses. She was a walking stereotype taken from the Australian gutters reminiscent of television shows like "Housos." It was no surprise that she behaved the way she did. She was probably high from taking a cocktail of 10 different drugs.

The subhuman whore walked up to his car and started pounding on his window. Bill did not have time for this. Now that she was outside her car, it was the perfect opportunity for Bill to drive off. He could just go find another suicide tree. Bill gently started accelerating but the bitch suddenly moved in front of his vehicle and started slamming the hood. She was also shouting incoherently.

"FUCK YOU YOU FUCKIN' CHING CHONG CUNT! OPEN THE FUCKIN' DOOR!" She kept shouting. Bill immediately hit the brakes. What the fuck was wrong with this cockroach? Why the fuck did these moron bitches all act so entitled? The road was not their fucking property, especially when she must have been driving close to 150km per hour. Bill gently pressed the accelerator again but the bitch refused to move.

Then Bill realised. Nobody knew where he was. Nobody was driving past. This was the perfect opportunity to murder a bitch. Random murders in the countryside? No possible way to solve them. Bill floored it. The bitch was thrown forward on the ground and landed right on the back of her head. She was not moving. Then Bill slowly drove forward until he could feel the bump of the car running over her body. He then reversed the vehicle. Then went forward. Then reversed again. Then repeated this at least 8 times. He lost count after a while. Then he drove the car onto the middle of her body and floored it with the accelerator again. Then he suddenly slammed on the brakes. Bill checked the scene behind him using his rear view mirror. He saw red. Well, it was time he drove off.

Bill's heart was pounding. He could barely believe what he just did. He did not have to plan anything. It felt like divine intervention. He had fully intended to commit suicide but he realised, if he was willing to terminate himself then and there without having killed anyone, what a wasted life that would be... Fate had handed him the perfect opportunity to kill. Now that Bill knew what it felt like to kill, Bill craved more. What the fuck was he thinking today? Suicide? Anna the tongue patient, the judge and the lawyers, they were still breathing. That and Dr Sung, the subhuman moron from Shellharbour. Those people all had to die. Heh, Bill thought, that subhuman bogan probably saved his life. She traded her life for his and helped Bill perform a public service.

Bill arrived back at his apartment with renewed vigour. He needed to do lots of preparation work. Bill inspected his car. There was no trace of blood unless he shined a torch underneath the car and used a magnifying glass to thoroughly check. Even then, there was so much dirt and grime it was hard to see. Unless someone actually witnessed the crime and informed on him, the police would never suspect him. Bill had no idea who he murdered. He would have to pay attention to the news for a while. Bill took the elevator up and turned on the donated junk computer. First, he looked up the judge in his case. "Justice Sandra Maxson" Bill Googled her name. Interesting. Bill then looked up the lawyers. As luck would have it, all the lawyers were now offering at home consultations due to the pandemic. They were even nice enough to advertise their home offices. Very interesting indeed. Bill spent a whole 10 hours doing research to plan for his upcoming endeavours.

For the next week, Bill attempted to sell off all his electronically traded fund holdings. He tried withdrawing cash but the banks kept repeating they had a limit of however much they had on hand on any particular day. After a week, Bill was only able to withdraw $30,000 then all of a sudden, one bank manager informed Bill there was a civil freezing order issued on his account. Fuck! Bill had received many letters from the court which he completely ignored. Bruce also attempted to contact him. Apparently he was supposed to be summoned back to court to declare his assets. Why the fuck would he do that? He would have gladly went if they allowed him to carry a gun in.

$30k might be enough. Bill also watched several news media outlets like a hawk, repeatedly checking for updates every hour. It took three days, and it was not widely covered either. "Hit-and-run fatality outside Ballarat," reported on ABC news, relegated to a minor spot under "Victoria" based local news. The "article," if it can even be called that, was about 10 sentences long and identified the cadaver as some "Jenny

Mills" and that police were looking for leads. They had nothing. Good. For the first time in years, Bill was able to endure 8 or more waking hours on any given day. He was motivated now more than ever.

There were certain purchases Bill needed to make. For the next three weeks, Bill started eating better, exercising and even sleeping some more regular hours. He managed to purchase a 2010 Toyota Hiace for $15,000. He bought several sets of "tradie" overalls and tools as well as a very heavy wrench. Bill ordered a hat with the NBN logo printed on it from eBay. Bill then retrieved a specially ordered, authentic sashimi knife from Japan which he kept in a nearby Kennard's Storage. It cost over $200 but goods made in Japan had quality he could trust. It was worth it. Bill also made some phone calls to set the plan in motion. Those morons had no idea what was waiting for them. They made the mistake of attempting to murder someone who had nothing left to lose.

Chapter 24

The most loving doctor

Bill drove to Anna the tongue patient's house. She was the easiest to locate. The twin morons Chao and Chaudry leaked her address in their court submissions. Bill mused in his head, did those morons have IQ below room temperature? Did those fuckwits completely ignore the fact that their correspondence submitted as evidence had her address printed as clear as day? No wonder they were begging around street corners offering "no win no fee" scams. Not to mention Bruce, that fucking moron handed Bill this information on a silver platter in the bundle of handouts from their final meeting.

All it took was ten seconds for Bill to search up Anna's Twitter feed and cross reference her house pictures with those on Google Maps. She was just like all braindead females. Did females even have functioning brains? To Bill, it was as plain as day that female "brains" operated like an algorithm which superficially mimicked real thought processes but in reality just rehashed the same logical errors in an infinite loop. There was zero probability that bitch ass whore could resist the temptation of dumping her verbal diarrhoea on the most brain-dead online platform for all her equally brain-dead, sub-zero IQ, cancer spreading sycophants to read. She had the fucking gall to gloat.

That animal had infinitely negative self-awareness. Bragging to the public about ruining a hard working man's life and thinking she was the hero. Moronically assuming she was about to get the payout of a lifetime while ignoring the fact that Bill *literally* had no money. That fucking bitch ass whore's payout from Bill's insurer would amount to so little it would not even cover her lawyer's fees. She was literally on the verge of bankruptcy. Yet she was on Twitter trying to celebrate some sort of win? Oh my God, Bill thought. It was honestly giving him tears just thinking about the possibility of allowing something so retarded to keep breathing. To persist in allowing the continued existence of this self-destructive animal was cruelty *beyond measure.*

It did not take long before Bill arrived at the correct address. Bill had checked this dilapidated street many times online. It reminded him of Detroit. These cockroaches lived in a small, wooden weatherboard dump in West Heidleberg. Everything screamed "poverty." Bill knocked on her door. It was Sunday around 11am. Nobody attended church these days so he would expect them to be in the house. While there was no current lockdown, people were still being pressured against public gatherings because of the pandemic which was still looming. Not that Bill cared. After a while, a man answered the door.

"Hello, I'm John from the NBN, there was a reported fault on this property listed under an Anna Williams, are these details correct?" Bill announced. Bill arrived wearing his NBN hat and blue "tradie" overalls. There was a large pouch slung across his left shoulder and he held a clipboard on his left hand followed by a large wrench longer than his forearm on his right.

"Uh yes, she's my partner, our internet is working fine so what's the problem?" the man answered.

"Oh it's nothing serious, our servers show there's been some throttling and micro-disconnections resulting in latency issues. You might not notice it during normal use. It's a known issue due to corrosion and we need to fix it otherwise it could crash the network. We've isolated the fault to these three properties. Now I don't have to enter your property, but if you could quickly guide me to where you receive the NBN outlet, that would make my job much faster," Bill explained making up a fake story with completely fake, meaningless terminology. These morons would not be able to know the difference anyway.

"No worries mate, follow me, name's Steve by the way, nice to meet you. Come to think of it, the internet does screw up pretty often, I'm glad they've finally sent someone through to check," the moron accepted it hook line and sinker. Bill walked inside and closed the door.

Now was the most important part. "Is your partner in?" Bill asked.

"Yeah, she's with the little one out the back-" then Bill slammed the large wrench against the man's head. The wrench was heavy. No man could stay standing after receiving a direct blow. Bill wrenched out his sashimi knife and slashed his throat multiple times. They were standing in a narrow hallway which led to a kitchen area. There she was sitting in the kitchen, breastfeeding. Bill hid the knife back in his pouch as if nothing happened. Anna was seated while bobbing her baby up and down making baby noises as Bill entered her field of view.

"There's daddy- wait, where's Steve? Who are you?" Anna suddenly started, shaken. Bill did not hesitate. He slammed the wrench against her head with all his force. Anna dropped her baby and collapsed, falling off the chair. Bill leaned down and said calmly.

"Remember me? You just couldn't fucking leave it alone could you? You fucking animal. All you had to do was take my money. But you just had to fucking gloat. You think you've won? Ha, ha, ha, ha, ha..." Bill could not help laughing. Anna seemed to still have some consciousness but was clearly too stunned to say anything. "Oh look at you, don't you see how pathetic you are? Don't get up," Bill muttered while grabbing out his sashimi knife. It was slice and dice time.

Bill stared at the mess beneath him and diverted his attention to the crying infant.

"Look at the mess you've created. Don't you see the tragedy Anna? It wasn't enough for you to harm society, you just had to metastasise and breed. You pollute our genepool with your malignant DNA without even thinking about the consequences of your own actions," Bill was sure she was beyond dead but it felt like he just had to say it. He bent over to pick up the infant.

"How can you raise a child in this fucked up environment? How can a fucking rabid dog raise their own child? It's even worse than biting another animal to spread your malignancy. You willingly created another rabid animal *from nothing*. I don't hate you at all. I once hated you but I've discovered that I love you more than any other person on Earth, even more than your husband. I can't live with myself seeing such a diseased animal struggle for survival. I can't in good conscience allow this suffering to continue. I hope that some day while you're rotting in Hell, you get to understand my love for you."

* * *

Fifteen minutes later, Bill was back on the road. Bill spent a few minutes cleaning up his messy tools and changing into another pair of overalls. Bill lovingly euthanised the entire household. Bill really ought to receive a public service award for all the good he was doing. This was all an act of love. Bill was such a loving person. Nay, Bill was the most loving person. He loved so many people he was overflowing with love. If only they could accept his love. Bill truly was misunderstood. He was the most peaceful, most loving person on Earth. Next on the list was Sandra Maxson. She lived in Toorak. Of course she would.

Bill knocked on the door of the double story mansion. It was a stroke of genius to find this place actually. Because that moron subhuman was elderly, she clearly did not know how to use technology. Her Facebook and social media were easily found with a quick Google search and were not set to private. She posted photos of her house and grandchildren as if they were some kind of "achievement." Typical degenerate. The only accomplishment she wanted to show off was fucking like an animal. It was not hard to track down her physical address with that information. Bill had the internet to thank for teaching him. "Doxxing" was an art. Being a hacker was not necessary to dox someone.

Bill heard the sounds of little children running around before the door opened. There she was, she looked even older and more used up than the photos in court. Supposedly she was 54 but she looked 70 at least.

"Hi there, I'm not interested in any sales thanks," Maxson said the moment she opened the door.

"No madam, not at all. I'm John from the National Broadband Network. I am not working for any service provider, I'm here to inspect a suspected fault," Bill replied.

"Oh? I've been having some internet connection issues but it has been working for today," Maxson explained.

"Our servers show there's been some throttling and micro-disconnections resulting in latency issues. You might not notice it but it during normal use. It's a known issue due to corrosion and we need to fix it otherwise it could crash the network. We've isolated the fault to these three properties. Now I don't have to enter your property, but if you could quickly guide me to where you receive the NBN outlet, that would make my job much faster," Bill spouted the same nonsense he said before. Maxson sighed with a haughty expression. Typical female. They do *not* gain self-awareness even when they're hell old, Bill thought.

"Oh I suppose. Ever since the switch it's always had issues. If you can fix it that would be great," Maxson said.

"May I come in, just for a few seconds," Bill repeated, since Maxson was not at all welcoming.

"I suppose. You have to watch out for the grandkids though," Maxson explained while gesturing Bill in.

The moment she closed her door, Bill slammed the wrench against the side of her head resulting in her head smashing against the glass window decorated doors separating the lounge room. Maxson collapsed in a heap then Bill knelt down and coldly stated,

"Do you even know who I am? *You* are the one who murdered me. I'm just returning the favour. You animals need to learn, don't mess with someone who's got nothing left to lose." Maxson was cradling her head with eyes half open. She seemed to be semi-conscious but responsive.

"That's right, you judged me and ordered me to pay everything I owned. That's the last name you're gonna hear before you die. William. Hastings. Parker," Bill stated before giving her the "sashimi" treatment.

Bill watched as the cockroach beneath him started spluttering through agonal breaths. Bill knew those breaths all too well. It was a very characteristic whistle which sounded as people's autonomic systems desperately attempted to draw even the faintest of final breaths.

"For your whole life you were judging others. Under whose authority I wonder? You think you get to say and do whatever the fuck you want just because some fuckwits put you on a stand and wrote 'justice' in front of your name? You know, funny story, I used to have a friend who always said the law didn't exist. Well today, I'm here to teach you some law. First lesson, the law does fucking exist. Second lesson, I am the fucking law. Third lesson, people deserve nothing but to live with the consequences of their own actions," Bill coldly stated as the agonal breaths finally faded.

Bill stood up. There were two boys who looked like they were between the ages of 3 to 5.

"What did you do to grandma?" one of them asked while the other was literally wetting himself.

"I was only giving her my love. Don't you love grandma too?" Bill stated chillingly while holding up the red knife.

Within another fifteen minutes, Bill walked out of the house. Bill inspected the soles of his shoes. There was a little bit of blood but it had dried up already and would not make a mess of his van. After giving his overwhelming love to the two grandchildren, an adult woman walked in and almost screamed before Bill "loved" her to death as well. Why was he so kind? Bill shook his head in disappointment. If only more people in society were like Bill. It would become a much more loving society. As it turned out, Bruce the incompetent also lived in Toorak. This moron publicly handed out his home address because he decided to "work from home." That just made Bill's job that much easier.

After a 5 minute drive, Bill knocked on the door of another Toorak mansion. There was no answer for at least 30 seconds. Bill knocked on the door again. Bruce answered.

"Bill? What? What are you doing here? Why are you dressed like that? Did you really change careers?" Bruce recognised him too quickly. Perhaps Bill should have changed strategies here. It was too late. Bill slammed the wrench onto his head while kicking him down. Then Bill quickly took the knife out and "sashimi"d Bruce's neck. Bruce started coughing blood but he stared back with full comprehension and sheer horror.

"You know, I made an important discovery looking through you lawyers' Facebook pages. One very interesting picture came up on Judge Maxson's page. You, her and those two morons Chao and Chaudry, were all in one photo hugging and laughing at some function. You almost had me fooled. I knew you weren't on my side but now I know the truth. The law is just some fucked up game you assholes play. MY LIFE IS

NOT SOME FUCKING GAME YOU PIECE OF SHIT!" Bill screamed before kicking Bruce's body repeatedly like a rag doll. With each kick, frothy blood escaped from Bruce's mouth. Speckles of red landed on Bill's overalls. It did not matter, he had spares.

"Bruce... Bruce, Bruce Bruce..." Bill uttered in rapid succession like a mother shushing her child, "I owed you those kicks so please forgive me. I'm sorry this happened to you. See? I apologised just like you taught me. I think you're special Bruce. I do actually feel a quantum of genuine guilt that we had to part ways like this. If only I were more loving, I could have prevented this altogether and euthanised that entire law convention from that Facebook photo. See how loving I am? It physically pains me watching all you rabid animals roll in your filth like this. *Physically* pains me. I'm not acting out of hatred or malice. I put aside my hate for you long ago. Now all I feel is love. I just hope that while you're rotting in hell, one day you'll finally be able to realise just how loving I am," Bill gave Bruce his last rites.

Bill watched as Bruce started his agonal breaths. Bill smiled as he saw Bruce's final breaths pass while he laid in a puddle of his own blood. There was a sudden shrill scream and Bill lifted up his head. There was an older woman there who quickly turned around and ran in the opposite direction. Bill gave chase into some kitchen area. There she was. She took out a slightly smaller knife than Bill's sashimi knife.
"Get away from me you fucking psycho!" she screamed, "I'm calling the cops!" Cold sweat poured down his back. This was the eventuality Bill wanted to see the least. He did not want to risk getting injured or perhaps even haemorrhaging to death. Bruce was dead anyway, it was enough.

Bill ran back out and closed the door then started power walking back to his van. Bill turned around but did not see any movement. Shit. The cops would be called immediately. However, his van was not parked in the vicinity so even if there was a manhunt out for Bill, it would still take them a few hours to put the puzzle pieces together. Bill used his

Korean name on the vehicle ownership transfer form. Vicroads might recognise the invalid name months afterwards. They were as useless as the DMV from the United States. It was a mild hindrance, but it would buy him some valuable time before they figured out which car Bill was driving. Bill was *not* intent on "getting away with it." He was probably going down in a rain of gunfire or slamming into a tree again.

Bill floored the accelerator and raced off to the Eastern suburbs where Chao and Chaudry both lived. He still had to drive below the speed limit so that no police officers accosted him. Now the clock was ticking. Chao and Chaudry both lived in Glen Waverley. Typical location for cashed up Asians. He once got lost driving to Cheng's place because Cheng also lived in Glen Waverley. However, it was supposed to be a dead easy navigation. All he had to do was drive down a straight line, Toorak road, which then became Burwood Highway. Previously, when Bill heard "highway" he thought he needed to turn onto Monash freeway. Only morons would name their roads like this, Bill thought.

It was 3pm by the time Bill reached Chao's Glen Waverley mansion. Cheng used to complain about not being in some "school zone" for Glen Waverley secondary college. Apparently Asian fuckwits all wanted to send their children there and for some reason that raised the real estate value of that zone by 100%. These morons deserved to fucking die. Chao and Chaudry were both mentally retarded enough to pay double to buy houses in this exact zone. Bill had to thank these Asians for being so stupid. Chao was up first. Bill knocked on his door. A young boy answered, he seemed to be about 10 years old. Too early for Glen High but fortunately, he would never make it, Bill thought.

"Hello?" the kid uncomfortably greeted.

"Who is it Mike?" a man's voice sounded from inside.

"My name's John from the NBN," Bill said loudly enough to be heard.

"NBN was it?" the man's voice from inside sounded, "invite the man in Mike, we're in luck." Bill was smart to choose to pretend to be an NBN worker. If Bill could rely on the NBN for anything, it was poor reliability.

"Uh, come in," Mike uttered. Bill walked in and was led into some lounge area. There he was, Chao the motherfucker was on his tablet. Chao made eye contact but did not recognise Bill.

"Hi, good thing you came, you know, we've been having -" Chao said before Bill slammed his wrench onto Chao's head. Mike was too stunned to act so Bill kicked with all his might. Mike slammed into the wall and collapsed. Bill took out his trusty Japanese knife and set to work.

In between slashes, Bill casually informed Chao,

"You better remember who the fuck I am. William Hastings Parker. You picked a fight with me because you were desperate to fuck someone over like a fucking parasite." Bill watched as his final slash rendered Chao to start drowning in his own blood.

"I'm not angry, Chao. I just want to help you. I have no other choice. The most loving thing anyone can do for a rabid animal is to put them down. If there were any other way to help you, I would absolutely do it. I'm doing this out of love and don't worry, I will spread the love to everyone here. See how much of a loving person I am? Maybe one day while you're rotting in hell, you can finally understand that."

* * *

This time, Bill did not change uniforms. He hurriedly washed the blood off his hands and tools. There were some splotches of Bruce's blood as well but he managed to hide it from Mike using his trusty clipboard. Bill drove three minutes to Chaudry's house and knocked on the door. There was no answer. There were also no cars parked out the back. Fuck! Bill knew that by now the police might have figured things out.

The likelihood was low. Bill had seen Victoria Police in action. They acted like their IQ was lower than room temperature and with as much motivation as a sloth. Plus, it was Sunday. Most officers were probably too busy snorting cocaine and fucking hookers. Even if they knew it was Bill, how long would it take to find him? Bill did not know how long he could wait. Bill looked at the time. It was 3:13pm. The family might have gone shopping. Who knows? Bill decided he could spare a maximum of one hour. If there was even a single police vehicle, he would definitely speed off.

Bill returned to his van and waited. Bill's heart was racing the whole day and he had to admit, he felt extremely lethargic. Bill checked the news online on his "burner" smart phone he paid cash for at the Chinese grocer. Huawei phones were tracked by the Chinese Government but he trusted 'dem Chahn-nese not to trade information with Victoria Police. So far, there was nothing online about any man-hunt. Not even a peep yet. Bill sat back down. His eyes felt droopy... Suddenly, Bill was woken up by the sound of a passing car. Bill looked at the time, it was 4pm. Bill sighed with relief. He did not sleep for long. Bill looked at Chaudry's property. There was now a Porsche Cayenne SUV on the driveway.

Bill knocked on the last door he planned for that day. It was Chaudry himself who answered.

"Hey, I've seen you before haven't I?" Chaudry said after looking at Bill's face. Bill laughed chillingly. Bill slammed into Chaudry's head with the giant wrench. Then Bill slashed up Chaudry's throat with his patented "sashimi treatment."

"That's what you get for messing with someone who's got nothing left to lose," Bill coldly stated and then spat on the corpse. Bill walked in with his dripping red knife in hand. Good, Bill thought. The family was busy cooking. Bill crept up and found a young girl hopping around her mother. Time to express my boundless love, Bill thought.

Bill stared at the red mess he created. It was time to perform their last rites.

"Ashes to ashes, filth to filth. I don't know if any of you can hear me but know this. I did this out of love," Bill remarked as he stepped over the puddles corresponding to Chaudry's wife and child. He could have sworn at least one body was still twitching. Good.

"It's not like I want to do this, I *need* to do this. Any lesser man would just let society wallow in its own filth but only an ubermensch like me has the will to power. I have the power to lessen everyone's suffering, especially yours. There has not been and will never be anyone as loving as me. One day while you're having a family picnic in hell, maybe you will finally realise just how loving I am."

* * *

It was dark. Bill had been driving for the past three hours. Bill had dumped his smartphone tracking device an hour ago after he entered the Hume Highway. Before he dumped the phone, he checked the news one last time, while driving, to find that there was indeed a manhunt issued for him. Bill safely crossed the New South Wales border and arrived in Wodonga. Now that he crossed the state border, Victoria Police no longer had jurisdiction. It would not take long before New South Wales police joined in but the likelihood they knew he crossed the border was remote. There was one more target Bill needed to hunt down: Doctor Samuel Sung. Bill could not help but feel like that moron started off all of this mess in the first place. That subhuman cockroach tipped over the first domino which eventually led Bill to this suicidal rampage.

It was a stroke of luck that Bill managed to take down as many targets as he did. Bill knew that all of them were going to be working the Friday preceding and the Monday following so they would not be out travelling. Bill checked by pretending to make appointments on the preceding Friday and the Monday following. Furthermore, Bill really had to thank COVID-19 for pressuring people to stay in their houses. If it were any other time prior to 2020, the likelihood of so many people being present in their homes would have been next to impossible. Bill almost did not make it today if he did not decide to wait that tiny bit longer outside Chaudry's house. It must have been fate at work. Bill reminisced about his love/hate relationship with fate. In the end, fate delivered so he really could not bring himself to hate lady fate.

Bill was struggling to stay awake. He almost swerved off the road multiple times. It was really difficult. Eventually, Bill was forced to drive onto a lonely side road and park on the gravel. Bill brought along a back-up smartphone which had no mobile network connection. It truly brought back some memories just looking at it. It was the same hunk of junk free phone that Bill used back in Shellharbour. What do you know, Bill thought. So many things led back to Shellharbour, the winter of Bill's innocence and summer of Bill's discontent. It was 1am and Bill could not keep his eyes open any longer. Bill set the alarm for 6am and closed his eyes.

Bill was woken by his alarm. It was pouring sunlight in but these days, that was not enough to wake Bill up. Bill shut the alarm off and started driving again. Bill did not need a GPS device to know where to drive. He was still on Hume Highway and he knew that he was close to Illawara Highway, where he needed to turn right. Bill was still lethargic from the extreme exertions of the previous day but he was determined to follow this through. After driving for about 90 minutes, Bill was in Shellharbour again. The memories started flooding in. That fucking cockroach boss had tortured him day after day in collaboration with his cabal of spies and backstabbers. Bill checked online before his rampage, Samuel Sung and Cynthia Huang were both there. If Bill were lucky, maybe Wendy the grandma would be there too.

It was still too early. Bill drove around the city first to take in the sights. He was back as a conqueror not a "loser" like Samuel Sung made him out to be. Veni, Vidi, Vici. I came, I saw, I conquered, Bill thought.

Bill took in the scenery for the last time as he drove through the town. Bill passed by the Warilla Mcdonald's and bought his last meal. Bill was not going to die on an empty stomach. He was going all out here. Bill decided to purchase the Presidential. After Donald Trump's victory, Bill decided to name the family McValue Box the "Presidential" because Trump often boasted eating a similar Mcdonald's feast for breakfast.

Bill paid in cash and sat in the carpark devouring the giant feast in front of him. Delicious, Bill thought. Every death row prisoner received their last meal request and so did Bill. Bill looked at the time again. It was 8:50am, still too early. To be safe, Bill needed to wait until at least 9:30am to ensure that the target dentists were working. With all this time to spare, Bill decided to visit the beach for one last time. Bill drove down south and parked his car. Bill walked out slowly and took in his surroundings. Bill thought back to all the troubled events of the past 6 years. Despite society's passive genocide finally killing him, Bill was the bigger man and paid society back only with love. It was ironic, the social justice warriors and fake feminists out there were always talking about love but they did nothing but harm. Yet Bill, the so-called "crazy" one was here handing out acts of love.

People just did not realise. Human civilisation was diseased. Terminal cancer. Stage 4. Massive, uncontrollable metastasis to every part of the body. The goddamn females and subhumans managed to destroy thousands of years of nature. Hard working men like Bill were genocided and instead society was rewarding all the most useless of fuckwits. For each murdered ubermensch like Bill, there were 1000 useless morons waiting in the wings to receive some victim trophy. Society just kept pumping out useless jobs like "Human Resources" and psychologists at the cost of real jobs like the kind of dentistry Bill performed. Fuck dentistry, it was curently not even an empty shell of what it used to be. This was the result of nosediving stagnation. The more society genocided men like Bill, the more society degenerated into the cesspit of filth it now became.

Therein lay the problem. Society had degenerated beyond the point of no return. Bill had thought and thought. Bill had investigated every possible means. There was no way. The prognosis was terminal. There were cases of spontaneous cancer remission, sure, but society was even beyond that. The cancer cells were proliferating so successfully that they basically replaced almost all the healthy cells. The remaining islands of healthy cells were slowly being killed off. Cancer cells, just like society, did not need to actively kill off healthy cells. Simply by scavenging all the resources from the body, the healthy cells would be starved of all sustenance.

Bill was high IQ enough to understand all of this. It was such a pity all those low IQ morons around him could not understand this basic, fundamental truth. Society was beyond help, the only option was to die. In a patient with better prognosis, the surgeon could cut out the tumour. For a while, Bill thought he could be that surgeon, surgically excising the cancer in society. How naive. If society itself became the cancer, then any surgery would conversely help reduce the remaining scattered islands of healthy cells. Society was well beyond desperate attempts at surgery. In fact, any form of treatment resulting in the destruction of cancer cells would leave an insufficient biomass to allow continued survival.

Bill pitied these cockroaches. It did not matter that they did not understand they were suffering. Bill remembered those North Korean defectors complaining about their garbage life in their motherland. Apparently many of their compatriots just accepted their way of life because they did not know better. If he were to have brought one of those suffering morons into the United States and showered them with a lavish lifestyle for only one week, they would understand just how much they were suffering. There was no way to enlighten the billions of untermensch. The final solution was the only solution.

Only a truly loving man could come to this conclusion. All the untermensch were happy to just let the cancer devour them whole but not

Bill. Society was like a terminally ill animal or a rabid dog being put down. It was the most loving, merciful thing that anyone could possibly do. If only Bill could cleanse the entire globe in nuclear fire. Bill was far too powerless to accomplish that but what he could do now was the next best thing. Bill started chuckling. He could not help it. Slowly but surely, the chuckle progressed to a laugh, which then burst the dam and Bill started laughing hysterically like the Joker.

Bill laughed and laughed. He could barely breathe. He did not know how long he kept laughing maniacally. Was it a minute? Was it 10 minutes? Was it an hour? It was easy to lose track of time when reminiscing.

"Hey, that's the guy!" Bill heard a man's voice in the background. "You there, yes you, hey! Stop!" Bill turned around. There was a crowd which formed. Bill must have scared some of the local residents with his laughing. Bill remembered. It was normal for homeless people to sleep in their cars because of the over-inflated real estate prices here in Shellharbour. Even if you had a job, there was no chance of buying a house here. As a result, there were always people in the beach carpark and unsurprisingly, a police presence. Bill saw a man pointing towards Bill, directing the attention of two officers adorned with protective vests. One of the officers started screaming at Bill. They probably recognised him from the photos Victoria Police posted online.

Bill leapt into action. Bill jumped back into his van and turned on the ignition. Bill floored the accelerator and raced towards King's dental. There was no holding back now. As Bill turned onto Shellharbour Road, he saw flashing lights from police vehicles behind him. Bill no longer cared about speed limits and the law. The law was for the living. Bill was a dead man so mortal laws meant nothing to him. Bill knew the way. He raced past a red light barely missing being T-boned by the traffic from the intersection. The police were unrelenting. Bill had no choice now. After a couple of very tense minutes, Bill charged into the parking lot of King's dental and slammed his foot down on the accelerator.

Bill instinctively shut his eyes as he heard and felt the shuddering crash. The moment Bill felt the impact, he instinctively slammed his foot down on the brakes just before he felt a second, softer thud. As Bill opened his eyes, he realised the world outside the van cabin was basically a blur. There was dust everywhere. He could barely make out a metre outside his cabin window. Amazingly, the instrument cluster was completely unscathed and the only difference to the interior was the deployment of airbags. The impact was actually so mild, Bill did not even notice the airbags being deployed. The windscreen had multiple crack lines but it still laid intact.

It only took a few seconds for Bill to collect himself. While his left hand released his seat belt, Bill pushed hard on the driver side door with his right. There was some resistance but as the anterior column was not deformed, the door still opened with barely a complaint. As Bill stepped out, he smelled the dust before it forced itself into his airways. Bill could not help but splutter and cough. Fuck that moron, Bill thought to himself. Of course that piece of shit fake Christian Korean asshole would renovate this dump with the rock bottom cheapest materials and labour. The Hiace was top quality Japanese design. This shitty Chinesium constructed dump did not stand a chance. That fucker probably used asbestos but fuck it, Bill's life expectancy was now measurable in seconds so why the fuck should he care about cancer?

Bill did not need to see, he instinctively knew his way around King's dental. The scars of his torture never left him. Bill knew the van must have hit the patient chair so Samuel Sung must have been lying to Bill's right side. Bill hobbled through the detritus and sure enough, there was a body lying on the floor. Within a second, Bill approached and recognised the pathetic form of a snivelling cockroach in human form he was all too familiar with - it was indeed Samuel Sung. His safety glasses must have been forced into his nasal bone because as Bill squatted down, he noticed a flattened, bleeding mess where Sung's nose used to be.

"Please, help," Sung groaned in agony as he made out Bill's form. Bill could not help but pity this cockroach with the memory of a goldfish. He clearly did not recognise Bill. In that fucker's brain, there was only enough real estate for his own ego plus a guide on exploiting people for money. Bill could barely stomach the revulsion of seeing this pathetic sight. Was there any existence more pathetic in the world? Bill could not imagine anything screaming "KILL ME" louder than that cancerous vermin on the ground. Yes, it was a fucking mercy to end this fucker.

Bill slashed at Samuel Sung's face and neck. Bill viciously slammed the knife down and slashed left and right repeatedly. Specks of blood were flying up and down while Bill screamed,

"THIS IS WHAT YOU GET YOU FUCKING COCKROACH! LEARN SOME FUCKING HUMILITY WHEN YOU MEET YOUR MAKER YOU FUCKING ASSHOLE!" while Bill heard the police officers yelling through a megaphone.

"THIS IS THE POLICE! GET OUT OF THE VEHICLE AND PUT YOUR HANDS WHERE WE CAN SEE THEM!" Bill heard them say. Bill attempted to look but there was so much dust from the collapsed wall and a bit of the roof as well. In fact the van was holding up part of the collapsed ceiling. He could only make out blobs outside the clinic.

Those donut addicted morons did not even realise Bill was already out of the vehicle. Was this fucking amateur hour? The LAPD would have charged in and beat his ass to Korea and back within this time. These weekend warriors outside saw a collapsed wall and they were too scared to enter. What the fuck was wrong with this country? Were they too fat to squeeze in? Did an itsy bitsy bit of dust violate their OH and S? Bill could not help but smile as he stood up and slid back into the van so that he could exit the other side. He knew the door to the rest of the clinic was on his left after all. He could make out some collapsed wall cabinets in front of the van. There was no way around that. As he opened the left door, he heard a quiet voice in the background declare, "I see some movement!" followed by the megaphone again.

"STOP! WE ARE AUTHORISED TO USE DEADLY FORCE IF YOU DO NOT COMPLY WITH OUR COMMANDS!!"

Fuck them, Bill thought as he power walked down the clinic's hall. As he passed reception, there was some new reception woman who must have spotted the blood soaked knife in his right hand. She let out a blood curdling scream which set off a flurry of activity in the waiting room as well. Bill moved past in an instant and stopped caring. He had only one destination - Cynthia Huang's room. As if to satiate her curiosity, Bill spotted that Chinese whore craning her head outside her room's door. The moment she saw Bill, she immediately turned around and slammed the door. There was no fucking point. Bill knew very well that King's dental had no locks on their surgery doors. How else would that cockroach be able to constantly barge in on Bill working?

When Bill was about two steps from entering Cynthia Huang's room, the couch potato police officers finally started entering the hallway, from reception. Those fuckers were too scared to encounter dust so they actually went the long way and entered from the proper reception entrance. Bill could not even make this shit up. Bill spotted two officers with protective vests on while holding standard issue Glock 22 firearms with shaky hands. Those fuckers were shaking in fear from Bill who was armed with nothing but a fucking sashimi knife.

"STOP! PUT THE KNIFE DOWN!" Bill heard one of them yell but it was already too late. Bill heard a loud BANG as there must have been a firearm discharge but it was clear they fired just for mere psychological effect because Bill was already in the room.

In it, Bill found the Chinese woman cowering in a puddle of her urine. How pathetic, Bill thought, exactly as he expected. Wendy was not there. Maybe she was pinned down by the initial impact and laid under the vehicle. She usually nursed for Samuel Sung anyway. For that matter, Bill did not have time to check if a patient was present either. Bill wasted no time closing the few metres between him and Huang with wide, menacing steps. Just as Bill was about to stab the snivelling mess, there were more loud firearm discharges. For some reason, Bill did not feel any pain. The bottomless cesspit of raw emotion driving him completely overwhelmed any sense of his pain perception. Bill stumbled and shoved the knife deep into Cynthia Huang's face. He basically fell on her using the knife as support.

"STOP! PUT THE KNIFE DOWN!" the officers continued to scream while Bill continued stabbing in a frenzy accompanied by the echoes of the explosive gunshots in the confined space. The last thing Bill experienced was the rhythmic swinging of the knife. Up and down, up and down, left and right, left and right. Ha, ha, ha, ha, ha...

Epilogue

https://www.[redacted].com.au/murdering_dentist2021005-YUCWELVNLYJZJPVU

MELBOURNE AFTERNOON HERALD

National World Politics Business Tech Popular

National > NSW > Crime

Mass murder committed by evil, "psychotic" dentist

Alexander Jones ◷ May 5th 2021 14.00 AEDT

On Sunday the 2nd of May, unemployed and disgraced dentist William Hastings Parker, formerly known as Jin-Woo Park, started his brutal campaign of targeted and meticulously planned murders around Melbourne and Shellharbour.

There have been 17 confirmed victims. In the morning, Parker murdered the young couple Anna Williams, 27, and her partner Stephen, 31, as well as their infant daughter, Lisa. Anna was Parker's former patient. Later, Parker murdered respected Supreme Court judge Sandra Maxson, 54, and her daughter Ellen, 31, and two grandsons, Max, 5, and Peter, 3. Parker then brutally murdered his own solicitor Bruce Mcintyre, 51, whose wife, Zoey, managed to defend herself to save her own life.

Zoey's brave acts first alerted police to the brutal rampage but it was too late for the victims that afternoon. Lawyers Brandon Chao, 38, and Aidan Chaudry, 37, from Chao and Chaudry solicitors at law were both murdered that afternoon. Chao's 10 year old son Michael, Chaudry's wife Melinda, 37, and daughter Aliyah, 5, were all murdered alongside their parents.

Victoria police initiated a statewide search for the dangerous Parker but unfortunately they could not stop him in time. On Monday the 3rd of May, Parker was identified laughing hysterically at Shellharbour beach by police and was pursued by car. Parker then proceeded to ram his van into King's Dental clinic, the clinic owned by Dr Samuel Sung, 41. The initial impact caused severe injuries resulting in the death of Dr Sung's assistant Wendy Johnson, 46, and patient Karen Waters, 41.

Police attempted to arrest Parker but the accident scene was described as "too dangerous" to enter by the responding officers. Amidst the chaos, Parker proceeded to stab Dr Samuel Sung repeatedly. Sung succumbed to his injuries on site. Officers managed to enter the clinic via its reception entrance and ordered Parker to stop but Parker refused to comply despite a warning round. Officers were unable to prevent Parker from stabbing Dr Cynthia Huang, 38, repeatedly.

Only through multiple lethal rounds was Parker's rampage finally stopped. Huang sadly succumbed to her injuries on site. An urgent autopsy later found bullet fragments in Huang's body. Trauma surgeon Associate Professor Robert Smith stated publicly that he believed the bullets "without a doubt" contributed to Huang's death.

New South Wales Police issued a statement denying any allegations of negligence and maintained the fact that the bullets were fired accurately and were essential to stopping Parker's rampage. The statement further lambasted any allegations of inadequate police training saying, "there is no amount of training that prepares officers for all situations."

Colleagues at Parker's former clinic, Mega Dental, have been shocked and horrified by the revelations. Dr Cheng Wang, one of Parker's closest friends said, "Bill made joke threats about killing all the time but I've never seen him even hurt a fly. I had no idea he was such a psycho. I'm so shocked by this experience. It's gonna haunt me for life. Now I'm looking at all my other friends with fear."

It has been alleged that Parker had a long history of mental illness. However, what finally sparked this incident was a long running court case over Williams's tongue injury resulting from Parker's negligent treatment. Judgment was handed down by justice Maxson only a month prior to the mass murder. Victoria Police revealed that inside Parker's apartment, Parker left 24 hand written notes of various sizes reading, "Don't mess with someone who's got nothing left to lose."

This incident has shocked a nation. New South Wales and Victoria Police have both vowed to improve cross-border communications and make changes to pursuit protocols. Application of deadly force will also be reviewed. Commissioner Christian Hayden of Victoria Police and Victorian Premier Nathaniel Morrows have both vowed to never let such an incident ever happen again.

"We need to invest more into mental health and we need to do it now!" Morrows said yesterday in a press interview.

"Dangerous individuals must be identified... and stopped before they cause harm," commissioner Hayden stated in yesterday's interview.

**If you or someone you know is suffering from depression, call Lifeline on 13 11 14.*

Related articles:

Ex-dentist con-man Henry Park arrested at airport attempting to flee using fake passport

Henry Park: from dentist to cult leader, how he stole

his millions

"Disgusting cabal" of Melbourne Dental School academics allegedly involved in decades of fraud, embezzlement and sex crimes

Comments (540)
Most upvoted comments below:
(Click here to view all comments)

Paulhewitt_86:
First!

based_bicthxXD:
Yo, this dude is a f#)king hero. I don't give a f#(k what all the fake news media says. This guy did all you morons a public service.

jparker_230:
@based_bicthxXD I can't believe there are people like this. Grow up. Go be edgy somewhere else. I've been too ashamed to even step outside because some psychopath decided to choose my last name.

based_bicthxXD:
@jparker_230 Ha ha ha ha! Another f#)king moron. You sheeple are just lambs to the slaughter. A martyr died for

our cause and you morons just keep spouting your NPC bullsh*@.

am_tr:
Lawyer here. I looked into his case. This guy was forced to stop working due to mental illness. I can't forgive the murders but I think a lot of people don't realise that he was pushed to a corner. With no income and no income prospects *and* no house, once the courts take his money, he's basically on the streets.

Flameice12:
@am_tr Being pushed into a corner is no reason to start committing murder. There is always Centrelink. Even if I were forced onto the streets, I would just have to accept that.

am_tr:
@Flameice12 After reading about this guy, do you honestly believe he would work his arse off to collect welfare payments? As I said, I would never even contemplate murder but I wholeheartedly agree that if I had no better option than to beg for money, I would rather call it quits then and there.

Stray_cato_o:
@am_tr Yeah dude, he doesn't look like someone who would accept begging on a street corner. The court system basically

gave him a death sentence. Everyone sees a monster but nobody is willing to ask, "who made this monster?"

ambrosia99:
I once saw this guy as my dentist! He was a bit weird but his work was great! I've had this problem tooth which all other dentists couldn't fix for more than a month but I still have his filling to this day! I would never have thought he would do this...

dmx:
I have to say, this guy finally opened my eyes. You fake news media keep labeling him as a "psycho" but the more I read about this guy, the more sense he makes. I have been bullied my whole life and I've been unemployed for years, all because of made up excuses. Recently I was rejected from a job because I was overqualified. I only have a bachelor's degree. I found out through some friends that they gave the job to some disabled woman with no experience and a foreign bachelor's in the same field. This was not an isolated incident. Society is diseased.

EmperorSigma:
@dmx I'm with you, fam. F#)k the mainstream media. You gotta check out www.provisionalgov.com for straight facts. Even if you got a job, you'll only be part of a corrupt system, and you might have ended up feeling like that 'psycho'.

Don't kid yourself that people at work will be better than the people who bullied you at school.

Chaos_chaser9:
Just saying, if everyone else on Earth thought and acted like this Bill guy, everyone would treat each other MUCH better. If I knew that any random guy I piss off might decide to kill me, I would not behave like an animal. Those who do, well... you know what would happen.

angelsky21:
@Chaos_chaser9 Are you insane? You honestly believe it's a good thing that everyone should be one step away from killing each other? You literally propose living in a tinderbox environment like Nazi Germany?

Randallm12:
It's disheartening to see people even dare sympathise with such a cartoonishly evil man. Not even a cartoonist would think up such an unbelievably exaggerated, psychotic character like Parker. I truly worry about the young ones growing up in a society with people like this. All you sympathisers have not lived through the horrors of the second world war.

teabag_urlife:
@Randallm12 OK Boomer. Whatever you say boomer. HITLER DID NOTHING WRONG!

bgone5:
Uhh... Why did I even bother coming to the comment section? So many trolls and edgelords.

jparker_230:
@bgone5 I know right. They're all just incels.